PRECIOUS LOVE

Standing alone in the tent, her hand pressed over her bruised lips, Amber let her tears flow freely. She felt dazed, betrayed, and more alone than she had ever felt in her life. How could she live as Tate Coker's wife, sold to him, her fate sealed? Drudgery and misery would be her constant companions.

Then she felt a hand on her shoulder. Had Tate Coker returned?

"Cusni ceya; don't weep, Autumn Dawn." The softly spoken Sioux words settled upon Amber's ears. She turned, and stared transfixed upon the Indian warrior who had once saved her from a bear.

"What are you doing here?" she whispered.

"Come with me. Come away from this place with me." The English words were spoken softly. His dark eyes gazed into her face with a tender warmth. "Come with me," he repeated, and held out his hand to her.

Slowly, Amber rose to her feet and tentatively slipped her fingers over the brave's hardened palm. Instantly, his fingers captured hers and his full lips drew back into a tender smile.

A smile that offered protection, and strength . . . and maybe even more. She knew she would never be able to look back if she held this hand and went with this man.

Taking a deep breath, she slipped her hand deeper into his . . .

TODAY'S HOTTEST READS
ARE TOMORROW'S SUPERSTARS

VICTORY'S WOMAN (4484, $4.50)
by Gretchen Genet
Andrew — the carefree soldier who sought glory on the battlefield, and returned a shattered man . . . Niall — the legandary frontiersman and a former Shawnee captive, tormented by his past . . . Roger — the troubled youth, who would rise up to claim a shocking legacy . . . and Clarice — the passionate beauty bound by one man, and hopelessly in love with another. Set against the backdrop of the American revolution, three men fight for their heritage — and one woman is destined to change all their lives forever!

FORBIDDEN (4488, $4.99)
by Jo Beverley
While fleeing from her brothers, who are attempting to sell her into a loveless marriage, Serena Riverton accepts a carriage ride from a stranger — who is the handsomest man she has ever seen. Lord Middlethorpe, himself, is actually contemplating marriage to a dull daughter of the aristocracy, when he encounters the breathtaking Serena. She arouses him as no woman ever has. And after a night of thrilling intimacy — a forbidden liaison — Serena must choose between a lady's place and a woman's passion!

WINDS OF DESTINY (4489, $4.99)
by Victoria Thompson
Becky Tate is a half-breed outcast — branded by her Comanche heritage. Then she meets a rugged stranger who awakens her heart to the magic and mystery of passion. Hiding a desperate past, Texas Ranger Clint Masterson has ridden into cattle country to bring peace to a divided land. But a greater battle rages inside him when he dares to desire the beautiful Becky!

WILDEST HEART (4456, $4.99)
by Virginia Brown
Maggie Malone had come to cattle country to forge her future as a healer. Now she was faced by Devon Conrad, an outlaw wounded body and soul by his shadowy past . . . whose eyes blazed with fury even as his burning caress sent her spiraling with desire. They came together in a Texas town about to explode in sin and scandal. Danger was their destiny — and there was nothing they wouldn't dare for love!

Available wherever paperbacks are sold, or order direct from the Publisher. Send cover price plus 50¢ per copy for mailing and handling to Penguin USA, P.O. Box 999, c/o Dept. 17109, Bergenfield, NJ 07621. Residents of New York and Tennessee must include sales tax. DO NOT SEND CASH.

PRECIOUS AMBER

KATHLEEN DRYMON

ZEBRA BOOKS
KENSINGTON PUBLISHING CORP.

ZEBRA BOOKS are published by

Kensington Publishing Corp.
850 Third Avenue
New York, NY 10022

Zebra and the Z logo Reg. U.S. Pat. & TM Off.

First Printing: June, 1996
10 9 8 7 6 5 4 3 2 1

Printed in the United States of America

To Charles and Betty McCall:
Thanks for always being there to lend your support.
You are both what family is all about.

Prologue

The Great Plains:
March: The moon of the snowblind

"Wakán Tanka! Hear me, oh Great One!"

The heartfelt cry escaped the lips of the warrior hanging in midair upon the sun dance pole. The sound of his prayers passed over those participating in the ceremony, and those sitting and standing around the sacred grounds. His cries rose upward, to be carried along the invisible path of the Spirit Trail.

Grandfather peyote, the dream button, had been placed beneath the warrior's tongue shortly before the Wicasa Wakán, holy man of the Lakota people, had pierced his chest and secured the claws of the sacred eagle within the incisions above the nipples of his breasts and beneath the tendons. Leather tethers tied to the top of the sun dance pole had been secured to the eagle claws, and as the warrior stood, chanting a prayer for strength and bravery, he had been hoisted into midair. He hung only by strips of leather, which drew the flesh and tendons grotesquely away from the upper portion of his torso.

Swirling colors of purple, red, blue, spinning yellow, silver, and gold collided within the warrior's inner vision, and left him hanging upon the very apex of the universe.

Wi, the sun, poured its life-giving rays down upon him, and gradually the tendons deep within his chest began to tear, inch by slow inch. All reality disappeared as he was carried upon the breath of the Spirit Touch. Feeling himself lifted out of the pain of the self-inflicted torture, he was delivered from his mortal body. Ascending upward, toward the heating rays of Wi, he looked down and glimpsed his body hanging upon the sun dance pole. He could hear the chanting of the old shaman, Medicine Cloud, and was enfolded by the noise of the eagle-bone whistles that were held between the lips of those dancing around the sacred pole.

Looking into the faces of his people, an overpowering love for these enduring Lakotas filled him to the very center of his being. His glance touched upon each one separately, and his memory was rekindled as to the love and guidance each had placed upon his life path.

As the soft flutter of eagles' wings settled around him, he was lifted to a loftier place. His sight drew in the beauty of a thousand or more conical-shaped dwellings that were stretched across the floor of the valley with a river slashing through it. It appeared as though a streak of lightning. He was carried farther, beyond the river's boundaries, and gently his feet were set upon the blessed earth that made up the sacred burial grounds of his people. The disturbance of eagles' wings lightly set into motion the ancient war lances, shields, and quivers that hung upon the head-poles of those that had long ago traveled down the Spirit Path.

The warrior walked there among the spirits of those that had gone on to join the sky people. He felt the touch upon his shoulder of his grandfather, Gray Horse, who had taught him how to hunt and fight when his father had been absent from the village. The old chief, Thunder Cloud, who had led his people to great victory centuries ago against the Cree, walked at his side. He spoke to those from ancient lore, as far back as first man and first woman. He was blessed with the knowledge of the Spirit People. They told him things that even the greatest Lakota shaman had lost knowledge of. They sang ancient, lost songs, for him to bring back to the people. They spoke to him of the sacred hoop that was the foundation of their being, of healing properties that long ago had been forgotten, and they told him of what was to come in the future.

That day his name was changed to Spirit Walker, and in the warrior's mind, he walked with the Spirit People for days, learning all that he could of the old ways, and that which one day would be. As he stood alone at the edge of the river, feeling blessed and overpowered with knowledge, he glanced upward and viewed the wings of the eagles coming once again for him. Before their touch settled around him, he turned back to the sacred burial grounds one last time. What he saw was not the vision of earlier. He viewed a young woman, her head crowned with fire-curls. She stood alone, her hands outstretched, and around her throat, she wore the claw necklace of the matóhota.

One

For a few minutes, which stretched out with unbearable tension, there was quiet in the cabin. The leather-hide covers had been drawn closed over the open-framed windows. The single room, in which the dwellers, ate, slept, and lived their daily lives, was held in semi-darkness. The glowing fire beyond the hearth made up most of the light. The pungent odors of dried herbs and meadow grass joined the harsher smells of vomit and blood.

The silence was short-lived as another scream, like that of an animal in excruciating torment, came from the corner, where a makeshift bed with straw-filled mattress, had been set up. The sound encircling the interior of the small structure seemed to linger overlong within the confining walls.

"There you go, Lizzy. Once more you need to push. Once more, and mayhap the babe will give way." The usual jovial features of Bertha Poole were tensed with worry and frustration at the unusually long, hard birth that she was midwifing. Her large brown eyes filled with pity, her soft tone bespoke her deep concern. Drawing her glance away from the suffering Lizzy Barrow, her eyes set upon the silent girl, standing pale and wide-eyed at the foot of the bed. Bertha's heart went out to the girl, because she knew her to be as helpless as herself, only able to stand by and watch her mother moaning in the depths of her agony. Some hours past, Elizabeth Barrow had stilled all movement. Only sharp, mournful screams and fevered moans escaped her dry lips. Her body had weakened long ago from loss of blood, which even now, lightly flowed out of her body in a steady stream.

"Amber girl, get your maw another cup of that herb tea. We'll try to spoon some of the liquid between her lips." Anything was worth a try. In the back of the midwife's mind, she had already given up all thoughts of a successful delivery. Lizzy Barrow was already old and worn out at the age of thirty-two. Her life as Mrs. Henry Barrow had brought her low these past six years, and her pregnancy had only aided in draining her of the small strength she had.

The young girl called Amber hurriedly did the older woman's bidding, praying silently with each step she took that the child would be delivered. If the crimson liquid seeping out of her mother's body would only still, perhaps she would have a chance to live. *Even if the child is brought into the world dead, dear Lord, please let my mother live!*

Returning to the side of the bed with the chipped cup containing the herb tea Amber met the pitying regard of Bertha Poole. Gently the midwife took the cup from her hand. As the girl's eyes lowered to her mother, she noticed that there was no movement from the pale woman on the bed, nor did she hear the sounds that had kept her pulses throbbing for the past twenty-four hours. Great, liquid tears instantly filled her eyes.

"Mother," she said the word softly at first, then more urgently. "Mother!"

"I'm right sorry, lass, but there was little that could be done for poor Lizzy. She's with her maker now, and I am sorry to say, but that's a much kinder place for her than living on this earth with Henry Barrow!"

The Barrow cabin was located on the outskirts of St. Louis, and there wasn't a soul in the area who didn't know old Henry for the whiskey-drinking, good-fer-nothing that he was. Lizzy and the girl were the best two people Henry Barrow had ever come across, and he had treated the pair worse than his dogs or mule. For a moment, Bertha's mind flighted over Amber's future. As the first sob shook the girl's frail form, she drew her into her arms, thinking now only of giving comfort.

Having grown numb hours ago, Amber sat in the hand-made rocker in front of the open stone fireplace. There was little movement from the slender frame, the chair remaining still. Every now and then, her delicate profile would turn toward the bed. At these times, fresh tears would fill the exotically slanted, cobalt-blue eyes. No movement was made to wipe away the salty liquid that silently fell upon the creamy-smooth cheeks; the moisture fell and dried without notice.

It was late afternoon when the cabin door was flung wide and a gust of late winter air swept within and circled the tiny cabin. "Elizabeth!" came a harsh shout. "What the hell you got it so dabbern dark in here for?" The man held a lithe-rangy appearance, large, but not slight of frame. A full growth of beard covered his chin, and a graying thin mustache covered his upper lip. His dull green

eyes searched out the interior of the cabin, which he had
built himself with the help of a few neighbors four years
earlier. As his gaze settled upon the girl in the rocker, the
first trembling fingers of doom touched his hard heart.
"Where's your maw, gal?"

The tears in the blue eyes renewed, but Amber held her
seat, the low heat from the fire beyond the hearth touching
her chilled form. Her head turned at the words, and she
held her gaze full upon the man in the doorway. "She
passed on this morning. The midwife came, but there was
little that either she or I could do other than watch Mother
bleed her life away. She was too overworked, and too old,
to have another child, Mrs. Poole said."

The green eyes beneath shaggy gray brows appraised
the girl before going across the room to the bed. For a
silent moment he studied the mound, still covered with
blankets; the form of his wife. For an added moment or
two some touch of sorrow filled his eyes, but he did not
show his emotions long. The bearded chin firmed in
resigned resignation. "That old bitch, Bertha Poole, don't
know what she's yapping about, gal. Your maw was a strong
enough woman. It wasn't no one's fault if her Maker called
her home."

Amber looked across the room at Henry Barrow, her
stepfather, and knew there was nothing she could say to
convince him to take any portion of the guilt over her
mother's death. He had wanted Elizabeth Barrow to give
him a son, that was all he had talked about from the
moment her mother had married him six years ago, and
had moved with him from Richmond, Virginia, to St. Louis.
Whatever Henry Barrow had wanted in the past, he had
tried to get. Now he had a dead wife, and no child to
claim, except her. The thought did not fill Amber with
any gladness.

Entering the room without thought to knocking the

mud from his boots as Elizabeth Barrow had always pleaded he do, Henry slung his heavy buckskin coat, with its fringed neck, chest, and sleeve ornamentation down upon the scarred wood table. His brass-mounted, half-stocked, plains rifle, which had been made by Sam Hawken, followed next. Making his way to the bed, for a few silent minutes he stared down at the still, pale, work-worn visage of his wife, where she had drawn her last breath. He moved his hand, as though he would smooth her brow, but unable to touch the dead women, he turned back to her daughter. "I reckon you had best get yourself down to town and call for old preacher Fletcher. Your maw always did have a hankering to step foot in his church. Now he can read a few words over her when she's put in the ground."

Amber bit her lip, forcing herself to still the condemning words that were held on the verge of coming forth. Words that would have reminded Henry Barrow that he had forbidden his wife to go to church. He had more times than Amber could remember cursed old preacher Fletcher for a skinny, do-good satanite, tilting his clay jug of whiskey up to his lips as he spoke the admonishment. Amber scarfed her head and nodded her agreement. It would do little good to hurl accusations upon her stepfather's head. At least her mother would be allowed a proper funeral. Rising from her chair, and still feeling numb, from her auburn curls to the ragged shoes upon her feet, she reached for the black-cloth cloak that hung upon the peg behind the cabin door.

"I reckon your my responsibility now, gal." Henry's gaze settled on Amber standing at the cabin door as she pulled the cloak over her shoulders and drew the clasp tightly at her throat. As her large blue eyes looked at him in question, he told himself that there was no way out for him. He was going to be saddled with the girl, whether he wished to be or not. "I told your maw, not more than a day or two past, as how I was going to sign on with Andrew Henry and William Ashley. I were just told, about these two blokes, placing an advertisement in the St. Louis, *Gazette*, for one hundred good men to go trapping in the mountains. I signed meself on yesterday, and I reckon as how you'll have to go along with me now that your maw's gone. I can't say it will be too bad having a woman along to do the cooking and helping with the skinning and curing. Your maw would have gone, except with the babe coming and all, I just thought you two would stay here in the cabin until I returned. Three years, that's the time I planned on being gone."

Amber froze in her tracks. *Three years! Cooking and skinning animals for Henry Barrow for three long years!* But all she could get out of her mouth was, "Go with you trapping?" all through the long day, she had sat before the fireplace and wondered what would become of her, but she had never imagined *this!* Her mother had no family for her to go to. Her natural father, having died when she had been but a child after a fall from a horse, also had had no kin. She frantically searched for some alternative to the problem. "I could stay with Mrs. Poole, while you're trapping. I'm sure she could use another hand around her place, what with all her children." She said the first thing that came to mind, *anything* that would save her from being forced to go with Henry Barrow.

"Bah, that old she-dog! I never did cotton to her. Always bragging on her midwifery. Well, you can see with your own eyes yer dead maw, over there on the bed. Bertha Poole ain't nothing but a sham! Why, when I left yer maw yesterday morn, Lizzy weren't even feeling a little peeky. More than likely, Old Bertha gave her one of them potions she's always fixing up! That's probably what killed your maw, and the babe, too! And shame, you wanting to go and live with your maw's killer!" With his green gaze held upon her, he continued. "Besides, you'll be a sight better company than an Injun squaw. Most trappers hitch themselves up with one of the filthy, flea-ridden heathens to pass the months with. With you along, there won't be much sense in me trucking with no redskins!"

She could well imagine that if her mother had lived and Henry Barrow had gone trapping alone, he wouldn't have been so choosy about hitching himself up to an Indian woman! At that moment, Amber could have spewed forth every abuse this man had ever inflicted upon her and her mother, but at fifteen years old, she had had six long years in which to learn that she never spoke back to Henry Barrow! He was a cruel and vicious man, and the memory of the lashings she had received at his hands only reinforced the need for her to clench her jaw tightly and not refute his words.

"We'll be leaving at the end of the week. The keelboats will be loaded with those trappers who answered the ad, and the supplies that Henry and Ashley promised." The keelboats would take the trappers up the Missouri, to the confluence of the Yellowstone, and from there it would be up to each man to proceed up the tributary to the hunting grounds. Henry Barrow, for one, aimed in three years time, to have himself a cache of furs big enough to enable him to buy that tavern he had always wanted. Once he owned the place, he would kick back, drink his fill, and watch the money roll in!

Three years . . . Three years . . . Three years! Those two words repeated themselves over and over in Amber's mind. She would be living in the wilderness, for three long years with this man that she despised, and she wouldn't have her loving mother at her side to soothe the way. Three years of hardship and drudgery, if she knew anything at all about Henry Barrow! Three years that would seem like forever!

* * *

Upon a little grass hill that overlooked the Barrow cabin, with preacher Fletcher reading from his old yellow-paged Bible, and Bertha Poole the only person other than immediate family in attendance, Elizabeth Barrow was laid at last to rest.

Amber cried anguished tears for the loss of her dear mother and for her own unsure future. Bertha Poole drew her to her ample bosom and tried to soothe her grief. Henry Barrow tilted his whiskey flask up to his lips as he watched the scene. He remembered another wife that he had buried years ago. His childhood sweetheart and their son, had been killed in a cabin fire. The only comfort he had gotten from the torment of their memory had been out of a whiskey bottle. He had turned hard and mean over the years, often beating Amber without the slightest provocation from the girl and now with the death of another wife and child, he knew for certain that there was no smiling deity looking down from above at him. That damn skinny preacher could wail aloud all the sermons for repentance that he wished, and that stepdaughter of his, she could shed a bucket of tears. It wouldn't be changing the way of things one bit. It wouldn't be changing Henry Barrow!

Two

St. Louis, Missouri, was a teaming frontier settlement. The docks were littered with run-down shacks and makeshift warehouses. Canoes, longboats, flatboats, keelboats, and even a paddle-wheeled steamboat littered the levee. It was an exciting time for adventurers and trappers. Those men seeking their fortune in the exploitation of fur trapping, and those having a mind to seek out new territory and routes west, marked their first step up the Missouri, from St. Louis.

Amber Dawson watched everything around her in wide-eyed amazement. She had never been around the dock area of St. Louis, and as the busy activity passed all around her, she clutched her worn valise tightly against her body.

"Stay over here, gal, out of the way, while I help these men load up the supplies in the keelboat," Henry Barrow ordered, and pointed out a corner next to some stacked crates along the wharf.

Too frightened to do otherwise, Amber nervously obeyed. William Ashley and Andrew Henry's keelboats

were loaded high with traps, provisions, and other gear
that the trappers would need in the mountains. There was
also a large supply of various items for the trappers to
trade with the Indians for furs and horses. There were
bundles of multicolored, four-point trade blankets, multicolored chevron beads, amber-bone hair pipes, wire-
wound beads, assorted glass beads, English-manufactured
flintlock trade muskets, and a supply of trade kettles and
pots.

Ashley and Henry had come up with the novel idea of
furnishing the trappers with all supplies and to pick them
up at the rendezvous at the end of the three years, at which
time the profit from the pelts would be split evenly between
trapper and employers. Not revealed to the trappers was
Ashley and Henry's idea that at rendezvous, they would
bring a quantity of goods with which they hoped to trade
for the trapper's portion of the profits at inequitable rates.

The goods were stacked upon the keelboats in canvas-
covered bales. There would be sparse room for the trappers. The keel, or the curved base of the framework of the
freight boat, was used for the sail. That would allow the
flat-based vessel to move easily up the Missouri when tides
and currents permitted. When the sails were not being
used, the trappers would row, or each one would man a
pole. Walking from bow to stern, they would pole themselves toward their destination.

As Henry Barrow worked next to his fellow trappers, he
kept a wary eye on his stepdaughter. If nothing else, Henry
Barrow was protective of that which he deemed belonging
to himself. When two Indian women appeared on the wharf
with two trappers who began to help load the first keelboat,
Barrow spat a stream of tobacco juice into the river, before
loudly ordering Amber to keep herself away from them
"Injun squaws." "He added, Ain't no daughter of mine
going to be cozing up to no redskin, woman or buck!"

Amber felt her face flush with her stepfather's words, but the two trappers didn't seem to pay any attention to the disrespect Henry Barrow showed their women, and the two women silently kept their distance from the girl, quickly realizing Henry Barrow was not one to be taken lightly.

Rolls of pigtail tobacco, kegs of gunpowder, as well as a supply of whiskey and boxes carrying paper cartridges filled with fixed ammunition, were the last of the goods loaded before the two trappers called for their Indian women to step aboard the keelboat. Henry Barrow directed his stepdaughter to sit near the back of the boat, on the bales of supplies.

Amber hurriedly made herself comfortable where instructed as the group of trappers manned the poles and began to push the keelboat away from the St. Louis docks. Looking to shore, once again Amber was reminded that she would be gone for three long years. With her valise sitting next to her on the canvas-covered supplies, she unlocked the clasp and drew forth the journal her mother had given her for her fifteenth birthday. She began to sketch the scene of the St. Louis levee, the river transportation, shacks, and warehouses. As the keelboats glided easily into the current that would take them up the Missouri, Amber made her first notation in her journal. *Today the keelboats left St. Louis. The first leg of the journey toward the hunting grounds is now under way.*

"Hey, girlie, write all you wanting in that little book of yours. There's a whole case of books with blank pages, under this canvas. I don't know what Ashley and Henry were thinking when they sent them to be loaded, but there ain't a man among us that can write, so I reckon you can claim the case for yourself."

Amber's blue gaze instantly went to her stepfather to check his reaction to the other trapper's words.

Without the slightest break in his poling, Barrow's head nodded in a single movement. "I reckon as how doodling in your book will help you pass the time, gal. If no one has any better use for the books, you can claim them."

Never knowing how her stepfather would react if she were to thank him for a generous gesture, Amber nodded her head, as though it was settled, she would become the owner of the case of journals. With a sparkle in her eyes, she retrieved her journal from her valise. As she watched the banks of the Missouri, she jotted down notes, writing more descriptively about this first day's passing.

She wrote in leisure, and also sketched the birds that flew overhead, and a deer and fawn that drank at the river's edge at midday. She treated her journal as her friend, writing down her thoughts, fears, and dreams and fashioning pictures of all she observed.

"Amber's excitement grew with each day that passed as the trappers trekked upon the same route Lewis and Clark had ventured upon some seventeen years earlier. Having lived in virtual isolation for the past six years, she greedily drank in every sight that passed in front of her. The beauty along the banks of the river was breathtaking. The river itself changed as rapidly as the scenery. At times, the trappers would have to pole the boat through shallow water, and other times, the craft appeared to glide over the surface with a speed that seemed unsurpassed. Often, Amber spied game down at the river's edge, and upon occasion, she caught glimpses of Indian women with vermilion-painted faces wearing buckskin dresses, filling parfleches with water and their braided willow baskets with firewood. One afternoon, she watched the picturesque scene of two Indian women gathering fish from the weirs they used as traps. Much of what she viewed, she sketched in her journal spending her days in a world unto herself.

It was a rare occurrence when the trappers were set upon by Indians, but occasionally a few arrows were let loose from a copse of trees along the riverbank. The trappers wasted little time in priming their rifles and letting loose a volley of shot in their direction. From her hiding place, Amber judged that no damage had been done to either side, and for that she was glad.

For the best part of the days, Amber sat in the back of the craft upon the canvas-covered supplies, writing in her journal or watching the passing countryside. In the evenings, if the trappers thought it safe enough to go ashore, she helped the two Indian women prepare the food and supplies that were available. At such times, she was not surprised to look up from the campfire to find Henry Barrow's gaze upon her. She spoke little to the women, not inviting their company, lest her stepfather find fault.

Often, before the keelboats would leave shore early in the mornings, a pair of trappers would scout the area and if lucky they would come across fresh game, which would become the main stay of their meals for the next few days.

It was here at Fort Mandan, at the very camp site where Lewis and Clark had spent their first winter with the Indians, that Amber received her first close look at wild Indians. That evening while sitting near the shallow, pit-fire that had been built in camp, not far from the keelboats, she sketched in her journal some of the sights she had viewed while the trappers had traded their goods with the Indian. Several haughty-appearing warriors, wrapped in painted buffalo robes and adorned with feathers in their long black hair, bright paint adorning their features, had wheeled their spirited ponies into the midst of the traders, and galloped through the Indian encampment, flourishing muskets, bows, and battle-axes before all in a threatening manner. Amber tirelessly worked in her journal, this scene, as well as one of a young Indian mother, a cradle-board strapped to her back, holding her baby.

With Barrow's harsh command that she put away her nonsense and get some sleep, she had promised herself that she would find time the next day to finish her drawings. As she laid down on her pallet, she could not help reflecting over this day. The natives at Fort Mandan had been nothing like she had expected. They appeared a happy, pride-filled people. There had been an air of excitement throughout the village and she had glimpsed a colorful pageantry in the people's dress and housing. They were nothing like the ill-kempt savages her stepfather had led her to expect.

The days passed. At last the keelboats reached the area where the Missouri came together with the Yellowstone. From here, the trappers continued up the tributary until they reached the mountains which were rich with wild game, their luxuriant pelts greedily desired by Europeans.

This same day the keelboats were unloaded near Ben Harper's trading post. The trading post was a ramshackle affair, with a lean-to roof, and hides covering windows and front door. As the last of the canvas-covered supplies lined the shore, a small band of Shoshone Indians leading a long string of ponies approached. The Indians expressed their desire to trade their animals for the goods the white men had brought to their lands.

Ben Harper was eagerly willing to help conduct the trading for his share of the goods, and as Amber watched in wide-eyed amazement, Henry Barrow traded a portion of his supplies for four sturdy-looking horses and a bundle of pelts. Beads, pots, blankets, one rifle, and several rolls of tobacco were traded. The only item that Barrow would not part with was his allotted two small kegs of whiskey. Shaking his fur capped head as a brave pointed to a whiskey keg, he indicated that there would be no bartering where his spirits were concerned. He would be in the wilderness three long years, and there was little enough whiskey to spare.

Sitting on a trade blanket next to Barrow's supplies, Amber sketched the scene along the riverbank as the Indians traded with the trappers. This would be the last day that the trappers would stay together. Come first light the following morning, they would strike out in different directions. Each man would set out in search of the best portion of the Rockies in which to do their trapping.

While Amber was busily sketching, a disturbance suddenly drew her attention away from her journal to her stepfather and two Shoshone braves.

Barrow was plainly angry. Bright red spots flamed upon his cheeks, revealing his temper as he shouted, "I won't be telling you again! The gal ain't for trade!" His hand tightened upon the rifle that he held in the crook of his arm. The two braves did not appear to understand, and seemed intent on claiming the young white woman for themselves.

Amber felt her cheeks flush, feeling the stares of both Indians, Barrow, and another trapper called Silas Benson. *Lord God above, they were trying to get Henry Barrow to trade her for a horse!*

Pointing to Amber once again, and then to his own hair, one of the braves said something in his native tongue.

"They ain't never seen a woman with copper hair before," Silas Benson stated. "You've got to admit Barrow, your little gal's hair is as bright as the underside of a shiny brass pot!"

"I still be telling these savages that, she ain't for trade!" Barrow shoved one of the braves aside, and making his way to where Amber sat on the blanket, he spoke sharply. "Cover your head with a scarf, gal. You want them heathens to be leering at you?"

"No, of course not!" Amber gasped, and hastily pulled a dark scarf from her valise to cover her bright hair. Tucking the long strands back up under her collar, she sighed out her pent-up breath as Barrow turned back to the Indians with a dark glare. She was never sure about her stepfather, and knew that if the mood struck, he was very capable of any sort of devious behavior toward that which he believed he owned!

The Indians appeared at last to understand that Barrow would not part with the girl, and shortly they gathered their goods and joined the rest of their band. With the finish of the trading, the Shoshones left Ben Harper's trading post, leaving the trappers with the horses and pelts they had gained.

That night as the group of men sat around the campfire they had built a short distance from the trading post, Silas Benson spoke to Henry Barrow in low tones. "Your little gal's a looker, Barrow. You best keep a sharp eye on her. Them bucks were anxious to get their hands on her."

Barrow looked at Amber, where she was fixing a pot of coffee and setting it against the hot coals. "She ain't much. Her maw was the looker." He spat a stream of tobacco juice into the glowing coals, and for a few seconds remembered the first time he had seen Lizzy Barrow. She had been beautiful back then, with flowing auburn curls and warm blue eyes.

To Silas Benson, fifteen year old Amber Dawson promised to be a woman of incomparable beauty. She was tall and willowy. Her shimmering curls caught light from the flames of the campfire and sparkled brightly. Her eyes were a dark indigo blue, and were fringed with thick, long lashes. Her lips, even at this young age, were full and lush.

Aye, she was a beauty, all right. If she were his stepdaughter, one could bet for sure that he would be keeping a sharp eye out for her. "If she's going to turn out looking like I think she will, when we meet up at rendezvous, I myself, might be wanting to trade you my whole cache of furs for her, Barrow!" He chuckled as though making a fine joke, but there was a slender thread of truth to his words.

Henry Barrow's glance sharpened somewhat as he took a closer look at Amber. She was passable enough, but as pretty as old Silas claimed . . . ? Well, he would have to watch her blossom over the next three years before forming any definite opinion, and over the next three years he would also think about Silas's words of trading his entire cache for his stepdaughter.

Three

The Rocky mountains were a lush wonderland of rising mountains, thick green grass-carpeted summits and valleys, and magnificent, towering pines. Only the hardiest of trappers had come this far into the mountains, and Henry and Ashley's trappers would find an abundance of badger, beaver, fox, wolf, black bear, grizzly, mountain goat, elk, and deer. It was a land ready for exploration; its vast lakes and game-filled streams beckoning to the hardy mountain men.

Henry Barrow and Amber Dawson set out that morning, with two pack horses loaded with enough supplies to see them through until rendezvous. Amber had stuffed as many of the journals from the case packed aboard the keelboat into her valise as she could possibly fit. What was left she kindly offered to Ben Harper. The older man smiled his appreciation, and offered his hospitality anytime she passed near his trading post. Her valise was strapped over the pommel of her Indian saddle. Amber had no wish for Henry Barrow to complain about the extra burden placed upon the pack animals and change his mind about her keeping the ledgers.

The first few days of travel, they pushed toward the higher elevations of the mountains, hoping by doing so, they would find the wildlife more abundant. Amber did not argue with the course set by her stepfather. On the contrary, the scenery was breathtaking, and it was all she could do throughout the days to take all within her regard and write everything down in her diary, of an evening, while she sat close to the campfire.

One afternoon, the pair traveled down a gorge. Its steepness made hard passage for their mounts, but the lush grasses and profusion of plant life covering the summit were beautiful to behold. Fuchsia blossoms grew in a crooked pattern, following the meanders of a small spring that oozed out of the ground and trickled downhill. Indian paintbrush and yarrow, growing in small, flat-topped clusters, dominated the hillside, appearing a vermilion with white tinge. Close to the ground were pussytoes, yellow penstemons, and cinquefoils, all so small, one had to bend low to fully appreciate their dainty beauty.

From the crest of the ridge, Amber looked down upon a small lake at the base of the glacier-scoured basin. With no words spoken, she followed Barrow down, and that night they camped along the banks of the lake.

It was not until the fifth day that Barrow halted his horse in a small clearing encircled by tall pines next to a swiftly running stream. He would build them a shelter here, and eventually a small cabin, he decided, after checking the stream and the area for sign of wild game.

Amber had no say in the decisions. She dismounted where her stepfather directed, and while he stripped the packhorses of their load, she began to make a fire and prepare a meal.

It was not until evening that she had a chance to write

in her journal and sketch the campsite. *Today, Henry Barrow chose his campsite. It is in an isolated area, deep in the mountains. I can't imagine living here for the next three years, without benefit of female company. I despair to think what I would do if not for my writing and drawings.*

The following morning, before taking up his traps and hoisting them over his shoulder, Barrow handed Amber a plains rifle, similar to his own except for the brass tack decoration on the stock. "There's a pistol in that leather haversack lying over there, gal." He nodded toward the supplies that were covered with a piece of canvas. "Stay here to camp. Don't be wandering off and getting yourself hurt or stolen by Injuns!"

Slinging the metal traps for both small and medium game, with their anchor chains, over his shoulders, Barrow headed downstream, leaving his stepdaughter to fend for herself until his return.

Amber nervously held the rifle across her lap, not daring to move far from the shallow pit-fire in the center of their camp. With Barrow gone from camp, the woods appeared to encircle her with an ominous presence, the quiet settling over her and lending eerie shadows where moments past she had not glimpsed them.

At last, she shook herself from her paralysis, and setting the rifle aside, she scolded herself for being childish. She had far too much work to do to sit like a frightened rabbit waiting for something to jump out at her from behind a tree. When her stepfather returned to camp, he would surely take a strap to her if he found that she had been lax throughout the day!

It had been several days since last she had been able to wash out their dirty clothes. Taking up a bar of strong lye soap and the parfleche of clothes that needed washing, she made her way down to the stream. For a few seconds, she thought about taking the rifle, but swiftly realized that if she were to be set upon by animal or Indian, she more than likely would not have the time to aim the rifle and fire. It would only be in her way and add to her nervousness.

She spent this first morning washing the clothes against a smooth, large lime rock, then hanging them over bushes to dry. After returning to camp and putting away the supplies and skillet she had used for breakfast, she dug through Barrow's haversack until she found a knife with a sharp spear point, with a shaped wooden hilt. She began to cut thick branches from the brush and trees around camp. The limbs would be used to shape the lean-to, which would provide shelter until her stepfather could build them a cabin.

By late afternoon, Amber was exhausted, but pleased with her work. The large lean-too, would be able to shelter them and their supplies from the elements. Setting a pot next to the glowing coals of the fire, she cut chunks of venison and wild onions together, to simmer for a stew.

Taking up the bar of soap and a fresh dress, she headed upstream to find a spot deep enough to swim and bathe. Freeing her long, glistening copper curls and pulling off her gown, she relaxed in the cool water. She had not been afforded such privacy since leaving St. Louis. Floating on her back, she looked up at the canopy of trees, and for the first time in weeks, felt strength welling within her. She had survived this first day alone in the wilderness. She would endure the next three years, she vowed silently, and then somehow she would make a life of her own, away from Henry Barrow.

The days in the mountains passed in a sameness of routine. Amber had counted off every week, every day she had been here. Eighteen months had gone by. Only eighteen more to go, she told herself.

It hadn't taken long before Barrow and she built the lean-to. When Barrow completed the single room cabin the lean-to became a shelter for the horses. Each morning, before daylight, Amber awoke, and sleepily made her way to the stone fireplace. Stoking the embers, she would place a few small pieces of wood on the fire to heat the cabin.

Breakfasts were the same each morning. Amber would put a handful of coffee beans into a skillet, and holding this over the fire beyond the hearth until they were coaled on the outside like charcoal, she would empty the skillet into the small coffee grinder that Barrow had brought with him from St. Louis; the coffee grinder that had belonged to her mother. Setting the coffeepot beneath the grinder, she turned the handle to grind the beans. Silently Amber went about her morning work, now and then throwing a glance over her shoulder in her stepfather's direction knowing, that at any moment, he would rise from the bed, which set against the cabin wall nearest the door. Putting some cornmeal into a box-through, she added a little salt and water. Working the dough with her fingers until it felt the right consistency, she pressed handfuls of the meal into the skillet. Some mornings, if lucky, there was meat left over from supper the night before. Occasionally there would be fresh fish to fry, caught in the stream, the day before.

With the scent of food cooking, Barrow began to stir about and drag himself from bed. More often than not, neither occupant of the small structure spoke. Amber set the tin plate, containing his food and his three-pronged fork, down on the wood table, and silently Barrow ate the food placed before him, and drank the pot of coffee.

This morning after pulling on his jacket and taking up his rifle, he reminded Amber, ''Don't be fergetting to make up some beaver scent today. I'm just about out." So saying, he pulled his ash-framed snowshoes from the peg on the wall next to the door. Closing the door behind him, he headed out to check his traps.

Amber enjoyed these early hours after Barrow left the cabin. When the weather permitted, she would go down to the stream and bathe. This morning, though, she knew, there would be a fresh supply of snow on the ground. Heating water in a trade pot over the fire in the fireplace, she decided to take a sponge bath, and after leisurely brushing out her waist-length hair, she took time to braid it into one plump braid that she left hanging down to her slender waist.

Pulling on the warm jacket she had made for herself at the start of fall from the hide of a mountain goat that Barrow had killed and brought back to the cabin, Amber made her way to the stream to get water for the cabin. She would put off making the beaver scent for as long as possible. When Barrow returned to the cabin this evening, he would demand to see the horn vial that would contain his precious mixture. She made a sour face, wishing that she could put off the ill-liked job until another day.

The stream was partially frozen, steam rising, the lush pines breathtaking at this time of morning, with their boughs decked with snowflakes. It would be Christmas in a week, she was reminded, and she would be seventeen. If her mother was alive, they would be preparing for the holiday. This time of the year had always been a special time of celebration. They would have a small tree, with cut-out paper decorations, hanging from its limbs, and there would be a present beneath the tree for her birthday.

Those days were now gone forever. She bent her back to fill the parfleche with water. There was little sense in bemoaning her fate. Returning to the cabin, she stoked the fire a little higher, placing another log on the coals.

After clearing away the breakfast dishes, Amber set the ingredients for the beaver scent on the small wood table Barrow had built for the cabin. Over the past year and a half she had learned much about skinning the animals her stepfather brought to the cabin, and tanning their hides. She was as good as Barrow with her horn-handled iron-bladed knife, which she used for scraping hides. The only task she truly despised worse, was making the beaver scent.

There was little help for it, though; she had the job to do. Taking up the vial, made from a deer antler, she poured the contents into a medium-size trade pot. Within were six stones, which had been taken out of beaver bladders. She added half a nutmeg, a dozen grains of cloves, and thirty grains of cinnamon into the pot with the stones. Finely pulverizing the mixture, she poured in oil, which had come from the beaver stones, until the mixture looked like soft mustard.

Earlier, before opening the horn vial, Amber had tied a scarf over her nose and the lower portion of her face, trying not to be forced to inhale the noxious smell. She tried to keep herself from gagging as she spooned the mixture into the vial and quickly pressed a cork on the top to keep the air out and not allow the beaver scent to lose its power. In four or five days, it would be ready for use. Barrow would entice beaver as far as a mile away by placing the bait on the point of a stick. The stick would then be pressed into the ground, in the water, over his traps.

Amber thoroughly scrubbed the table and utensils, trying to rid the cabin of the scent. Pulling the scarf from her face, she went to the cabin door, and for a few minutes allowed the cold northern air to sweep within.

As she was standing within the open portal, she heard the call, "Hello, the cabin!"

Breaking through the forest of pines, and stepping into

the clearing that circled the cabin, two trappers
approached. Amber hurriedly shut the door, and pushed
the wood latch into place. Taking up Barrow's extra rifle,
she made sure it was primed and ready before once again
stepping to the door. Sliding the lock aside, she opened
the door only a few inches and peered out, her gaze settling
on the two trappers.

"We saw the smoke from your cabin some ways into the
woods, little lady." The largest of the pair sported a full,
dark beard, and a beaver cap covered the crown of his
head, allowing straggling, rough edges of his oily hair to
lie along his collar. Eyeing the woman through the crack
in the door, he easily glimpsed her nervousness. "Where's
yer man?" he questioned, his dark eyes shifting around
the outer portion of the cabin.

"My stepfather is out trapping. He should return most
anytime now." Amber didn't like the way the man was
looking her over, and her hand tightened on the rifle, her
finger settling over the trigger.

The other trapper, who was short and slender, noticed
the rifle, and keeping a weathered eye upon the woman
standing with only a crack of the door open, he cleared
his throat before speaking. "Why don't you let us in the
cabin, to get warmed up by your fire? It's colder than a
dead whore's arse standing out here in this snow!"

Trying not to show her distaste at his words, she stated
coolly, "The best I can offer, until my stepfather returns,
is the lean-to over there." She nodded her head in the
direction of the structure. "Our horses are stabled there,
and it's a sight warmer than outside."

With her reply, the large man took a step closer to the
cabin door, as though he held a mind of forcing his way
into the cabin. His friend, at his side, stayed him with a
pull on his hide jacket. "I reckon that will do for the time
being." Women and rifles didn't mix, in Red Clayburn's

book. The little girlie might get spooked any minute, and him or Big Mike might take a bullet in the gillet for their pushy ways. As they left the front of the cabin and started toward the lean-to, Red questioned, "Didn't ya see the rifle the wench had in her hands, Big Mike?"

"All I saw was that soft peachy skin, and those purple-blue eyes. I sure would be liking meself some of that sweet meat!"

"Yeah. We should have gotten us an Injun woman to keep our blankets warm."

"An Injun, hell! I've got me a mind to taste some of that red-haired little split tail before we leave this place!"

Amber sat before the fireplace in one of the two chairs Barrow had made for the cabin. The rifle rested across her lap, and with each noise from outside that reached her ears, she drew her hand back to the stock of the weapon. There had been something about the two men she had not trusted. There had been a few other trappers over the past months who'd approached the cabin, but the others had held more respect when they had spoken to her. These two men had looked her over with a greedy glance that left her feeling unclean and nervous. She hoped that her stepfather would return to the cabin early in the afternoon, as he had been doing the past several weeks, because of the cold weather.

Henry Barrow did return a short time later. After finding the two trappers settled down in the lean-to with the horses, he grunted in Amber's direction, after entering the cabin, "You did good, gal. I'd've tanned your backside if I came home to find Big Mike and Red, in here warming their arses by my fire! Now hustle us up some grub to eat. Me and the men have some drinking to do." A few minutes later the two trappers entered the cabin and were making themselves comfortable on the plank seat Barrow had made on the back side of the table.

While Amber busily cut up some deer meat in the skillet, and set a pot of mountain turnips to boil, Barrow uncorked one of the iron-bound whiskey kegs and poured a tin cup for each man and a healthy draught for himself.

"You sure got a nice right place here, Barrow," Big Mike stated as he reached for the cup of whiskey set before him on the table.

"I ain't never been one to shy from work, if the payment in the long run holds true. I aims to get myself a little tavern, at the end of my three years of trapping," Barrow boasted as he thirstily drank down his cup of whiskey.

"I reckon then that you ain't heard that Ashley and Henry's trappers will be meeting at Bear Lake fer rendezvous. The Injuns are raiding up and down the Missouri, so word's being sent out that rendezvous will be at the foot of the Unita mountains, along the border of Utah and Wyoming."

"Thanks fer letting me know, Red. Here, have another drink of my whiskey." Barrow refilled the cups. "My gal will be having some vittles ready right quick." His glance as well as that of the two trappers, went across the cabin to Amber, who was stirring the meat in the skillet before mixing the cornmeal in the box-through and making cornbread.

Feeling their gazes upon her, Amber shifted nervously around so that her back was to the men, but this action brought about no peace when she imagined the heat of their glances caressing her.

"I reckon you value yer stepdaughter pretty highly?" Red, whose nickname was reflected by his shaggy red locks, spoke softly before taking another sip of the strong brew.

"Yep. She's right handy in the cabin, what with cooking

and tending to my hides." Barrow's voice was loud, his words bringing a flush over Amber's cheeks.

"I just bet she can warm a man's blankets right well, too." Big Mike grinned across the table at Barrow.

"The gal's as fresh and pure as the snow outside my cabin!" Barrow drained his cup. He couldn't blame the men for looking upon his stepdaughter in the fashion men have of looking at and lusting upon a woman. The gal had changed over the past year and a half. She was blooming into a real beauty, there was no denying the fact. More than once, he had found himself looking at her in a not very fatherly fashion, but always he had been reminded of her mother's image, and thoughts of Lizzy instantly held the power of cooling down his ardor.

Big Mike looked hard at Barrow, and in low tones, he questioned, "What're you holding back for, man? She ain't your blood kin."

As Amber set the tin plates on the table, and then the food, she self-consciously avoided eye contact with the men. Not having an appetite herself, she went to her bed, and taking out the dress she was making from a bolt of cloth which had been aboard the keelboat, she quietly sat down and began her sewing.

"Your right about one thing, Barrow." Big Mike spoke with a mouthful of food, pieces of cornbread falling in his thick beard. "Your gal can surely cook. Me and Red ain't had any home-cooked vittles since we came to these mountains."

"I reckon as how, you could gett yerself some extra money toward that tavern you're wanting, if you had a mind to let yer go for a price?" Red was not as blustery as Big Mike, and spoke only after chewing his food. His dark gaze held upon the woman across the room as he waited for Barrow's reply.

"I might do just that when I reach rendezvous," Henry

Barrow said between mouthfuls of his supper. Silas Benson had planted a seed in Barrow's head that night before they separated from the trappers aboard the keelboat. The girl was blooming right well here in the mountains. Come another year, and she would be ripe and lush for the attentions of men such as these two trappers, who had been isolated in the mountains for the last three years.

"Maybe then, you've a mind to let us have a go at her for the night?" Red felt his guts tighten with the thought of having the girl's shapely form beneath his body. It had been a long time since he had had a woman with half her looks!

"I ain't no weasely pimp, where my own stepdaughter is concerned. When I sell the gal, I'll be doing it for good, and not cheap! She'll be going to the highest bidder!" Barrow was not about to let these two men sample his stepdaughter's charms. He was smart enough to know that he could get more for her if she were still a virgin. He would wait until they reached rendezvous. Turning toward Amber, Barrow spoke out gruffly. "Get yourself under them covers, gal. It's time for you to turn in for the night. Me and the boys here have some more drinking ta do before they go back out to the lean-to." Barrow had considered letting the pair spend the night inside the cabin. They could have slept on the floor, near the fireplace. On second thought, he knew he couldn't trust either one of them as far as Amber was concerned. He sure as hell didn't want a bullet in the back of his head while he slept because these two blokes were too horny to control themselves!

For a second, Amber thought to remind him that she would need to clear away the supper dishes, but feeling all eyes resting upon her, she did not argue, but put away her sewing. Without changing into her nightrail, as she usually did while Barrow was checking on the horses for the evening, she climbed beneath her blankets wearing the same clothes as she had throughout the day.

Long into the night she heard the men talking and laughing, often hearing her own name being spoken. She could only hope that her stepfather did not become too inebriated to handle the two trappers.

It seemed to Amber that she lay there pretending to sleep for hours before the two men finally left the cabin. In loud voices, they told Barrow that they would be leaving at first light, and that they would see him again at rendezvous.

"Perhaps between Big Mike and meself, we'll have that price you were talking about earlier in the evening, Barrow." Red laughed loudly, right before the cabin door was closed behind both of them.

Four

Like a fallen cloud, the morning mist drifted past the open slopes that guarded the towering pass, opening into a lush meadow. The boundaries of which encircled the forest that sheltered Henry Barrow's cabin.

Early one morning while fishing along the stream bank, dense with red cedars and old timber and dewdrops spangling over an emerald tapestry of oak ferns, Amber discovered the meadow, a place that dazzled her eyes with a vibrant blur of color. The meadow was ablaze with a galaxy of flowers, a heady collage of red, yellow, pink, white, purple, all displayed against a background of resonant green.

At one end of the meadow, melting snow rushed down a stairway of rocks and boulders and cascaded into a sparkling lake, which fed the stream flowing near the cabin.

This morning, like so many since summer first began, Amber made her way to her secret meadow. As soon as Barrow left to check his traps, she rushed about getting her chores for the day out of the way, and then following the stream bank, with blanket and journal in hand, she made her way to the lake. Clumps of beargrass were in bloom. A solitary, bulbous cluster of creamy white tufts atop each stalk dotted the meadow, and were surrounded by mountain heather, scarlet Indian paintbrush, white yarrow, and purple daisies.

Arriving in the meadow, Amber freed her glorious hair, and with the peacefulness of the early-morning hour surrounding her, she spread out her blanket atop the lush grass near the lake and began to write in her journal. Her life, her hopes, her expectations, were all recorded here among these pages. Those sights that had caught her eye, she had delicately sketched Henry Barrow's three long years of trapping were at last drawing to an end. More and more of late, he had begun to talk about his plans to start out to rendezvous with his hides, for the purpose of meeting the rest of Ashley and Henry's trappers.

Amber felt excitement growing with the expectation of finally leaving the mountains. She had changed over these past three years. She was no longer a child, but a young woman grown. She held the same hopes and desires of every young woman, only she knew that for her to accomplish anything with her life, she would have to get as far away as possible from her stepfather.

Such thoughts no longer filled her with dread. She had had three years to come up with some plans for her future. She expected that Barrow believed she would go on with him, wherever he would decide to purchase his tavern. From there, she would become his servant without pay. Her own plan was different. Once they reached rendezvous, she would request that her stepfather pay her passage back to St. Louis in exchange for her hard work these last three years. Once in St. Louis, she would get a job. Perhaps she would be able to find work as a seamstress, or even cleaning and cooking in one of the boardinghouses or hotels along the levee. She would work and save her money until she had enough to get her to Richmond, Virginia, the place where her mother and father first started. In Richmond, she would begin a new life. Eventually she would take a hard-working man for her husband, and they would have children. Love did not enter her plans; she was more practical than to believe she would be granted such happiness. Henry Barrow had been the only male figure in her life, and after years of living under his cruel hand, she believed she could be content to find a man who would not abuse her or her children. If she could find such a man, she told herself, she would ask little more out of life. She could endure hard work and hardship in order to find this small taste of happiness.

All these dreams she wrote down in her diary, savoring the day when she would leave these beautiful mountains, and Henry Barrow, forever.

With the finish of the day's entry, she set the journal aside, and as the sun touched the meadow with warmth, she shed her clothes and for a while swam in the cool waters of the lake.

When she had had enough, she dried her body with the blanket and put on her dress. As she sat among the flowers, her fiery hair drying beneath the rays of the sun, she wove a crown of meadow grass, heather, and daisies. "It will be wonderful, when at last I am free," she called softly to a chipmunk that scampered over a nearby decayed log. As a blue dragonfly lazily fluttered over the flowers near her feet, she laughed aloud and set the crown of flowers atop her flaming head.

Stepping to her feet, she began to twirl, her arms outstretched as though she were dancing with a favorite beau. The birdsongs throughout the meadow served as, her music. It was a glorious morning to be alive, to be young, and to have hope.

* * *

From the crest of the mountain, two horsemen sat silently looking down into the meadow at the strange sight of a wasicun winyan, white woman, all alone and performing some strange dance. She wore flowers in her hair, which glowed the color of the glittering rocks found in the Paha Sapa, the hills of Dakota which were home to the Wakinyan, the sacred thunderbirds of their people.

"The wasicun winyan surely must be touched with strong wówasake; power." Thunder Hawk, a war chief of the Lakota Sioux, spoke to the warrior at his side, Strong Elk.

As an eagle swooped down over the meadow and shrilled loudly, Strong Elk stated, "She must be touched by the power of Wi. Her hair is a cover that shines with brightness even at such a distance. Perhaps she is a Wanági Winyan; Spirit Woman."

"Perhaps," Thunder Hawk replied thoughtfully. When they returned to their village, he would tell Spirit Walker all they had seen this day. If anyone would know the meaning behind this wasicun winyan here in this meadow, it would be Spirit Walker.

The warriors watched the woman unobserved, until at last she gathered her blanket over her arm and disappeared into the forest, following the stream.

Perhaps he and Strong Elk had joined together to witness a powerful vision, Thunder Hawk thought to himself, looking down into the meadow vibrant with colorful flowers. There was no longer any sign of the wasicun winyan; perhaps Strong Elk had been right, and she was a Wanági Winyan, and not real after all.

A sweat lodge had been constructed along the banks of the river, which flowed through the Lakota Valley. In the sacred manner of the people, it had been fashioned with sixteen willow sticks, each one tough but resilient, and easy to bend. The sticks had been forced into a beehive-shaped dome. Two buffalo hides were stretched over the framework, allowing a small entrance flap. The floor of the lodge was covered with sage. In the center, a circular pit had been dug to receive the burning wood, which would be topped with rocks. Wood was also piled outside the lodge to ensure the fire remain hot. After the fire burned down to coals, white lime-rocks would be placed in the center-pit. The lime-rocks had been gathered from the hills, those with green moss on their smooth surface etched with secret, spirit writing. The dirt from within the pit was piled in a small mound outside the lodge, which represented Unci; Mother Earth. A sacred prayer was said when the mound of earth was piled. Outside the entrance flap a buffalo-skull altar had been set up; tobacco ties were fastened to the skull's horns.

Arriving in the village late the night before, it was not until early the next morning that Thunder Hawk and Strong Elk had a chance to seek Spirit Walker out and tell him about the Wanági Winyan they had seen in the meadow, several days prior. Approaching the river, they spied the sweat lodge, which Lame Deer, Strong Elk's brother-in-law, had told the braves Spirit Walker was constructing near the river.

"I am pleased that my brothers have returned to the village," Spirit Walker called out in greeting. "I have made a sweat lodge for you to renew yourselves. Come," he commanded, the fire has been started, and the brave has been chosen to tend the fire."

Strong Elk looked at Thunder Hawk at his side, and then back to Spirit Walker. "You knew that we would be in the village this morning? You have prepared a sweat lodge for us, and have begun the fire?" But how could it be that Spirit Walker knew of their return to the village when they had arrived late into the night? Few in the village, besides their family, knew they had returned from their hunting trip. Surely no one would have anticipated that they would come to the river this morning to speak with Spirit Walker.

Spirit Walker did not answer the brave's questions. A smile filtered over his lips, then widened as he looked at his closest friend, Thunder Hawk.

It was not necessary to explain to Strong Elk about Spirit Walker's unique powers. Thunder Hawk was wise enough to know that something special was to occur in the sweat lodge this morning. Strong Elk would have his answers before this day was finished.

The three warriors discarded their leggings, moccasins, and breechcloths before bending and entering the sweat lodge. As Thunder Hawk and Strong Elk sat down, Spirit Walker uncovered his pipe, which was wrapped in a hide bundle. The pipe stem had been made from the leg bone of a buffalo, the bowl from red pipestone.

The fire-tender pushed aside the entrance flap. Carrying each lime-rock in the fork of a deer antler before placing it within the fire-pit, Spirit Walker touched each rock with the bowl of his pipe.

When the rocks were all brought into the lodge, Spirit Walker filled the pipe bowl with kinnikinnick; Indian tobacco made from willow bark. Holding the pipe over his head, he called on the spirits to bless this sweat lodge ceremony. After evoking his prayers, he settled his lips over the mouthpiece of the pipe and inhaled deeply before passing it on to Thunder Hawk, seated at his right.

Silently, the fire-tender reached through the lodge entrance, and taking up the gourd of cool, fresh water, poured a small amount over the lime-rocks, which had been sprinkled with green cedar. The air filled with an aromatic odor, as steam hissed over the rocks and filled the lodge.

Strong Elk gasped aloud as the heat instantly settled over him. Spirit Walker and Thunder Hawk relaxed, as though welcoming the purifying steam.

A few silent minutes passed. As the steam began to clear from the interior, Spirit Walker bent forward and studied the rocks with their secret spirit writing etched over their surface. Turning toward Thunder Hawk, he stated, "There is something that you wish to speak of. You have seen something that you question."

Strong Elk looked in Thunder Hawk's direction, waiting for him to tell Spirit Walker about the Wanági Winyan; Spirit Woman in the meadow.

Thunder Hawk nodded his head. His body feeling languid from the heat, he spoke slowly, "You are right, my friend. While on our hunting trip, Strong Elk and I saw something that we have spoken about often between us, though we do not understand its meaning."

Before the conversation could continue, the fire-tender poured more cool, fresh water from the gourd over the stones, and immediately there was a hissing noise in the lodge as more steam filtered throughout.

The heat intensified as the flap was secured back in place. Strong Elk drew in large breaths of heated air, thinking at any minute he might be forced to bolt; so hot was the inside of the lodge.

Spirit Walker leaned back and silently drew upon the pipe, the smoke mingling with steam. As he closed his eyes, his large, lithe frame felt weightless, and his mind swirled beyond the presence of the sweat lodge. He traveled without boundaries, soaring as one with the sacred eagle that had caught up his spirit.

All things were viewed through the eyes of the eagle. He glided over snowcapped peaks, swooping over trout-filled streams and blue-green lakes that mirrored jagged ridges stabbing the sky. The tiniest creature to the largest was viewed as he crested the treetops. The eagle's wings were weightless as he effortlessly spiraled Mother Earth, the north winds carrying him onward.

The fire-tender once again poured water from the gourd over the rocks, but Spirit Walker held no touch with the world of beings; he was in the realm of the spirit, carried to that place of unreality where the sky people and the spirits join as one.

The eagle flew over a meadow spectacular with heady color, water from snowcapped peaks rushing down the mountain, its shimmering droplets falling into a lake that glittered diamondlike beneath the morning sunlight. His wings extended as he swooped closer to Mother Earth, the eagle's eye, the vision that was the center of Spirit Walker's being, held upon the woman whose head was crowned with the blaze of fire-curls, the meadow flowers twined within the backdrop of long, glittering tresses.

Spirit Walker could feel the vibration of his heartbeat as he viewed the woman of his vision. As she turned in dance, her beautiful features directed upward, he felt his spirit calling to her, the sound coming out in the shrill loud cry, expelling from the eagle as he flew over the meadow.

Spirit Walker had viewed this same woman before, in another vision, but until this minute, he had not known the reason for her presence. His heart spoke to him, telling him all things. She was that part of his soul that waited to be joined with his spirit, to be claimed as one. She was the reason for the beating of his heart. Each pulse beat of his body pushed the blood flow to his heart, with but the purpose of singing her praise. She was the woman who would complete his life-circle.

As the eagle circled and soared, he viewed the two

horsemen sitting silently against the crest of the mountain, and with regret, he watched the woman gather her belongings and disappear through the forest.

He longed to follow her, but the eagle flew through the slopes guarding the meadow. Flighting among the clouds, he returned to the river that ran through the Lakota Valley.

Spirit Walker expelled a long, ragged breath as his spirit was returned to his body. Opening his eyes, he viewed the fire-tender pushing aside the entrance flap.

Thunder Hawk and Strong Elk looked upon him, neither speaking, awaiting Spirit Walker's words. Both warriors had watched as he had lain back as though one having passed from this world to the other side with the sky people. It seemed as though hours had passed before he revived. They knew without being told that he had been blessed with a mighty vision.

"The woman that you saw in the meadow is not a Wanági Winyan but a two-legged, like you and I."

"How do you know about the woman?" Strong Elk sat up straighter, his eyes wide as he stared at Spirit Walker. He had always known that Spirit Walker was different from the other braves of the village. His strength in combat was well known, he had counted coup on many enemies. His wisdom also was revered throughout the Sioux nations, but Strong Elk had not realized he had such strong power.

"One day, the woman's path will be joined with that of the people. She will be known among the Sioux, as Ptanyétu Ánpo; Autumn Dawn."

Thunder Hawk, unlike his friend, did not question that which Spirit Walker said. He knew that all would come to pass as he claimed.

With the finish of the sweat lodge ceremony, the three warriors dove into the cool, reviving waters of the river, cleansing away the impurities of flesh and mind, which the sweating had drawn.

Before the two braves left the river, Spirit Walker pulled Thunder Hawk aside and invited him to join him for supper in his lodge. There were things he needed to ensure were taken care of, before he left the village in search of the woman with the fire-curls.

Five

It was a glorious day for Amber Dawson. Midmorning saw the finish of the supplies and furs strapped across the two packhorses backs. Amber's valise was stuffed full of journals and personal belongings, and tied once again over her mount's saddle pommel. It was a warm day, the forest filled with birdsong. Henry Barrow kicked his horse's flanks and directed him away from the cabin tucked away in the wilderness. Amber followed silently behind as her stepfather started the long trek by following an invisible path along the bank of the stream.

Her three long years were finally up! Once they reached rendezvous, and she gained the means to return to St. Louis, her future would at last begin. Her stepfather had said little to her about his plans after he sold his furs. She assumed that he expected her, as his stepdaughter, to do his bidding, and follow wherever he would lead. She wisely knew to keep her own plans to herself until they reached rendezvous. Once there, she would request a small portion of his three years profit in order to return to St. Louis.

She was not sure that he would comply with her request, for she knew him well enough to be aware that he could be tight-fisted when it came to his purse. There was one thing, though, that she did know for sure; she would not leave with him from rendezvous. She was a woman grown, and would no longer be treated like a piece of chattel. She owed him the respect a parent was due, nothing more.

Henry Barrow halted his horse, less than two miles downstream in an open meadow. Dismounting, he handed the reins to his mount and packhorse over to Amber. "Stay put here with the horses, gal. I got me some traps along the stream-bed a'ways up. I don't aim to leave them here, when I can sell them for a few coins at rendezvous."

Holding the reins to Barrow's horse, as well as those of the pack animals, Amber sat atop her mount and watched her stepfather stride off into the forest. She was enjoying the warm summer afternoon. Meadow grass was belly high to her mount, dwarf huckleberry patches, beargrass, and buffalo berry bushes were in abundance. The meadow itself was encircled on three sides by a thick forest of pine, the same forest that sheltered the Barrow cabin.

Swatting away a pesky fly, which seemed intent on plaguing her, Amber held the reins loosely in one hand and allowed the animals to feed on the tall sweet grass. Pulling a handkerchief from her pocket, she unbuttoned the top buttons of her blouse and wiped away the perspiration from her neck and forehead.

Lost in thought, as once again she excitedly began to plan her future, she was taken unawares as the horses began to pull nervously against the leather reins. Her own mount began to shy and sidestep, and automatically Amber's thighs tightened as her hands clutched the reins in a firmer hold. "What is it, boy?" She tried to soothe the animal with gentle tones, at the same time looking around the field of tall grass.

For seconds her voice appeared to calm the animals, but shortly they again displayed nervousness. Amber knew something was distracting them, and still unable to find the cause of their agitation, she wished her stepfather would return. With her hands occupied with the reins, she could not retrieve the pistol from her stepfather's haversack.

Trying as best she was able to calm the horses and keep hold of the reins at the same time, her attention was drawn to a disquieting noise some distance away. Turning in the saddle to face the direction she heard the noise, panic instantly claimed her heart as she was met with the sight of a huge grizzly. The meadow grass had hidden him from view until this moment. Rising up on hind legs, he was several hundred yards away, his piercing gaze held directly on Amber and the horses. For a split second beast and human made eye contact. A fierce, blood-letting growl spewed forth from his massive throat; in that same instant, he lunged forward in attack.

Amber's thoughts frantically went to the extra rifle strapped along with the packs on one of the horses. If she could only fire the weapon at the bear, perhaps there was a chance he would turn direction in fear of the noise. She was not sure if even this would work. She had heard numerous stories of grizzlies attacking humans even as they were being fired upon, but even with such knowledge, she knew she had to try something to chase him away.

With each passing second, the grizzly was gaining distance. The sounds emitting from his throat were frightening to hear. Everything seemed to be happening so quickly, Amber knew that her only chance now was to flee. Clutching the reins, she tried to control her mount, and with a yell, she kicked him into motion.

Ears straight back, nostrils flaring, her mount nervously sidestepped and circled, not obeying his mistress's commands, his fear heightened with each passing second. A loud whinny escaped him as the seven-foot, eight-hundred-pound, man-eating grizzly bear lunged toward them. The great animal's three-inch-long razor-sharp claws struck out and tore flesh from the rump of one of the packhorses.

A piercing scream escaped Amber's throat, and with a final jerk, the three horses broke free of the hold she had on the reins. With as much effort as she could possibly gather, Amber tried to keep her seat. Frantically she kicked out at her mount's sides, trying to spur him into motion. Even as she heard the bear's low growls and could smell his scent, she tried to race for her life.

The horse's eyes enlarged as a fear unlike any he had ever known gripped him. Whinnying noises escaped him as his ears were lain back against his head. Feeling his mistress's movements atop him, he was caught up in wild panic. Rising up on his hind legs, his only thought was of dislodging the woman on his back and gaining his own freedom from the attacking beast.

Spilled to the ground, without a second to spare over damage to her person, Amber leaped to her feet and began to run. As the great beast rose up on his hind legs, his mouth opened wide and a ferocious growl filled her ears. Amber knew in that passing minute that her fate was sealed. A trembling, terror-filled scream left her lips and filtered throughout the encircling forest. The noise coming from her throat had no end as she felt the animal's breath upon the back of her neck, and her nostrils filled with his horrible stench.

Time seemed suspended as a loud, piercing cry from the edge of the forest intermingled with Amber's own and drew the attention of the ferocious animal. Suddenly a Sioux warrior broke through the edge of the pine forest, his deadly war cry proclaiming to the beast his desire for combat.

The grizzly growled a loud warning at the intruder, his glance, for the time being, taken away from his prey.

The warrior's war cry broke the still afternoon air. His large, prancing war-horse rose up and pawed at the air as man and beast gave clear warning before charging head-long in the direction of the grizzly and woman.

Amber dared not even breathe, fearful of drawing the attention of the ferocious animal back to herself. Her blue eyes were wide as she watched the bronze warrior, with war club held high over head, kick out at the black stallion's flanks. His war cry erupting from his throat, he shook a painted shield in the direction of the sun, and then bent low to touch it to Mother Earth as he boldly approached the bear.

Appearing to have entirely forgotten about the woman, who only seconds ago had been within his reach, the grizzly turned fully to face his attackers: man and horse. Amber did not hesitate, knowing this might well be her only chance to get away from the deadly attack of the grizzly. She began to run in earnest toward the shelter that the forest could provide.

"Ayeeeyeeee!" The deadly war cry rang throughout the meadow once again, the warrior knowing that he was facing a deadly opponent. There were many stories among his people of warriors giving their lives up to the strength of the mighty matóhota. From the corner of his eye, he saw that the woman had reached the forest, and kicking out harder against the stallion's flanks, he rushed directly at the beast. Bringing his war club down in a brutal arc, he struck the great bear on the side of the head, barely missing the ravaging assault of his deadly claws as the grizzly swung out at his attacker. A gash was opened by the war club, the bear screaming in fury and pain.

The warrior turned his mount sharply, ready to charge once again, but the grizzly was launching his own attack, racing on hind legs toward horse and man. Making sure that the woman could no longer be seen near the edge of the forest, the warrior allowed the grizzly to give chase, luring him to the opposite side of the meadow from where the woman he would call Ptanyétu Ánpo had disappeared into the pine forest.

Within the shelter of thick trees, Amber turned back in the direction of the meadow. Breathlessly she watched as the grizzly bear chased after the Indian warrior. After a few moments Amber collapsed back against a large pine tree, so great was her relief that by some miracle she was still alive.

A noise behind her caused her to jump as her heart hammered wildly in her chest. Turning with a weary eye, she saw that the horses were feeding there among the forest underbrush. Her breath wished out in grateful exhale. Approaching the animals, she gently cooed to them, sensing that they, like herself, were still very nervous.

With much relief she remounted and gathered the reins of the other animals, silently staying hidden within the boundaries of the pine trees. There, within her shelter, she watched for any sign of the Indian who had saved her life.

It was not the Indian and his black stallion that Amber saw stepping out into the meadow a short time later, but Henry Barrow. Leading the horses out of the pine forest and heading in his direction, she easily glimpsed from a distance that he was not pleased with her.

"I thought I told you to stay put, till I got my traps back" were the first words to leave his mouth. More than likely she went to the forest to shade herself from the afternoon sun, Barrow thought in irritation as he began to stow away the beaver traps in his packs. His glance soon went from the pack animal's rump, back to his stepdaughter. "What the hell happened to this here animal?'' The ugly claw marks left by the grizzly were bloody and gaping.

"That's why I was in the woods with the horses. We were attacked by a grizzly." Amber was still breathless. Even as she spoke, her violet-blue eyes circled around the meadow as though expecting the vicious beast to renew his attack and to lunge once again out at them.

Securing the packs back in order, Barrow looked sharply at Amber. "I reckon as how you're pretty lucky then, gal, to have gotten away from a bear like that." By the marks on the packhorse, it was plain that the grizzly had been pretty big. "Most hungry grizzlies don't give up easily. It were smart thinking to head fer the forest with the horses. If I had lost my animals and furs, it would have been a waste of three years work." Barrow had to admit that Amber was braver than most females; he would give her that much. Another would have more than likely took off and saved her own hide without thought to his supplies and animals.

Upon first seeing her stepfather, Amber had considered telling him about the Indian who had rescued her, but on reflection, she had kept quiet about that part of her story. All Henry Barrow cared about anyway was that his horses and furs were safe. If he knew that she had been saved by an Indian, she wouldn't put it past him to go into the forest to search for the warrior. It wouldn't sit good with Henry Barrow that his stepdaughter had been rescued by an Indian. More than likely, he would make sure that the grizzly finish off the Indian before they would be allowed to continue on with their journey.

Late that evening after clearing away the supplies and skillet used for supper, Amber had a few minutes to herself. She sat upon her trade blanket near the edge of the camp-fire and wrote the happenings of the day down in her

diary. Reflecting back over the afternoon, she realized how
brave the Indian had been to come to her rescue. All she
could do now was silently pray he had not been harmed
by the great bear. If only he had returned to the meadow
before her stepfather, she would have been able to thank
him for saving her life, and would have been assured that
he had been unharmed.

At the finish of her entry, she painstakingly sketched
the proud warrior sitting atop his black stallion. Drawing
the image of him as his horse had risen up on his hind
legs, she searched her memory for each detail. When she
had completed the sketch guided by the firelight, she
looked fully down upon her handiwork. The warrior's features were darkly handsome. He had worn a breechcloth
about his hips, and over his chest was a pipe-bone breastplate, with strands of horse hair and brilliant blue beads
embellishing both sides. His bronze muscles had glistened
as he had held war club and painted shield in hand. His
long midnight hair fell loosely down his back, an eagle
feather hanging over his left ear, from the beaded headband secured around his forehead. A soft sigh escaped
her. She wondered if she had ever seen a more handsome
man, Indian or not. The warrior had appeared out of
nowhere, like a knight in shining armor, saving her from
the very claws of sure death.

For a few added moments, she seared the likeness to
memory before putting the diary away and stretching out
on her blanket. Looking up at the star-brilliant night, she
felt strangely at a loss. Was the Indian, this minute, also
looking at these same stars? Why had he risked his life to
save hers?

Six

From a distance, gunfire, riotous yelling, and shouts of every description could be heard coming from the valley below. Bear Lake glistened brightly as the afternoon sun reflected off its surface. The numerous hastily erected lean-tos constructed a short distance from the lake were intermingled with canvas-covered wagons, canvas tents, and Indian tepees. The valley floor itself was dotted with grazing Indian ponies. During the span of the last three years, because of the Indian hostilities and hardship of travel, Andrew Henry had backed out of the partnership he had made with Ashley. But William Ashley an enterprising man who easily caught up a challenge, led an overland pack train into the Rockies, and down the Green River. At the appointed date for rendezvous, he and his supplies were at Bear Lake waiting for his trappers and those free trappers and Indians who wanted to trade, or bargain a price for their furs.

Ashley's trappers, as well as free trappers, turned out for the venture. Rendezvous meant contact with the out-

side world for the first time in three years. There were
letters from home. The St. Louis, *Gazette*, dated only two
months previous, was passed around and avidly devoured.
There was also talk with men who had read papers all
through the winter and spring, and those who had lived
among civilization on a daily biases.

Amber, as well as Henry Barrow, felt excitement growing
as their mounts drew closer to the activity of rendezvous.
With a shout and a loud whoop, Barrow kicked his horse's
sides, and pulling his rifle from its scabbard on his saddle,
he fired it into the air, setting his mount into a gallop,
with the packhorse running on his heels. Henry Barrow
eagerly rushed toward the first form of civilization he had
seen in three years. Amber also kicked her mount's flanks
as she raced after her stepfather.

Hearty shouts, calls of welcome, feminine laughter, gunfire, grunts and groans from fistfights, and drunken
whoops greeted Henry Barrow and Amber Dawson as they
halted their mounts in the center of the rough encampment. Rendezvous was one big free-for-all, where drunken
brawls, gambling, women—both Indian and white—were
swooped up in the arms of a trapper and carried away to
the nearest bush or shelter. Foul language could be heard
all about, and more than one death was not an uncommon
occurrence. Amber watched everything around her in
wide-eyed amazement.

"Stay close to me, gal. I don't want any of these blokes
to be thinking that you're free with your favors like those
whores over yonder." Barrow nodded his beaver-capped
head toward a canvas covered wagon. Next to the vehicle
was a line of trappers. They were being tantalized out of
their money by two barely clad women, who smiled invitingly from the open back portion of the covered wagon.
A small man with a dusty jacket and a trim, round-cornered
hat held out his hand for the desired coin. As a trapper

was shoved out of the wagon by the pair of women, the next in line was pulled within.

Henry Barrow would get no argument from his stepdaughter. The atmosphere at rendezvous was wild and dangerous, and Amber had no desire to be forced into a situation where she would have to fend for herself against these rowdy backwoods men.

"I see that you finally made it, old son!" Silas Benson was the first trapper to make his way to Henry Barrow's side and greet him and Amber properly. As Barrow and Amber dismounted, the other man's gaze shifted to the young woman. "And I see that you made it just fine in them there mountains. You're looking right fit, miss." His glance took in the womanly length of Barrow's stepdaughter. Her long, copper-colored curls were even more beautiful now than when they had started their trip up the Missouri three years earlier.

"Why, thank you, Mr. Benson." Amber was pleased to see a face she recognized amidst the group of trappers that were beginning to encircle them.

Her smile was sheer radiance as violet-blue eyes sparkled warmly. For a single minute, Silas Benson stood before her mesmerized, unable to speak, his breath clutched tightly in his chest. She was the prettiest thing he had seen this side of the Rockies—and admittedly up the Missouri, and even beyond. He had never seen a woman quite as fair as Amber Dawson. Looking at her now, he wondered how old Barrow had held onto such a rare treasure these past three years. It was indeed a wonder that an Injun or trapper hadn't put a bullet in Barrow's gullet and taken the girl for his own.

"If you're done gawking at my gal, Benson, you might tell me where to take my plumes to sell," Barrow gruffly spoke out. Watching Silas Benson and the other trappers encircling them, staring at Amber as though they had never

seen a white woman before, he was inwardly pleased. He
would let them all look to their hearts' content. Soon
enough, he would be finding out which man among them
would be serious enough about his stepdaughter to be
parting with his hard-earned money!

The trappers standing around were more than happy
to supply Barrow with the desired information, hoping
that somehow they would gain the young woman's eye in
the process. Eagerly, several men pointed to one of the
open lean-tos in the center of the encampment.

"Ole Henry, ain't in the fur business anymore, so you
just got Ashley to be dealing with, and he don't want to
part with any more than six dollars a plew, prime." It was
Silas Benson, coming to his senses at last, who after giving
Amber one last smile, supplied the information to Barrow.

"Six dollars, you say? Well, me and me gal's got a right
good cache here. She's a fine one to help with the skinning
and curing. More than likely, Ashley'll find that my plumes
are the finest he'll be seeing this year at rendezvous."
Barrow eagerly declared his stepdaughter's virtues as his
helper to all those standing around. At six dollars a plew,
prime, and whatever he could profit from Ashley, he would
have himself a nice little nest egg to go toward that tavern
he had been dreaming about all these years.

There wasn't a man in the group who disputed Barrow's
words about the talents of his stepdaughter. If the old
trapper claimed that the young woman could skin and
cure animals better than the lot of them, so be it! With
her rare beauty, each man among them was sure that she
could do anything she set her mind to, and even if she
couldn't, what trapper in his right mind would truly care
anyway?

As Amber closely followed Barrow and Benson, she was
greeted with wide smiles and calls of greeting. Men, both
in their cups and sober, made an effort to tip their fur-

trimmed caps. These were lusty men of the mountains, and Amber could hear their admiration of her beauty as they whispered among themselves, *"Did you ever be seeing anything as fair, Jeb? Why, her hair fairly shines! It be brighter than a fox pelt! I'd give anything for jest a touch of them pretty curls!"*

"She's a lady, old Hos. I wouldn't be touching without permission. Ye be wanting a feel, ya best be going on over to that whore wagon. Fer the right price old Slim will let you feel any one of his girls in the back of the wagon."

"It just wouldn't be the same, Jeb. Slim's girls can't be holding a flame to her."

Amber hurried her steps, not wanting to be far from the protection that her stepfather offered. Having lived in the wilderness these past three years without male companionship other than that of Henry Barrow, she had not realized that men such as these surrounding her could be attracted to her. When she had left St. Louis at fifteen, the men she had known and met on the keelboat had paid little interest in her.

Henry Barrow let go the reins of his horse and pack animal as he approached Ashley's lean-to. Unstrapping his furs, he took up an armload of pelts before starting through the entranceway. Pushing two drunk, arguing trappers aside, Barrow spread out his pelts on a table set up for the selling and trading of furs. "Me packs are piled high with such pelts. I expect the best price you're offering, Ashley." He spoke loudly, without hesitation, to William Ashley and the large black man at his side.

"Well, Barrow, I see that you made it to rendezvous." Ashley had met Henry Barrow when he had first signed on to go trapping with his men. At that first meeting he had taken an instant dislike to the rough-edged man. He had to admit, though, as he ran his hand over the beaver pelt spread out before him that he was a passable enough trapper.

"Me and my gal made it well enough in the mountains," Barrow admitted. Several of the trappers who had signed on with Ashley and Henry had not been so lucky. One reportedly had been found two winters past, frozen solid where he sat beneath a tree, his hand clutched to the stock of his rifle. Two trappers had been killed by grizzly bears, and Indians were claimed to have murdered a few others.

William Ashley's glance rose up from the pile of pelts and traveled over the young woman standing behind Barrow. So this was his stepdaughter. He had heard that she had left St. Louis on the keelboat with Barrow. A slow smile curved his lips. She was certainly a beauty, and by the glances of the men standing around the lean-to, Barrow would be having his hands full while they remained here at rendezvous. "Will you be wanting credit for more supplies?" His gaze shifting back to Barrow, Joseph pulled forth a pad of paper to write out the necessary credit slips to the supply wagons.

"Naw, I want cash fer my pelts this year. I ain't so sure if I'll be going back to the mountains just yet." Barrow was wise enough to keep his plans for a tavern quiet for the time being. The amount of money he made off his cache was entirely up to this man. After Ashley took out his portion for the supplies he had advanced him three years ago, Barrow hoped to still have a tidy bankroll.

"Most of the trappers are taking credit slips for their portion." Ashley looked directly at Barrow with a hard frown. Too many like this one and he wouldn't be in business very long. Ashley made his profit from the trappers spending credit slips on whiskey and supplies. "Why don't I give you half of your profit in cash and the other half in credit slips?"

Barrow was adamant. He wanted cash for his cache, and

he wouldn't take any less. "Naw, that ain't good enough. Like I said, I might not go back to the mountains for a year or so. There's some business I need to tend to in St. Louis." The business of finding himself a tavern.

There was no more that Ashley could do to sway Barrow, so, he nodded his head in Joseph's direction. The black man pulled out the cash box from behind the table, and Ashley began to count out the money slowly. "Like I said, Barrow, these are fine pelts. It'll be a shame to let a year pass, when you could be making big money for another cache like this."

"Can't be helped," Barrow answered gruffly. Henry Barrow figured he had done his time as a trapper. All he wanted now was to get back to St. Louis and find that tavern he had been dreaming about all this time he trapped in the mountains.

A short time later, Barrow, with Silas Benson still at his side, and Amber close, left the lean-to. "Come on, Barrow, you and little sis here can bunk down with me. I'll show you where you can tie off your mounts and put away yer gear. Pete Tanner and me got a tent. I won it in a game of poker from some greenhorn who headed back to St. Louis the day afore yesterday. You and the girl are welcome to share it with us, while you're here at rendezvous."

Henry Barrow nodded his beaver-capped head in agreement to the invitation. It was not often that he was treated so graciously. This was a benefit, he knew, that was coming his way because of his stepdaughter. Old Silas was smitten with the girl, and it was clear he wanted to make sure she had some kind of shelter over her head while here at rendezvous. There was no fool like an old fool, Barrow thought. He, along with many of the trappers at rendezvous, would be more than willing to bid for the honor of the gal's company when he decided to put her up for sale. He ought to wait a few more days before he announced his intention to sell the girl, he decided. The group of men that had followed them to the lean-to, and even now were tagging behind them, acted as though they hadn't seen a fair woman in some time. It might just prove more profitable to flash the gal around for a day or two, and whet more appetites. On second thought, he might be ready to head out to seek his future after a good night's rest. He would see the mood of things come tomorrow morning.

As they left the lean-to, only several yards away from where they stood a fight broke out. An Indian had apparently come out of no where and attacked a buckskin-clad trapper. As Amber watched the grisly contest of strength, the Indian clutching a sharp-bladed hunting knife in one hand and a tomahawk in another, she saw the cool, death-like control cross the bearded, mountainman's features as he drew forth his own wicked hunting knife.

The fight was over shortly after it started. Amber gasped as she quickly turned her head away from the sight of the trapper pulling his knife out of the brave's chest.

"What the hell was that all about?" Barrow asked Silas Benson.

"The best I can tell you, Barrow, don't be hanging around ole Samuel there for too long of a time. This sort of thing happens on a regular basis to him."

"What's his story?" Henry Barrow looked back over his shoulder, wishing that Silas wouldn't be in such a rush. It appeared that the action wasn't over yet. There was still a crowd milling around the prone Indian and the trapper.

"Well, to hear tell of it, Samuel took himself a Flathead Injun squaw a couple of years back, and they had themselves a kid. He was out trapping one day, when a half-dozen Crow bucks come upon the woman and kid. When Samuel returned to their lodge, he found his woman and kid dead. Them Crows had been vicious with the two."

Silas didn't elaborate on what he had been told had been done to the pair, because of Amber's presence. He was sure that Barrow would hear the entire story again before he left rendezvous, and at that time he could be filled in on all the gory details.

As they made their way to his tent, he continued. "Well, I reckon that ole Samuel went a little crazy. He loved that woman and kid. He tracked the braves down and killed 'em one by one. Only thing, he cut open their chests, pulled out their hearts and ate 'em."

Silas Benson heard Amber's gasp of horror as the grisly image crossed her mind. His look as he went on appeared apologetic to her sensibilities. "Crows aren't exactly the forgiving type, if you know what I mean. They believe that the spirits of those braves that Samuel killed can't go on to the happy hunting ground, because their bodies weren't intact. Now it's a regular pattern that they send a warrior out against him. Each new warrior is stronger than the last. So far, ole Samuel has taken 'em all on, and been the winner. Odds are, though, his time will run out sooner or later, and I wouldn't want to be around when it happens!"

"So that's what he was doing back there. Cutting the Injuns's heart out?"

Silas nodded. "The Crows believe he has much power. All Samuel wants is revenge for the death of his squaw and kid, and each Crow warrior wants the honor of being the one to kill him."

"That's terrible!" Amber exclaimed softly, her features pale, her hand clutching her slender throat as though she might well be ill at any moment.

"It's a hard life here in the mountains, sis. I reckon as how us trappers takes what's given out and tries hard to give back a little worse than the other fella."

Arriving at Silas's tent, the trapper showed the two where they could stow their gear. "If you like, Barrow, little sis here can stay here in the tent while we go and get ourselves a drink of whiskey.'' He was sure that Amber would appreciate some time to freshen up and rest after their long days of travel.

"Naw, the gal will come along with us. She ain't no prissy sass that ain't never seen a man in his cups." Henry Barrow wasn't going to let Amber out of his sight. He needed her if he was to have enough money to purchase his tavern. He wasn't about to take the chance that one of these women-hungry trappers would get at the gal before paying his full due!

"She'll be safe enough here inside the tent, Barrow. Silas Benson was taken by surprise at Barrow's protectiveness toward his stepdaughter. It didn't seem at all like the Barrow he knew. The last time he had seen Barrow and the girl, the trapper hadn't had that much affection for her. These past three years must have softened his heart. "No one's coming in this here tent uninvited. She'll be safe enough till we return. Come on, old son, that whiskey's waiting fer us!" He didn't see any reason why the young woman couldn't rest for a while. She looked near tuckered out.

"Like I already told you, Benson, the gal goes where I go." Barrow's voice hardened. He didn't appreciate Benson's pushiness where Amber was concerned, and for a minute, began to reconsider the offer of staying in the other trapper's tent. It was plain enough to see that he was soft on the gal, but Barrow knew better than to allow any mollycoddling where his stepdaughter was concerned.

Silas Benson caught the other trapper's mood swing. "Whatever you want, Barrow. I didn't mean nothing by saying she could stay behind in the tent. I just thought she could rest herself here fer a spell."

Barrow ignored the apology. "Brush out your hair, gal, and come along." He had noticed Amber's disheveled appearance. He wanted her to look her best when they left the tent and strode out among the trappers.

Amber was more than a little surprised at Barrow's order. Pulling her comb out of her valise, she gave no argument. After the long days of travel to reach rendezvous, she would have been more than willing to wash her hair and her body. But knowing that she would not be afforded such a luxury here at Bear Lake, she could at least run the comb through her tangled curls and brush the dust from her skirts.

Pulling the sides of her copper hair back, she secured them with a pair of leaf-design hair combs that had belonged to her mother, allowing the full length to hang down her back, reaching her waist. Turning back to her stepfather and Silas Benson, she saw the glint of satisfaction in Henry Barrow's dull green eyes as they traveled over her.

Seven

There were over one hundred trappers at this first rendezvous, and many over that number of Indians. Booths and wagons were set up for entertainment, sales, and bartering. Bolts of material, beads of every variety, pots and pans, flour, coffee, whiskey, sugar, spices, all were available at extravagant prices—five, sometimes ten, times the going rate on the streets of St. Louis.

The Indians appeared as light hearted as the hearty mountainmen in this carnivallike atmosphere. Besides gambling, the young bucks loved the attention and applause they received as they galloped about showing off their favorite Indian pony. Horse races, field sports, mock battles were all openly displayed at any time of the day. The trappers joined in these activities and displayed their skills, which often were as good, or even better, than those of the braves.

As Silas Benson led Amber and Henry Barrow to the lean-to that had been erected as a saloon, Amber noticed that a long-rifle shooting contest was taking place between two trappers. The winner shouted aloud as his bullet hit the mark, the loser promising a round of whiskey in a good-natured voice.

Whiskey, or what was called whiskey—because in truth it was raw alcohol thinned with water from the lake—was consumed at five dollars a pint. Silas Benson placed his money on the plank table, purchasing the first round.

Amber stood silently next to her stepfather, uncomfortable with the stares she was receiving. She tried to pull her mind away from the attention of the men by watching the antics of an Indian on horseback who was racing through the encampment, loud whoops escaping his parted lips. Boldly, he displayed his trick riding. With ease, he held on to his pony's mane as he pressed his lithe body to the animal's side, appearing to be riding beneath the horse. Those standing around the lean-to stopped to watch him. In one motion he slipped to the pony's back, but this time he was riding backward. All of a sudden, his pony took a sharp right turn in order to avoid a drunken trapper who was weaving unsteadily before him. The brave on horseback took a sudden fall to the earth.

Raucous rounds of hearty laughter followed his fall. "That's Ole Winter Owl's youngest son, Little Eagle. He tries that same trick most every day, and his arse hits the ground as many times!" Benson's laughter joined in with the rest.

"Injuns ain't got no good sense anyway you look at it!" Barrow grinned, watching the young brave rubbing his backside as a pair of trappers helped him to gain his feet, then placed a pint of whiskey in his hand as payment for their entertainment.

"Some Injuns, like Little Eagle's pappy, might have more sense than you reckon," Silas stated as he took up his whiskey glass. "To hear tell, Winter Owl claims to know where there's a place in the mountains that's crawling with beaver. I heard one fella say that all you need is a club to hit the critters over the head. You don't even need to set any traps!''

"You don't say?" Barrow drank down a big swallow of the harsh-tasting whiskey and wiped the dampness on his mustache with the back of his hand. "Now if I could find a place in the mountains where the beaver are that thick, I might just trap for another year. It don't take no time at all to trap out a rich stream bed, and I can't say a few more coins in me pocket wouldn't come in right handy."

"Maybe this evening after little sis here settles down, we'll take a stroll on over to ole Winter Owl's lodge and see what the chief has to say on the matter fer himself. Most everything I done heard so far has been from some drunken buck. We might as well get the directions to this spot in the mountains from ole Winter Owl himself. We'll take him some whiskey and a few beads. He's got himself three young squaws. The presents should come in right handy for the women, while the whiskey loosens up the ole Injun's tongue."

This time, Barrow didn't object to letting Amber stay behind in the tent while he went to Winter Owl's lodge. Thoughts of such a cache of beaver plumes was a mighty temptation. With what he hoped to profit from his step-daughter added to what he had made for his three years of hard work in the mountains, he hoped to have enough for his tavern. But with such a wealth of hides as Benson was describing, he envisioned a larger tavern, with plenty of rooms upstairs for weary travelers to rest themselves throughout a night.

As the two men conversed, Amber paid them little atten-tion, watched instead two men rolling on the ground in a fistfight. Lifting her gaze from the pair, she found her regard instantly captured by a pair of compelling ebony eyes. Her heartbeat instantly intensified, her breath coming out in small gasps, her knees weakening because of this chance glance. *It was him! The Indian warrior who had saved her from the grizzly bear in the meadow!*

For a few seconds, Amber squeezed her eyes tightly shut as she tried to steady her breathing. Not knowing what she expected, she slowly opened them to find him still standing there staring at her as though they were the only two people in the world. He did not have the look of the other Indians standing around the whiskey lean-to. He appeared haughtily regal even in these lowly surroundings. Around his shoulders was wrapped a buffalo robe, painted with the scenes of his triumphs on the hunt and in warfare. In his left hand, he held a lance with eagle feathers hanging in decoration. Also in this hand, he clutched his shield, the facing painted with the warrior's depiction of a buffalo. Eagle feathers, and red trade-cloth strips had been beaded in a pattern at the top and bottom of the shield. But what held Amber's gaze was the warrior himself. His ebony hair hung loose below his shoulders, an eagle feather hanging in a downward position above his right ear. On this same side of his head, near the crown was ermine fringe, the tips of the snow-white fluff painted vermilion. Around his throat he wore a necklace of dentalium shells and elk teeth. As her blue eyes strayed over his face, she sharply inhaled once again. He was by far, Indian or not, the most handsome man she had ever seen. His skin was bronze, cheekbones high, lips full and sensual. His nose was aquiline, with a hawkish angle, which added a rugged appeal to his striking face. His ebony eyes framed by raven-black brows held the power to mesmerize and capture.

"Dab-berned it, gal, what's come over you?" Barrow's elbow against her forearm all but knocked her over. "I asked you, if you're ready to go on back to the tent and fix me and Benson here some grub? We've got things to do and ain't got time fer any of your lallygagging around!"

"Yes . . . yes, of course I'm ready," Amber stammered, looking at her stepfather as she caught herself with a hand on the edge of the wood-plank board that served as the bar in the lean-to. As she started to follow Barrow and Benson out of the shack, she cautiously looked back in the direction that the Indian had been standing.

He was nowhere to be seen.

Eight

*The Indian warrior was not dead after all, as she had feared
. . . he was here at rendezvous!* It was not until late that same
evening, after she had put together a meal and Barrow
and Silas had left the tent, that Amber found the chance
to write her thoughts down in her diary. Then, she sketched
every detail of the warrior's appearance. Amber felt her
heart racing wildly in her chest as she looked down at
her handiwork. She had captured the handsome, virile
magnificence of the man upon the page before her. She
had feared that he had been killed by the bear, but now,
remembering how he looked this day, Amber knew that
not even a fearsome grizzly could harm a warrior such as
he. He seemed invincible to her.

Fleetingly, she wondered what he was doing here at
rendezvous. Perhaps he had brought furs to trade or sell.
He had seemed to stand alone, not in the company of any
of the other Indians. She had not seen him participating
in the drinking and gaming along with the other Indians
or trappers. Their chance meeting in the whiskey lean-to

had been so short that she could not put answers to these questions.

Perhaps he was here at rendezvous with a band of his people. Perhaps his family or wife and children were somewhere nearby. Surprisingly, thoughts of the warrior having a wife and children left her feeling strangely ill at ease and a little let down.

Scolding herself for being silly, she tucked the journal beneath the blankets of her bed. Why should, his reasons for being at rendezvous matter to her, or, in fact, if he did have a family here with him? He had saved her life and for that she was grateful. If she found the opportunity to thank him, without her stepfather being nearby, Amber told herself that she would do so.

It had been a long, tiring day, and she tried to lose her thoughts in the darkness of slumber. The noise at rendezvous seemed to intensify with the lateness of the hour; gunfire, whoops, and shouts seemed to come from every direction. With eyes shut, her inner vision instantly filled with the image of the warrior. She tried to chase from her mind the power that those ebony eyes held as they looked upon her. She reminded herself that it was time for her to talk to her stepfather about her need for money so she could return to St. Louis. Tomorrow . . . she told herself. Tomorrow she would approach Henry Barrow with her request for money. This would be the first step toward her own future. She would take whatever money he would offer, and never look back upon the past!

By noon the following day, Amber had seen no further sign of the Indian; or as she was beginning to think of him, *her* Indian. She had awakened early and had cooked breakfast over the open fire for Barrow, Benson, and the other trapper who shared the tent. Barrow had left with

Benson shortly after the meal. He had administered a stern warning for Amber to stay near the tent, and not to talk to any of the trappers who might happen to come nearby. After putting away the dishes and straightening out her pallet, Amber went outside and sat down on the log that had been drawn up near the open fire. Silently she watched the activity around the encampment, her gaze often wandering in search of her Indian.

One of the most crowded places of business was the covered wagon that offered a lady's entertainment for the right price to the trappers. From early morning till the late hours of night, the long line made its way to the back of the wagon. Amber watched the activity around the wagon from where she sat, her laughter mingling with the others around her as one of the women from the back of the wagon, who boasted an overabundant bosom and flame-red hair, stuck her head out the back entrance and cried loud enough for all to hear, "Enough, Slim! You might not need a break out there holding your hand out for money, but me and the girls are done in! Our arses are near to raw and chafing!"

The slender man called Slim looked abashed and red-faced with her outcry. Bowing low from the waist, his dapper hat clutched in his hand as he swung it in a wide arc, he quickly replied, "Yes, ma'am, Miss Calico Kat, whatever you say, my dear, whatever you say. Gentlemen, there will be a fifteen-minute resting period for the ladies!" he called down the line of men.

"Fifteen minutes, hell, you money-pinching skinny little whoremaster!" the red-haired bawd shouted as she climbed down from the back of the wagon. Skirts rising up her thighs were given no notice as she stood before the little man, both hands firmly placed on abundant hips. "I didn't come out here to this wilderness to die upon my back! Me and the girls will take an hour break, and if you don't like that, you can climb up into the back of that wagon yourself!''

Slim's face flushed brighter as the trappers standing around the wagon rolled with laughter at the fiesty whore's loud rejoinder. ''Whatever you wish, my dear, whatever you wish.''

''Well, I say that four whores aren't enough for these horny bastards! The next time I agree to come along with you, Slim Farley, you better have more girls!'' With that, the woman called Miss Calico Kat stomped off in the direction of the Whiskey lean-to, eager to quench the thirst she had built up while lying on the mattress in the back of the whore wagon, moaning and groaning as though she held only one desire in life: to pleasure a man!

Amber's blue gaze followed the woman's swinging hips as she strutted across the encampment. Though Amber did not condone the woman's occupation, she had to admit that she admired the way Miss Calico Kat had stood up to the little man! Amber wished that she had an ounce of the woman's backbone that she could stand up to Henry Barrow in a like manner. All morning, she had tried to decide how best to approach her stepfather about her plans to return to St. Louis. If worse came to worst and he refused to give her any money, she told herself that she would somehow find other means to get to St. Louis. Perhaps she could approach Mr. Ashley, and ask if she could join his party on the return trip. She would be more than willing to work hard for food and shelter. He had seemed a nice enough man when she had seen him yesterday in the lean-to where Henry Barrow had bartered hides for a price. He might take some pity on her, if it came down to it.

Shortly after the incident at the wagon, Henry Barrow approached the tent with two men at his side. One man was tall and burly, his features covered by a thick, dirty-blond beard and scraggly mustache. Long, stringy, brownish-blond hair hung against the collar of his buckskin shirt. The other man was much smaller and stayed in the background. He wore a tattered suit that had seen far better days; to Amber's eyes his appearance was that of a young dandy.

"Gal, this here's Tate Coker." Barrow introduced the large trapper, while ignoring the young man as though he wasn't worth a glance. "Get yourself up, gal, and turn about, so Coker can get a fair look at you."

For a full minute, Amber looked at the three men in surprised hesitation. What on earth was her stepfather up to? Why should she do what he ordered her for this filthy man? She sat where she was upon the log.

Barrow reached down a strong arm and jerked her up by the forearm. "Most times as not, she does what she's told right quick enough," he quickly began to explain, giving Amber a hard shove that almost sent her to her knees in front of the two men.

Amber managed to catch her balance, and for the first time that she could remember, she openly glared her full hatred upon her stepfather.

"Yeah, I'll be bidding on her, Barrow." The trapper spat a long dark stream of tobacco juice toward the open fire, the contact making a hissing sound, before he turned around and headed back to the whiskey lean-to. The man at his side looked quickly from Henry Barrow to the girl, his features showing disbelief as he pulled a pad of paper from his suit coat pocket, then, turning, followed the larger man across the encampment.

Amber stared in stunned disbelief after the two men. She turned back to her stepfather. "What did he mean when he said he would 'bid on me'?" Fear the likes of which she had never known before traveled over her length and covered her with gooseflesh. What could Henry Barrow be up to? she wondered, but could gain no knowledge of his plans on Barrow's closed features.

"I'll tell you what you need to know, when it's time. You just do what you're told, and you won't feel me fist on the side of your head. Get yourself inside and wash up. You've got a smudge of dirt on yer cheek, and your hair's all tangled."

Once again her stepfather appeared concerned with her appearance. Twice in as many days was two times more than he had ever given notice to her looks before. Suspicion grew, but Amber knew by his threats and harsh tone that she would be told no more until he was ready to reveal his purpose. Inside the tent, she dampened a cloth and washed her face and arms. She tarried for a few minutes as she brushed out her long copper curls.

Looking on with hearty approval, Barrow smirked with the finish of her toilette. "Come on with me, gal, to the whiskey shack. I aim to buy myself a pint of brew."

The chilling glint in his green eyes, the sound of his voice, and the pressure of his heavy hand upon her forearm as he started her toward the tent flap, all told Amber that she had no choice but to do as he ordered. If she had been made of braver stuff, she would have turned on him, then and there, and demanded her release and enough money to see herself to St. Louis. But having lived under this cruel man's rule for so long, she could not muster the courage to break free of his grip and face him without falling in a heap to her knees.

Barrow did not release her arm, but led on, a steady purpose clear in his mind as he entered the whiskey lean-to. Throwing the required coins on the plank table with his free hand, he demanded a pint of whiskey.

The whiskey lean-to was surrounded with trappers and Indians, all looking toward Barrow and his stepdaughter with some expectation. Amber shuddered as a dark premonition seized her. Silently her blue gaze traveled over those standing around viewing her and Henry Barrow with open curiosity. Seconds later, she lowered her eyes, unable to endure the greedy leers that were being cast in her direction.

"Come on out here with me, gal," Barrow demanded, her arm still in his tight hold. With one hand, he both clutched the pint of whiskey and dragged a chair along with him, outside the lean-to. "Get yourself up here on this chair, gal, so everyone hereabouts can be getting a real good look at you." His watery green eyes slipped from her face to the chair.

"I will not!" Amber gasped aloud, and tried to jerk free from his grip. She would certainly not agree to do anything so degrading to her person.

"You'll do as you're told, or I'll strip you naked right here and now in front of every man jack here, and lash your backside to teach ye yer manners!" Taking another long swallow from the pint, Henry Barrow set the rest of the contents of the mug down next to the chair, and with a quick motion jerked Amber upright until her feet touched the flat wood surface of the chair.

Amber's features flamed as she stood there silently for the viewing of the men surrounding her and her stepfather. She had no choice. Henry Barrow would do exactly as he threatened without hesitation if she tried to fight him for her release!

"What do you say, men? Here's my gal, just like I told you, and she's ripe and ready for the taking. She's fresh and innocent as a new-born fawn, and can cook whatever you can kill. She can skin and tan a hide better than any man among you, I'll be wagering. Now I ain't parting with her cheap, 'cause she's right dear to me!"

A loud, disbelieving gasp escaped Amber's lips and circled the area. She could not believe what her stepfather had said to this crowd of unwashed, foul-smelling mountain men! She would have jumped down from the chair and fled, except for the fact that Henry Barrow clutched the back of her gown, making it impossible for her to move. She would have screamed aloud for help, but glancing around in terror, she knew there would be no help forthcoming from this crowd of rowdy onlookers. These men were a law unto themselves. There would be none willing to step forward and defend her against Henry Barrow.

"I'll give you fifty dollars for her, Barrow!" A shout came from the back of the crowd.

"Fifty? Shit, I'll give you a hundred!" another called.

"She's worth ten times that!" Henry Barrow exclaimed. "Why, take a look at her hair. When it's washed and dried in the sun, it fairly shines like pure gold! She'll do whatever you tell her. She ain't afraid of hard work, and she'll train right well in bed! What more could any man here be asking for?"

Amber could no longer look up. Her head hung low, her humiliation complete. Her stepfather was selling her, as though she were no more than chattel. These men, who had been womenless for the past few years, were drawing closer like a bunch of starving wolves, moving in on the kill.

"I give five hundred white man's dollars for the woman with the sun in her hair!" Little Eagle, old Winter Owl's son, shook a small leather pouch full of money over his head.

Henry Barrow didn't cotton with selling his stepdaughter to an Indian. His glare conveyed these feelings as he stared hard at the brave and then looked back around at the crowd.

"I'll give you one thousand dollars for the girl, Barrow." An audible gasp went through the crowd as Slim Farley stepped forward. "Miss Calico Kat is complaining there aren't enough girls in the wagon to go around for all the men here at rendezvous. Your daughter could earn back the thousand and then some in no time at all." Farley had admired the young woman's beauty yesterday when she and Barrow had arrived at rendezvous; he would never have believed that luck would favor him so kindly as to deliver her into his hands. He would make a fortune with her right here in this encampment. Once he returned to St. Louis and put her up in the Blessed Paradise, his fancy house, as he liked to call it, she would attract men for miles around with her radiant beauty.

"Aye, she'll be doing whatever you demand of her, Farley!" Barrow cried, and taking hold of Amber's skirt hem, he started to pull it upward for the men's viewing, hoping by showing a little of her creamy thighs, he could drive the price even higher.

Kicking out at the hand at her hem, Amber glared hatred upon her stepfather. He had degraded her unmercifully; he would go no further without her fighting back!

Barrow relented, not pushing the matter fully. Shouting out in the hopes of working the crowd up that much more to his benefit, he sung her unseen praises. "She be a tempting gal beneath these skirts, men! Why let old Slim have her so cheap, and share her among you, when one of you can have her treasures all for yer own?"

"Two thousand!" It was Tate Coker who raised the bid. Leaning against one of the wood posts that supported the whiskey shack, with the slender man in the suit feverishly writing upon his pad of paper not far from his side, Tate's hard eyes traveled around the group of men in an intimidating manner, as though to ward off any more bidders.

"Well, I guess I could go as high as twenty-five hundred, but she had better be worth it, Barrow." Slim Farley's glance traveled over Amber as though he were trying to assess her true value. It would take time for her to earn out this much cash.

"Three thousand!" was the response from Tate Coker. Folding his brawny arms over his wide chest, he waited for Farley to respond to this new bid.

"That's too steep for me!" Farley replied, backing out of the bidding with some regret. Miss Calico Kat would be mad as hell when she heard that he had had a chance to get another girl and had allowed that chance to slip out of his hands. But he just couldn't force himself to part with so much money for a woman. Why, the girl could run off during the night, or she might already be diseased, and cost him more than he bargained for. Who could take the word of a man like Henry Barrow that the girl was untouched? This was a ruse he himself used upon occasion at the Blessed Paradise. Often when he got a new girl, the word was spread that the girl was a virgin. Every man liked to believe that he was the first!

Three thousand dollars! Henry Barrow couldn't believe his luck! He had not dreamed that the girl could bring him so much money! "Sold!" he shouted in Tate Coker's direction. He could forget ole Winter Owl's wild murmurings about a place in the mountains where beaver were as numerous as the stars in the sky! He wouldn't never have to work another day in his life!

The crowd parted as Barrow pulled Amber down from the chair and began to drag her toward Tate Coker.

"I will not let you do this to me!" Amber cried. "You can't make me go with him!"

"Shut up, gal, or I'll club you with my fist!" Barrow raised his hand as though to strike her.

"Go ahead and hit me, I don't care!" Amber replied. She had been beaten by her stepfather plenty of times in the past, and would endure another beating before she would willingly go with this large, ill-kempt trapper who had to buy himself a woman.

"I don't want no fight on my hands every time I'm in need of some loving, Barrow. 'Specially after paying such a price fer her!" Tate Coker looked from Barrow to the woman he was dragging behind him; it was plain to see she was not keen on the idea of being sold to him, or any other man.

"Are you really going to buy this young woman, Mr. Coker?" Arnie Atsworth, a reporter for the St. Louis *Gazette*, questioned with much animation, hurriedly writing down everything that was happening on his paper pad. He had been assigned the task of covering this rendezvous, and having come out to Bear Lake with Ashley and his overland wagon train, he had quickly hitched his coattail to this rough and rowdy trapper, Tate Coker. He jotted down much of what the trapper said, and described fully everything he did; from fights he appeared to relish to this afternoon's adventure of purchasing a young woman who he intended to take back to the mountains with him.

"What do I got to do, greenhorn? Swat you like a pesky fly? I told you that if you going to be staying underfoot, you've got to keep your mouth shut!"

"Where the hell did this damn pilgrim come from?" Henry Barrow glared at the young man, wanting to strike out at someone for the aggravation his stepdaughter was causing him.

"He's all right, Barrow. He's going to do an article for the paper about me." Tate Coker puffed out his chest. "Like I was saying, though, I prefer my women willing."

"She'll be willing enough all right," Barrow assured, and pushed Amber closer to the larger man. "Just hand over the three thousand dollars, and she's all yours."

"I am not willing, and never will be!" Amber was just as quick to cry out her feelings. "I will never willingly give myself to a man without a proper marriage ceremony!'' Tears stung her eyes, glittering like diamonds on her pale cheeks as she shouted out the first thing that came to mind; the only response that she hoped would save her from the awful fate her stepfather intended for her.

Henry Barrow had not even considered his stepdaughter's refusal or that someone would take her desires seriously. He saw Coker's interest in the girl clearly written upon his scraggly features, but he also noted his reluctance to have a woman it would be necessary to force at every turn. And even then he'd never know if she would run away from him. *Three thousand dollars . . . three thousand dollars!* The thought of such a large amount of money stimulated Barrow's brain into feverish machinations. Without further hesitation, he looked at Amber and declared, ''So be it then, gal. You'll have your ceremony. Get yourself back to the tent, and wait for me there.'' Releasing her arm, he turned and watched her run through the crowd back to Silas Benson's tent. Turning around to face Tate Coker, he grinned, ''The little gal wants a ceremony, why not give her one?''

''I hadn't planned on marrying her, Barrow. I'm sure not the marrying kind. All I want is someone to go along with me to the mountains. Them winters can be hell, and right down lonely without a woman. On second thought, I might just find meself an Injun squaw instead of wasting my money.''

''Who said you're going to really wed the gal? I'm sure we can find someone here at rendezvous who has heard a marriage ceremony before and can say a few words that'll convince the gal she's wed. You can tell her the truth whenever you think it wise.''

Tate Coker grinned widely, and at the same time reached into his buckskin jacket and pulled out his wallet. ''I reckon your smarter than I took you fer, Barrow. I also reckon a ceremony can't be hurting none, if it'll make the little lady willing."

A round of laughter followed this remark as the two men left the crowd in search of someone to perform the marriage ceremony for Tate Coker and Amber Dawson.

Nine

It was Arnie Atsworth who posed as a preacher a short time later. Standing before Amber and Coker, he settled his wire-framed spectacles on his long, thin nose as he drew a little Bible from his jacket pocket. The young man had no desire to take part in this phony marriage ceremony, but having been bullied by both Coker and Barrow, and truly fearing for his life, he had at last agreed, confessing to the two trappers that he had a Bible tucked away in his saddlebags. "I'm truly sorry about this, miss" were his first words as he looked at the young woman's distraught face. It was obvious she had been weeping, and given the two, hard-looking men standing at her sides, he didn't blame her one bit.

"Don't be paying this skinny greenhorn no mind, gal. He's a preacher and that's all that matters. You wanted a ceremony, and your going to have one. Ain't that right, Coker? Your willing to marry the gal, ain't you?"

"Yeah, you're right there, Barrow. Get to it, Atsworth. I ain't got all day. I got some celebrating to do before I have myself a wedding night." Tate Coker's guffaw filled the air, and sent chills of fear for the night ahead running the length of Amber's young body.

In a trembling voice, and stammering every now and then over the words, Arnie Atsworth began to read from the pages of his Bible, and at the finish, asked Amber, "Will you take this man for your husband, miss?"

Everyone standing around the area looked at the pale-featured, woman and silently awaited her reply to the question put to her. Adamantly, Amber shook her head in refusal. "No, I will not take him!"

"Your damn right, she takes him!" Barrow grabbed a handful of her bright hair at the back of her head and moved her head up and down. "You can see for yerself that she's hot to become his bride!"

Snickering laughter from the encircling crowd came to Amber's ears. Arnie Atsworth turned to Tate Coker and asked him the same question.

"If I didn't want her, I wouldn't have given Barrow all that money, now would I?"

In a real marriage ceremony, a yes or no was required, but Arnie Atsworth only wanted to be away from these men and not have to look into the pale features of the woman any longer. "Then in the name of . . ." There was simply no way he could say, "in the name of all that's holy" so instead he said, "Then in the name of this first rendezvous, I now pronounce you man and wife!"

The crowd cheered, and Barrow beat Tate upon the back. "She's all yours now, Coker, she's all yours!"

Ignoring Henry Barrow, the large, foul-smelling trapper turned to the young woman he now could claim as his own. He grabbed her around the waist and pulled her up tightly against his chest. "I reckon as how I should kiss the blushing bride now!" Before his head descended, his laughter joined the sound of merriment circling around him.

Amber only had time to press her slender hands against his broad chest, as though this action could somehow ward him off. "No . . . no, please don't!" she shrieked.

Coker pressed his full lips over hers in a hungry assault, the kiss brutal and emotionless. When at last he released her, he grinned down into her tear-stained face, "That's something to hold you and keep you thinking about your man, until I return to fetch you wife! You'll be getting plenty more kisses and a whole lot more tonight!"

Amber's hand went to her lips, and without care of what Coker would think, she began to wipe her mouth. The moistness from his tobacco stained lips sickened her, as did his taste and the stench that lingered long after he had lifted his head. Her knees shook and her head swam with utter disbelief that this foul man believed he held ownership over her.

"I'm going to join my friends for a round of drinks to celebrate my wedding day, woman. Get your things together and be ready to leave when I come back fer you." Tate Coker noticed her distaste of him, and a feeling of pure power swelled his chest. He would teach the little bitch that she wasn't any better than him. By the start of winter, she would be begging for what he planned to give her tonight! Without another word, Coker turned away from Amber and amid hearty shouts and well wishes of congratulations, he and Barrow headed for the whiskey lean-to, while Amber turned and ran back into the tent where prying eyes could no longer be witness to her humiliation.

Standing alone in the tent with her hand pressed over her bruised lips, Amber's tears freely flowed. She felt dazed, betrayed, and more alone than she had ever felt in her life. Blinded by her tears, she fell upon her blankets, great sobs of heartbreak escaping her throat as she reviewed, over and over in her mind her future as Tate Coker's wife.

All she had ever wanted was a small amount of happiness, and someone with whom to share her life. Thus far, life had not been easy for her, and her expectation of the future had not been so different. But, she certainly had wanted more than to be sold and wed to a man such as Tate Coker. Her fate was now sealed. She would live the rest of her life as the wife of a cruel trapper. Drudgery and misery would be her constant companions from this day forth. Dreams for a happier future were now dashed aside as if they had never existed:

She lay in misery, her body shaken by sobs, all her hopes destroyed in a single afternoon. Fear and sorrow made her jerk away from the hand that gently laid itself over her shoulder, then pulled her into an upright position. Not able to see clearly through the blur of her tears, she assumed that Henry Barrow or Tate Coker had returned for her.

"Cusni céya, Ptanyétu Ánpo; Don't weep, Autumn Dawn." The softly spoken Sioux words settled upon Amber's ears, and drew her instant attention. Brushing away hot liquid with the backs of her hands, her violet eyes stared transfixed upon the Indian warrior who had saved her from the bear.

"You!" she softly gasped. "What are you doing here?" Her gaze darted around the interior of the tent, fearing she would see Henry Barrow or someone else bursting through the entrance and finding the Indian bent down near her blankets.

"Come with me, Ptanyétu Ánpo. Come away from this place with me." The English words were spoken just as softly as his earlier request that she not weep. His dark eyes gazed into her features with a tender warmth, the likes of which she had never viewed before from any man.

"But . . . why . . . why do you want to help me escape?"
She realized he was offering her a way out of the situation
that had been thrust upon her; a way out of the abject
misery that was fast becoming her fate. He had saved her
life in the meadow, by purposely drawing the grizzly bear
away from her, and now he was offering to save her from
Tate Coker.

"Come with me." He held out his hand, and rose to his
full, imposing height.

For a moment, she stared at the hand offered to her,
her mind clouded with indecision.

What is the matter with you, girl? her inner mind's workings
questioned. *Do you think you have a choice in this matter? Your
only option is to flee rendezvous with this Indian, unless you
would rather stay here and suffer the foul attentions of Tate Coker!*

For another person, perhaps such an offering would
have been easy to reach out to, but for Amber Dawson,
who had taken orders from Henry Barrow for so many
years, it was the hardest decision she ever had to make.

*Get up and go with him, and for the first time in your life show
the strong stuff that you are made of. Your mother would not
want you to be such a coward!* Once again, that hidden part
of her nature tried to instill some much-needed backbone
to her character.

Slowly, Amber rose to her feet. Seeing that he only waited
for her to place her hand within his, Amber tentatively
slipped her fingers over his hardened palm. Instantly, his
fingers captured hers, his full lips drawing back into a
tender smile; a smile that offered protection and strength
for the ordeal ahead.

Leading her toward the back of the tent, she noticed
for the first time a large slice in the canvas, which had
been made by the warrior's hunting knife. She also noticed
the implement was now sheathed at his side. Parting the
canvas, he stepped through, and pulled Amber with him.

The black stallion, which she recognized from that day in the meadow, stood waiting behind the tent. Releasing her hand, with a lithe movement the Indian swung up onto the animal's back, and, once again, his hand reached down to her.

Looking around, she saw that no one was paying them any attention. Taking a deep breath, she stared at the tan hand with its long fingers. She would never be able to look back if she reached out to that hand once again.

What do you have to look back to, anyway? that inner voice quickly questioned.

She grabbed the hand without further hesitation, and within seconds, was sitting behind the warrior, her hands lightly resting against his sides as he kicked the stallion into motion.

A few hours later, shortly before dusk, Tate Coker led the lively procession of trappers toward Silas Benson's tent. Henry Barrow and Silas were close at his side. Shouts and calls to the bridegroom incited Coker to hurry his steps to claim his bride.

"If your all real quiet about it, I'll let you watch me mount the little wife right here in Benson's tent!" he slurred drunkenly. The image of this group watching him as he took the beautiful, proud Amber, whom he had paid three thousand dollars for, evoked a lusty picture that kept blood flowing wickedly in his veins and his manhood hard pressed to be freed.

Pushing the tent flap aside, Coker bent his tall frame, and stepped within. A call for his bride to get her clothes off was already out of his mouth before he noticed that the tent was completely empty! Turning back to the trappers squeezing through the entrance flap to get a better look, the large trapper purposely strode back to Barrow's side and grabbed a handful of the front of his hide shirt. "Where the hell is she, Barrow? She's flown from her cage!"

Henry Barrow grabbed the hand and cast it from him, but even in his drunken state, he realized Coker's enormous strength po*sessed*. "She's around here somewhere." He stomped over to her pallet and kicked at the pile of blankets, as though expecting to find her hidden beneath. "More than likely, she jest stepped out fer a breath of night air." He turned back to face Coker.

"You think so, do ya? Well then, what the hell's that tear in the back of the tent for? Didn't she know to step out the front flap?" Drunk or not, Tate Coker's eyes were sharp.

"A tear in me tent?" Silas Benson shouted, and hurried over to the back of the tent to get a better look. "Barrow, you're going to have to pay for this! You brought the gal here, and you treated her bad enough to make her run. You're responsible, and I damn sure can't sleep in a tent with a big hole in its side!"

"That ain't all your going to be paying fer, Barrow!" Coker turned on him. "I'll be taking back my three thousand dollars! No girl, no money!"

"Now just hold it a damn minute! We don't know if she even made that hole in the tent. Why, where would she get off to anyway? I'll bring her back, don't you worry. And when I find her, Benson, you'll talk to Coker here about getting you a new tent. The gal ain't mine no more, remember?"

"She ain't yours, if she's here at rendezvous," Coker reminded. "I ain't throwing me money on a runaway!"

Pushing his way through the crowd of men standing at the tent door, Henry Barrow made his way to the back side of the tent to see if he could make out Amber's tracks. More than likely, she went down to the river for a drink of water, or went out in search of something to fill her belly, he told himself, not believing that she would disobey him and run away. As his hard, green eyes searched out the area, a cold glint of recognition settled in their depths.

"You see any sign of her tracks?" Coker questioned as he joined Barrow.

"Yeah, I see sign all right. There's prints from an Injun pony, and that's where the gal's tracks disappear."

"Injun?" Coker stated in surprise. "What damn redskin would be brave enough to run off with my woman?"

Ten

For the first several hours after leaving rendezvous, Spirit Walker pushed his mount at a hard pace, hoping to put as much distance between himself and Amber, and Bear Lake. It was not until the sun lowered and the moon rose high in the velvet-dark sky that he allowed his horse to slow its gait. Following an uncharted trail, they traveled silently across country. It was not until the early hours of the morning, when they entered a forest of tall lodge-pole pines and cottonwoods, that Spirit Walker at last halted the stallion.

"We can rest here for a time." He turned and looked at Amber, able to see her exhaustion by the moonlight filtering through the canopy of trees.

Amber was too tired to respond. It took an effort for the slight nodding of her head.

With one movement of his powerful body, Spirit Walker dismounted, then reached up to help Amber to gain her feet. "Are you hungry?" Concern could be heard in the husky tremor of his voice.

"I think not. Just weary." Amber smiled up at her rescuer, not wanting him to think she was a weak-kneed girl that couldn't hold her own. "Do you think that it is safe to stop here? By now, Henry Barrow would have found her gone from the tent and would be searching for her. She knew her stepfather well. He was not a man to take her disappearance lightly. She could well imagine that he was fuming with anger over her running away from the horrible man he had forced her to marry. A shudder traveled her length; fear of what he would do if Henry Barrow caught up with her and this warrior caused frightening images to flash within her mind.

"We will be safe here for the rest of the night, Ptanyétu Ánpo. I will build a small fire so you can get warm and sleep until morning." Spirit Walker had directed his horse over ground that would be hard for anyone to follow, and several times he had backtracked before they had reached the forest. They surely would be safe enough for a few hours.

Taking his blanket and trappings off the stallion, he spread out the colorful trade blanket upon a bed of pine needles. With a glance toward Amber, he invited, "Come, Ptanyétu Ánpo, lie here and sleep. I will watch over you and give warning if there is danger that someone approaches."

Amber did not have the will to resist. She was weary of mind and body. She wanted only to shut her eyes for a few minutes and forget everything that had brought her to be alone in this forest with the handsome Indian. Silently, she sat down on the blanket, her glance stealing over the warrior, as though she were unsure if she should trust his offer of protection. The thought fleetingly traveled through her mind that perhaps she would need protection from him.

Spirit Walker did not miss her look of apprehension. Gently he reached out, his strong hand pressing her down upon the blanket. "Sleep. I will build a fire and tend my horse."

His words held the power to assure her, and as soon as her head touched the blanket, her eyes shut and soon she slept.

Spirit Walker built a small fire in a shallow pit close by the blanket in order for Amber to feel its warmth. For a few minutes, he silently remained squatted near the fire, his dark gaze studying this woman of his vision. She need not fear that he would allow any harm to befall her now that he had found her and had her at his side. Not only was he a spirit man among his people, but he was also a war chief. He was wise in the way of war, and could protect that which he believed belonged to him.

Minutes later, Spirit Walker stood next to his horse and with handfuls of sweet grass he rubbed down his damp flanks. Speaking in soft tones to the beast, he thanked him for his swiftness and endurance on the trail. The animal reacted to his master's gentle hand with soft, blowing noises of affection.

"When we reach the mountains, my friend, you will be able to rest, and eat the tender shoots of grass growing along the banks of the lake." Spirit Walker smiled fully as the stallion rubbed his forelock against his chest. The mountains would be a place where *all* could rest, he thought with anticipation, his ebony gaze drawn, again and again, to the woman sleeping upon his blanket.

Throughout the rest of the night, Spirit Walker silently kept vigil over his small camp. He had learned at an early age to rest lightly. The slightest noise that was out of place from the usual forest noises coming to his ears caused his hand to tighten its grip upon the handle of his tomahawk. The call of an owl, high in a tree, relaxed him with assurance that all was well.

* * *

With the first traces of the morning sun breaking through a pinkish dawn, Spirit Walker stood facing the morning star, his prayers of thanksgiving soft upon his lips. "This warrior has much to be thankful for, Great Spirit." He lifted his head to the One Above after murmuring prayers of welcome to the four powers that ruled the lives of his people. "You have given into my charge this gift of my vision woman. I ask that you give this warrior the strength to protect her from all harm, and the knowledge that will be needed to keep her at my side."

With the finish of his prayers, Spirit Walker returned to the fire and stoked the dim embers back to life by feeding the growing flames small twigs.

Some small noise broke through Amber's sleep, and opening her eyes, she was greeted with the sight of the large warrior bending down to the pit-fire. "The name that you called me yesterday, what does it mean?" In her sleep she had heard the Indian words repeated over and over.

Dark, warm eyes rose from the flames and held upon her heart-shaped face with a tender perusal. "You are a woman of many changes. Your fire-curls the shade of the leaves that fall in early autumn. You are also a woman of the morning." Spirit Walker remembered his vision in the sweat lodge, as he had viewed her in the meadow, through the eye of an eagle. "Your smooth flesh has been kissed with the cast of early-morning dew. Ptanyétu Ánpo." He spoke the name as though a caress. "You are Autumn Dawn."

Amber felt her face suffuse with warmth, and pulling herself upright on the blanket, she forced her eyes to break contact with his dark, searching regard. No man had ever said such things about her! Expelling a soft breath, she tried to sound light, even though his words and husky tone had affected her more than she was willing to admit. "I could use some of that food now that you spoke about last night." She had eaten little for breakfast yesterday morning, and nothing else throughout the day and night. She felt her stomach's rumbling and hoped that the mention of food would draw the warrior's attention away from her physical being.

Spirit Walker's smile widened to a grin. He had noticed the instant flush that came over her features, and admired her ease in turning the conversation to food. Reaching into a rawhide parfleche near the fire, he drew out some pemmican and handed her a piece.

"What is this?" she questioned as she examined the fine mixture in her hand.

Spirit Walker was surprised that she had not eaten pemmican before. Many trappers and frontiersmen made a soup from pemmican, which they called robbiboe. "It is called wakápapi wasná; pemmican. My people make it from the meat of tatanka; buffalo. Our women pound the dried meat to powder and mix this with berries. It is good." He took a bite and nodded his head in her direction, indicating she should do the same.

Amber took a small bite, and finding it tasteful, took a larger one. "You speak English far better than most of the Indians back at rendezvous," she stated, in between chewing the pemmican. It was strange, but she held little fear of this man. He had saved her twice, and she had survived the night without any difficulty. She was uncertain of the reasons for his actions, but she was fairly sure that he meant her no harm.

"My cousin, Two-Owls-Cry, lives a far distance north of my village; when I was younger I visited him. There was a black robe living among his people, and this one taught me the wasichu's tongue." He left out explaining that the sky people from his vision had told him to go to his cousin's village and seek out the black robe. The ancestors had told him, that day long ago, of his need in the future to know the ways of the pale men.

"A black robe? Oh, you mean there was a priest in your cousin's village." Missionaries went to certain tribes and attempted to convert the Indians to the white man's God, so she was not surprised at his answer. He handed her a small leather water pouch, and she thirstily drank from it.

Some minutes later, she thanked him for sharing his food and water with her. "Thank you for everything . . . I'm afraid I don't even know your name." Her wide blue eyes looked at him in question.

"I am known as Wanági Máni; Spirit Walker." He pronounced the Sioux name first.

"Wanági Máni, Spirit Walker," Amber softly repeated, and again she felt the compelling power of his dark regard. "My stepfather will follow us. How long do you think it will take to reach St. Louis? Perhaps you could take me as far as Harper's trading post; from there, I am sure I will be able to find someone who will help me get to St. Louis." If she could get there before Henry Barrow, she could go to the authorities, explain her circumstances, and request protection. She could also make certain Tate Coker had no legal rights to claim her as his wife.

Spirit Walker was not sure how he was going to explain that he was not taking her to this place called St. Louis, nor was he taking her to Harper's trading post. He had prayed to the Great Spirit to help him say the words that would open her inner vision, to the knowledge that she was meant to stay with him, but at the moment, he was at a loss. "What will you seek in this place called St. Louis, Ptanyétu Ánpo?" He rose to his feet and kicked dirt into the shallow pit fire before gathering the parfleches and water bag.

Amber also stood to her feet, and assuming that he was ready to get back on the trail, she picked up the trade blanket and shook the leaves and pine needles from it. "I hope to be able to find employment in the city." She was not really sure what she would find once she reached St. Louis, but she did know that she had to make a start somewhere. Amber had only herself to depend on, and the sooner she could find a job, the sooner she could start building some peace and security for her future.

After the two mounted the horse and started down a trail that led them into the forest, Spirit Walker's masculine voice questioned some more. "Why is it that you believe you should go to this place?" He turned to look at her as he waited for her reply.

Amber was not quite sure how to answer, but as his dark regard held, she knew she had to speak the truth. "I am not really sure where I should go," she admitted softly. "All I know is that I can't return to my stepfather, or that terrible man, Tate Coker."

Spirit Walker agreed with her on this one point. There was no way he would ever let the man with the lifeless green eyes have any say over her again. He had seen the treatment that this man she called stepfather had handed out to her at rendezvous. He was aware of Barrow's selling her and then forcing her to join with the large trapper who had treated her with little respect. Never again would this woman be treated in such a fashion, he swore silently as they made their way through the forest.

"My mother and father were from Virginia. It is very far away, but I thought I might go there." Amber revealed her thoughts to him.

"And when you go to this faroff place, what will you do, Ptanyétu Ánpo? Do you believe that you will find the happiness you seek in this place called Virginia?"

Happiness? the word seemed alien to Amber, and she

had no answer to his questions. All she desired was peace. If she found more than this, she knew in her heart, she would be forever grateful.

By midday, Amber was hot and irritated, as much from the uncomfortable ride as from her thoughts about her future. Her dress was torn in several places, the hem seeming to catch every bush or briar that came near, her hair gnarled and hanging wildly down her back. When at last Spirit Walker halted the horse for a break in the hurried pace, she unbuttoned the top two buttons of her blouse, with hopes of catching a cooling breeze. "Are you sure we are going in the right direction? It seems that we are going more north than east. I have really gotten turned around here in the forest, but it seems like we should head more in that direction." She pointed in the direction she believed they should travel to eventually reach Harper's trading post.

Spirit Walker helped her dismount, and silently handed her the water pouch. He would have to try and explain their destination. He would have to tell her that he was not taking her to Harper's trading post, that they were traveling higher into the mountains with each passing hour. His gaze was drawn to her slender fingers, as she dampened them and pressed the moisture to her throat; droplets of liquid trembled downward into the valley of her bosom. "You are tired and hot, Ptanyétu Ánpo. We can rest here for a time until you are ready to go on."

"Go on where?" Violet-blue eyes looked up into bronzed features, and locked with warm obsidian. Amber felt herself beginning to tremble as she was made aware, for the first time, the depths of this man's feelings toward her. "You aren't taking me to Harper's trading post, are you?" The words were spoken softly; barely was she able to push them from her throat.

"You are trembling, Ptanyétu Ánpo. Come and sit here upon this log." Spirit Walker knew that the moment had come, but still, he searched his soul for the words that would reveal to her the truth. It would be an easy thing to frighten her, and he had no desire to do this.

Amber shrugged away the hand he placed on her elbow. For the first time, she began to fear that she had made a terrible mistake. "You have to tell me where you are taking me. Why did you help me run away from rendezvous?" She should have asked him these questions sooner, and her nervousness increased with each passing second. Yesterday, she had only thought of escaping Henry Barrow and Tate Coker; she had not thought ahead to this minute, when she would be alone in a forest with a powerful Indian warrior.

Spirit Walker saw the fear upon her features, the blue eyes looking at him filled with apprehension. "Sit and rest while I explain these things to you," he coaxed, wishing to put her back at ease.

Amber complied, only because she had to know, even though she dreaded hearing what he would tell her. Tentatively, she sat down on the log, watching as he did likewise. His long, muscular legs, encased in buckskin leggings, stretched out comfortably, as his dark gaze studied her.

A pent-up breath escaped his chest before he began to speak. "Among my people, there are ceremonies that are performed to honor the promises that one makes to the Great Spirit, or to acknowledge a deed or gift bestowed upon one by Wakán Tanka. I received these scars upon my body while performing in such a ceremony." He drew fingers over the pale scars on his bare chest. He watched Amber's glance go downward to his chest, and then back to his face, as yet not understanding what he was talking about.

His voice was tender with a touch of masculine huskiness that was not lost upon Amber. "It was during such a ceremony that I received the name Wanági Máni. This day, I was blessed with a vision of much power. Power that enabled me to teach my people many things which had been lost to them with the movement of time."

Amber shook her head, totally at a loss. "What has all this to do with me, and where you are taking me?" All she wanted was for him to take her to Harper's trading post, or some other place where she could get help to return to St. Louis.

Spirit Walker would not be rushed, and softly tried to explain all. "As I told you, I was gifted with much power during this ceremony. I was also gifted with knowledge of what was to come into the future of my people. Because of this vision, I went to my cousin's village and learned from the black robe all that he could teach me."

Amber wasn't sure if she believed a single word he told her. How could anyone be shown things which were to come in the future? Wisely, she kept her thoughts to herself. She had no wish to antagonize this man. He was her only hope of reaching civilization. "So . . . so what was it that you learned about the future, Spirit Walker?" she questioned, having some genuine interest in this story that sounded more like a fairy tale to her.

"This day while I hung upon the sundance pole, I saw you for the first time."

Amber's eyes widened with disbelief.

"At first I was not sure of the meaning of your presence in my vision. You stood alone, next to the river that runs through the valley of my people. Your arms were outstretched, your fire-curls gleaming beneath the morning sun, and around your neck you wore the claw necklace of the matóhota; grizzly bear.''

Amber's hand automatically went to her throat. This was crazy! It was impossible!

"I was sure of what your presence meant in my vision the second time that I saw you."

"The second time?" He must be insane if he thought that she was believing this nonsense:

"While in a sweat lodge, I was gifted with a vision, and in this vision, I saw you in a meadow, abundant with colorful flowers. There was a lake nearby."

"It could have been some other woman that you saw in this vision." Amber tried to sway him to be reasonable. Of course, he hadn't seen her in a vision. Perhaps he had dreamed about her after the incident with the grizzly bear; after all, she had dreamed of him several times before reaching rendezvous.

"Entwined within your fire-curls, you wore a crown of flowers and meadow grass. Your arms were outstretched as you danced to a rhythm known only to yourself."

Amber's cobalt eyes widened as remembrance stole through her thoughts. "You were watching me in the meadow?" That day shone vivid in her mind. It was the beginning of summer, and she was looking forward to Henry Barrow saying that it was time to leave the cabin and head for rendezvous.

"Thunder Hawk and Strong Elk, two braves from my village, were in the sweat lodge with me. They had come to tell me about the woman in the meadow who they had watched from the side of a mountain. They were uncertain if you were real, or a wanági winyan; spirit woman. They did not need to tell me what they had seen. I saw all within the vision that I was gifted with there in the sweat lodge." He did not tell her that he had seen her there in the meadow himself. If he claimed to have seen all through the eyes of an eagle, she would find his story even more impossible to believe. Such things happened among his people, but he had never heard of them happening among the wasichu.

He had to be making all of this up, Amber told herself, but looking at him this minute, she did not see any traces of deceit on his features. "You say that you know what this second vision means?" She only wanted to try to understand what he was getting at and then convince him to take her to Harper's trading post.

His dark gaze held her softly, the sound of his husky voice encasing her warmly. "The moment that I viewed you in my vision, there in the meadow with your beautiful fire-curls unbound and glistening brightly beneath Wi; the sun, I knew in my heart that you were to shortly come into my life path. As I watched you turn in dance, your carefree features turned upward to Skan; the sky, I knew that you and I were created by Wakán Tanka for this moment of life upon Mother Earth. My life circle will only be complete with you at my side, Ptanyétu Ánpo. You are that portion of my heart that has been stilled throughout my manhood. I have existed only for the day when my heart will beat with yours as one, when you have joined your life path with mine."

Amber shook her head in denial. What on earth was he talking about? "Join my life path with yours? Your life circle is not complete? You can't be serious? These . . . these visions, that you claimed to have had, you must know that you were dreaming! You can't believe what you are saying!"

Spirit Walker's gaze held steady upon her, assuring that he indeed believed every word he spoke. She was the woman of his heart. She might not know it this minute, but with the passage of time, she would learn what was meant to be. "A vision is much like a dream, Ptanyétu

Ánpo, but there is much more meaning to a vision. It is a gift that is bestowed upon one by the One Above. There is no doubt in my heart of what I have told you. I did not expect that you would understand everything quickly; that is why I have waited until now to reveal this to you." His patience was long-enduring. He would have every day of his lifetime to convince her to his heart. Her disbelief would one day turn to belief, he silently reasoned. She was his vision gift, and the Great Spirit would never reveal a thing to him if it were not meant to be.

"So, this is the reason that you helped me escape Henry Barrow and Tate Coker? She was truly becoming alarmed. Was this Indian mad? Had she fled rendezvous only to find that she had placed herself in a worse fate? Later, upon reflection, she would realize how absurd this thought had been. What fate could possibly be worse than that which her stepfather had had in mind for her at rendezvous?

"I would have helped you to leave this man that you call stepfather, anyway, Ptanyétu Ánpo. He is a cruel man, with an evil heart. But I speak the truth, when I say that I would not have been at this place called rendezvous to offer you a way to flee if I had not been searching for you."

And of course, he had only searched her out because of his insane visions, she told herself. "Well, now that we have met, you must realize how impossible this thing of joining our life paths together, really is." Drawing in a deep, ragged breath, she decided the best possible way to handle this situation was to try to remain calm and talk some sense into this man.

"I have learned in this life, Ptanyétu Ánpo, that many of the seemingly impossible ventures are those that stand out most in my life. The Great Spirit lends us wisdom in our time of need, and understanding will come. He has a plan for each of our lives. If we will only listen with our hearts, we will learn of His desires. If anything, now that I have met you, I am more sure that our joining as one was meant from the beginning of creation.''

How could he just sit here next to her and make such statements? He didn't know anything about her! *Neither did Tate Coker when he bid three thousand dollars for you! All men are alike, she concluded, they have only their own selfish pleasures in mind.* Away from her stepfather her conscience appeared hard at work. *Don't allow yourself to forget your mother, and the treatment she was handed out by a man that had promised her much in the beginning, but from whom received only abuse and mistreatment! What does this Indian offer that would be any different than what Tate Coker would force upon you? The only difference is the one visible to the eye. Where Tate Coker was foul and ill kempt, this warrior is distractingly handsome. But still, is this enough to give over the rest of your life for?*

Adamantly, Amber shook her head. She could not allow herself to be lured by this man's warm gaze and under- standing tone. The first years of her life had already been wasted; she could not afford to waste more! If forced, she would have to fight for what she wanted, and this, too, would be for the first time in her life. ''What you are offering, Spirit Walker, would perhaps sound inviting to another woman.'' Looking at him as he watched her every movement, she was certain that any number of women would willingly take his offer to join their life path with his. ''But you must understand my feelings. All I want is to be taken to some form of civilization. I want nothing more.''

For a moment, silence hung between them as Spirit Walker's gaze traced the delicate curve of her features. The soft, creamy texture of her unblemished skin drew him, the bow-shaped petal-rose lips beckoning for his own to press against them. The tight control he usually maintained over his emotions slipped. Long, bronze fingers reached out and gently caressed the soft flesh that laid over her cheekbone, her paleness alabaster against his sun-bronzed flesh. He heard the slight sucking of her breath, and even as his dark head leaned toward those sensual temptations, he knew that he was putting her at a disadvantage.

Tate Coker, was the only other man who had ever kissed Amber, and as Spirit Walker's intent became clear, she reacted in quick panic. Her first thought was to push him away, to run, to flee; not to suffer such abuse as she had in Coker's grasp. But all too quickly, she was surrounded by strong, powerful arms, his ebony gaze searing her to the depths of her soul, his sensual lips lowering, and surprisingly settling so very tenderly over her mouth. She was powerless, but to attempt an ineffectual effort at winning her release, her hands pushed against the hard-muscled broadness of his chest.

He withstood her efforts for release as though they were nonexistent, his lips making contact with the honey sweetness of her mouth. Tenderly at first, he plied her, then as his passion mounted, his heated tongue caressed the pinkened morsels, gently pushing against her resistance until she opened to him. With a heady assault, his tongue swirled, and sought out each hidden crevice. As his sensual actions continued, he felt her hands, which were pushing against him, slowly splay against his chest as she leaned into his body, her sweet lips now willing to his exploration.

Amber did not realize the moment that resistance turned to desire. All she was aware of was the taut, muscular flesh beneath her hands and the heated, sensual plying of his mouth over her own. His moist tongue sought out and filled her mouth, and the action left her melting into him, desiring more of this delicious blending of their lips.

It was Spirit Walker who at last gathered the self-control

to draw back. How could he have know that this simple act of joining his mouth with hers could be so pleasurable? He was no unseasoned warrior. There had been many maidens in his past who had been more than willing to lie upon his sleeping pallet, but never could he remember tasting paradise in another's arms. He was as surprised as she at what they had discovered. Fortunately, he had had years of perfecting the art of discipline over his body and emotions. Looking down into her passion-filled eyes, he held her at a disadvantage. Her actions told him everything; she was completely untutored to the ways of men and women. Still, he held her against his chest, his finger lightly tracing her rosy lips. "I am not taking you to this place St. Louis, Ptanyétu Ánpo. We are going high into the mountains."

"But we can't go to the mountains." Her words came out feebly, even to her own ears. Her senses felt drugged. Her body felt as though it had melted from within. He surrounded her, and she could only make half-sense out of his words. She wished that he would quit talking and kiss her again!

Spirit Walker knew that her resistance was low, and taking full advantage, his head bent to her again, his mouth a blend of heady seduction and gentle pursuit. When the kiss ended, he ached with unbridled passion as he looked down into closed eyes, her thick lashes lying lush and long against soft cheeks. "Come away with me, Ptanyétu Ánpo. I will not force you to do anything which you do not desire. I ask only that you come with me. We shall learn of each other as friends. If you do not wish to remain at my side after the winter snows melt away, I will take you, then, to this place called St. Louis." He knew that he would never be able to release her, even as he made the promise. But he also knew he needed more time, time in which to win her over, to show her the full depth of that which could be between them.

"But so much time has already been wasted." Believing that the past three years in the wilderness with Henry Barrow had been a wasted part of her life, Amber had been anxious to start her future. But now, held within this warrior's arms, looking up into warm-jet eyes, all her plans seemed scrambled in her mind. *He had said that we would just be friends. Would it be so terrible to go to the mountains with him? Perhaps during the time it takes for the snows to melt, Henry Barrow will have forgotten all about you, and when you return to St. Louis you won't have to worry that he'd try to force you back into some terrible situation.*

Her worries over time were those of the young, Spirit Walker thought. Tenderly, he brushed back stray strands of her bright copper hair. "We are not in control of time, Ptanyétu Ánpo. The Great Spirit's hand guides our path, and the steps that we make down it. If we learn all that we can, as we are led, then there is no wasted time."

"You sound very wise, Spirit Walker," she said softly, her senses beginning to clear.

"Come with me, and I will teach you about your purpose here on Mother Earth. Come with me, and you will learn to treasure each moment. You will never again think of your life as being wasted." He knew that if she did not agree to come with him to the mountains, he would be forced to take her against her will, and he didn't want this to be the start of their relationship.

"As a friend, you will teach me all these things?" It was insane, but Amber was beginning to think going to the mountains with him might be in her best interest. Henry Barrow, and more than likely, Tate Coker, were out looking for her. They would never find her in the mountains. As long as it was friendship that Spirit Walker was offering her, and nothing more, she might well consider the idea.

A lazy smile settled over Spirit Walker's lips as he looked down into her face. "As your friend, I will teach you all that I know." The words were a promise made from his heart. He truly desired to be her friend. He wanted her to trust him, confide in him, and eventually fall in love with him.

This promise of friendship was something entirely new to Amber. She had never had a friend before. Besides her mother, she had only the midwife Bertha Poole to confide in, and her only occasionally. "You promise that you will take me to St. Louis after winter's end, if: I don't want to stay in the mountains with you?" As she waited for his answer, for some strange reason, Amber wanted to believe him.

This would be an easy enough promise to make, for Spirit Walker intended on spending every waking moment guiding their friendship into something more. Silently he nodded his dark head.

"Do . . . do friends kiss like that often?" she nervously questioned, her senses still clouded by the kisses they had shared.

Spirit Walker's smile turned into a wide grin. "Do you like this thing of joining our lips together, Ptanyétu Ánpo?" With the slight nodding of her head, he warmly replied, "It will be my pleasure, as your friend, to kiss you as often as you wish."

Eleven

Word traveled swiftly throughout rendezvous that Henry Barrow's stepdaughter had disappeared and there was evidence that an Indian was involved. No one had seen an Indian speaking with the young woman, nor had anyone seen an Indian near Silas Benson's tent. It appeared that the girl and the Indian had simply disappeared!

Henry Barrow was seething with anger as he gathered up his gear from Benson's tent. Tate Coker had given him two days time in which to return his money or produce Amber. Coker himself would ride along with Barrow as he tried to track the Indian pony and reclaim his stepdaughter.

If the girl had run off with any other man besides an Injun, he would more than likely just have demanded his money back from Barrow, but his hatred of Indians bound him and Barrow strangely together. More than likely, the girl had been stolen, and Tate Coker swore that no Injun was going to get away with stealing what belonged to Tate Coker! "Damn it all, Barrow, hurry up in there!" The sun was already climbing the sky and the burly trapper reckoned that they had already lost enough time. They had been too drunk to chase after the Injun and the girl last night, but he had wanted to get off to an early start this morning.

As Henry Barrow was gathering up Amber's sleeping pallet, he found her journal tucked beneath her blanket. Stuffing the articles of bedding into a parfleche, curiosity caused him to retain the diary. Thumbing through the last several pages, he let loose with a stream of foul words. Looking down at the pages, he recognized the sketched drawings of an Indian. Slamming the book closed, he swore, "When I get hold of you, gal, I'll strangle you with my own bare hands!"

Stomping out of the tent, Henry Barrow threw the journal in Tate Coker's direction. "Why, the little Injun-loving bitch drew a picture of the damn buck right here in her journal!"

"What's all this scribbling here next to the picture?" Coker questioned as he studied the drawing, not able at all to read. Thumbing through the pages, he came across another picture of the same Indian. "Here's another picture of the Injun, but he's on a horse, and it looks like he's fighting off a grizzly bear."

Barrow looked at the picture, and remembered the day they had set out for rendezvous. Amber had claimed that she and the horses had been attacked by a grizzly. No wonder the damn animal had left her alone; the Injun must have come to her rescue! Barrow was as curious as Coker to find out what the words on the pages meant. "Where's your fancy friend, Atsworth?"

"That two-bit greenhorn ain't no friend of mine! He ain't no more than a damn pest!" Coker wondered what Barrow was aiming at.

"He can read, can't he?"

"I reckon he can. He read from his Good Book yesterday." Catching on to Barrow's idea, he added, "Yeah, I reckon he can tell us what your little gal wrote down here about this Injun. It appears by his dress that he's Sioux." Tate Coker studied the hair-bone breast plate, and eagle feather in the Injun's hair. The girl had spared no detail in her drawings of the savage!

"Yeah, I was thinking the same thing."

"Them Sioux ain't the sort of Injuns to be playing around with." Coker began to lead Barrow toward Arnie Atsworth's tent.

"You want your property back from that thieving buck, don't you?" Barrow's dull green eyes searched Coker's hard features with meaning.

"I wanted the girl enough to spend my money for her." Coker wasn't pleased by this turn of events. He had desired the girl's body, wanting to snuggle up to it on a cold winter's night while he trapped in the mountains, but he had not counted on running up against the Sioux. Still, with Henry Barrow staring at him, he displayed bravado.

"I reckon you're right, old son, about the damn red devil stealing what belongs to me, and his needing to pay for his thievery. I'll help you trail them two, and when we find them, I'll kill the Injun myself!" He fingered the hilt of the sharp hunting knife sheathed at his side. He had killed Injuns before, and wouldn't mind killing another. He hoped, though, that they would come upon the buck and girl before they reached his village. The Sioux were about the fiercest Injuns a man could come up against, and he didn't cotton to the thought of having to face the savage heading up a war party.

Arnie Atsworth was busy packing up his belongings. Having gathered enough information about rendezvous, he was anxious to return to civilization to write out his story. Ashley was sending three of his men back to St Louis for more supplies, and Arnie had accepted the invitation to ride along. The minute he saw Barrow and Coker entering his tent, he swallowed nervously, knowing that whatever these two trappers wanted would not be healthy for him.

Tate Coker was one of the reasons he was in a rush to leave rendezvous. The trapper was getting meaner and meaner by the day, and he didn't want to feel Coker's sharp-bladed hunting knife cutting into his flesh. "What's going on?" he nervously questioned, his dark gaze going from one man to the other, not noticing the small book Barrow held in his hand. He had heard that Barrow's stepdaughter had disappeared. Rumor had it that an Indian was involved. He couldn't say that he blamed the girl. An Indian couldn't be any worse to live with than Tate Coker!

"We need you to read something for us." Coker took the book from Barrow and held it out to Atsworth.

Arnie was not in the least surprised that neither one of these trappers could read, and taking the offered book, he pulled his wire-framed specs from a jacket pocket, then studied the page that Coker had held open. "This is someone's diary." his dark gaze turned away from the personal account of the writer's life, and looked back at the two trappers.

"Yeah, we know what it is. Just read what it says."

Arnie would have liked to refuse them, feeling it was none of his business, nor was it the business of these two men, to hear someone's personal thoughts. But with the two men staring at him, he didn't have the nerve. "This was written a few weeks back."

"Yeah, more than likely the day we started out for rendezvous," Barrow acknowledged.

The journal must have belonged to Barrow's stepdaughter, Arnie deduced. The two must be trying to figure out where she had run off to. Reading past the entry date, he

looked from the writing to the sketch of the Indian warrior.
"The Indian saved her life. She was attacked by a grizzly
while you were getting your traps. She writes that she is
unsure of his fate. The bear chased him into the forest,
and she never saw him again." He did not state that Amber
had written in her journal about her stepfather's hatred
of Indians and that she had not told him about her rescue.
Why should he add more fuel to the blazing fire of hatred
this man possessed. There was no one to say that this
was the same Indian who had taken the girl away from
rendezvous. She had written down that she had not seen
him again.

Barrow reached out a calloused hand and turned the
pages of the diary until he saw the other sketch of the
Indian.

"Read!" Coker demanded.

The warrior was certainly handsome, in a primitive sort
of way, Arnie thought as he viewed the drawing of the
Indian standing with a buffalo robe about his shoulders
and the eagle-feather decoration secured in his long dark
hair. Silently, he read the page next to the drawing, then
looked up at the two trappers. He knew that he couldn't
lie to these two rough, burly trappers. They might find
someone else to read the journal, if they thought he was
holding out on them; what choice was left to him but do
as they demanded? He could only hope that the Indian
had already put some distance between him, the girl, and
rendezvous. "The Indian that saved her from the grizzly
was here at rendezvous. She writes that she saw him the
first day she arrived. She doesn't say that she spoke to him,
or saw him again, only that she saw him standing silently
and watching her while she was with her stepfather in the
whiskey lean-to."

Barrow reached out and grabbed the journal. "I knew
it was the same Injun!"

Coker nodded his head. "Couldn't be no other."

"What do you plan to do?" Arnie Atsworth found the nerve at last to question.

"We aim to find the gal, and the Injun, and what's going to be left of his hide when we're done with him ain't going to be fitting for the buzzards to pick over!" Barrow declared, right before he and Coker left Arnie standing alone in his tent.

Several hard days of travel which took Spirit Walker and Amber higher into the mountains ensued before they finally reached their destination. With each passing day, Amber questioned herself about the hasty decision she had made to come with this warrior instead of trying to convince him to take her to some form of civilization. The prospect of running into Henry Barrow or Tate Coker had seemed ample enough reason to agree to go to the mountains with Spirit Walker. But now, the reality of her decision pressed home the point that she would be alone with this man for several months.

Throughout these long days of hard travel, Amber had had plenty of time to reflect over everything Spirit Walker had told her about his visions, and also his belief that their life paths should be joined. Visions . . . sacred ceremonies . . . sweat lodges. All he had revealed about his world seemed like some crazy dream. She was forced to acknowledge that the kiss they had shared had dulled her senses enough to agree to this insane idea of going to the mountains with him, then staying until the snows cleared.

Amber, had reflected upon their one kiss more times than she could count. Spirit Walker had not attempted to kiss her again, but the simple act of her own fingers touching her lips brought about instant remembrance of her body pressed closely up against his chest, his mouth covering her own, his tongue caressing and seeking. Each time she thought of the kiss, she felt her face heat with flame, and she tried valiantly to push such thoughts from her mind.

She had promised, in a crazed moment, that she would go with him into the mountains and that she would be his friend. The rest of the summer, and the long winter ahead, now seemed like an endless span of time to her, and she wondered why she had not considered this fact the day she had agreed to go with him.

She had thought to try to talk to him again about taking her to Harper's trading post, but always in the back of her mind she held the image of her stepfather. Her fear of what he would do if he found her and Spirit Walker had the power to keep her from stating her desires.

Amber could not overlook the fact that Spirit Walker had been kinder to her than anyone for so long. She hated the thought of hurting him. She had lost any fear she might have had of the bold and powerful warrior as the days had passed. He seemed anxious to please her, taking breaks throughout the day, which she was sure he would not normally have done, allowing her time to stretch her legs and drink from his water pouch. And in the evenings, when they made camp, he demanded nothing from her. He would build the fire, and if he had killed a rabbit or some other small game on the trail that day, he would be the one who would cook the meat over the open flames.

He had begun to teach her his Sioux language, pointing out different objects and animals in the forest, then repeating the name in his language until she responded with similar words. During these nights, he would sit by the fire and sing songs for her about his people. Last evening, as she had lain upon his sleeping pallet spread out near the fire, she had lost all thought as she listened to his strongly masculine voice telling her a story about an

Indian brave who had fallen madly in love with the most beautiful maiden in his village.

Spirit Walker had sat near the campfire, enjoying the sight of the firelight reflecting off Amber's glistening copper curls. He had desired nothing more than to lie down next to her on the blanket and run his fingers through her soft fire-curls. Instead, he held control over his baser emotions, and began his entertaining story.

"There was once a young brave whose heart had been stolen by a beautiful maiden in his village. The young man worried day and night over the maiden, and prayed to the Great Spirit to help him win her heart. Waiting for some sign to come to him that would assure his being singled out by the maiden, the brave sat within his grandmother's lodge next to her fire.

"One afternoon, while the young man's grandmother sat sewing beads upon a pair of moccasins she was making for her grandson, he glimpsed the maiden through the entrance flap of the lodge, going to the river with her water pouch. His heart hammered heavily in his chest, as it did each time he looked upon the maiden. But this day, he knew that he had to do something to gain her attention. He was afraid that another brave from his village would have the same thoughts of the maiden and that he would be too late to win her affections.

"Seeing his grandmother's old, worn moccasins near the fire, he rose to his feet and stepped into the loose-fitting shoes. When his grandmother looked at him with questioning eyes, he assured her he would return to her lodge shortly. She said nothing, because she was pleased that her grandson had at last decided to go out into the village once again.

"Making his way to the river, the young brave watched the maiden dip the water pouch into the river. Gaining her side, he reached out and took the pouch from her hand. "Let me get the water for you, maiden," he said. As she watched, he stepped into the river, the moccasins still on his feet.

"The beautiful maiden smiled shyly at the young man, and as he handed her the water pouch back, their hands touched.

"The brave took this simple touch as the sign he had been waiting for. Worried that he might not have another chance, he took a deep breath, and looking down at his grandmother's wet, sloppy moccasins, he spoke: "You must come with me and be my woman."

"Why should I do this?" the beautiful maiden asked.

"Because, as you can see, I need someone to make me a pair of moccasins. These that I now wear are far too big and old. I need a maiden such as you to sew for me and take care of my lodge."

"The beautiful maiden was surprised at his answer, and at first shook her head in refusal. But as she again looked down at his shoes, she reconsidered. Handing him her water pouch, she said, "I will come with you to your lodge and I will be your woman. You speak the truth. Someone needs to make you a better pair of moccasins." The beautiful maiden and determined brave left the river that day and went to the brave's lodge."

Amber softly laughed at the finish of Spirit Walker's story, and as she gazed up at the star-brilliant heavens, she wondered if life could ever be as simple and innocent as such a story. "Do you think the maiden and brave lived happily ever after?" She remembered the tales her mother used to tell her when she was a child, and, always, the ending concluded with these happily-ever-after words.

"Happiness is found when one opens one's heart to direction. The young man knew that he had to make the beautiful maiden his own. He could find no rest until he accomplished this. If one does not follow the purpose that the Great Spirit has designed for one's life, then unhappiness and strife will follow. Happiness is gained with the knowledge that we are led by the guidance of an inner wisdom much wiser than our own.''

Amber remained silent. She knew that his words held a message, but she was too tired from the long day's trek to sort out the meaning now. Feeling secure with Spirit Walker close by, her eyes closed, and shortly she was asleep.

As the sun was beginning to lower and the amethyst hue of dusk settled over Mother Earth, Spirit Walker directed his horse along a path, which soon opened into a lush valley. Near the center a large lake glistened invitingly, and against its bank a tepee had been constructed.

As they entered the valley, Amber's attention was immediately drawn to the lake and the lodge. She had never seen a tepee up close, and as Spirit Walker halted his pony and helped her to dismount, she was filled with curiosity. "Is this your home?" She questioned. There was no one else around, and by Spirit Walker's actions, she assumed that this valley had been his destination from the start. The setting around the hide lodge was indeed beautiful. The valley was alive with a colorful profusion of plant life and the sparkling surface of the lake added a touch of tranquil beauty.

Silently, Spirit Walker nodded his dark head. He would tell her about his village and his people at a later time. For now, she could believe that this valley was where he lived. "Are you pleased?" he asked, watching the curiosity play upon her features.

"I have never looked inside a tepee before," she confessed. Her glance darted, going back to the buffalo-hide structure, with its heavy seams and artful paintings depicting several types of animal, including a large eagle.

The front of the lodge was held tightly together with wooden pins, allowing a small entrance door at the bottom which faced the east, as was the Sioux custom. It also faced the glistening lake. At the top of the lodge, the lodge-poles, at a height of twenty-five feet, escaped through the smoke flap hole. The lower edges of the lodge were secured with heavy hardwood pegs, driven into the ground through holes in the hide.

"Would you like to go and look within?" Spirit Walker had not seen the inside of the lodge since it had been set up here in the valley. He had sent Thunder Hawk to do everything, while he went in search of Autumn Dawn. He saw her hesitation, and quickly offered, "I will go and unpack my horse, and allow him to graze." He turned away from her, hoping that she would feel more at ease to go into the lodge.

Amber held back as long as she was able. As Spirit Walker busied himself with taking the trappings from his horse, she made her way to the entrance flap of the lodge. Pulling the leather hide aside, she peered within the dim interior.

The inviting coolness of the lodge drew her further. As she stood within and looked around, she was surprised at the amount of space. Everything appeared to be neatly in place. In the center floor, a shallow pit had been dug. Small stones were situated around the inner edges and a small pile of wood was stacked and ready to be used. There was a colorful willow backrest, beautifully beaded and propped in an upright position near the fire pit by its stout wood braces. The lower portion of the backrest was rolled up, but when stretched out, one could rest back on it much like a couch.

Along one side of an interior wall, leather strappings secured a rawhide Sioux pipe bag. The flap was decorated with white and green glass beads, with a blue-beaded eagle formed in the center. Next to this hung a breastplate of

bone hairpipes and blue and green glass beads, similar to
the one that she had seen Spirit Walker wearing the day
he had saved her from the bear. Tied to one of the leather
straps was a bandolier of china tubes and blue glass beads,
boasting an otter fur pendant. There was a bow case and
quiver made from the fur of a mountain lion, with a red-
and-white-beaded strap for the shoulder.

Near the bow case and quiver was a tomahawk, the shaft
painted vermilion, with strips of red trade cloth and two
eagle feathers dangling from the bottom. Near this was a
war shield, larger and more decorative than the one Amber
had seen Spirit Walker holding at rendezvous, and next
to this hung two decorative war bonnets; the smaller one
claimed a trailer of eagle feathers.

Drawing her glance across the lodge, her eyes rested
upon a bed of lush furs. After her days on the trail, the
bed looked very inviting, and for a moment Amber was
tempted to ease her body down upon its apparent softness.
But she was wise enough to consider that the invitation
made by Spirit Walker to be friends did not extend to
laying claim to his bed.

As Spirit Walker entered the lodge, his glance immediately fell upon the woman of his heart. Instantly he felt an
inner sense of well-being. He had waited for this moment
all his life. As she turned, and he glimpsed the caution in
her blue eyes, a small sigh escaped his throat. He was
reminded that it would take time to win her total trust. "I
thought that you would like to swim in the lake before we
eat." He hoped that a refreshing swim, and, later, a good
night's rest, would help her adjust to her new life.

It had been days since Amber had been able to do more
than splash water on herself whenever Spirit Walker halted
his horse near a stream. A swim in that beautiful lake would
be heavenly! She glanced down at her torn and dirty dress,

and once again wished that she had thought to bring some clothes with her.

Spirit Walker appeared to have read her thoughts. Going across the lodge, he placed his parfleches down against the hide side, but before he did, he took out a vest and breechcloth, then held them out in Amber's direction.

"What is this?" Amber's eyes widened as she looked at the small vest and breechcloth.

"After you swim, you can wear these. You will find them comfortable." Spirit Walker resisted the grin that threatened to come over his lips as he looked upon her surprised features.

"I could never . . . I mean . . . I couldn't wear something like that!" Amber clutched the folds of her skirts, and as she did she felt her finger poke through a hole in the material, made by a briar. "Well, perhaps I could wear them while I wash my dress," she relented, seeing no other way in which she would be able to wash out the clothes she now wore.

Spirit Walker smiled thoughtfully as she reached out a tentative hand and took the leather vest and breechcloth, then turned toward the entrance flap of the lodge. Watching her retreating back, a small smile tugged at the corners of his mouth. He anticipated the pleasurable sight of Autumn Dawn wearing the brief Indian garments. He would give her a few minutes of privacy before he joined her in the water.

Twelve

The first traces of evening slowly descended over the valley, leaving the edges of the lake in shadows, as Amber nervously eased her dress and underclothing off and waded into the cool water. Several times, her searching gaze turned in the direction of the lodge, to assure herself Spirit Walker was nowhere in sight. Leaving her clothing, and the vest and breechcloth along the bank, her intentions were to wash her dress after her swim. If she were lucky, the clothing would quickly dry, and she would not be seen in the skimpy Indian apparel, which even now as she thought about caused a flush to grace her cheeks.

The water was refreshingly cool as it passed over Amber's tired limbs, and for a short time she forgot about the soreness of her muscles, due to the days of hard riding. She also cast from mind all thoughts of Henry Barrow and Tate Coker as she floated upon the lake's crystal surface, copper curls twining around her body as they spread out in a glistening display beneath the shimmering moonlight.

The sound of a large splash suddenly intruded upon

her peaceful interlude. Instantly her body lowered into the water, senses alert as she looked around to find the cause of the disturbance. "You!" she gasped as Spirit Walker's dark head broke through the surface, not more than several feet away from where she stood.

His response was a wide grin. "I needed water for the lodge. Seeing you enjoying your swim so much, I could not resist the temptation of joining you."

"But you can't . . . you can't do this!" Amber's face flamed. He had been watching her while she was floating on her back! If she had been able, she would have turned and fled. But she was trapped there where she stood. "It is not proper that you are here in the water with me, Spirit Walker!" She prayed that he would heed her words and leave her to her privacy.

"Proper?" Spirit Walker sounded the word upon his tongue as though it were strange to him. "I see nothing wrong with our swimming together. From early childhood my people bathe and swim in the river." He did not tell her that the men and women bathed separately. It was the children who swam together daily in carefree abandon.

Amber looked at him with wide blue eyes, shocked that he would make such a confession to her. "Perhaps such conduct is appropriate among your people, but it is not among my own!" *Savages.* The word instantly came to the forefront of her mind.

"Why is this, Ptanyétu Ánpo? Do two people among the wasichu, who are friends, not share all with one another?"

"Friends?" He was once again claiming that all he was interested in was her friendship. His handsome features seemed straightforward enough. His dark eyes searched her face, as though waiting for some opinion on the matter. "I . . . I guess that friends do share certain things, but this is surely different. I am . . . I am . . ." She was about to say that she was naked beneath the cover of the water, but she couldn't force the words beyond her throat.

He read her thoughts with ease.

"If you fear that I will see your nakedness, put away your worries. The water is dark from the shadows of early evening. Why can we not enjoy this time together as two friends?" Spirit Walker's smile was attractively disarming.

How could she reply to such persuasion? Looking down at the swirling water around her, she noticed that he was right that the dark depths revealed little of her body; and once again, he had used that word friendship. Amber wasn't sure how to respond. She had never had a friend before, and certainly she had never swum with anyone, male or female. She had taught herself how to swim at an early age, in the pond behind the Barrow cabin, but always she had swum alone.

Spirit Walker was not lost to her look of indecision, and not wishing to give her more time to consider his invitation, he dove underwater and playfully caught her slender ankle. Giving a slight tug, he set her on her backside with a loud splash.

With a nervous eye cast in his direction, Amber watched Spirit Walker dive into the water. As she wearily searched over the surface waiting for him to reappear, she felt something take hold of her foot; in the next instant she was falling backward. She rose up out of the swirling depths spitting water and coughing, eyes wide as she tried to catch her breath.

Spirit Walker's husky laughter filled her ears. "That was but a friendly dunking, Ptanyétu Ánpo."

Amber's blood began to race excitedly through her veins. Even though a small portion of her mind told her that this wasn't right, she couldn't help feeling playful and carefree. "You could have drowned me!" She forced herself to remain breathless, but in truth, she felt exhilarated by the prospect of romping in the water with this handsome warrior. She watched concern slowly cross Spirit Walker's face, then lunged at him unexpectedly. Pushing his broad chest with all the strength she could muster, she set him on his backside. Without lingering to watch him resurface, Amber turned and kicked out strongly behind her as she began to swim out of his reach.

Spirit Walker broke the water in time to glimpse a rounded hip and one shapely leg. A wide grin split his features as he dove into the cool depths and gave chase. He was enjoying this camaraderie they were beginning to discover. With thoughts of her shapely flesh so vivid in his mind, he held back somewhat, not wishing to overcome her but longing to keep her in his sight.

Amber's musical laughter mingled with his masculine tone as she raced to the side of the lake. Glancing over her shoulder, she spied Spirit Walker fast approaching. With another tinkling laugh, she kicked off and headed back the way she had come. "I'm a strong swimmer, Spirit Walker. There was little entertainment for me during the summer months when I was a child, other than swimming!"

"I am sure that you were a wonderful child, Ptanyétu Ánpo," Spirit Walker called as he also turned back, keeping a small distance between them for his own peace of mind.

Her childhood now seemed so far away. The hardship of living with her stepfather had caused her to feel much older than her years. Pushing these thoughts away, she turned unexpectedly and dove beneath the water, coming up behind Spirit Walker. She giggled as he swung about in surprise.

Cupping a handful of water, he squeezed his fist together, and a showering spray hit Amber full in the face. Laughter overtook them both as Amber drew closer, to try and see for herself how he could make the water spray out so far.

Spirit Walker delighted in teaching her to cup her hands; as well he delighted in her carefree playfulness, and her closeness as she stood only a foot away from him. Slowly he would gain her trust, and with it he would eventually win her heart.

They swam and played in the lake a while longer. It was Spirit Walker who suggested, "Let us return to the lodge, Ptanyétu Ánpo. It is getting dark, and I have grown hungry."

Amber also felt the full force of her hunger. It had been a long day, the swim a welcomed diversion, but now the weight of her tiredness was creeping up on her, as well as her own hunger. As the pair started toward the bank, Amber hesitated. The night air touching upon the upper portion of her naked flesh reminded her that her clothing was lying on the bank. As Spirit Walker turned to face her, she looked at him, wondering how on earth she was going to leave the lake, and dress, without him watching her every movement.

Instant recognition of her dilemma came over Spirit Walker. "I will go on to the lodge, and await you there."

Amber gave an audible sigh of relief. Turning her back in his direction, she waited for him to leave the water.

Spirit Walker smiled to himself at her innocence. He silently stood there along the edge of the lake for an added moment. His night vision was sharp, and even though the water was dark, he could make out a portion of her shapely curves. His loins tightened as he thought to the day when she would welcome the caress of his eyes upon her naked flesh.

Amber was pleased when she heard the noises made by Spirit Walker as he gained the bank. She had been holding her breath, waiting for him to leave. She waited an extra minute before turning around, and finding no sign of him, she made her way to the bank. In the past days, since leaving rendezvous, she had grown to trust Spirit Walker, but this evening, she was strangely more cautious. As soon as she climbed to shore, she hurriedly put on the vest and breechcloth.

She found that the garments did little to conceal her body. The vest fit snugly across her shoulders and over her breasts. A slender piece of leather strapping tied the two front portions together, and the fullness of her breasts was revealed as they strained against the hide material. The breechcloth was just as revealing. It tied about the hips, leaving her long, shapely legs fully exposed, as well as her midsection.

It was better than wearing nothing, she told herself, picking up the dress and underclothing. Rushing back to the water, she began to hastily wash the garments. Perhaps Spirit Walker would have some thread and needle for her to mend the tears. Seeing a smooth lime rock near where she was standing, Amber began to dip the gown in the water and rub it against the rock.

Within short minutes, she realized she had made a mistake. The dress had been her oldest, and now the telling marks of age and use were apparent upon the material. As she held the dress up for inspection against the moonlight, she gasped aloud in horror. There was a large rent down the skirt, and the upper portion was fairly covered with small holes caused by washing the garment against the rock, as well as the abuse suffered along the trail.

"Oh, no!" Amber moaned softly, knowing, as the moonlight filtered through the material, that the dress would be impossible to repair. She realized that she couldn't wear the dress, that it would be even more revealing than what was now covering her body!

"Well, I can't wear what Spirit Walker gave me. Not

something this skimpy!'' Amber's chin firmed. He had to
have something else he could lend her. Surely he had a
shirt of some kind. She remembered the buffalo robe she
had seen him wearing at rendezvous. With the remembrance, she gained some hope. She was handy with needle
and thread. If he had some hides that she could use, she
could fashion something in a short amount of time.

Wringing the dress of water, she decided to go back to
the lodge with the dress held up against her body in order
not to expose her body to Spirit Walker's regard.

Some small noise near the entrance flap drew Spirit
Walker's attention from where he sat next to the blazing
fire he had built in the center of the lodge. Looking in
the direction of the doorway, which earlier had been
secured with a leather tie, he saw Amber standing anxiously
outside, her dress held up beneath her chin. ''Come, Ptanyétu Ánpo. Come and warm yourself near the fire. I will
have something for us to eat soon.''

Amber dared not set foot within the lodge, for to do so
would be to reveal a great portion of her body to his gaze.
She was vainly trying to cover the front part of herself with
the dress; it was impossible to cover both back and front.
''I . . . I need something else to wear,'' she nervously stated,
glancing down at the dress in her hands, believing that
there was no need of further explanation.

''Do you not wear the vest and breechcloth that I gave
you?'' His dark gaze searched her features, not fully understanding her discomfort.

Slowly, Amber nodded her head, ''Yes . . . yes, I am
wearing them, but they . . . they just aren't appropriate. I
need something else.''

Spirit Walker's expression did not change. ''Did they
not fit?'' He had made certain to instruct Thunder Hawk

to pack these items, and had told him the garments were to fit a small woman.

"They fit fine, Spirit Walker. It is just that . . . that they reveal far too much of my body!" There she had said it.

Now he understood. "The wasichu worries too much about the outer body," he said patiently. "What matters lies within a man's heart."

"That's just fine," Amber acknowledged, "but I am not a man, I am a woman, and your garments cover far too little. I need something else!" She couldn't believe that she was standing outside the lodge door and arguing with him over clothing.

"I know fully well that you are a woman, Ptanyétu Ánpo. I did not mean these words for you. You have been raised by the wasichu, so you know no better than to believe this way. The Great Spirit made our bodies, and there is nothing wrong with that which the Great Spirit has made. You and I are the only ones here in this valley. We are friends. No other will look upon you, except me."

That was exactly what Amber was afraid of! His words sent chills of gooseflesh dancing up and down her spine. She forced herself to ignore the husky tone which held such strange power over her. "What about the buffalo robe I saw you wearing at rendezvous, Spirit Walker? Can I borrow it, until I can sew myself something better?"

His dark head slowly shook in the negative. "The robe holds special power, Ptanyétu Ánpo. This power would be lost if anyone other than myself were to put it on their body."

Amber's sigh held great aggravation. Was this man deliberately trying to bait her? Special powers, indeed!

Before she could say more, Spirit Walker stood to his feet and began to approach the entranceway. "Why do you not come near the fire and warm yourself? It is late and soon we will sleep. Tomorrow you can worry about covering your body.''

Amber knew she was making little headway with this man. The night air was chilly against her body, the damp dress adding to her discomfort. The warmth of the fire was inviting, but still she hesitated. "Then a fur from the bed?" Her blue eyes left him and went across the lodge to the comfortable-looking bed of furs.

A generous smile spread over Spirit Walker's face, and turning away, he went to the bed. Retrieving a lush otter pelt, he returned to the entrance flap with his hand outstretched, the fur a prized offering.

There was not the slightest hesitation on Amber's part. Grabbing the pelt out of his hands, she pulled it in front of her body, smoothing the edges over her sides. Amber had been raised to be frugal, and even the torn, tattered dress might well have a use in the future. Turning away from the doorway of the lodge, she hung the threadbare material over a tree limb to dry. Tomorrow, she would see if any part of the dress was salvageable.

Entering the lodge, she silently stood near the entrance, watching Spirit Walker pulling food from a parfleche.

Looking up from where he once again sat near the fire, he smiled invitingly. "Come, Ptanyétu Ánpo." He held out a hand in her direction. In his palm rested a piece of pemmican. Leaning back against his willow backrest, Spirit Walker's dark eyes held hers of deepest blue.

Swallowing nervously, Amber started toward the fire, the piece of fur held by one hand over her bosom. Seeing the food, she felt the full force of hunger, her belly growling in protest to the fast. As she began to sit down across from him, on the other side of the fire, her free hand reached for the pemmican.

Spirit Walker drew his hand away. "Come here, Ptanyétu

Ánpo." He motioned for her to draw closer to where he was sitting against his backrest.

Amber moved only a small distance closer, still holding her distance.

The dark eyes were teasingly tender as he drew the food closer to himself, and farther from her reach. Parting his legs, he patted the space between his muscled thighs, then lured in a husky tone, "Come and sit here by me, Ptanyétu Ánpo. I am your friend, I will not harm you in any way."

Weary azure eyes looked fully into his handsome face with defiance. He had to be insane if he thought she would sit on his backrest. Between his thighs! "I am comfortable where I am sitting, Spirit Walker." she replied, trying to force calmness into her tone.

Spirit Walker nodded. His hair which had been freed before swimming now hung in shimmering, inky rivulets over his shoulders and down his back. Instead of handing her the piece of pemmican, he brought it to his own lips and took a bite from it. Chewing the tasty food, he smiled thoughtfully in her direction.

Amber refused to beg him for food. Instead, she forced herself to look away. She would forgo dinner this evening!

Spirit Walker had prepared a fragrant-smelling tea made from lavender hyssop. He now poured himself a small amount in a wooden bowl and drank thirstily, the effect causing Amber's stomach to rumble in rebellion.

"The tea is good, Ptanyétu Ánpo, are you sure you do not want some?" He moved one leg further apart on the beaded backrest, as though he only waited for her to come near so she could eat and drink her fill.

Adamantly, Amber shook her head in denial of her hunger. "I am fine, thank you." She tried to take her mind off of the food and delicious-smelling tea but had little success as Spirit Walker displayed full enjoyment of the meal.

"Tomorrow, I will set a snare for a rabbit, or perhaps I will come upon a deer. Many animals come to the lake to drink." He seemed content as he set the bowl aside, then stretched out against the backrest.

Amber did not reply. She was too busy berating herself for ever thinking that this man was kind! To think that she had agreed to stay with him for the next several months! "I am tired," she announced softly. Her voice quivered as though she had to use control not to weep in front of him.

"I also am tired. I will comb out your hair for you. Then we can go to my sleeping couch and rest."

"What?" Amber had had about enough of this high-handedness. First he wanted her to practically sit on his lap and eat, and now he voiced his intention of combing out her hair. She feared to even think about the meaning behind his words that they could "go to his sleeping couch and rest!"

Spirit Walker did not reply, but instead turned to one of the parfleches lying on the floor near his backrest. Within short seconds, he produced a beautifully carved quilled comb. "Your hair is very beautiful, Ptanyétu Ánpo. Am I not your friend?"

When his dark, fathomless regard held upon her, she was at a total loss. By slow degrees, lost within the heat of his ebony gaze, her rebellion began to melt. She could only nod her head in agreement.

"Is there anything wrong with a friend brushing another's hair?"

She searched her mind, coming up with a thousand reasons why she should not allow him to brush out her hair, but none of these reasons rose to her lips. She had felt this strange sense of power that he held over her while they had been on the trail, but here in his lodge it was even stronger. Silently she shook her head.

This time, instead of demanding that she come to him,

he moved his lithe body swiftly, and within seconds he was standing behind her, his strength surrounding her as he drew her with him. His legs stretched out on the backrest, gently brushing against her thighs as he pulled her down before him. An instant flush of heat traveled from her cheeks to the points of her breasts. She could say no words that would make him move away, nor could she force herself to get up and put some distance between them.

"Have you ever had a friend before, Ptanyétu Ánpo?" His husky tone easily traveled over her entire length. She trembled slightly from the sound of it as she felt the comb easing through her long hair.

She held no power to speak; all she could do was shake her head.

"Augh, I thought that you had not." He remained quiet, only his hand moving to gently comb the length of her hair from crown to curling tips, which, sitting as she was, reached beyond the lodge floor.

"A friendship is a serious thing. I have had only a few true friends in my life. There have been many people in my village that I have been close to, but few have been my close friends. Perhaps I could count them upon my hands. Now I add the name Ptanyétu Ánpo to this small list."

Amber drew in a deep breath and forced herself to respond. If she didn't keep a tight grip on her emotions, she would soon be succumbing to his touch, melting back against his sturdy chest. "What makes these that you call friends so different from the rest?"

"The difference lies in trust. Do you trust me, Ptanyétu Ánpo?"

"Why, I am not . . . I don't know," she stammered her answer.

"You speak the truth when you say this. Time is needed for trust. You will learn with the passing of each day that you can trust. When there is peace in one's life, people are better able to glimpse the heart of those around them. This valley is such a place to find this peace. Why do you not allow yourself to learn of inner peace? You will find that you can open your heart and trust.''

Enveloped by his soft, masculine voice, Amber indeed felt at peace. She remembered as a child how her mother would sit in her rocker and brush out her hair. She felt the same comfort now.

"Your hair shines with the life of fire-curls, Ptanyétu Ánpo.'' Spirit Walker marveled at the beauty of such hair. "You have been blessed by Wi; the sun." He had been doubly blessed by being gifted with this woman, he told himself.

With the touch of heat radiating from the fire in front of her and Spirit Walker behind and encircling her, she felt her senses swirling upon the downy illusion of total bliss. So content, was she that she had even forgotten her hunger.

Spirit Walker felt the fierce racing of his heart as his long, tan fingers lingered upon the silky tresses. His glance touched upon the soft flesh of her back and legs, and he longed for that day when he would be able to reach out and touch her tempting body. "Would you like me to carry you over to my sleeping couch?'' he questioned softly, sensing both her weariness and her contentment.

"No!" Amber gasped aloud, at last coming back to her senses. Her hand clutched the piece of fur tightly against her chest, as though this would ward off any such actions.

Spirit Walker laughed softly. "Your hair is dry, Ptanyétu Ánpo. I will go and check on my pony." Regretfully, he rose to full height. Casting a backward glance in her direction, he saw the rosy flush on her cheeks, and noticed that she held her eyes closed tightly.

Amber's sigh filled the lodge after his leavetaking. She felt her entire body trembling as she rose to her feet. Upon wobbly legs, she crossed the lodge, and stood looking down upon the bed of thickly inviting furs. Surely, Spirit Walker would stretch out across the lodge. She climbed quickly beneath the furs. She would pretend sleep, and, when he returned to the lodge, believing her thus, he would sleep elsewhere, as any gentleman would.

Without second thought, Amber rolled over on her side, away from the interior of the lodge, and shut her eyes.

The cool night air helped to bring about a semblance of control over Spirit Walker's emotions. He was finding it more difficult, now that he was here at his lodge, to keep body and thoughts under control while in Autumn Dawn's presence. He tossed back his hair from his shoulders, his strong profile gazing up to the sky as he sucked in deep breaths of night air. "I thank you, Wakán Tanka, for my vision gift. I ask now that you help me in my hour of need, when I must win Ptanyétu Ánpo's trust and eventually her heart."

An eagle flew high overhead upon the night sky, traveling the path of the moon. Screeching sounds filled Spirit Walker's ears, giving assurance of promised strength and wisdom to the one who cried aloud for the help of the Great Spirit.

By the time Spirit Walker finished his prayers and had secured his pony before his lodge for the night, he found that the fire in the shallow pit had burned low and Autumn Dawn was already asleep. His ebony gaze held upon the slender curve of her back, the burnt-copper curls glistening against a backdrop of rich furs. This woman was everything he desired. He would risk his heart and all that he was and would one day be to make her his own.

Silently, he stretched out his large body on the opposite side of the sleeping couch. A soft, dreamy sigh escaped Amber's throat, and his heart instantly swelled with tenderness toward her. He was well aware of the life she had lived with her stepfather, and knew this to be the reason for her distrust of people. A protective instinct welled up inside him as he silently gazed upon the beauty of her heart-shaped features. Never again would she know such hurt and brutality as she had in her past, he swore inwardly, vowing to offer his life in protection of her.

More than once throughout the long night, Spirit Walker awoke, his sable eyes instantly seeking out the woman lying upon the sleeping couch next to him. During the night she had cast aside the furs which had earlier covered her, and now he glimpsed the slender, shapely length of her exposed body. His heartbeat accelerated. Her flesh was so soft and pale compared to his muscular, bronze limbs. She softly moaned, in sleep, one slender leg crossing over his own. His breath was drawn from his body, and for a full moment he dared not inhale. With a will that was dredged up from the depths of his soul, he remained still. Closing his eyes tightly, he tried to force sleep, knowing that to give response to the temptation of Autumn Dawn lying so close would surely break the small trust that was slowly building between them.

Thirteen

Amber awoke to find herself snugly drawn up against Spirit Walker's wide chest, her leg thrown over him, and one hand comfortably lying along the hollow of his throat. Stunned disbelief caught her unaware, as she stared at her pale hand lying so familiarly against bronzed skin. Quickly she jerked herself away from him, her face burning with heat from her embarrassment.

Spirit Walker had found little sleep throughout the night. Since dawn first broke he had been lying still, enjoying the feeling of Amber's body pressed against his length. He had not wished to disturb her sound sleep, nor did he wish to break the spell cast by the moment. With regret, he heard the sharp intake of her breath and felt her pull away from him. Rising up on an elbow, dark eyes warmed as he looked into her face, and a tender smile pulled back his lips. "It is good that you rest well, Ptanyétu Ánpo."

Amber moved farther away from him, clutching a fur beneath her chin. She forced her gaze away, as she murmured softly, "I didn't think that you would sleep here on this bed with me." She had tried to stay awake last night to insure that he made himself a bed across the lodge, but the soft bed of furs and warmth of the fire had been heady inducements toward sleep.

Spirit Walker's husky laughter filled her ears. "There is but one bed here in my lodge, and there is nothing wrong with friends sharing it." Pulling himself upright, he made his way to the fire to stoke the embers to flame. Now and then, his gaze returned to the sleeping couch as he began to prepare food to break their fast.

This man kept Amber in constant confusion. He appeared to think little of the fact they had slept in the same bed. Once again, he had claimed that they were friends, and apparently he believed that such things could take place between friends.

"Are you hungry this morning, Ptanyétu Ánpo?" His dark glance touched her, softly breaking into her thoughts.

With the mention of food, once again, Amber felt her stomach rebel. Silently, she nodded her head, wary of what he would demand of her.

"Come." Once again, he held out pemmican in his hand as a tempting offer.

Swallowing hard, Amber knew that if she wanted anything to eat, she would have to give in and go to him. Silently, she sat up on the bed of furs, and still clutching the pelt over her breasts, she slowly made her way to the fire.

Spirit Walker sat against the willow backrest, and patiently waited for her to sit before him, moving his legs slightly apart.

Watching him, knowing what he wanted, she realized that his will was more determined than her own. She was hungry, and if she did not comply to his demands, she would not eat. With downcast eyes, she silently sat between his thighs and waited for him to make the first move.

Spirit Walker softly smiled, but Amber did not see the movement of his lips. Reaching around her, he took up the bowl of tea he had poured from the parfleche, then had heated with hot rocks. "Wahpé Kalyápi," he said the Sioux word for tea.

At first Amber did not respond, but as she reached for the bowl, he pulled his hand back, and she realized that he wanted her to repeat the words. "Wahpé Kalyápi," she replied, feeling her face beginning to pinken.

Pride in her ability to learn quickly filled Spirit Walker's chest. "Wahpé Kalyápi," he nodded as he held the bowl up to her lips.

Amber wanted nothing more than to snatch the bowl from his hand, but she restrained the impulse. The tea was delicious. She had come this far, and she didn't want to do something that would put a halt to the meal.

Breaking off a piece of pemmican, Spirit Walker spoke aloud the Sioux name for the food, as he had the tea, "Wakápapi Wasná." He waited for her reply.

Hunger as her motivating force, she willed her voice from trembling as she slowly repeated, "Wakápapi Wasná."

Again, Spirit Walker repeated the words, but instead of handing the piece of pemmican to her, he brought it to Amber's lips with his own fingers. As a young brave, Spirit Walker had found a mountain lion cub and had wisely trained him to his scent and voice by allowing no other to feed or tend to the cat's needs. He had fed him daily with his hands, and had gentled him with words of understanding. The cat had become a constant companion until the day he disappeared, leaving Spirit Walker to believe the wild animal of the forest had returned to his own kind. Wishing to draw Amber close to him, Spirit Walker had

decided, while still on the trail, that to teach her to trust
him, he would use these same methods on Amber.

But Amber instantly jerked her head away, rebelling at
his feeding her as though she were a child. "I can feed
myself!" she snapped.

"I wish to do this, Ptanyétu Ánpo, as your friend."

Was this some strange custom of his people? Amber was
at a loss. Her hunger mounted from the tantalizing smell
of food. Silently, she slowly opened her mouth, and allowed
him to place the piece of pemmican within.

Inwardly Spirit Walker smiled. This was the beginning
of her trust in their relationship.

Spongy chartreuse mosses, clusters of tan mushrooms,
and white Indian pipes matted the damp green pine nee-
dle-strewn earth deep within the forest. Flames of orange
lichens splattered rocks and climbed blackish-brown tree
trunks. Delicate maidenhair ferns reached out with beckoning, slender tendrils to delicately brush against the limbs
of intruders who dared enter their silent domain.

Forced to endure breakfast with Spirit Walker's large
body surrounding her, and then, voicing no complaint as
he had brushed out and braided her hair, Amber would
have been content to spend the rest of the morning recu-
perating from the closeness of him, but the handsome
warrior gave her no reprieve. Shortly after breakfast, he
announced that they would go into the forest to hunt for
their evening meal. With those blazing ebony eyes staring
at her, there had been no way for her to refuse.

Amber initially thought to try to keep the piece of hide
with her to cover those portions of her body revealed by the
vest and breechcloth. But even before leaving the lodge,
Amber knew that her efforts to cover herself were being
wasted. The pelt was not large enough to cover her legs

as well as her upper body. Glimpsing Spirit Walker's grin of amusement, she straightened her spine, took a deep breath, then threw the hide upon the pile of furs that made up the comfortable bed.

Feeling uncomfortable with her body exposed, Amber tried to keep well behind Spirit Walker as they traveled through the forest trails. She soon found that Spirit Walker would not allow shyness to keep her at a distance. As the morning progressed, he would stop and draw her close to his side at the sight of any creature they glimpsed. With soft, patient tones, he would repeat the Sioux name for the animal, over and over.

"Wáblosa," he spoke, pointing at a redwing blackbird, his fingers gently curled around her forearm in almost a caress. He stated the word once more before they would walk on. A short time later, he said the word mastínca for rabbit, and hetkála for squirrel.

Spirit Walker appeared as one with the forest and the nature which surrounded them. His steps were silent, his dark eyes sharp enough to spot the smallest of wood's creature. Soon, Amber began to willingly repeat the names of plants and animals, his husky tone goading her on.

This portion of the forest was cool and pine-scented, the rays of early-afternoon sun shimmering through the canopy of trees. Spirit Walker led Amber toward a small, rushing stream. Before they reached the flowing water, the warrior lightly touched her arm. She stilled, blue eyes wide as she glimpsed a large buck deer with antlered head bent low. She watched him drink from the swiftly flowing stream.

"Heháka." Spirit Walker murmured the name of the animal next to her ear.

Feeling a shiver of excitement race up her spine from his closeness and his warm breath against her ear and throat, Amber watched his hand reaching over his shoulder to the quiver of arrows. Setting the arrow against his bowstring, Spirit Walker pulled. The wooden bow bent with the pressure, at the same time the smooth muscles in his arm bulged. The twang of the arrow flying through the air caught the deer's attention a split second before the large beast fell to the earth.

"You got him!" Amber gasped, wide blue eyes darting from the fallen animal back to the man at her side.

"You held doubts, Ptanyétu Ánpo?" Spirit Walker turned to her with questioning eyes.

Amber had watched Henry Barrow hunting the woods around their cabin in St. Louis, then had lived in the mountains with him. She was no stranger to the fact that animals were killed for their meat and hides. Her surprise stemmed from the ease with which Spirit Walker had accomplished the task. Many times her stepfather had spewed forth a verbal tirade after missing his target. Having watched Spirit Walker down the deer at the distance that separated them from the stream, she was impressed by his archery skills. "No . . . no, of course I didn't doubt that you would hit him," she hastily replied. As he gave her a last smile before starting toward the animal, admiration shone in her cobalt eyes.

Pulling his sharp-bladed hunting knife from the beaded sheath at his side, Spirit Walker bent over the deer. Softly spoken words filled Amber's ears as she silently approached. "Sunkáku heháka; brother deer, I thank you for giving up your life so that my belly can be filled. I will honor your strength by remembering this day. Thank you, Mother Earth, for giving up one of your children to this warrior." So saying, he began to skin the hide from the animal and cut the meat into quarters.

Amber stood and silently watched Spirit Walker as he labored over the dead beast; as she did, she wondered about him. She had been taught by Henry Barrow that all Indians were savages. But what sort of savage gave a prayer of thanksgiving over a felled animal? As she watched the lean, strong fingers at their task, she marveled at the wisdom and respect he held for those things of the forest. She had never met a man such as he, and a small inner voice told her that no other could compare to him.

Amber would have offered to help butcher the animal, but she did not have a knife. Spying a smooth-surfaced rock near the edge of the stream, she sat down, and while Spirit Walker cut two stout poles and fashioned a travois to carry the meat, she watched several fat trout swimming up stream.

"This evening we will have plenty of roasted venison." Spirit Walker threw her a wide grin as he packed the meat upon the piece of hide, the fur on the outside, then tied the hide together to secure it upon the travois. Afterward, he approached the spot where she sat, and, bending down, he washed the blood from his hands.

Whenever Spirit Walker was near, Amber found herself at a total loss. Silently, her eyes appraised the muscular power of his upper body. His bronzed back glistened with rippling strength, leaving her somewhat breathless. Her fingers ached with a sensitive will of their own, needing to reach out and trail a pattern over the enticing flesh.

Turning his head, Spirit Walker's jet eyes caught her look. The instant flush of heat that traveled from her face down her slender throat did not escape. He wondered at her thoughts, but kept questions to himself. "Have you ever caught fish from a stream, Ptanyétu Ánpo?" he instead asked.

Swallowing, Amber nodded her head, wondering if he had noticed the embarrassment that had stolen over her after his glance.

With a slight movement of his hand that was by far quicker than the eye, he clutched a wriggling trout in his fist.

"How did you do that?" Amber gasped as she leaned closer over the rock, peering into the water, then at the fish in Spirit Walker's hand. "I have caught fish before, but I always used a hook and line!" She was utterly amazed by his quick ability.

"It is a simple thing." Spirit Walker opened his fist and allowed the fish to escape back into the water. "Brother fish is willing, if one is fast enough."

"Let me try that." Amber crouched upon the rock on her hands and knees, close to him, peering down into the crystal-clear depths. Soon, she glimpsed a fish between two small rocks. This should be an easy one, she thought. Slowly her arm moved and her hand opened above the water. The fish appeared patient for the moment. Drawing in a deep breath, she lunged, arm plunging into the stream. Misjudging the depth of the water, Amber completely missed her target, and lost her balance where she was leaning over on the rock. She was all arms and legs as she splashed into the stream's cool depths.

Spirit Walker could not suppress his mirth at the suddenness of Amber's fall and the total surprise on her lovely face. His husky laughter circled the area. As she spat out a mouthful of water, he reached down a hand to help her out.

Embarrassment and a tinge of anger from his laughter scorched Amber's cheeks to a healthy rose blush. Seeing the proffered hand, Amber's own reached out. With a quick tug, she pulled Spirit Walker off balance. Her own laughter soon replaced his as he fell headlong into the water, only inches from where she was sitting.

The water felt refreshing after the morning's long walk through the forest and the work Spirit Walker had done to ready the meat for the travois. The sound of Amber's laughter fell upon his ears and set his heart to racing. He gazed directly into her grinning face, and thought he had never seen such radiance. Her wondrous hair gleamed with diamondlike droplets of water as the afternoon sun shone fully upon her. Her wide blue eyes sparkled with devilment, laced with good humor. Here indeed was a woman beyond compare, and if in his power, he would keep her happy every hour of the day.

Cupping his hands together beneath the surface of the water, he made a spiraling spray of liquid shower in her direction. As she gasped aloud, Spirit Walker too, grinned. "It is a fine afternoon to enjoy a swim, Ptanyétu Ánpo," he said good-naturedly.

Amber had not intended to engage swim with the man. She had already learned that he was far too dangerous to her senses while they were in the water together. The slight caress of his hands on her body while they swam together held the power to leave her totally unnerved. Trying to stand and gain her footing upon the slippery bottom; she hastily began to amend his suggestion, then tried to get his thoughts back to the meat that needed to be taken back to camp. "We . . . we had best return . . ." Suddenly her foot slipped, and a shriek escaped her throat as she fell once again into the water.

Coming up coughing and sputtering, Amber glared at Spirit Walker. This time, she crawled on hands and knees to the edge of the stream, and with one last heated look over her shoulder cast at him, she pulled herself out of the water.

"I don't know what you're grinning at when there's work to be done!" She stomped away from the stream toward the travois, his husky laughter following her steps. *Better to cloak yourself with anger than endure the heat of his strong hands. Surely you would have felt that touch if you had stayed in the*

water with him! Her inner voice surfaced, assuring Amber
that she had made the right decision.

Spirit Walker's ebony eyes warmed as he watched the
gentle swing of her backside. Her glorious hair wound
down her back, below her waist, in a plump, damp braid.
Her pale arms and legs had a pearllike sheen as she angrily
stomped away from him. He groaned as he felt the swiftly
rushing flow of blood settling in his groin. He shut both
eyes tightly as he willed his emotions to settle, his heartbeat
to calm.

The trek back to camp was much slower going than their
easy morning walk through the forest. The extra burden
of the travois kept the pace slow as they wound their way
through the forest paths. As the afternoon heat had pene-
trated the cool forest, Spirit Walker suggested Amber take
off her vest. He knew from experience that the dampened
leather could chafe unmercifully.

"Absolutely not!" came Amber's instant rejoinder. How
dare he even make such an unseemly suggestion!

"There is no shame in the beauty of a woman's body."
As she looked at him with a dark glare, he added, "There
is little thought when a man wears only a breechcloth about
his loins. What difference in a woman being free to be
comfortable, especially when she is with a friend?"

Amber's features flushed but she dared not reply. What
he was saying almost made sense to her. She must be going
mad, she told herself. She was beginning to act as insane
as he! She silently rebuked that side of: her nature that
was growing freer with each passing day. She would never
go about without clothing to cover her upper body, no
matter *what* this Indian suggested!

"I am thinking only of your comfort, Ptanyétu Ánpo."

Spirit Walker added as he saw her flushed face, and the slight frown that marred her delicate brow.

It was midafternoon when they finally arrived back at the lodge. Amber was hot and irritable, her mood plainly unfriendly.

"Why do you not go down to the lake and swim while I place the meat on the drying rack and start our dinner?"

Instant guilt swept over Amber, at his suggestion that she leave him to tend the deer meat alone. But without a will to resist the invitation for a swim, she eagerly jumped at his offer. Without hesitation, she made her way to a secluded spot along the bank of the lake, and taking off the vest and breech cloth, she hung them over a bush to fully dry. Standing naked for a brief minute, she grimaced at the angry, red welts beneath her arms and along the upper fullness of her breasts. With some relief, she dove into the cool water, the aching soreness of her body responding with pleasure at the reprieve the water lent.

For some time, Amber swam in the blue-green depths, and as the sun began to lower in the western sky, she idly floated on her back, her thoughts troubled as she reviewed the strange situation she was in, here in the mountains with Spirit Walker. She should never have agreed to come here with the handsome warrior. She was once again reminded of those dark-warm eyes caressing her, and felt a slight shudder travel the length of her body. She had been a fool to ever agree to go away with him. She should have stood her ground and demanded that he take her to Harper's trading post, or some other place where she could have secured the means to go back to St. Louis.

Even Amber's knowledge, that she had come with Spirit Walker, in part, because of her fear of Henry Barrow, did not give her peace of mind. Though she was innocent to the feelings that stirred throughout her body when Spirit Walker was near, she was wise enough to know, that he was more than a little dangerous with his good looks and gentle manner. After all, he was an Indian and she a white woman, who, though she hated to admit the fact, was also married to a man she could not stand.

Fourteen

As the first traces of dusk settled over the valley, Amber entered the lodge. Spirit Walker looked up from his position near the shallow pit-fire, an inviting smile on his face. "Come, Ptanyétu Ánpo, our meal is ready," he welcomed. "I have been waiting for you. ' He changed position to make room for her to sit between his legs.

Amber inwardly groaned as her gaze filled with his handsome features. If she wanted to eat, she would have to comply to his wishes to sit close to him. The tempting odor of the roasted venison forced her to slowly advance in his direction. If his actions toward her had been harsh, or in any way uninviting, she would have been able to resist him; but with his lips drawn back over straight white teeth, and dark eyes sparkling with inner lights of warmth, she was powerless to do other than what he requested.

As she silently settled herself between his powerful thighs, he poured a bowl of the fragrant-smelling tea. Without words, he brought the bowl to her lips. Throughout the long day, Spirit Walker had bombarded her with Sioux words, and this meal was no different. Before she was allowed to sample what he brought to her mouth, she was required to repeat the name of the food in his language.

Amber had little trouble repeating the Indian words, or even, remembering their meaning. Spirit Walker took pride in her abilities, and after she drank from the bowl, he brought a piece of the roasted meat to her lips. ''The venison is good, Ptanyétu Ánpo.'' He delighted in watching every movement as she opened her lips to accept the piece of meat, then eagerly chewed.

As they ate, he spoke of inconsequential things, hoping to put her more at ease. He told her about the first deer he had killed with the bow his grandfather had made for him. He took pleasure in the way her beautiful eyes fastened upon him as he told her how his father had instructed him at an early age to give thanks to the animal that fell beneath his arrow and never to forget that Mother Earth was the provider of all life, and could give or take as she saw fit.

Amber silently listened to all he had to say. The warmth of the fire and his large body surrounding her affected her as though she had been drugged. She ate the food he placed between her lips, his masculine voice engulfing her, lulling her emotions.

After they finished the meal, Spirit Walker once again began to comb out her long, shimmering fire-curls. Amber did not resist his ministrations. In truth, his actions were too pleasurable to turn away from. Her back brushed against his chest, and she was hard pressed not to allow herself the luxurious sensation of fully leaning against his strength. He was spinning a web of tranquil seduction over her senses, and she was doing little to ward him off. ''You are like the touch of the sun, Spirit Walker, she softly murmured, remembering when he had said similar words to her.

"How is this, Ptanyétu Ánpo?" His voice was huskily soft as his bronze hands gently ran the comb through her hair.

Without thinking, she answered, "You warm me." Even the heat of his hands upon her head touched her deeply within.

"Then come closer, Ptanyétu Ánpo. Receive my warmth with welcome. Know that the sun within my body is there only to draw you to my heart." Tenderly, his hand caressed from her cheek to chin, and with the touch, he drew her closer to his chest.

No longer able to bear restraint, with a soft sigh, she leaned backward, feeling the heat of the man as though a candle drawn to flame.

With a slight movement, Spirit Walker turned Amber within his embrace. She lay across his lap, cheek pressed against his chest. Inhaling her clean, flowery scent as his hand twined within the silken strands of her hair, he said, "Do you feel the heat, Ptanyétu Ánpo? Does it burn your tender flesh?"

"No . . . I . . . I am warmed through, as though sunlight filtering through the treetops rested fully upon me during a warm spring afternoon."

"Then feel the sunlight, little one. Learn my scent . . . the beat of my heart . . . the touch of my hand."

Amber was powerless but to comply to the inviting request. His manly-fresh scent filled her nostrils, the thundering of his heart filled her ears and set a pace with her own beating pulse as her cheek rested against the muscular ridges of his chest. One hand lay against the bulge of his hard, muscular thigh, the dark strands of midnight hair falling over his shoulder softly brushing against the fullness of her breasts. Amber turned more fully against him, lost to the sensual power that this man held over her mind and body.

His voice came to her from some far distance, the pounding of his heartbeat in her ear overcoming all thoughts of the right or wrong of her own actions. "Learn also of my taste, Ptanyétu Ánpo." His head bent, lips very softly covering her own.

With the first impulse of self-preservation, she jerked back in his embrace, but when their gazes fused, she knew this kiss was meant. Her breathing drew in raggedly as she moved back into the warmth of his embrace; the sapphire-blue jewels disappearing as both eyes closed, lips trembling with anticipation.

If Spirit Walker's heart had not already been captured by this woman, this moment surely would have sealed his fate. His lips met hers in a tender, breathless kiss, which held the power to set his blood boiling, his maleness responding with an uncomfortable tightening. "Your taste is pure and sweet," he breathed against the side of her mouth with the finish of the kiss.

"And yours, is an inviting wildness. If possible, I would capture it for my own." Amber held no guile, and spoke only those words from the heart.

Her ragged breathing stilled as his lips took her once again. This time, the kiss was languorously long, exploring the full draught of passion's pleasure. Spirit Walker's heated tongue probed and plundered, leaving her clutching his shoulders for support.

Honey-sweet nectar filled Spirit Walker's mouth as the kiss was yet again prolonged. Her lush curves pressed against his body, goading the sensual pull of the moment, until, at last, he knew that for his own sanity he had to pull away. As his tongue drew back, he caught hold of her bottom lip and sensuously suckled.

This new assault touched off a flame deep in the heart of her womanhood, an ache of unbearable wanting come to life. Without conscious thought to her actions, Amber began to lightly press against the hardness of his maleness.

The squirming of her bottom against his loins had the power to drive all caution and control from Spirit Walker's mind, but the small moan escaping the back of her throat strangely forced him to pull his mouth away. She was a novice to the desires that were filling her. Looking down into her upturned features, with kiss-swollen lips and closed eyes, he knew that this was not the right time for them to come together as one. He wanted her totally—not just her passion, but her heart . . . her soul.

Pulling herself from the grips of the seductive spell that had been cast around her, Amber's eyes slowly opened, her lips slightly parted as she would have pressed herself closer to his chest to recapture the earlier moment. "Don't . . . don't stop," she whispered brokenly, the hungry ache still throbbing in her lower regions.

Restraining the impulse to pull her back to his body and sate his fierce desires took every ounce of Spirit Walker's self-control. But patience had ruled his life. He knew that the pain inflicted would be that much sweeter in victory, when he would hear Amber's cries of need coming from her inner feelings for him, not just her body's desires. His hands reached out and gently traced a path over her forearms as he spoke. "Another time there will be more kisses, Ptanyétu Ánpo." His raging desire was at last forced into submission, even as he glimpsed Amber's face lose its passion-laced glow.

His words were spoken tenderly, but they no longer held the husky, seductive power of moments before. More than likely, he had at last remembered that she was a married woman; the thought sprang to life in her mind, and with it, she told herself that she should have been the one to remember such a thing! Jerking from his embrace, she almost fell from his lap. The quick movements caused her to release a groan of pain as she felt the inflamed welts caused by the rough leather of the loaned garments beneath both of her arms being rubbed raw by her movement.

Spirit Walker held her captured between his legs, wishing he could recall those earlier moments. But for now, it was best that he control these strong feelings that raged between them. He wanted no regrets for either of them later. Spirit Walker had seen the look that had passed over Amber's face when she had fully realized the truth: that she had allowed herself to turn her passions fully over to his own. He had also viewed another reaction, but had been unsure of its meaning. He had been sure, though, of her look of pain, and hearing the small groan escaping her lips, he knew he had done nothing to cause such hurt. As she tried to pull herself from his hold, he glimpsed her pain-filled grimace.

"What is the cause of such hurt, Ptanyétu Ánpo?"

"It is nothing, just let me loose!" Amber could not believe that she had allowed herself to so easily fall prey to his charms. The pain of her body was nothing compared to the agony of her peace of mind.

With one hand, Spirit Walker captured both her slender wrists. Under loud protest, he pulled both hands above her head, and with his free hand, he drew the leather vest away from her breasts. He plainly saw the raw, bloody welts that crisscrossed the pale, tender flesh above and below her full breasts. Silently, he allowed her arms to fall back into place.

As quickly as he released her, Amber scampered away from him and the warmth of the fire. She desired nothing more than to hide herself away from his dark, seeking regard. Going to the sleeping pallet, she sought the cover of a lush pelt, her eyes warily watching him as he crossed the space of the lodge and began to search through his medicine pouch.

As he turned and began to approach her with something

in his hand, she gasped softly, not sure of his intent, "Don't you come near me with whatever you have there, Spirit Walker!"

Spirit Walker was surprised to see the mixture of fear and caution on her face. "I would never hurt you, Ptanyétu Ánpo." He held out a horn vial containing a mixture of crushed meadow rue and scarlet mallow for healing and wood lily to give the mixture a fragrant odor. "What I have will heal your wounds."

Amber shook her head. There was no way on earth that she was going to let this man apply his salve to those parts of her body that had been chafed by the wet leather of her vest and breechcloth!

Spirit Walker bent toward the bed as she scampered to the far side. His features held a determined look as he reached over and caught hold of her wrist. "If you will not take the vest off in order for me to tend your wounds, I will remove it for you." Her modesty aside, Spirit Walker would not allow her to remain in misery, even if she were foolish enough to resist his offer of help.

"You will do no such thing!" Outrage over his statement filled Amber's voice, but as she glimpsed the dark determination on his features, she knew he would not be denied. She tried to pull her arm free from his grip, but to no avail. Using little of his strength, Spirit Walker gently pulled her, an inch at a time, toward him, even as she struggled against his touch.

"All right! You don't have to do this! I'll remove the vest myself!" Amber had little choice in the matter. She knew that if she desired any sense of modesty left to her, she would have to be the one to remove the vest. Snatching her hand away, as he released her, she turned her back toward him and began to unlace the leather bindings.

Patiently, Spirit Walker watched her every movement. As he saw the vest fall to her side, he silently marveled at the beauty of her curling, flame-tresses as they contrasted starkly against the pale smoothness of her flesh. As he peered at her nakedness through the veil of her copper hair, the thought struck somewhat belatedly that perhaps he had made a mistake in insisting that she allow him to treat her wounds. His heart hammered heavily in his chest as he waited for her to turn around to face him. In his heart he knew that he could have as easily handed her the ointment and left her to her privacy in order tend her wounds.

Drawing in a deep breath, Amber dropped the vest to the pallet. With her back remaining rigid, out of sheer desperation she reached out and drew a piece of fur over the swell of her bosom.

Seconds passed . . . the silence of the lodge drawing into an eternity of spinning emotions. Feeling in control of his body and emotions, Spirit Walker reached out a hand and drew Amber around to face him.

For a few silent seconds he looked at her, his glance taking in the lowered eyes and the slender hand tightly clutching the piece of fur which hid her breasts from his viewing. His husky voice entreated her to relax. Bringing the horn vial beneath her nose, he softly instructed, "Smell the sweet scent of the lily, Ptanyétu Ánpo. I promise nothing will harm you." His free hand lightly brushed the brassy curls away from the side of her breast, exposing the raw, angry welts. His breath caught at the sight of the raised inflammation. With a movement, he poured a portion of the ointment into his open palm.

The scent coming from the mixture swirled around Amber's senses. Spirit Walker's seductive voice filled her ears, and with the knowledge that those dark, fathomless eyes were boldly scanning the outline of her bosom, she felt a shudder ripple the length of her body. She looked

up from beneath thick lashes, watching as he poured the
liquid into his large hand.

"Lift your arm." The words were a husky command,
and without will, Amber complied, lifting her arm for him
to tend the places where her skin had been rubbed raw.
The area was so sensitive to his touch, she felt as though
her body would start trembling and she would have no
power to control herself.

The coolness of the ointment-covered palm lying against
her heated flesh as he gently rubbed the moisture over
the chafed area caused Amber to gasp softly. At the same
time, her heart dashed fiercely against her rib cage. The
earlier kisses compared little to what he was now doing.
His long, tan fingers lightly massaged the outer swell of
her bosom, their gentle touch, more than the ointment,
soothing her hurt. A small moan escaped her lips before
she could halt it.

Spirit Walker fought against the need that quickened
within his body. With fierce control, he leashed the spurs
of passion that threatened to demand fulfillment. Lowering her arm to her side, he drew in a ragged breath as
he shifted his body and lifted her other arm. Here also
he saw more redness, and without words, he poured the
ointment into his open palm and rubbed it over the tender
flesh.

His doctoring seemed to go on forever. Clenching her
teeth together, Amber tried to hold her body still. She
couldn't allow the trembling that threatened to take complete control. As he bent to her, for an insane minute, she
thought to reach out and caress the long, shining length
of midnight hair.

When his arm relaxed, Amber believed him at last finished; but soon enough she found she was mistaken.

Reaching out, taking hold of the piece of fur which she
valiantly tried to hold over the fullness of her breasts, his

dark gaze held hers as he gently tugged. "Let me see the extent of your hurt, Ptanyétu Ánpo."

The huskiness of his tone, as well as the knowledge that the piece of fur was slowly being removed, brought a dark flush over Amber's upper body. There was little she could do to stop him. After all, he was the stronger, and ever so determined. In order to salvage any pride at all, she was forced to endure what was next to come.

Perfection. The single word filled Spirit Walker's thoughts as he looked upon the fullness of the twin, pale globes with their dusty-rose nipples. For a second he dared not move for fear that his hand would shake while he tended the fiery welts across the top swell of her breasts. He fought the desire to cup the perfect breast in the palm of his hand. He summoned all his control to restrain himself from bending his dark head to savor a pinkened crest. Capturing a ragged breath, he poured the liquid on the tips of his fingers and gently spread it over the afflicted area. "In my village, many of my people come to me with their hurts or illnesses." He forced himself to say something to try and distract that baser side of his needs.

"Then, you are a doctor in your village?" At last Amber was able to respond to something he was saying. As she grasped the meaning of his words, she told herself that if this man was a doctor, then what he was doing was not as improper as she feared.

Spirit Walker's fingers lingered overlong atop the soft, pale flesh as he replied, "A healer, a medicine man . . . there are different names among the Sioux for those who use their skill and knowledge to help their people." In fact, many among his village called him a Wicas Wakán; a holy man. Reluctantly, he finished tending the inflamed flesh, and, reaching down to the bed, he handed her back the piece of fur. "Do not put the vest back on this night," he instructed. As her eyes rose to his, he added, "Let the ointment have a chance to heal the raw flesh before the vest once again rubs against it.''

Amber did not answer, but instead, she clutched the fur over her chest and moved as far as possible to the other side of the sleeping pallet.

Spirit Walker stood, and without a glance in any direction, he exited the lodge, heading in the direction of the lake. He was in desperate need of a swim, to cool down the raging fervor that flowed fiercely throughout his veins, the passion that had settled with a searing heat within his loins. He did not know how long he would be able to be around Autumn Dawn and not show her the powerful need that raged within him.

Awakening early, Spirit Walker did not leave the lodge in order to greet the morning star as was his usual habit. Instead, he lingered upon the sleeping couch. As his dark gaze swept over the woman at his side, he forced himself to remain still, barely daring to breathe as he silently appraised her. Against the backdrop of the dark furs, her beautiful countenance appeared relaxed and trusting. The guarded look he usually saw in her blue eyes was now absent as he admired thick, long lashes resting against high cheekbones. His feasting gaze roamed over the perfect, heart-shaped face and brilliant tawny curls which cascaded over the lush furs to twine in lengths over her pale shoulders. As his gaze lowered down her smooth throat and the delicate curve of her collarbone, the beating of his heart increased. Sometime during the night, her grip had loosened on the fur, leaving her naked upper torso fully exposed to his searching regard.

A dream-crested moan escaped her parted lips, but the sound did not distract Spirit Walker's perusal. Her beauty was astounding. Her breasts were full and firm, the peaks

crested with a rose blush. Her slender rib cage and waist
tapered down to shapely hips and long, slender legs. The
breechcloth hindered the treasure that was concealed
beneath, and Spirit Walker could only guess at the splendor
of her woman's jewel.

As though able to feel the heat radiating from his intense
gaze, Amber turned in her sleep, her hand thrown out as
though she would shield her breast; lightly it settled over
Spirit Walker's chest. For a moment, he admired the
shapely hand as wholly as he had the rest of her splendid
body, his jet gaze devouring the sight of slender fingers
with trim, pearl-tipped nails.

Amber awoke to a feeling of total well-being. As her
eyelids fluttered open, and the soft blue topaz jewels within
looked directly into sable depths, a warm smile instantly
came over her lips. In those few seconds of contentment,
while Amber's mind was somewhere between sleep and
wakefulness, Spirit Walker felt his spirits soar with happiness as she looked upon him.

Quickly, reality settled around her. Realizing where she
was and whose chest her hand was lying on, she gasped
softly, "I'm sorry!" She jerked her arm down to her side.
With the movement, Amber also realized that she was
totally bare to his gaze. In a frenzy of utter embarrassment,
she snatched up a piece of fur and quickly covered herself;
her chin and flushed face now all that remained to be
seen.

Spirit Walker's warm smile never faltered. Even in her
state of discomfort, she was by far the loveliest woman
alive. "It is good that you wake with a smile, Ptanyétu Ánpo.
There is no reason to hide yourself from me; remember we
are friends."

"Why do you keep insisting that because we are friends,
such conduct is all right?" Tears of frustration instantly
filled her eyes and delicately spiked her long lashes. Her

voice slid low as she added, "You know that I am a married woman, and until I can do something to change that fact, I am bound by God to Tate Coker. Why do you wish to torment me so?" All the tension and torment Amber had endured over the past few days laced her trembling voice. She was tired of fighting off the attraction she felt toward this man; but at the same time, she knew she had to be strong. Even if she wished to give in to this weakness that beset her each time she looked at Spirit Walker, or was the recipient of that husky, gentle tone, she knew she had no choice but to stand firm.

Spirit Walker heard the anguish in her voice, and would have reached out to draw her against his chest to comfort her, but the resolve in her eyes was plainly evident. As though reading his thoughts, she drew herself farther away from him. He knew she still did not trust him enough to turn her fears over to his keeping. It would take more time to gain her full confidence. Looking at her, a tender smile touched his lips. Spirit Walker had plenty of time. This was the woman of his heart; he would wait forever if need be, to glimpse the trust in her gaze that would one day come. When she discovered the feelings of her own heart, there would be no dark shadows lingering in her thoughts about the man she had been forced to join with at rendez-vous.

Fifteen

Time passed swiftly in the mountains. A week went by and then soon another. Several times Amber had approached Spirit Walker about taking her to Harper's trading post, but each time she broached the subject, he would quickly direct their conversation down another avenue. Their friendship was growing daily, and, as well, the attraction she held for the handsome warrior, one which she valiantly fought against. Amber did admit, though, that she had never felt so at peace, as she did here alone in the mountains with Spirit Walker. There were no restrictions placed upon her, no harsh words or demands. Each day they wandered the forest near the lake; they hunted, fished the streams, and swam whenever they pleased.

Amber was finding in Spirit Walker a man of wisdom and sensitivity. He seemed never to tire of explaining his knowledge of nature to her, and he tirelessly taught her the Sioux language. Many evenings as she lay upon the sleeping couch, she listened to the sound of his masculine voice as he sang songs to her and told her stories of his people.

As each day passed, she was finding it more comfortable to be around the large warrior in her state of partial undress. She no longer reached for a piece of fur in order to cover herself when she felt Spirit Walker's gaze holding full upon her, nor did she hold back when he invited her to sit between his legs and he would feed her with his fingers. It seemed a natural thing now, and the tantalizing kisses they shared were excused in her mind as only an expression of the friendship building between them. Lately she was pushing to the back of her mind all thoughts of the ceremony that she had been forced to participate in at rendezvous. Here in the wilderness with Spirit Walker, her earlier life seemed to be part of another lifetime.

This evening the sound of Spirit Walker's flute circled the interior of the lodge. Sitting upon the sleeping couch, with light given off from the shallow pit-fire, Amber worked over a piece of hide that she was fashioning into a shirt for herself. With a bone needle and sinew which had been taken from alongside a buffalo's leg bone, Amber silently made her stitches as the music from the flute held her senses enthralled. She had never heard the music of a flute before, nor had she ever seen an instrument such as Spirit Walker held to his lips. The flute had been crafted from a piece of cotton wood, extending at least three feet in length. At the opposite end of the mouthpiece, a bird, with the features of a woodpecker, had been skillfully crafted. The bird's head had been painted vermilion, and rawhide fringes decorated the length.

The intensity of the music was poignantly beautiful. Amber was well aware that Spirit Walker was lending much of his inner self to the wondrous sound, which was escaping through the parted beak of the bird.

With the finish of the music, Spirit Walker lowered the

flute from his lips. He gazed across the lodge to the pallet to look at Amber. Her eyes rose from her sewing and locked with his as she softly spoke. "That was beautiful, Spirit Walker. You are a man with many talents."

"I am a man who seeks to hear the words that are hidden by the heart."

The power of those husky words, and the ebony eyes that held hers relentlessly, forced all thoughts of sewing from Amber's mind. "What would you have me say?"

Her words touched him so softly, he almost had to strain in order to hear them. "I would have you speak aloud of what you feel, Ptanyétu Ánpo." He glimpsed the frown that marred her soft brow and added, "It is an easy thing to search one's inner spirit for that which should be. Your heart burns to release that which you force to remain hidden."

"How do you know this?" Could he so easily read her thoughts? Or was he such a wise man, he could see into her heart? She felt the instant sting of tears gathering as her inner feelings demanded that she no longer hold back what was in her heart. She remembered her feelings of only moments past as she had watched him playing the flute. He was so tender and kind toward her, and by far the most handsome man she had ever seen. *Why was it so wrong for her to have these feelings toward him?* her inner conscience questioned. *How could it be so wrong, when daily she felt herself more attracted to him?* But was there a right or wrong in this matter? She knew that there was little time left for her to search her soul for the feelings that she held for this man. "What I feel is not right," she whispered softly.

Spirit Walker felt his heart skip a beat. For the first time she had confessed that she had feelings for him. He was determined, now that she had declared a small portion of her heart, that he would not give up until she shared more with him. "And why is this, Ptanyétu Ánpo? Is it not right for you to walk in the light of these inner feelings? Is it not right that you allow that which you feel in your heart to be brought forth, so you can know true happiness and inner peace?

How could she ever explain to him about the beliefs that had been instilled in her since early childhood? A married woman did not harbor such intimate feelings for man other than her husband. In Amber's mind, there was no distinction between marrying a man because you love him and being forced to endure a ceremony with a foul brute. "What happiness can be found by doing that which goes against the laws that man has been taught of God?"

Placing the flute at the side of the fire, Spirit Walker crossed to the pallet, and sat down on the edge. "And does your God wish you to be unhappy?"

"Of course not!"

"Then why do you hide the feelings of your heart?"

"I am not hiding them, I just don't want to think about them."

A tender smile settled over Spirit Walker's lips. She was so innocent of nature and the knowledge of life. "Did the one you were joined with fill your heart then with happiness?"

"No!" Amber gasped. Tate Coker had been repulsive to her. The one kiss he had forced upon her had been foul and unwelcomed. There had been no comparison to the kisses she and Spirit Walker had shared.

"Do you think that your God wishes you to be happy?"

With him sitting so close, his warm eyes searching out her every nuance of expression, it was hard for Amber to try to explain. "God wants me to be happy, as He does all of his children. The point is not my happiness. Even though I was forced to endure the ceremony, words were spoken from a Bible that day at rendezvous. I am not free to explore, or even think about these feelings I have for you." Her face flushed with her confession.

"In my youth, I learned some things of the white man's God, from the black robe in my cousin's village. I do not think that He is so much different than the Great Spirit of my people. My people pray to the forces here on Mother Earth, but all forces of power lead to the Great Spirit. I think that He would forget the words that were said that day, Ptanyétu Ánpo. I believe that your God would want you to know love and happiness."

"Do you truly believe what you are saying?" Amber jumped at any reprieve offered. She had felt bound by ties of matrimony which she had never wanted, and to a man that she despised. Could it be possible that Spirit Walker was right; that God had never condoned the ceremony that had taken place at rendezvous?

Spirit Walker recognized the glimmer of hope that filled her eyes. "Is not this God of yours loving and good to His children? Does He not know, that all things in our life path are meant to be? You were never joined by the heart to this man. Your heart, Ptanyétu Ánpo, has always been mine."

What could she possibly say that would refute such assured words? Looking into his eyes, she knew that everything he had told her about their life paths destined to be joined was true. He was the man who filled every corner of her heart. This Indian warrior, this savage among men, was the reason that her past had brought her to this minute. She could feel the warmth of his love as he looked at her, the strength of his promise of protection as he reached out and drew her across the pallet and into his arms.

"Your heart is forever joined with mine, Ptanyétu Ánpo. You are the woman that will make my life circle complete. I am the one that will show you the happiness that lies in your heart, just waiting to come forth." Lightly he placed his hand against the upper fullness of her breast, his voice husky with emotion.

Amber was lost before the dark sea of his eyes, his words wrapping around her in a golden promise for all her tomorrows. As his head lowered and his lips brushed against her own, for the first time she allowed herself to fully accept his passion.

His mouth covered hers, his tongue swirling within her honeyed depths with a heated grace of seeking and sampling. There was no holding back on Spirit Walker's part. He felt her response, her hands clutching his shoulders as she pressed her length fully against him. He had waited forever for this moment, when she would acknowledge and accept her feelings for him.

Amber's lips parted, welcoming the warm intrusion of his tongue as he sought out the hidden bounty to be found there. Without second thought, not caring to try and call reason back to the moment, her arms went to his shoulders for support. Her fingers clutched at the firm flesh as her body leaned into each muscular curve.

For a span of time they were lost in the sheer taste of each other. Their kiss grew deeper and their desire heightened. "You are my destiny . . . my soulmate in this life and throughout the eternities to come." His husky words mingled with the fiery kisses he rained against her lips, then over all the contours of her face.

A soft moan escaped Amber's lips as she felt a simmering heat growing in the very depths of her being. His words of love heightened her passion as his fingers lightly splayed against her throat. His mouth placed fevered kisses over her lips, eyelids, cheekbones, and along the fragile line of her jaw.

Spirit Walker knew Amber had at last discovered the truth, that she was meant to share her life with him. This tempered the urgency he had felt before while holding her in his arms. He wished to take his time and teach her the rare delights the two of them could share. Soon, the branding flame of his searing lips trailed a path down her shapely throat, his hand lowering and teasingly entangling with the leather tie that joined the vest over her breasts.

Succumbing to the raw ache of wanting that gripped her, Amber gave herself over to the heady seduction of his lips and hands. Her body trembled as his mouth covered the pulsebeat of her throat, his branding tongue stroking her flesh as though he would savor her very taste. Acknowledging somewhere in the passion-drenched recesses of her mind that her breasts were now free from confinement, her shivers of awakening expectation caught her unawares.

Sheer carnal desire flamed throughout her body as Spirit Walker's lips lowered over the fullness of her breasts, heated moistness settling over one rose-point nipple. An eternity passed during which Spirit Walker seemed satisfied to feast upon the sweet-tender bud.

Amber clung precariously to her clutch upon sanity as Spirit Walker lovingly lavished one breast and then the other. Passion's embers were ignited into towering flames of desire. She ached for something, though she knew not of its existence. She knew only a need to find release. As she pressed her passion-drenched body fully against his, she felt the pulsating length of his manhood hard against the lower portion of her body; the contact between them seared with intensity.

The force of her mounting desire was not lost upon Spirit Walker; his body raged with a burning need that fully matched her own. Holding only the thought of worshipping every glorious inch of her, Spirit Walker's mouth reluctantly left her breasts. For lingering seconds, his agate eyes looked down into her passion-laced features, and his heart thundered inside his chest. At last, all evil thoughts that had stood between them had been vanished.

His glance lightly traced the beauty of her heart-shaped face, his gaze slowly lowering over the slender column of her throat. As his gaze rose upward, his hand released the leather tie of her breechcloth, and with one quick movement, the cover was cast to the side of the sleeping couch. For a breathless moment, he stared down at the luscious curves of female perfection. Searing every inch of her flesh. He reveled in the fullness of the twin globes with their dusty-rose buds, then left them to roam down the length of her trim rib cage to the tiny indent of her navel, across the womanly flare of her hips, and down the long, shapely legs. His gaze caressed her delicate ankles and slim feet, and drawing halfway up, his eyes filled with burning desire as he boldly looked upon the junction of her womanhood, its feathering of auburn curls contrasting against the creamy-pearl iridescence of her skin.

As his gaze returned to her face, Amber's lips parted, his name escaping upon a single breath, "Spirit Walker."

Spirit Walker forced himself to go slowly. He had desired her for so long, he would not allow himself to rush the moment, now that it was at hand. He rose to his feet at the side of the pallet, his hand lowering to release the tie that held the breechcloth about his hips.

As he stood next to her, Amber drew in a deep breath as she gazed upon the hard, bronze flesh that covered smooth, strong muscle. He stood an added moment to allow her to view the perfection that could be found in a male body. And indeed, as he stood before her, he was a worthy example! A warrior in his prime, unequaled by any!

The breechcloth fell to the floor of the lodge as Amber's flashing cobalt gaze traveled slowly over the jet-colored hair lying against massive, tanned shoulders. His forearms and chest bulged with unleashed strength. Muscle-rippled flesh covered his ribs and tappered down to a narrow waist and hips. Only a glance was given to the tight contours of his buttocks and powerful thighs as her attention was captured by the throbbing shaft protruding from his lower body. Amber drew in a ragged breath as her eyes rose upward. Though she had caught glimpses of his nakedness when they had swum in the river, she had never allowed herself to fully appraise this portion of Spirit Walker's body. Momentarily, fear shone in the depths of her sapphire eyes.

Without another second's wait, Spirit Walker lowered his large frame to the bed and gently drew her into his arms. The warning sounded in his brain to go slowly, but his body instantly reacted to the feel of her soft flesh; the contact goading heat anew into his loins. He knew it would take little to inflame her desires once again to fever pitch, and that was exactly what he set out to do. He slanted his mouth over hers, his tender kiss chasing away her fears. His hands moved seductively down her arms, caressing her soft flesh until her supple arms rose up, fingers entwining in the dark strands of midnight hair lying against his shoulders.

Amber made no attempt to still her moans of soft delight as Spirit Walker's mouth and hands roamed over her length. Feathering kisses, licking and nibbling, he ravished both breasts, straight white teeth caressing the underflesh, driving her mad with need. Another moan, louder this time, escaped from deep in the back of her throat. His dark head lowered to her ribs and to the tempting curve of her waist and hip.

His hands splayed over the firmness of her belly to press her hips closer to his heated lips. His tongue sent flames shooting throughout the lower portion of her body as he laved the inside of her thighs. As his mouth touched her woman's jewel, Amber's body bucked in surprise as sweet, forbidden pleasure snaked its way throughout her very core.

With her heart hammering wickedly from his assault of new sensations, Amber clutched tighter to his hair, as he, in turn, opened her gently with his fingers. With a swirling motion of his tongue, he delved into her. Casting her headlong into a torrent of boundless rapture, the seductive movement of his tongue filled her again and again with stroking heat.

Her senses were spinning out of control as a vortex of exquisite pleasure raced throughout her limbs. Hot flames of molten desire spread throughout her body and pulsated wantonly within her womanhood. She was on fire! The flames shot higher, then erupted! Her head and shoulders rose from the pallet as a cry of utter pleasure burst from her lips and her body shook with a satisfaction she had never known existed.

Without mercy, Spirit Walker continued his love play, his tongue delving into her moist, sweet depths, then lingering over the sensitive nub as shudder after shudder gripped her. Her cries filled his ears and added fuel to his desire to pleasure her to the fullest.

As the trembling of her body slowly subsided and the fingers within his hair lessened their tight hold, Spirit Walker rose from his position between her thighs. His lips seared branding kisses over her body as he once again pressed his full length against her. His sable eyes witnessed the sated passion upon her face before he covered her mouth with his own.

When, after what seemed an eternity, Spirit Walker released her lips, Amber softly gasped, "I had no idea anything could feel so . . . so . . . wonderful."

Spirit Walker delighted in her innocence. Her pleasure so far was but half measure; she would soon learn that the full draught of their lovemaking would be unequaled!

So, this was that secret thing that went on between a man and woman, Amber marveled as Spirit Walker ravished her lips, his hands roaming over her body, stoking the fires banked within her to flame once again. As his lips plundered hers with a hunger that seemed even more insatiable, her mind fleetingly, relived these past few moments. Never before had she experienced such wonderful feelings as those brought to life by his touch. The things he had made her feel were truly astonishing, yet some inborn womanly knowledge told her that he was still not finished with her. He molded himself to her body, his throbbing shaft pressed between them, seeking out the place where only short moments past, his lips and tongue had worked their magic and left her trembling with hot desire.

Amber opened to him, too swept up in steaming rapture to resist. As Spirit Walker's kisses increased his tongue filling her mouth, his pulsing maleness slowly lowered, pressing against the moistness of her opening. Without a will to do otherwise, she pushed upward to meet him.

Spirit Walker's buttocks drew upward, and as he entered her inviting warmth just an inch, he felt the tightness of her passage. Dark eyes held crystal blue as he pressed another inch and felt the velvet trembling of her inner sanctum. "From the beginning this moment was meant, Ptanyétu Ánpo. Eternities past, it was written in the stars that you and I would become as one. You are the portion of my heart that has been waiting for completion in order for my life cycle to be complete. My love for you is beyond anything I have ever known in this lifetime!" Slowly he began to penetrate her deeper. Forcing extraordinary control over himself, he strained to avoid causing her more pain than was absolutely necessary.

The instant Spirit Walker breeched her maidenhead and heard her small gasp of pain, he drew back as though feeling the pain deep in his own heart. The look upon her

face was one of accusation, of hurt and betrayal. Without
words of apology spoken, he quickly caught her lips with
his own.

The kiss shared was the most tender Amber had ever
known. All Spirit Walker's feelings of love and regret over
the pain were within the touch of his lips. His sensual lips
caressed, pulling her thoughts away from pain, rekindling
desire. "Never again will there be such pain, my heart.
You will know only pleasure while we lie together, from
this moment forth. Trust me, Ptanyétu Ánpo, trust in what
I say, in the love that I hold for you."

In those few seconds, Amber could have easily drowned
in the love she saw on Spirit Walker's face, his words
entreating her to trust in what he told her. The pain had
already diminished; only her fear of the unknown
remained; thought his tenderness quickly chased this from
mind. In the depths of his warm, sable eyes, she was held
for a timeless second by the promise of what lay ahead, if
she could but trust in him. Slowly, she moved her body as
though adjusting to the weight atop her and the fullness
between her legs. She would have spoken her feelings
aloud, but was still unsure of what these feelings were that
she harbored for this man.

Her movement stoked the passion between them to full
wakefulness. Spirit Walker's lips descended in a kiss that
caught her within a tender budding and slowly grew to a
tempting hunger. His body slowly began to move atop hers,
and she welcomed the movement, her hips undulating
temptingly beneath him.

Spirit Walker's only thoughts were of pleasing this
woman who so completely filled his heart. Her softly yield-
ing body was a seductive temple of love to him, quenching
his incredible thirst, setting his soul afire. His body slowed,
keeping in mind to have a care for her virgin's flesh. He
moved back and forth, not allowing the full thrust of his

massive size to claim her, but instead, going slowly deeper, then withdrawing. He plied her with skillful seduction until she held him in a tight grip, her head thrown back wildly as the fullness in her loins drove her toward a frenzy of mindless ecstasy. Each time he drove into her depths and stirred, her body moved toward the fullness. Her legs slowly rose as she sought to capture the entire length of him within her sleek, hot sheath.

Over and over, he continued to fill her, then ease from her depths, leaving her wanting more of the throbbing length of him. The motion set off a glorious sensation which grew in the very depths of her being. For the very first time, Amber knew of true sensual pleasure; her body trembling, caught up in the blinding rapture of fulfillment.

Spirit Walker caught hold of her buttocks, and with a talent borne from past lovemaking, maintained a strict control over his body. Even as he felt the shuddering beginning again within her depths and traveling the length of his manhood as her sheath deliciously trembled and tightened, he inhaled deep breaths of air, willing himself not to release the true power of his passion.

Rippling shudders of pleasure coursed through Amber's body. She slipped beyond control of rational thought as her body thrashed about, her hips jerking convulsively as she was swept up into desire's realm.

Spirit Walker knew the full power of her release, and for a moment longer, he fought the heated need racing through his loins. He watched her face, blurred with passion, and heard the moans from deep in her throat. Each thrust became torture-laced as he fought off the aching need for fulfillment, desiring to prolong the moment to the very limit of his control. Only when he felt the trembling in her body receding did he give in to his own body's demands and give full vent to the searing desire of release.

Sixteen

Spirit Walker tenderly drew Amber up against his broad chest the both of them settling back down to reality. Her naked limbs entwined about his own on the fur-soft bed as his fingers laced through her fire-curls and his loving eyes looked deeply into her passion-sated features.

It took Spirit Walker a few minutes to conquer the disbelief that filled his mind as he relived what had just taken place between him and this woman of his heart. He had never doubted that he would find passion in her arms. Their joining had been destined from the beginning of time, but he had never expected to find more pleasure with her than he had ever known in the arms of any woman. His loins tightened, with the realization that he had never before been driven to such powerful feelings of passion. He had not forgotten that this had been her first time to lie with a man. His concern was apparent as he questioned, "Are you all right, my heart?" His chest swelled with tenderness for her as his embrace tightened in a protective hold around her.

A wild side and abandoned of Amber's nature came forth. The pain that she had felt at the start of their love-making was the furthest thing from Amber's mind at the moment. She was totally saturated with the most delicious feelings of languor. Her body still tingled from his touch, her thoughts dwelling on the incredible pleasures he had awakened deep within. She had never imagined that this act of joining oneself with a man could be so utterly wonderful! Not yet able to draw the strength needed to speak, she shook her head in response to his question.

For a time he held her against his heart. Neither spoke as they marveled over what they had shared. As the embers of passion slowly banked, Spirit Walker rose from the sleeping couch. Crossing to the pit-fire, he placed several glowing rocks into a pouch of water. After warming the water, he turned to the side of the pallet and silently dipped a piece of trade cloth into the leather pouch. With the tenderest of care, he drew the cloth slowly over her breasts and across her abdomen.

At first, Amber felt uncomfortable with his attention. Rising on her elbows, she moved her hand as though to take the cloth to wash herself.

Spirit Walker's dark eyes tenderly resting upon her face stilled her movements. "I would do this for you this night, Ptanyétu Ánpo. I would show you with my touch the feelings of my heart. A warrior must be aware of the gifts that the One Above has given unto him. This evening, I will cleanse your body. When you give birth to my child, I will do the same, and when you are sick with old age, I will find the greatest of pleasure in doing this service for you." His hand holding the warmed cloth slowly moved over her body, washing away the flecks of virgin's blood from her inner thighs.

Both the gentle caress made by his hands against her womanhood and his heartfelt words caused a trembling to take hold within her depths. She had thought no further than being held in his arms and experiencing the power that his body held over her own. She had given no thought to tomorrow, or living her life at this man's side. His words stirred the question to life in her mind: could she so easily give up her dreams of starting a new life in some distant place? Could she stay here in the mountains with him, be happy having his children, grow old with him? What about Henry Barrow and Tate Coker? Where they to be so easily forgotten? Confusion gripped her. It was hard for her to dwell upon anything except Spirit Walker. His dark gaze consumed her as he finished the loving task. Setting the water pouch and cloth aside, he looked upon her pale body lying upon the lush furs, and within his dark regard, all of his thoughts were plainly revealed. She had never been made more aware of her beauty. Her breath caught in her throat. For the first time ever she realized her woman's power. She gasped as his head slowly descended toward her and covered her lips in the tender flame of a love-filled-kiss.

"I know that these feelings of the heart are all new to you, Ptanyétu Ánpo. There is no need for you to worry of what tomorrow will bring. This moment is enough for now; Wakán Tanka will take care of all else in our lives." His husky voice settled around her, letting her know he was fully aware of her thoughts.

With a small moan, she wrapped her arms around his neck and drew him to her. "Oh, Spirit Walker, do you know me so well that even now you can be so wise and understanding?"

"All understanding comes from the One Above. I know your fears, but also know that this is meant to be, this that is between you and me will only grow." He wrapped her within his embrace once again as he stretched out on the pallet, delighting in the feel of her lush curves pressed against him. "To some it is an easy thing to walk the right path in this life. It is only through mistakes and practice that we can allow ourselves to be guided by one much wiser than ourselves."

"And are you always right in such matters?" Amber drew her chin up from where it was nestled against his chest, to look him full in the face.

A bold smile trembled about his sensual lips. "It is a smart woman who learns early that her life-mate is wise in most things," he warmly teased.

Amber playfully punched at his chest. With ease he gathered her hand within his own and gently pressed her cheek back against his chest. "Listen to how my heart beats a song of love for you, Ptanyétu Ánpo. Listen as you rest. Know that for this evening you need not worry about what tomorrow will bring. My feelings for you will not vanish; there will be time for you to learn your heart fully, to know the steps that you must take."

Amber did as he bid, his words gently ringing in her mind as she was lulled to sleep by the steady beating of his heart: he had called himself her life-mate.

Amber was awakened early the following morning by a thin stream of morning light entering the lodge and falling upon her bed of soft furs. Her vision filled with Spirit Walker's naked body as he stood only a few feet outside the lodge. In his strong hands he held a pipe which was raised upward in supplication toward the morning star. His forceful, masculine voice called out reverent thanks to the four powers which ruled his world, and to the higher power, known to him as the Great Spirit.

As her gaze greedily devoured the sight of him, her blue eyes roamed over his strong muscular back and buttocks, she recalled what had taken place upon the sleeping couch.

She knew that what they had shared was rarely found. He had awakened her deepest passions, and had met all of her desires. Nowhere in her girlish daydreams had she ever expected to find a man such as Spirit Walker. He had taken her to the very heights of rapture and had also given her his friendship and protection. Still, that wayward side of her nature would not allow her total happiness. Looking at him standing thus, in prayer to his gods, she was reminded that he was not of her own people. He was an Indian warrior, and she was still pricked with worries over the ceremony that had taken place at rendezvous. *Adulteress*. The single word filled every corner of her mind.

Finishing his prayers, and finding his heart lighter than it had been in some time, Spirit Walker turned back into the lodge. Automatically, his gaze went to the sleeping pallet, and though, Amber appeared to be deep in rest, he knew better. He had felt her gaze upon him as he had stood outside the lodge, and he could hear the change in her breathing. With a tender smile on his lips, he hurried to her side. "Come, Ptanyétu Ánpo. Let us greet the morning together."

Amber drew back, keeping her naked body covered by a piece of fur. With the slender threads of first light entering the lodge, she felt self-conscious about her nudity. Even her memories of last night on the sleeping couch were unsettling. "I . . . I . . . will stay inside this morning, Spirit Walker, to fix our meal. You go ahead," she offered, trying to think of anything that would give her more time to come to grips with this new situation she found herself in.

Spirit Walker easily guessed her thoughts. He was determined that things between them would progress. She needed time to become comfortable with him and these intimate feelings of the heart she had discovered. He was more than willing to give her time. But he would share this time, and teach her that his love for her would see

her through the most difficult times. Gently his hand
reached out and eased the cover away. His other hand
turned her head in his direction as she shifted her gaze
away from him. "We will do no more than take a swim in
the lake together, as we have many times in the past."

Amber knew nothing would ever be the same for her.
Last night had changed her: she was no longer the Amber
Dawson she had been. Looking into the warm, dark eyes
staring down at her, she swallowed nervously. "Can I put
on my vest and breechcloth?" she requested.

Her soft words touched Spirit Walker's heart with their
innocence. "If that is your wish, Ptanyétu Ánpo, but once
we reach the lake, you will only remove them." He
restrained the impulse to allow his gaze to roam over the
perfection of her body as it was now exposed.

Silently, she drew the fur back over her breasts and a
small smile of relief came over her lips as she sat up on
the bed and looked about for her clothing.

Spirit Walker stood next to the sleeping couch, his dark
eyes falling upon the vest and breechcloth where he had
discarded them the night before. "I will wait for you outside," he offered, and was instantly rewarded by the sound
of her pent-up sigh; he knew she was relieved by his offer.

Amber dressed slowly before leaving the lodge. She felt
strangely nervous and reluctant to be in Spirit Walker's
presence after what had taken place the night before. She
wished he had decided to take this day to go hunting or
fishing. She might have convinced him to leave her at the
lodge, and then she would have had more time to sort
out her feelings towards him. But such was not the case.
Drawing in a deep breath with the hopes of steadying her
nerves, she anxiously made her way through the lodge
flap.

Spirit Walker was waiting only a short distance from the
lodge. He appeared so at ease that for a minute, unreason-

able anger touched Amber's heart. He had changed her life so completely, but seemed himself so unaffected as he stood there calmly looking over the lake.

Sensing her presence, Spirit Walker silently turned and held out his hand.

Looking at the strong bronze fingers, Amber recklessly thought to turn back into the entrance and refuse to swim with him. Perhaps now was the moment she should demand to be taken to Harper's trading post! But the hand stretched outward never wavered, and Spirit Walker's patience finally won out as Amber silently placed her hand in his.

She would still demand that he take her to the trading post, she decided, but at the moment doing anything other than taking his hand would only make her look foolish.

There were no words spoken as they walked the short distance to the edge of the lake; nor were words exchanged as Spirit Walker made a movement of his hand which freed the leather ties that held his breechcloth about his hips. Without modesty he stood before her unclad for a few lingering seconds before he dove into the cool, clear depths of the lake.

Rising up out of the water, droplets of sparkling liquid cascaded from Spirit Walker's black hair and torso as he stood in chest-deep depths. His dark gaze rested on Amber where she stood on the bank. "Come, Ptanyétu Ánpo, the water is refreshing."

Regaining some of her sense, as he dove into the water and she no longer looked upon his muscular beauty, she was finally able to speak. "Please, turn around while I undress."

His dark head shook in the negative. "Why should I turn my eyes from that which fills my heart with gladness?" He hoped he would not frighten her and cause her to flee, but he would never again turn away from the sight of her naked perfection. He would not touch her again until she wished him to, but she would never get over her shyness if he was not firm on the issue.

Amber's heart skipped a trembling beat. His dark eyes caressed her with a warmth that was vibrant and alive, and for a full moment she stood in indecision. If she returned to the lodge, she held no doubt he would come for her. Turning away from the water, she went behind a bush and silently began to undress.

Spirit Walker watched her every movement. At first, he'd feared that she would go back to the lodge and decline his invitation for a swim. This would have been a grave disappointment, because he hoped that this morning's swim would lead to a deeper closeness between the two of them.

Standing naked behind the bush, Amber knew that she had to reach the cover of water in order to claim any modesty. Peeking out from over the bush, she could see that Spirit Walker was watching for her to step out. "Damn, and be double damned! she swore under her breath, and in the next instant, made her way as quickly as possible back to the lake's edge and dove instantly into the aqua surface.

Breaking through the surface, Amber pushed copper curls away from her eyes as she looked for Spirit Walker. He was gone! Then suddenly, she gasped in strangled surprise, arms flailing about wildly as her ankle was encircled by a tight grip and she was pulled under the water.

Sputtering, Amber kicked out and made contact with a broad expanse of chest. She pushed away and propelled herself over the crystal top of the water. The few yards distance created between them allowed her to ward off Spirit Walker's playful antics.

Only yesterday, they had frolicked in the water in this same carefree manner, but Spirit Walker knew that this morning was different. It would take Amber time to adjust to this intimate side of their relationship. Silently, he watched her retreat, jet eyes filling with heated lights as he watched the soft flesh of her shapely buttocks tantalizingly revealed by the kick of her legs against the water. "Where will you flee, my heart?" he laughed aloud with a self-assured tone, and Amber turned to look back in his direction.

He was gaining on her! Spirit Walker had allowed her no time to remain uncomfortable in his presence, and as the enjoyment of the moment filled her, she prepared for his attack with a gleam of playful revenge twinkling in her blue eyes. Hoping to take him unawares, she measured her distance, and when Spirit Walker was at arm's length, she rose up out of the water and with all the strength she could gather, she pushed against his chest, knocking him off balance and backward beneath the water.

She hurriedly swam toward the other side of the water's edge. A tinkling round of feminine laughter filled the air as she delighted in dunking him thoroughly.

Spirit Walker quickly recovered, and gave chase. His powerful body skimmed the surface of the water. As he closed the gap between them, once again he disappeared.

Rising up from the blue-green water, Spirit Walker held Amber tightly against his body. The silken feel of the liquid surrounding them cast a sensual spell of pleasure about them.

As her hands wound around his broad shoulders, Spirit Walker lifted her legs into the curve of his arm and cradled her against his chest; his mouth hovered above hers before slowly lowering.

This was what Amber had feared would happen; though this thought now was far from her mind. His masculine power, the ebony eyes regarding her so warmly, and the feel of her naked flesh rubbing against his chased away all rational thought.

His mouth hovered above her, then slowly he lowered his lips until he stole Amber's breath. Feeling her body going limp in his arms, Spirit Walker suddenly released her.

Splashing down to the bottom of the water, Amber instantly shot back up. She spat out a mouthful of water as a feral look in her eye was directed at the beast that would dare such a dastardly deed. "Why, you . . . you . . ." She darted after him as he swam away.

Spirit Walker's husky laughter filled her ears. "All is fair, my heart!"

"I'll show you what's fair!" Amber's strokes increased as she pushed harder to gain distance.

The morning was given over to this carefree abandon. Their antics caused Amber to lose much of her nervousness. Spirit Walker was the recipient of many tender looks cast in his direction, and they shared lingering caresses as their bodies met in the water.

When exhaustion claimed them, they made their way to the edge of the lake. It seemed the most natural thing when Spirit Walker wrapped his arm around Amber's waist and gently drew her against his chest. "Between us there is friendship which we have built over these past days, and now there is also this . . ." His dark head lowered as moist, cool lips lightly settled over hers.

Gasping, Amber spoke without guile. "Your kisses leave me breathless, Spirit Walker, and your closeness makes me weak." When she leaned into his body, his arms tightened around her. To fight off this attraction that held her spellbound was an impossible task. Her entire body ached to share with him once again the passion she knew him capable of stoking to flame within her depths. Her eyes closed as the familiar heat began to spread upward, the throbbing between her thighs resounding in her blood.

With a graceful ease Spirit Walker lifted her slender body into his arms. He stepped from the water and carried her to the lush, grassy slope at the lake's edge.

Employing the tenderest of care, he placed her golden body down among the splendor of the sweet-smelling emerald grasses; his ebony eyes locked with those of sparkling violet as he stretched out next to her.

Amber had made her choice. Right or wrong, she told herself, as she looked into his warm regard, there would be no turning back. Last night she had been taken to the very heights of passion. She was a woman true, educated into the delights of the body by strong and passionate yet gentle and tender man.

Swept away with the total pleasure of the morning, and both knowing that they wanted this moment to go on forever, they gloried in a wild, tempestuous joining that knew no restraints.

The smell and feel of the grass and soft, moist earth beneath them, as well as the sun's warmth and the cool, dampness of their wet bodies served as heady inducements to the surging rapture that stormed through their bodies. Amber gasped softly as Spirit Walker rose above her, his swollen manhood probing as his lips and tongue stole a flaming path from her mouth to her full, straining breasts. As he entered her tight velvet depths, his mouth drew and suckled upon a pouting bud.

She cried out as her lips parted; a contented, sound of pleasure circled the area as he filled her, her hands clutching his muscled back.

Spirit Walker sank deep inside her, his breathing ragged. Pleasurable sensations stormed through his body. He had almost believed last night to be a dream, but she was far better than any dream; the feel of her tight and smooth around his shaft drove him mad when she lifted her hips to draw him in more completely. Swirling enchantment streaked up his spine and expanded throughout every portion of his body.

As Spirit Walker took up a languid rhythm, Amber's hand stole down his muscular back and pressed against the base of his spine, driving him onward as he braced his feet against the earth and glided in and out in a primal dance of tantalizing passion.

She wanted this to go on forever. She wanted to feel him over her, hands against his flesh, their bodies entwined, filling her to the farthest reaches of her body. In his arms was endless pleasure . . . incomparable bliss!

With his heart pulsing harshly against her breasts and his mouth plundering hers, Spirit Walker held nothing back. He thought only of pleasing this woman who laid claim to his heart. Never had he felt such earth-shattering pleasure.

Her breathing, intensified in the flashing of a heartbeat as he pressed deeper into her trembling core. With each exquisite sensation, Amber's rhythm increased. Spirit Walker matched her it, following Amber fully into her satisfaction. When keening sounds escaped her parted lips, Spirit Walker drove in, holding himself hard against her womb as Amber arched into the hard length of him and clung to his shoulders as though he were all that truly mattered in her upside down world. As her shuddering intensified, he poured into her with a surging intensity that exploded in his depths and carried them ever higher.

Gasping for air, Amber's heart racing with rapture as he clutched her tightly against his body, Amber kissed his mouth, his eyes, his cheeks, her lips covering his face as she breathlessly attempted to express her feelings. "It was wonderful . . . I have never known . . . feelings like this . . . Thank you . . . thank you . . . thank you . . ."

Spirit Walker loved her kisses, her slender arms wrapped around his neck as though she would never let him go, testaments to the ultimate satisfaction she had received. "It was my pleasure," he grinned warmly into her glowing features.

"Truly?" She wondered if he had felt the same pleasure she had, or if he meant what he said and had taken pleasure in her reaction to his body.

"Truly." His grin never wavered. "Truly, it is my pleasure to join my body with yours, and truly you stir me to the very depths of my soul."

Reading the dark eyes that looked down into her own, she knew he had indeed spoken the heart felt truth. "Is it possible . . . do you think that we could . . . I mean, maybe later . . . after you have rested . . ." She didn't wish to sound greedy, but Amber wondered now if every time would be like this one, or if such pleasure would only be experienced some of the time. She certainly would enjoy learning more about these intimate matters between a man woman. With the slight pricking of her conscience, Amber pushed all warnings to go easy aside. She had already given herself to this man; what harm now if she fully explored all the joys that were to be had in his arms?

Spirit Walker's grin widened, his mouth covering hers. With the kiss he felt his manhood surging to life once again in her sweet depths. "I think it more than a little possible, my heart," he whispered against her soft lips.

Seventeen

Lingering within their grassy bower, Amber and Spirit Walker explored twice more, this newfound passion that flared up with slightest provocation. The sun was high in the cerulean-blue sky, the late-afternoon shadows encircling the area as Spirit Walker led Amber back to the lodge. With hands clasped, occasionally stopping to share a kiss, giving no thought to the fact that they had left their clothing near the lake, they made their way to the lodge, and, entering, Spirit Walker drew Amber to his chest.

"I seem not to be able to get enough of your honey taste." His lips lowered and covered hers passionately.

Amber felt her body melt against him, and that strange wanton need flared to life in the center of her womanhood. Never would she have imagined she would desire this man so strongly. *She* could not get enough of *him!* Each time he filled her was better than the last, and this fact, inflamed her desires to a higher peak. "I fear that you are starving, Spirit Walker, and only say these things to me because of your need for food." Her words came out shakily as he released her lips. In the dim recesses of her mind, she remembered that they had not eaten this day.

"I starve only for you, Ptanyétu Ánpo. When I join myself to you, it is as though I am reborn in your tender flesh."

"I know precisely how you feel," Amber confessed.

Spirit Walker laughed aloud, and, lifting her off her feet, he swung her around the center of the lodge. He had never known such happiness as that which now filled his heart.

Amber's giggles mingled with his laughter. It was strange, but she felt no guilt over her relationship with Spirit Walker. In fact, she felt giddy and carefree for the first time in her life. She was determined to enjoy this time with him here in the mountains, not allowing her thoughts to leap ahead to the day when reality would settle about them, and their happiness would surely come to an end.

They fell upon the sleeping pallet with limbs entwined. Spirit Walker's warm eyes danced with joyous lights as he looked into her smiling face and marveled at this gift that the Great Spirit had bestowed upon him. His look turned more serious as he smoothed back her fire-curls against the lush furs, "I admit I have been greedy in my desire for you, Ptanyétu Ánpo. But I will go and fix us something to eat." He had not thought of food until she had reminded him that they had not eaten, and now guilt rose up at depriving her of sustenance.

Amber seductively wriggled her bottom beneath him, blue eyes alight with desire as she locked both hands behind his neck and brought his mouth down on her own. Before their lips touched, she whispered, "Later, Spirit Walker. Together we will fix something, but later."

It was not until dark that the two of them left the sleeping pallet and Spirit Walker stoked the embers in the pit-fire back to life. Together they fixed a stew of venison, wild onions, and mountain turnips. Side by side, they sat facing to the fire and ate. Spirit Walker delighted in feeding Amber the choicest morsels of meat from his bowl. Amber savored the taste to the fullest as she seductively licked the juices from his fingers. Their appetites were hearty, for the food as well as for each other.

Later that evening, their supper long forgotten, the couple lay upon their pallet of comfortable furs. Amber gently pushed away Spirit Walker's hand, her words shyly touching his ears as she murmured a protest, "No more tonight, Spirit Walker. I am too sore." Even though she verbally expressed her need for reprieve, she felt a quickening response deep within her womb.

Spirit Walker was not a man to be denied. With soothing strokes, his lips and heated tongue roamed her body from her mouth to her breasts. "Relax, my heart. I will take away your soreness."

Amber felt her entire body tremble from the husky promise of his words lying still beneath him and allowing him his way.

He blazed a trail of scorching heat over her body. Positioning himself then lower on the pallet, his hand gently reached out and caressed her swollen womanhood. "You are so small, I fear that my size has caused this soreness, but there is a remedy." His ebony gaze was filled with desire as he drew it over her creamy-smooth thighs, then for a few seconds, examined the jewel of her womanhood. Spreading her thighs wider apart, he heard her small gasp of excitement, and settled his body more comfortably, his head resting on her inner thigh.

The silken length of his midnight hair caressed her soft flesh, his warm breath drawing closer as his mouth brushed against her womanhood, moist tongue tracing, then gently easing inside.

Amber's reason quickly fled, her body restlessly stirring beneath this passionate assault. Her fingers reached out and twined in the strands of jet hair, her breathing quickening as his fingers parted her fully and his tongue pressed deeper.

Feeling the sweet liquid of desire saturating her swollen depths, she lost herself to the familiar heat rushing throughout her limbs. Her cries of passion filled the lodge as his tongue teased and swirled, sliding deeper to test the bonds of rapture. No longer was there any soreness; there was only scalding desire, bold wanting, and exquisite need.

He tempted her with the magic of his mouth until her entire body ached for fulfillment. Positioning himself above her, his engorged manhood entered the moist, velvet heat of her sheath just an inch. "Is your soreness now gone, Ptanyétu Ánpo?"

She could not answer, but he felt her need as she clung to his neck.

"You will learn with time to trust me for all your needs," he murmured huskily before his mouth covered hers. Instantly merciless pleasure swept her away as she arched and he filled her with pulsing heat.

Afterward, exhausted, their limbs entwined, their passions replete, they slept as the first mauve colors of predawn broke the morning sky.

The days left them in their mountain seclusion were lazy, indolent hours passed in discovery of each another. They walked through the forest, swam in the lake, and made love whenever the mood struck. Amber no longer worried about covering her body. She took delight in glimpsing the admiration in Spirit Walker's eyes as he looked upon her naked flesh. Rarely did she wear more than her breechcloth when they ventured away from the lodge. Everything around her now seemed to take on new meaning. She viewed all through Spirit Walker's vision, and delighted in the discovery of the simple things she had overlooked in the past. He was a patient teacher and lover, and with each passing day, she knew her feelings for him were growing.

She did not allow herself the time to analyze the feelings that burned in her heart for this powerful warrior, fearing that if she did, she would be confronted with the full meaning of the situation. To love Spirit Walker could only bring heartache in the end. Their culture and backgrounds were worlds apart; there could be no easy road for them to travel if they stayed together. For the present, here in this valley, she pushed such thoughts away. Amber would steal moments of happiness, for they were so new to her, she had neither heart nor will to deprive herself.

As the two of them silently sat upon the surface of an age-smoothed lime rock, their feet dangling in the cool water of the stream that ran through the forest, Spirit Walker's regard adoringly appraised the beauty of the woman at his side. She wore only her breechcloth. Her exposed breasts were perfectly shaped, full and tempting with lush rose-tipped nipples. Her hair, the color of the autumn leaves of the cottonwood trees, curled and twined down her back and fell over her shoulders. Each day her beauty grew in his eyes, his heart full of the love that he felt for her. "We will leave soon to go to my village." He had put off this announcement as long as possible, wanting her to become accustomed to him here in the mountains before sharing her with his people. But the time had come for them to start their life in his village. He was anxious to live a normal life among his tribe, with this woman at his side.

"Your village? But why would we leave this place?" Fear of the unknown instantly filled Amber's blue eyes.

"Summer is almost at a finish; we should go to my village and help prepare for the winter months ahead."

"But can't we stay here?" Amber felt secure here with Spirit Walker, she didn't want anything to change; not while this closeness between them was so strong.

Since they had discovered the raging passion that quickly sprang between them with the slightest provocation, Amber had said no more about her desire for him to take her to Harper's trading post. Spirit Walker feared she would again request this of him once he announced they were leaving the valley. He hoped that her bond with him would keep her at his side. Looking at her worried features, he was not sure of her feelings, or if they were strong enough for her to brave her fears. "I am needed among my people, Ptanyétu Ánpo," he repeated. "The time that we have had alone here was needed for us to learn of one another. Now, the time has come when we must return to my people."

"But they are your people, Spirit Walker, not mine." Amber's thoughts filled with horrible images as she imagined being looked upon as an intruder in his village, and being treated as an outcast.

"My people will love you, Ptanyétu Ánpo, just as I love you."

"How can you be so sure?" he had told her many times in the past weeks that he loved her, and each time Amber felt uncomfortable, because she could not exchange such a declaration. She was unsure of her emotions, and dared not put a name to them.

"My people will know that you are my vision gift; the woman that the One Above placed upon my life path. This will be enough at first; later they will love you for your kindness of heart. Each day, they will view the happiness on my face and know that you are the one that has brought the sun into my life."

What could she say to such words? Amber knew that she was not yet ready to make the decision to leave his side. Spirit Walker had awakened in her the very meaning of womanhood; each time he touched her, it was as though the first. Could she so easily turn away from these feelings? *Why do you worry over such matters?* She chastised herself. *Go with him to his village and see if this attraction between the two of you remains. You can always demand that he take you to the trading post if you are not happy.* The adventuresome side of her nature spoke in her mind, and Amber gave in to the need that Spirit Walker had awakened in her. She needed more time before she could begin the life she had planned for herself before she had been taken away from rendezvous. Straightening her back she firmed her chin and looked into his warm regard. "I will go with you, Spirit Walker, but as you promised when you brought me here to the mountains, you must also promise that you will not make me stay in your village if I do not find happiness among your people."

Such a promise was easy enough for Spirit Walker to make. She was his heart; he would live each day with the sole purpose of making sure she was happy. The Great Spirit had brought them together; there could be no question she would find the happiness which she had been searching for all her life. At his side, and in his village, she would find this happiness.

Their last night together in their secluded mountain valley was rapturously fulfilling. A late-summer shower displayed its full force upon the valley floor; shuddering thunder shook the earth as flashing lightning lit up the darkened sky. Amber and Spirit Walker sat, side by side, upon a piece of fur before the entrance flap of the lodge and watched the fury of the elements.

"Wakinyan; the thunderbird, is restless this night," Spirit Walker announced, drawing Amber tightly to his side.

Amber sighed softly as she pressed her cheek against his broad chest, the steady pounding of his heart lending additional security. It was a beautiful night. The reflecting lightning mirrored jaggedly upon the surface of the lake and the thunder rumbling around them stirred the valley floor. "The elements seem fit for our last night here," Amber said, lightly kissing the spot above his heart, reveling in the feel of his smooth flesh beneath her lips.

"I have something for you, Ptanyétu Ánpo." Spirit Walker enjoyed the attention she was giving him, but he had planned to give her his gift while they were still in the valley and feared that there might not be a better moment tomorrow.

Amber anxiously watched him go to one of the leather parfleches and sort through the contents.

Returning to her side, Spirit Walker held out a necklace made from bear claws; between each of the three-inch-long claws was placed a nugget of gold. "The necklace of the matóhota will give you strength and courage. He is sacred to our people because of his power." Spirit Walker slipped the necklace over her head, allowing it to rest against her collarbone, the nuggets glittering as brightly as her copper hair. Looking at her, he was reminded of his vision; that day, too, she had wore the necklace of the matóhota.

Amber's hand reached up, her fingers lightly caressing the necklace; the claws had been bluntly rounded, the gold cool against her flesh. "It is beautiful, Spirit Walker. Are these claws from the grizzly that was attacking me in the meadow?"

Spirit Walker nodded his head to her question, hoping to somehow aid her time of insecurity when she would meet his people. "His strength was great; this necklace will give you much power."

"Thank you, Spirit Walker." She knew the gift was intended to give her courage, and as her heart surged with emotion, she marveled once again at her feelings for this man. Could it be possible that what she felt was love?

Spirit Walker allowed little time for her inner reflections. His hand reached out to tenderly caress the soft flesh around the necklace, his bronzed fingers lowering to stroke her breast. His thumb and forefinger gently rubbed against the darkened nipple. Hearing Amber's sharp intake of breath, his eyes rose upward and met hers. "Your body is very beautiful, Ptanyétu Ánpo." He marveled at the smooth, round breast which appeared to be straining against his hand for further attention. One day, these same breasts would give nourishment to his children. With such thoughts, he felt his loins fill with heated blood, his man-hood growing hard within his breechcloth.

Amber would have spoken about the pleasure his body brought to her as his hand kept caressing. But lost within the warmth of his gaze, she could not speak; it was hard enough to even draw a breath.

"Why do you not show me all of your body?" His husky tone circled her and sent shivers of anticipation coursing over her body.

Without saying a word, she stood to her feet and allowed her breechcloth to fall to the floor.

"My gift holds little beauty compared to your own, Ptany-étu Ánpo. You are without equal." Spirit Walker's dark regard slowly roamed over her length, taking in each nuance of perfection.

Amber felt the heat between her legs flame, then begin to throb. She would have willingly lain down with him upon the piece of fur, but Spirit Walker's voice held her standing before him.

"Does your body ache with need, Ptanyétu Ánpo?" His ebony eyes locked with hers, not allowing her to turn away, demanding an answer to his question.

"Yes," she got out of her dry throat on a ragged breath.

"What is it that your body wishes, Ptanyétu Ánpo?"

Amber felt her face beginning to flush, but those sable eyes would not release her. "I want you, Spirit Walker." Her words were spoken in whisper.

"Do you feel your need deep inside?" His words were a husky caress.

The interior of the lodge was as electrically charged as the dark night, his question a potent seduction over Amber's senses. Her legs felt leaden, her gaze breaking from his to travel over his length where he reclined upon the piece of fur.

Before she could speak, his voice touched her once again. "Come, my heart, help me take off my breechcloth." Their passions heightened by this interchange of words, Spirit Walker watched silently as she moved toward him. Silently, her hands reached down and, with a movement, the leather tie was unlaced. With the shifting of his hips the breechcloth fell away, his hardness jutting upward with a need only this woman could satisfy. His hungry gaze witnessed the parting of her lips as her glance slid over him and she inhaled a ragged breath.

Amber felt the ache in her lower depths widen, then spread upward to fill her gaze with the sight of his magnificent body. Her gaze locked with his, and lost to the heady spell, she bent to her knees between his powerful thighs.

The tantalizing caress of her fire-curls brushed softly against his groin and over his muscular thighs, the contact intimate and stirring. Even with such passion gripping him, Spirit Walker held himself still, not allowing himself the pleasure of reaching out to her to draw her down against his body.

Amber felt the inner trembling of her body as her slender hand reached out to lightly brush against Spirit Walker's hardness. With that slight touch, she felt the full force of her woman's power. A long-held breath escaped her lips as fingers enclosed around the heated shaft, the blood-pulsing thickness filling her hand with a velvet hardness. She explored with her fingers that which brought her so much pleasure, and as though a most natural thing, her head bent, lips pressing softly upon the sculpted head, moist tongue swirling around the heart-shaped tip. A small moan rose up from the back of her throat and mingled with the groan that escaped Spirit Walker's lips.

The fine strands of her titian hair flowed across the lower portion of Spirit Walker's body, one hand resting against his inner thigh, the other encircling the base of his shaft as her heated tongue slowly roamed the length of him.

Unable to endure more of this exquisite torture, Spirit Walker reached downward, fingers gently encircling her chin. As her gaze caught and held with his, there was no need for words.

She saw the searing desire, his need to join with her, in the depths of his eyes. Not thinking to hesitate, her body moved, hips rising, buttocks lowering until she felt the throbbing heat of his manhood as it brushed against her moist entrance.

With gazes locked, her slender hands splayed across his broad chest, her hair a finespun curtain shrouding them in a private world, the lower portion of her body slowly leveled down upon the branding heat of him.

Inch by slow inch, her velvet-warm sheath captured him, her breathing coming out in small ragged gasps. As she felt him pressed against her womb, an inner tremor caught deep within her depths and a convulsive trembling took hold as she tightened around his massive length.

As his hands reached out and settled over her hips, he set the pace, his body moving beneath her to a tempo of sensual undulation.

Incredible satisfaction flared and expanded as Amber rode the wave of flourishing passion. Spirit Walker's upper body rose up to meet her, his mouth capturing a full, ripe breast. Savoring the tempting rose-crested peak, he suckled greedily, thusting deeper.

At the exact moment lightning crackled across the darkened sky, a jarring clash of thunder exploded and shook the earth beneath the lovers. Amber lost all reason as molten heat traveled from her breasts down to her womanhood. As Spirit Walker moved beneath, her entire body shook with the force of her release.

Sweet tempting alluring satisfaction ingrained itself in every portion of Spirit Walker's body. Her passion was his passion, her satisfaction his own. His manhood surged as Amber reached the peak of fulfillment, and at last, he gave vent to the powerful urge of his own release.

An animallike groan escaped his lips as the liquid fire of pure gratification rushed upward and erupted in the depth of her. Amber clung to him as she rode out the tempest of his raging climax.

Later, Spirit Walker carried Amber to their bed of furs, no words shared, nothing needing to be expressed.

Eighteen

Immeasurable pride filled Spirit Walker as he looked upon the woman of his heart. She wore her fire-curls fashioned in one long plump braid reaching the center of her back. Copper strands of hair on each side had been left free to flow over each shoulder and a beaded headband secured over her forehead held the style in place. The hide shirt she had painstakingly sewn for herself had been artfully decorated after Amber had found Spirit Walker's paints. She had spent days sketching, then painting the design of an eagle on the back of the shirt. Along the sleeves and front, she painted small birds of the forest. She had also painted birds down the sides of the leather leggings Spirit Walker had given her. The necklace of bear claws and gold nuggets circled her throat.

"I am an honored warrior to have a woman such as you at my side, Ptanyétu Ánpo," Spirit Walker stated after they had packed up the lodge and their belongings on the travois that would be pulled along behind Spirit Walker's pony.

Amber looked at him with questioning eyes. She had done little this morning to deserve such praise. Her nervousness about going to his village had her feeling rather clumsy; it had been Spirit Walker alone who had disassembled the lodge and packed everything on the travois.

"The women of my village will visit my lodge often after seeing the shirt and leggings that you wear. They will wish for you to paint such drawings on their clothing."

Amber was well aware that the shirt had been crudely created with the sewing implements she had found in Spirit Walker's provisions. It was the paintings on the hide shirt and leggings that were outstanding. Amber was proud of her artistic talent; it had been the only thing that she claimed as her own during the years with Henry Barrow, and now, glimpsing the pride in Spirit Walker's eyes, she did not shy from his words. "Thank you, Spirit Walker." She hoped he would be right, that she would be able to make friends among his people. Her life, until she had met Spirit Walker, had been lonely; she welcomed the thought of sharing with other women.

"You do not need to thank me, Ptanyétu Ánpo. The Great Spirit has gifted your talent, and I will forever take pride in all you do. My people will also feel this pride and welcome you among them."

"As a child, and until the day I left rendezvous with you, I kept a journal and sketched pictures of the things that happened in my life." Amber enjoyed sharing her past with this man. He never looked down at her and always appeared interested in whatever she wished to tell him.

"Among my people there is an old man called Sky Weaver," Spirit Walker informed her. "He also keeps a record of the years of the Lakota. The Sioux calls these drawings that Sky Weaver sketches upon hide Winter Counts."

Amber filed away the name Sky Weaver. She would seek out the old Indian man and view his work.

"Is it a very long distance from your village, Spirit Walker?" Amber questioned as she took the hand he offered down to her from atop his horse.

As she settled behind him, Spirit Walker replied, "We will reach the winter valley of my people as Wi lowers from the sky."

She had thought they would have a few days travel before reaching his village.

"During the moon of the black calf, September, my people move from their summer camp high in the mountains to the Lakota winter valley," he explained "We will follow the trail of the river and find my people encamped in a valley that is protected from the full force of the winter. It is a valley that my people have journeyed to for more years than any in my village can remember." Spirit Walker did know how long his people had sought out this valley for protection during the winter months. In his vision, he had spoken with the fathers of the past. They had told him that long ago, even before his people had horses, there was a great war chief known as Whirling Heart; it had been he who had found the winter valley, and for the people's survival, he had begun the migration that had brought the people from high in the mountains to their winter valley. Spirit Walker had revealed his vision to Medicine Cloud, the shaman of his village, and had shared some things with Sky Weaver, but Spirit Walker knew that a vision was a sacred gift, and it was wise not to reveal all to people too quickly. Though Amber was the woman of his heart, he cautioned himself not to overwhelm her with the spiritual aspect of his culture. She would learn all in time, he told himself.

As they traveled away from the place that now held so much meaning for both of them, the place where they

had discovered each other, Amber remained quiet with
her thoughts as Spirit Walker directed his mount along an
invisible trail that wound through the forest. Fear plagued
Amber. How would Spirit Walker's people receive a white
woman coming into their midst to live with one of their
braves? Spirit Walker had declared that they would treat
her kindly, but what if he was wrong? What if he was blinded
because of his feelings for her and she found only hostility
in his village? She should never have agreed to go with
him to his village! She should have insisted that he return
her to Ben Harper's trading post! But even with such
thoughts, she secretly knew, why she had consented to go
with him: She could not bear to be away from him. While
riding behind him on his mount, she felt the attraction
that kept her at his side. Her fingers touched the tight
flesh that ran along his muscular sides; her face was close
enough to inhale his masculine scent. His manly power
aroused her sensual need whenever she was in his presence. She could not leave him now Though she knew
living with an Indian warrior went against everything she
had ever been taught, she could not give him up!

As the sun climbed higher in the afternoon sky, Spirit
Walker halted his horse in the forest. Helping Amber
down, he smiled tenderly as he brushed a wayward strand
of copper hair away from her forehead. "We will let the
horse rest for a time while we eat." He sorted through
one of the parfleches strapped on the travois, withdrawing
a small water pouch and a rawhide parfleche containing
strips of dried venison and pemmican.

The forest was cooly inviting. Sitting down upon a cush-
ion of early-autumn leaves and pine needles, Amber rested
back against a fallen log. She allowed her thoughts to
wander. She wanted to remain in the forest with Spirit
Walker at her side. Here in this isolated part of the forest
there would be no intrusion from the outside world. Nei-

ther Spirit Walker's people nor her own would be able to pass judgment on them for the feelings they shared.

"Why do you worry so, Ptanyétu Ánpo?" Spirit Walker sat on the log next to her; her unease easily discernible upon her delicate features.

"I can't help it, Spirit Walker." A touch of impatience crept into her tone. "I have always had a fear of the unknown."

"It is normal to fear that which we do not know. Every small child faces these same fears daily. It is a process of learning and accepting, also trusting. As a small child places his trust in those who are older than he who wish to teach him, so must we trust."

She gave voice to some of her fears as she looked deep into Spirit Walker's eyes. "But what if your people don't like me? What if they hate and shun me for being a white woman? What if they resent me for coming among them to live with you?" If the situation was reversed and an Indian woman went among the whites to live with a white man, she would certainly find no welcome from either man or woman.

"Would you have us live in a world apart from others?" Spirit Walker queried. "How long would you be happy with such a life?"

"I would be happy, Spirit Walker! I could stay in this forest with you forever!" She looked up at him with liquid-bright eyes.

Handing her the water pouch, Spirit Walker smiled softly. "You would grow weary of such a life, Ptanyétu Ánpo." Though the image she conjured was a pleasant one, he was wise enough to know that neither of them would remain happy for long living a life of isolation.

In her heart Amber knew that he was right; still, her fear of going to his village made her try to persuade him to give her more time to adjust to the idea of living among

Indians. "If you truly care for me, you wouldn't force me to go to your village. You would give me more time." Perhaps, given more time, she mused, this infatuation would wane and she would be able to leave him to get on with her own life.

It was impossible for Spirit Walker to believe she did not know the depths of his feelings for her. His smile no longer played over his lips, but his dark eyes held amusement, for he knew the womanly ploy of trying to sway him over to her desires. In any other matter, he would have willingly conceded, but he knew that it was time for them to join his tribe. She would soon learn that her fears were wasted. With an ease, he lowered his frame to the bed of leaves beside her. Though she attempted to resist him for a few seconds, he drew her into his arms, her head pressed against his chest. "Know this, Ptanyétu Ánpo," he spoke softly. "Each beat of my heart knows the feelings that I hold for you. As each heartbeat is stilled, and another reborn, my love for you rushes throughout my blood. You are my life, my heart, my woman. I will always be at your side to offer protection; trust in me, Ptanyétu Ánpo."

How could she do any less than to trust in such words? Her heart ached with feelings of tenderness his words of love and devotion stirred. These feelings within her heart remained unnamed; nonetheless they grew in her breast daily.

Her thoughts were clearly revealed on her features. "Know this also in your heart, Ptanyétu Ánpo; I would never lead you into danger, or take you to a place where you would not know happiness."

Her head pulled away from his sturdy chest, her eyes captured tenderly by his. As his head lowered toward her, her lips parted beneath the gentleness of his kiss. When Spirit Walker held her, all reason fled. Amber knew only the need for his strength and love.

*　*　*

Shortly before dusk, Spirit Walker once again halted his
mount along the winding forest path. As Amber drank
from the water pouch and rested, Spirit Walker pulled an
assortment of paints from his parfleches. With painstaking
care he painted the left side of his face black as he had
been instructed in his youth by the wicasa wakán; holy man
of his village. The dark paint represented that part of Spirit
Walker's inner being that was not shared with another.
Upon his right cheekbone, he traced a line of vermilion
and yellow, vermilion representing the blood of the sky
people who had died in battle or on the hunt, the color
yellow, honoring Wi; the sun, for giving energy to all life.

Amber had never glimpsed this side of Spirit Walker.
Silently, she watched as he groomed himself for his homecoming. His hair had been unbraided throughout the day,
held back by only a leather headband. After running his
tortoise shell comb through the thick, ebony length, he
twined an eagle feather near his temple on the right side
of his forehead. The eagle feather hung in a downward
position. Above the feather, he placed a headpiece of
ermine fringe, the tips of the snow-white fluff also painted
vermilion. Amber recognized the headpiece and eagle
feather, and also the necklace of elk teeth and bone beads
that was tightly drawn around his throat. She had seen
him wearing these same decorations at rendezvous.

Pulling his buffalo robe from a parfleche, she at last
spoke. "The robe is very beautiful, Spirit Walker." She
had admired it that day at rendezvous, but now she had a
better view of the painted designs that displayed his bravery
while hunting, and fighting his enemies. She would have
asked him who had made such a beautiful robe for him,
but something held the words still in her throat. She had
asked him few personal questions, and looking at him now

in all of his savage splendor, she realized that she did
not know him very well. Perhaps he had a girlfriend! If
questioned, he might respond that some beautiful Indian
maiden had tanned the buffalo hide to its yellow-buff color
and had also spent hours painting a recording of his victo-
ries on the front and back of the robe.

What if there was no girlfriend awaiting his return to
his village. Spirit Walker was a handsome, virile man; what
had prevented him from marrying before meeting her?
She had been told about Indian men taking more than
one wife into their lodges! Why, one of the Mandan chief's
had professed that he had four wives!

Spirit Walker did not notice her silence. He was occupied
in replacing the parfleches on the travois. Taking up his
war shield and tomahawk, he tied the shield to his horse's
mane; the leather strap at the base of the handle of the
tomahawk easily slipped over his left wrist.

His overall appearance was dangerous, his stance pride-
filled. His hand reached out to her. Noticing her drawing
back away from him, Spirit Walker's gentle tone belied the
savagery of his appearance. "It is the custom of the braves
of my village to prepare themselves when they have been
away from our village. The people rejoice at a warrior's
return, knowing *that* he has not been defeated, but returns
the victor."

The victor over what? she wondered. *Victory at bringing a
white woman among his tribe? Would his people believe her a
captive? Though she wore the clothing of an Indian, at first
glimpse of her flame hair and pale skin, every man, woman, and
child in his village would know that she did not belong among
them!* Fear of the unknown again washed over her.

Rounding a bend along the forest trail, Spirit Walker's
horse broke through the enclosing forest, and for a few

silent moments the couple upon horseback stared down
into the valley. Amber's gasp of surprise was directed at
the beauty stretched out in a spectacular setting before
her eyes. They sat overlooking a lush, green valley, and as
though viewing a masterpiece painted by a master's hand,
she regarded the scene of more than a thousand conical-
shaped dwellings resting along the dark depths of a wide
river, which slashed, as though a streak of lightning, over
the valley floor.

Anticipation surged through her as Spirit Walker kicked
his horse's flanks and began the ride from the summit,
which drew them closer to his village. Everywhere she
looked she viewed primitive beauty. Tall lodges with lodge
poles reaching up through smoke flaps had been artfully
decorated with brilliant colors. Each was painted and decorated with emblems of the dwellers' visions and dreams,
and many were replete with religious symbols. The savage
pageantry held her spellbound. As they entered the village,
she viewed the dwellers of the lodges curiously looking in
their direction. They stood or sat near their outside fires,
many of the women preparing the evening meal. Amber
glimpsed a woman taking strips of meat from her drying
rack, which had been constructed next to her lodge. Other
women were bent over fires stirring blackened trade pots,
which rested against the open coals.

Shouts of welcome were called aloud to Spirit Walker
as villagers came from their lodges. Others, curious at the
commotion caused by the barking dogs nipping at his
horse's heels, stopped what they were doing and openly
stared at the returning warrior and the white woman with
him.

With any luck at all, Amber thought, Spirit Walker would
keep riding until he reached his lodge. Once there, she
could hurry within the safety of the hide walls and not
have to be confronted by these villagers until tomorrow.

This thought strengthened as he held his pony to a steady pace. Returning the calls directed at him, he appeared to have a destination in mind. Amber prayed it was to his lodge they were now going.

Her displeasure was evident when Spirit Walker halted his horse in the center of the village as a large warrior stepped in front of them, blocking their passage.

"I see that you have returned safely, Wanági Máni; Spirit Walker. It was Thunder Hawk who approached them and spoke loudly enough for all to hear. His gaze swept over the woman with the fire hair, the woman he and Strong Elk had believed a spirit woman.

Amber was not lost to the brave's close perusal of her, and automatically her grip tightened upon Spirit Walker's sides.

Spirit Walker warmly greeted the brave, who was one of his closest friends. "I have returned with my woman, who is called Ptanyétu Ánpo; Autumn Dawn." He spoke in the Sioux dialect, his voice carrying to all those standing around. "Ptanyétu Ánpo is my vision gift from the One Above. She is now one of the people."

Amber understood much of what he was saying, and knew his declarations carried throughout much of the village. She heard several gasps of surprise at his words, but as she looked around, she viewed none of the resentment she had expected. She was now thankful that Spirit Walker had introduced her to his people right away. These people appeared to hold him in high respect, and none voiced objections to his announcement that he had brought a white woman to live among them. A soft, audible sigh escaped her parted lips.

Spirit Walker heard the sound of relief. At that moment, he desired nothing more than to turn on his mount and take her into his arms. The first part of her ordeal was almost finished, and Amber saw that she was safe. Summoning all his control he restrained his desire to reach out to her. "Has my lodge been set up near the river, Cetán?" he asked instead.

Before the large warrior could reply, an ancient Indian man, with unkempt gray hair and a robe of bear hide wrapped around his frail frame, approached the group. Holding a rattle made from a gourd in his right hand, gnarled fingers tightened as he shook the rattle resoundingly in the direction of the couple on horse back.

"Wíhmunge . . . wíhmunge . . ." He pointed a long, bony finger directly at Amber, his feverish black eyes glaring distrust and hatred for all whites as he spat out cruel accusations that the woman with Spirit Walker held witch medicine.

Protectively, Spirit Walker's hand covered Amber's slender fingers which now rested on her thigh. His heated look of anger settled upon the old man who had a history of trying to provoke discord among the tribe.

The old man claimed to be a holy man, but in truth had little or no power. "This woman is my wife, Cut Finger," Spirit Walker explained, "Ptanyétu Ánpo is my vision gift; a gift from the Great Spirit. She is not to be insulted by any among my people, even you old man!" His husky tone issued the challenge.

"She turns your head already from the path of respect! A wicása wakán has ways to deal with those who call him an old man!" He turned around, taking all standing close within his hard glare.

Many villagers turned their heads. Some were not certain Cut Finger had no validity to the claim of holy man, and did not wish to take the chance he did. Others, knowing well the old man's antics, held back their mirth as he worked himself into an agitated rage before the entire village.

"The wasicun winyan; white woman, has the signs of

wíhmunge; witch medicine, in her hair. She deceives Spirit Walker, but she cannot fool Cut Finger. I know her for what she is!''

Spirit Walker's anger kindled as he heard the old man shouting out his hatred. ''If you were a younger warrior, Cut Finger, I would not hesitate to challenge you; then all here would know the evil one amongst the people. But you are an old man, and I would only bring shame upon myself for making such a challenge! The people here before you know your words are false. The Great Spirit would not bring wíhmunge among his children!''

Murmurs of agreement stirred around the couple on horseback. The villagers knew Spirit Walker well. His wisdom was honored among the Sioux; few could make such a claim about Cut Finger.

Cut Finger had hated Spirit Walker for years, just as he had hated every other shaman or holy man of this village, because they threatened his own claim of power and spiritual knowledge. Few of the people came to his lodge seeking out his help or wisdom, but he had seen many young braves near Spirit Walker's lodge, testing his guidance. Shaking his rattle wildly in their direction, his eyes burned brightly as they stared straight at Amber. ''You will regret bringing this wíhmunge among us, Spirit Walker! One day you will seek me out with your need to cast this woman's evil from you!''

Spirit Walker laughed outright at the old man; the sound of his husky humor carrying over the villagers and putting them back at ease. ''That day you will not see, Cut Finger! Ptanyétu Ánpo is the woman of my heart. She will be at my side long after you have passed over and joined the sky people!''

Cut Finger's dark eyes glared hatred at the couple as he watched Spirit Walker set his pony into motion, continuing on through the village with the white woman. They were headed toward the bank of the river where Spirit Walker's lodge had been set up. Cut Finger swore that he would reveal her witch medicine to his people! As the two of them disappeared from sight, an idea caught and burned brightly in Cut Finger's head. If he could prove that the woman Spirit Walker called Ptanyétu Ánpo was in truth evil, as he claimed, he would at last be honored as the holy man; he had always wanted the people to believe him!

Nineteen

To Amber's relief, there was no wife or girlfriend waiting for Spirit Walker when they reached his lodge. She certainly could not have contended with a jealous woman and crazy medicine man all in one night! Standing near the entrance flap to the lodge, as Spirit Walker began to build up a fire in the circular fire-pit, Amber made an effort to control the trembling that had overtaken her body. She couldn't put from her mind the hatred and ill will she had seen upon the old Indian man's features as he had shook his rattle at her. No one had ever openly displayed such contempt toward her. "Why does that man hate me so much?" she questioned Spirit Walker, who fed wood to the growing flames.

Spirit Walker heard disbelief and confusion in her voice, and as he straightened to his full height, his dark gaze took in the paleness of her features. Cut Finger's words had held a potent effect on her. "Cut Finger is one whose spirit cries for that which he can never have. He would be more than what he is before the people. He is an old man,

and knows that he has not many more winters before he
will join the sky people; he will try anything to gain the
attention he desires.''

"But what has any of that to do with me?" Amber shook
her head, as though trying to clear her thoughts to better
understand what Spirit Walker was trying to share.

"Come near the fire, Ptanyétu Ánpo, you are cold."
Spirit Walker drew her to him and felt her trembling. "I
will comb out your hair as I try and explain."

Without second thought, Amber sat down between his
thighs. "I still don't understand why he would hate me so
much." She sensed there had been more than his aversion
to her color to the old man's meanness. Secretly, in her
heart, Amber had hoped that Spirit Walker would be right,
that his people would accept her because of him. She knew
now that this would not be the way things would turn out.

Unbraiding her hair, Spirit Walker ran his fingers
through the curling strands of fire-curls, his senses filling
with her clean earthy scent. He began to run the tortoise
shell comb through her shimmering tresses. "Cut Finger
is a man who has known little happiness. He had a good
wife, and has a fine son and grandson, but still he longs
for recognition that is beyond his grasp. He has no power
or dreams to share with the people. Because of this, he
does not receive the respect as a shaman that he believes
he deserves."

"So he thinks that he will gain this respect by turning
your people against me?" Amber turned on his lap, her
breasts pressing against his chest as she looked full into
his face.

"Those were his thoughts, but you saw for yourself that
the people know his intent. None believe his evil tongue."

"But how can you be so sure? What if they do believe
him, and because he says that I am . . . what did he call
me . . . wíhmunge?''

"In the white man's tongue, it means witch medicine," Spirit Walker supplied.

"What if your people believe that I do have this witch medicine?" Her body trembled anew as she imagined the hate-filled looks she would receive tomorrow if she dared to step foot out of Spirit Walker's lodge. She could even be attacked by some of Cut Finger's believers!

Spirit Walker drew a long, bronze finger across her cheek, his gaze direct. "My people will not judge you because of Cut Finger's words. They will give you the chance to prove yourself to be kind and generous of heart."

He sounded so confident, sure of his people and her ability to gain their respect. Amber had lacked self-confidence in the past, but in Spirit Walker's presence, she was made to feel as though she could accomplish anything, be anyone she wanted to be, do anything she wanted to do. If he believed that his people would accept her, then she could do no less. A small smile passed over her lips as she was warmed by the love in his gaze. Looking into his eyes, she believed everything he said would come true.

A call from outside the lodge broke the spell. With some resentment at having been disturbed, Spirit Walker rose from the fire. "Cetán wishes to speak with me. I will not be long. You should ready yourself for sleep," he suggested. "It has been a long day on the trail."

Amber nodded as she watched him leave the lodge. For a few minutes she sat upon the edge of the backrest and stared at the flickering flames. The die had been cast; she was here among the Sioux and knew that Spirit Walker would not agree to take her to Harper's trading post unless she made the effort to fit in with his people. The image of Cut Finger shaking his rattle at her, his wrinkled features holding contempt, filled her mind. But instead of giving in to the fear that filled her heart, she left the fire, making her way to the comfortable-looking sleeping couch.

The interior of Spirit Walker's lodge was much larger than the one Amber had shared with him near the lake. There was plenty of space, and more of Spirit Walker's possessions in evidence.

The sleeping couch was piled high with thick furs, those strapped on the travois having not been unpacked yet. Looking at the inviting bed, Amber began to unlace the leather ties of her shirt. Spirit Walker was right, it had been a long day, and Amber desired nothing more than to lose all thought in the tranquility of sleep. Tomorrow would be soon enough to face the people in Spirit Walker's village. Tomorrow, she would learn if they believed that horrid man's claim that she had some kind of witch medicine!

Allowing the entrance flap of hide to fall back in place, Spirit Walker silently appraised the woman of his heart as she stood next to the sleeping couch. With a noiseless tread he approached her, the slender curves of her exposed body drawing him closer, his heartbeat escalating with each step. As his hand reached out and gathered the full weight of her bright hair, the shirt held in her hand slipped to the floor.

Pressing closer to her, he inhaled her womanly essence. With a solitary motion, his other hand slipped around her, cupping the fullness of a breast in the palm of his hand, his head lowering to her shoulder, where his lips rained kisses over the graceful curve of her neck and along the bow of her shoulders.

Amber sighed with pleasure. This was why she was in this Indian village, the reason she had followed willingly where Spirit Walker led. This magical sense of rapture filled her each time he was near, and made her a willing recipient to the pleasures lying in wait.

His hand stole from breast to waist, and with a slight movement, her breechcloth fell to the floor with the shirt. She stood in beaded leggings and moccasins, the curve of her buttocks molded against him, the hard length of his shaft straining against his breechcloth. His body curved against her, her woman's shape arching toward the heat of his manhood.

His kisses increased, tongue swirling seductively over her flesh as he nibbled the delicate column of her throat, creating a searing path to her earlobe, where he whispered Indian love words in praise of her beauty.

He allowed the heaviness of her hair to drape over a shoulder, one hand slipping to the tie of his breechcloth. As it fell, Spirit Walker settled both hands over her hips and lifted Amber from the floor.

Breathless sighs escaped, then mingled as the velvet heat of Spirit Walker's manhood pressed against Amber's passion. Slowly, his hands drew her hips downward, the trembling heat of her tight passage encapsulating his hardness deep within her depths.

As quickly as he filled her, his hands upon her hips brought her upwards and then back down against him, escalating the friction of their passion. Tightening her leather-encased legs against the powerful muscles of his thighs, Amber's movement increased with the aid of his hands upon her hips. Taking him fully into her, she was stroked and then filled, until she was mindless but to the waves of crashing pleasure that spiraled throughout her body.

Spirit Walker's fiery strokes never wavered in depth and sureness. He welcomed the slight pressure of her legs against his own. His body was tuned to every inch of her soft flesh as her slender back pressed closer to his chest, her curvaceous buttocks molded tightly against his muscular abdomen. He gloried in filling her.

As he pressed further an explosive shudder rippled through Amber. The fiery center of her desire exploded in one stirring contraction after another. The cry of his name traveled around the interior of the lodge. Her head thrown back, eyes tightly closed, Amber was carried to new heights of passion.

Spirit Walker controlled his climax for as long as possible. When restraint was no longer a choice, he cried out harshly as his release gushed forth inside her like a firestorm. He held her within his fierce embrace, as though he could not get close enough to her, or deep enough inside her. Amber felt the pulsebeat of his fiery, shuddering release. Still joined, they collapsed upon the bed of furs.

"This is all that matters, Ptanyétu Ánpo, this that is in our hearts, what is shared between us. I will not allow anything, or any person, to destroy that which we have found." Spirit Walker settled her in his arms, his heart filled with love, his body sated.

She believed everything he said.

"Goddamn Injun, I'll slit you from crotch to gizzard with a dull deer antler, if you don't get the hell away from me while I'm playing poker!" Tate Coker hefted his mug of ale up in a beefy fist, his other hand reaching to the knife tucked in his waistband. A booted foot kicked at the chair the old Indian was sitting in, near the table where Coker and Barrow were playing cards.

"I don't cotton how old Ben can abide these pesky redskins around all the time." Henry Barrow threw a dark look at the Indian known around Harper's trading post as Whiskey Luke. A more appropriate name for the ancient Indian would have been Anything-To-Drink Luke, Barrow reflected as he watched the Indian lurch from his chair and away from Coker's reach. The stupid savage just didn't know when to quit! Looking at the cards in his hand, he threw down another coin. "I'll see you, Coker." By God, he was sick of playing cards, and he was sick of waiting for the winter months to pass!

Tate Coker cast one last glare in the Indian's direction. Draining the dregs of his mug, he slammed it down on the plank-board table, pushing the point home to Whiskey Luke that he was tired of his begging for a portion of his drink. And the point that he had best stay clear from here on out, if the damn Injun valued his red hide, Coker thought before throwing down his cards on the small pile of coins in the center of the table. Fours and sixes showed face up; a full house.

"Ah, shit!" Henry Barrow threw in his cards. He had a pair of queens.

A wide grin split Coker's lips. "Want to play another round?"

"Naw. Maybe later." Barrow rose from his seat, reminded that he had never been skilled at poker. It would be easy, sitting across from a man like Tate Coker, to lose all of his hard-earned savings. "I think I'll just walk around the post for a while."

"I'll come with you. Maybe we'll see Mavis bent over her wash tub again. I swear, even old Ben's ugly wife would do me some good." Coker stood, rubbing his crotch.

Henry Barrow made a sour face as he imagined taking the very overweight, very homely Mavis Harper to bed.

"Don't be knocking it, till you try some of that stuff, Barrow. I heard tell that you can be throwing a corn sack over a woman's head and you won't know the difference in her looks noways!" At the moment, Coker was willing to try throwing a sack over Mavis's head if it meant finding some much needed release for his aching balls!

"I think you might need yourself a real big sack for that

woman!" Barrow laughed outright, and Coker's own gruff laughter joined in agreement.

"It just don't seem natural that a place like this wouldn't have more women about. I'd even settle fer an Injun squaw every now and then," Coker relented, knowing that Ben Harper would more than likely shoot his balls off if he caught him sniffing around his wife.

"I know what you're saying, old son. I ain't pushed my pecker into a honey pot since rendezvous." For a few lingering seconds, Henry Barrow reminisced over the pleasure he had found in the back of Slim Farley's whore wagon. "That Miss Calico Kat sure was something, wasn't she, Coker?" He remembered the feel of her soft, voluptuous body beneath his own, and could feel the bulge in his pants beginning to stir to life.

Tate Coker's mind filled with the image of another woman, a woman with the color of flickering flame in her hair and a body that would make any many man's fingers itch to strip the clothes from her body. "I swear, Barrow, when we catch up with your daughter, she ain't going to be able to sit or stand for a week!" Again, Coker's hand rubbed at his crotch. "I'm as horny as a stallion having taking scent of a filly."

Henry Barrow didn't doubt a word Coker spat out. He had learned in the months since he and Coker had joined up that the large trapper was as randy as a stallion. He thoroughly believed Coker would treat Amber just as he said. "Well, you'll sure be primed to have a go at her by the end of winter. It's too damn bad that we can't just go on up into them mountains and steal the gal away from the savages like we planned."

"Better sitting here at the post for a month or two than having our scalps lifted," Coker reminded. "It was only luck that we ran into old Black Crow and were told about them Sioux holding themselves some big gathering of their tribes and bands. We could have walked right into a touchy situation. Them Sioux can be pretty mean, and get them all together, and you're asking for trouble by going anywhere near the lot of them.''

"You're right there, Coker. You ever heard of a sun dance ceremony? Old Black Crow said that they mutilate their own bodies in order to please their gods. I can just bet that my gal will be right pleased to see me and you coming to her rescue, come spring.''

Twenty

Like falling clouds, the morning mists drifted past the open slopes that stood sentinel over the Sioux Valley. This morning, like several during the past weeks, another band of Sioux noisily made their presence known throughout the encampment. Not only were the bands and tribes part of the Oglalas, but also the Hunkpapas, Brules, Yanktons, Minnecoujous, and all the rest of the Lakota tribes. The entire Sioux nation was holding a tribal gathering, where they would send forth a tribal beseechment in expressions of thanksgiving to their god; this ceremony was known to the Sioux as the sun dance.

Amber had been in the village for three weeks. Gradually she was becoming accustomed to the people and lifestyle of the Sioux. Her fear that Cut Finger would turn the villagers against her had been proven untrue the morning after their arrival in the village. Strong Elk's wife, Running Moon, in the company of her small son and mother, Yellow Fawn, had arrived at Spirit Walker's lodge with a bowl of early-winter berries and an invitation for Amber to join

them for their morning swim at the river. Amber shyly
went along with them, and by midmorning, she and Running Moon had become fast friends. Each day after, she
joined the two women and little boy at the river where
they would gather firewood and water for that day's use.
They also swam and bathed as they visited with the other
women of the village.

Cut Finger had said little else, at least in Amber's presence, about her living among his people. But whenever
Amber glimpsed his bent, ancient frame as he made his
way through the village, she couldn't ignore the heated
look of hatred that he cast in her direction. She believed
that the old man was only biding his time for attention to
be drawn her way before he would declare her to have
witch medicine once again and attempt to influence his
people against her.

This morning, after joining the women at the river not
far from Spirit Walker's lodge, Amber was reminded by
Running Moon that this was the day the Indian women
had promised to take her to meet Sky Weaver. Amber had
been kept so busy, she had forgotten about the old man
in the village who kept a record of the tribes' affairs by
sketching them out on bleached hide.

Walking back to the lodge with Little Bird held upon
her hip and Running Moon and Yellow Fawn at her side,
Amber was greeted warmly by Spirit Walker who stood
outside the lodge with several young men of the village.
The greeting was not spoken aloud, but the tender warmth
from Spirit Walker's glance as he viewed her carrying the
little dark-haired child in her arms was not only felt by
Amber but witnessed by the other two women.

Taking Little Bird from her white friend, Running Moon
spoke low so that the men would not hear her words. ''You
are very lucky, Ptanyétu Ánpo, Spirit Walker carries much
love in his heart for you.''

Giving the child over to his mother, Amber looked toward Spirit Walker and the men who were now deep in conversation. Spirit Walker stood out in Amber's eyes, but now as his attention was no longer directed upon her, she wondered at Running Moon's words.

"I see in his eyes as his glance is directed upon you, as does every other woman of the village, that Spirit Walker's love runs deeply."

"You mean that other women can see this?" Amber was surprised by Running Moon's words. She had glimpsed the tenderness in his gaze often, but she was surprised that others noticed as well.

Running Moon's laughter drew the men's attention back to the women standing outside the lodge. "Everyone in the village is happy for you and Spirit Walker. Only those maidens, envious that it is not they who share Spirit Walker's sleeping pallet, or those who wish to steal something from Spirit Walker's power, are not happy to see a warrior so content in his lodge."

Amber had not even considered envious maidens. Running Moon's words reminded her of Cut Finger's scornful attack that first night in the village. Looking at the young woman who had befriended her, Amber smiled weakly, glad to have a friend who spoke her mind so easily but uncomfortable to be talking about her relationship with Spirit Walker. Thus far, the two of them had not shared such confidences, but Amber knew that the closer they grew, the more open Running Moon would become. It was the nature of her character to be curious and straightforward. She would not feel strange about talking about such matters as closeness developed. "You won't forget that you promised to take me to Sky Weaver's lodge this afternoon?" She tried to turn the subject away from herself and Spirit Walker.

Running Moon's smile held about her lips. The young

Indian woman had always freely spoken her mind. She
had discovered in her new white friend a reserve that
seemed to hold her back from fully enjoying life. Autumn
Dawn did not fully appreciate the relationship she had
with Spirit Walker. As her friend, Running Moon hoped
she would be able to influence Autumn Dawn to open
herself up. To Running Moon, there was no more pleasure
to be found than that of being wife to Strong Elk, and she
wished her friend to realize the joys of the heart and to
take life a little less seriously. "As soon as Little Bird goes
to sleep I will return, and we will go to Sky Weaver's lodge,"
she promised her.

Amber was cutting up wild onions in a pot of buffalo
meat and water when Spirit Walker entered the lodge. He
watched her from near the entrance, remembering how
he had glimpsed her earlier with Running Moon and her
mother. Approaching the lodge, she had been laughing
and talking with the other women, Strong Elk's son riding
upon her hip, his chubby features carefree as Autumn
Dawn or one of the other women paid him attention. He
felt a tender ache build in the depths of his chest. He
prayed for the day when he would view his son in this
woman's arms, when their child's laughter would call out
to them throughout the long days and nights.

Looking up from the pot, Amber was unsure of Spirit
Walker's thoughts. "Is something wrong?" she softly questioned, wondering if the men he had been speaking with
had brought bad news.

"There is nothing wrong, my heart." His steps led him
to the backrest where he silently sat and watched her as
she continued to prepare their evening meal. Over the
weeks, she had appeared content enough in his lodge. She
had made friends with some of the women of the village.
Almost everyone accepted Amber as his woman. He knew
only the greatest pleasure when he was in her company.

She filled every inch of his heart. He still refused to push Amber into making a declaration of her feelings, knowing that the pleasure of hearing the words leave her lips of their own volition would be that much sweeter to his ears. He ached to know her inner heart, that portion of herself that she kept hidden from him. Once he had heard her call out that she loved him while they were both deeply lost to their passions, but later when she had not repeated the words, he had been unsure. Perhaps he had wished to hear her confession of love so badly, he had imagined the words coming from her lips.

"Running Moon is taking me to Sky Weaver's lodge this afternoon." Amber interrupted his thoughts to explain why she was preparing their meal so early in the afternoon.

"You will like Sky Weaver, Ptanyétu Ánpo. Do not feel hurt, though, if he does not seem overly friendly. At times, he remains aloof, not willing to share his thoughts with others. But everyone in the village has much respect for him. You and Running Moon will be lucky if you find him alone today. With another tribe arriving in the village this morning, Sky Weaver's time may be taken up with those needing his advice about the sun dance ceremony."

Spirit Walker was probably right, Amber thought. The Sioux village was teeming with new faces daily. A man in Sky Weaver's position was more than likely very busy. "I only wish to see some of his work and perhaps view how he puts the history of your people down on hides."

"Go and meet Sky Weaver this day, Ptanyétu Ánpo, but keep in mind he might not show you these things you wish to see until after the sun dance." Spirit Walker did not tell her that Sky Weaver had already asked about the woman with flame in her hair who was living in his lodge. The old man was just as curious about her as she was him. But his curiosity did not mean that he would be willing to show a stranger, and a wasicun winyan at that, the secret power of his work.

Amber was not sure about this ceremony the Sioux nation called the sun dance. She should question Spirit Walker more closely about the great event that was to take place in a week here in the valley. There would be sacrifice, feasting, and rejoicing, but she was not sure why. It had something to do with their religion. She knew it was a happy time for Spirit Walker's people, and the village had taken on a carnivallike atmosphere to match the event.

There was little time to talk to Spirit Walker about the sun dance ceremony now. Shortly after she set the trade kettle containing the buffalo meat stew next to the heated coals of the pit-fire, Running Moon called to Amber from outside the lodge.

Amber wore her best doe-hide dress and the bear claw necklace with gold nuggets Spirit Walker had given her. Making her way through the village with Running Moon, she hoped her appearance was suitable. Though the villagers were now used to seeing a white woman with copper hair walking through the village, she still received many curious looks, especially from the newcomers who had arrived in the village. She hoped that Sky Weaver would not be reluctant to talk with her because of her white skin.

"Few in our tribe knows exactly how old Sky Weaver is," Running Moon told Amber. "My mother said that when she was a child she remembered that his skin was dry as stretched leather and, his hair the color of the snow on the mountaintops."

Amber had not imagined that the man would be so old. Spirit Walker spoke with much respect when he talked about Sky Weaver, and had led her to believe that many in the tribe sought him out for his wisdom. If he were as ancient as Running Moon was stating, how was it possible that he could keep track of the tribe's records?

"You will see for yourself," she explained. "When I was younger, the other children of the village and I would often go to his lodge and wait for him to have a few minutes to spare for us. He would tell us many stories of days long past."

Arriving at Sky Weaver's lodge, the two women instantly noticed they were not the first visitors this afternoon. There were several men standing around in a tight circle in front of the lodge. Amber and Running Moon glimpsed the figure of a man sitting on the ground, the braves standing around him and paying close attention to everything he was saying.

For a few minutes, the two women patiently stood off to the side of the lodge. Perhaps this was the wrong day to approach Sky Weaver, Amber thought nervously. As the braves and old man conversed, Amber gently tugged on Running Moon's fringed buckskin sleeve.

"Maybe we should come back another time." She spoke in low tones, not wishing to disturb the men.

Running Moon lightly patted her hand, the smile directed upon her friend one of patient understanding. "Often one must wait their turn to speak with Sky Weaver. There is no better day."

Sensing that the old man must have heard their conversation but knowing that he could not possibly have understood the words beyond their low tones, Amber watched as the old man parted the crowd around him with a movement of the ceremonial staff of otter fur and beadwork, which he clutched in his hand. As the braves moved aside, he directed his full gaze upon the two women.

The braves turned and looked in the direction the old man was staring, and for a tense few minutes, quiet settled around the lodge as Sky Weaver's glance held full upon Amber.

"Come." With another movement of the staff, he indicated that the women were to draw nearer.

Amber swallowed hard. Now that the moment of meeting the old man was at hand, she wondered what on earth she was doing here. What did it matter if he recorded the history of the tribe with sketches? What concern was any of this to her?

Running Moon grasped her elbow and pulled her along until the two women stood before the old man. "This is Ptanyétu Ánpo, Sky Weaver. She has come to speak with you."

The dark eyes staring from features that were wrinkled and appeared as dry as old parchment looked Amber up and down for a full minute. Slowly, his lips drew back in a wide smile, revealing several missing front teeth. "It is good that you have come. I have been waiting for you to appear."

A smile trembled over Amber's lips. Though she was unsure of exactly the hidden meaning of his words, his warm welcome put her at ease. Her glance took in the frail frame sitting on the ground, and she wondered if perhaps age had made him somewhat feeble in mind as well as body. She noticed the slight trembling of his hand as he clutched the staff and, using it once again, indicated to the braves that he was finished with them for the afternoon.

As the braves began to disperse, Amber had a few seconds to fully appraise the old man as he slowly pulled himself from the earth. He was slight of frame, age having ravaged his body of weight and height. His snowy hair was fashioned into two braids plaited over each shoulder; the rest hung down his back. Around his head he wore a turban headdress of otter which was surmounted by four golden eagle feathers, symbolic of some outstanding deeds he had performed for his tribe in his youth. His shirt was made from tanned elk hide with porcupine quill decoration down the front and along the upper portion of each sleeve. It was also adorned with a V-shaped neck flap with hide fringe around the flap, on the bottom of the sleeves, and down each side. His breechcloth and leggings were made from tanned elk hide and had been painstakingly fringed down each side. Around his neck he wore a magnificent necklace of grizzly bear claws attached to a collar of otter skin.

Appearing to wait until Amber was satisfied with filling her gaze, Sky Weaver finally spoke. "Let us go inside near my fire, the air is chilly out here." Without waiting for the two women to respond, he turned and slowly made his way within his lodge, expecting they would follow.

Running Moon seemed not to think it unusual for the two women to go along with Sky Weaver, and Amber followed her lead. Within the lodge, Amber looked around in total amazement. There was not an inch of the hide lodge that had not been painted with some view of nature. On one entire wall there was a scene of a waterfall, the cascading water appearing real as it shimmered over rocks and puddled near the floor. There was another scene of two deer feeding near the side of a swiftly running stream and another of a forest thick with foliage and small animals such as birds and squirrels.

Following Running Moon to the central fire, Amber noticed a piece of hide stretched and pegged to the floor of the lodge in one corner of the space. Next to the hide, she saw several small, hollowed stone mixing bowls, a turtle-shell mixing bowl, and numerous small buckskin bags used for paints. There was a variety of small bone brushes, as well as large bone brushes laid out on a piece of bleached doe hide.

Taking added minutes to settle himself down upon his beaded backrest, Sky Weaver smiled in apology. "I am an old man," he sighed. "In my youth, I could hunt and run like the other young braves. Those in my youth are gone now; I am the only one left. This aching body refuses to join those in the sky, even though my heart is willing."

Amber was tempted to ask him just how old he was, but did not dare. Like Running Moon, she just smiled at his remarks.

"The Great Spirit has allowed me to linger for a reason, I am sure." Looking directly across his fire at Amber, he questioned, "I am told that you also enjoy making pictures on hide?"

Amber had not expected that he would have been appraised of her identity and her ability to sketch. Silently, she nodded her head.

"When I was a young man, I was taught by a wise teacher how to make the pictures that would tell the story of my people." Sky Weaver enjoyed talking of the past, and did not seem to mind that his company remained quiet as they listened to him. "Two Feathers was my teacher's name; he was an old man when he taught me all he knew. Not as old as I am. None of the people have ever been as old as I am, but he was patient and kind. He taught me where to find the reddish-yellow rock that when crushed, makes the color of vermilion, and where to find the warm-colored earth to make the color yellow. Also, bull berries, the moss on pine trees, and buffalo gallstones are good for this color. Two Feathers taught me many things, as a good teacher should."

"And have you taught another all these things?" Amber softly questioned. Running Moon looked in her direction and appeared as surprised as Amber that she questioned the old man.

With dark eyes holding on the white woman, Sky Weaver

slowly shook his head. "I have not found the one to share my knowledge. The history of the people, our winter counts, is a sacred thing. The one chosen must be chosen with much care."

"Has there ever been a woman who kept the winter counts for the people?" Amber asked out of curiosity.

Running Moon's mouth fell open at her friend's question. She had never heard of any woman in the history of the people keeping the winter counts. This had been a male tradition handed down to the worthy throughout the years.

"I keep the records of the people. There has never been a woman that has done the same." Sky Weaver's eyes held unflinchingly upon Amber, as though wishing to witness her reaction.

This seemed unfair to Amber, but she held her tongue, not wishing to go against tradition; she was the outsider here.

"When I was younger, I enjoyed going to the lakes where the wild ducks were plentiful, to gather duck manure to make the color of blue. Now I am old, and it is a chore for me to venture so far from camp." Sky Weaver continued as though Amber had never interrupted his earlier conversation.

"I would be happy to help you gather your supplies for your paints." Amber spoke up again without giving thought to her offer. "I mean . . . that is . . . if you need someone to help you?" she added a little belatedly as she felt Running Moon's hard stare once again.

Sky Weaver did not answer, but his dark gaze seemed to brighten. "I have begun to record the arrival of the tribes and bands for the sun dance ceremony. This is a special time for our people. It has been many years since the sun dance was held in our valley."

"Ignoring Running Moon's confused looks in her direction, Amber questioned, "Is that what that hide is for?"

Sky Weaver nodded his head in affirmation. He looked across the lodge to the piece of buffalo hide, which had been scraped and treated with brains until it was smooth, soft, and bone-white. Now it was pegged to the floor of the lodge, hair side down. "Tomorrow, I will apply the glue that will allow the color of the hide to show through, and will also hold the colors of the paints. This hide will tell the story of the entire Sioux nation encamped along our river valley. One day it will share with the people the days of the sun dance ceremony."

Amber could only envision the pageantry of the tepees and herds of horses that now partially covered the valley floor. It would be wonderful to paint such a scene for everyone to view. "You use glue to hold the color of the paints?" she questioned the old man with curiosity. She would never have imagined that these primitive people would be so advanced in the knowledge of treating paintings with a substance to keep its color.

Sky Weaver nodded his gray head eagerly, seeing in Amber a young woman thoroughly interested in his craft. "The glue is from the tail of the beaver, or from skin scrapings boiled in water," he explained. "The glue will aid in holding the hide's color at first. After the painting of the acts of the people have been placed upon the hide, the glue will again be applied to preserve the color and give it a look of gloss. The pictures will also have the effect of being outlined in white."

Amber had never heard of such a thing. "I would love to watch you work, Sky Weaver," she spoke out enthusiastically.

Running Moon was more than a little shocked at Autumn Dawn's manners. A woman did not invite herself to watch a warrior work, especially a man who held Sky

Weaver's position in the tribe. All she could do was stare openly at Amber and wait for the old man to take offense and request they leave his lodge.

"I will begin work tomorrow morning. It will please me if you are here to watch me," Sky Weaver warmly invited to Running Moon's total amazement and Amber's pleasure.

Twenty-one

Wiwanyank Wacípi, the ritual of the sun dance, had begun. The first four days of the ceremony were given over to the pleasures shared by all the people from the tribes and bands of the Sioux congregated here. Feasting, visiting, games, and courting between young men and women.

The next four days were to be held by the villagers as sacred. On the second day, a maiden of pure virtue, accompanied by assistants who claimed the title of chaste, went in search of the cottonwood tree that was cut and shorn of most branches and deemed sacred. The tree was carried to the sun dance camp. On the third day, the sun dance pole, a fork of limbs in its top boughs, was erected. Placed in the fork was a bundle of chokecherry brush, sweetgrass, bison hair, sage, an effigy resembling a human made from buffalo hide, an effigy in the shape of a buffalo, and long, slender sticks with small tobacco bags attached. These sacred objects represented the nest of the sacred thunder birds. Around this center pole, the sun dance lodge was built in the fashion of a framework wall of posts and covered with green tree branches. To the mighty Sioux, the lodge's shape represented the placement of the universe.

The afternoon before the dancing was to take place, Spirit Walker held a sweat lodge ceremony for some of the participants. Medicine Cloud had been selected to be the sun dance leader of this ceremony, but several of the young men who would undergo the piercing and dancing the following day had sought out Spirit Walker for his wisdom and power.

Amber sat upon the soft furs that made up the sleeping pallet in Spirit Walker's lodge and painted the scene upon the hide that she and Sky Weaver had discussed that afternoon. She listened to the words that Spirit Walker spoke to the young braves as he passed his pipe among them.

"Who is there among us who can offer the One Above his horse, his pipe, the deer that he killed with a straight arrow? Do not all these things already belong to Wakán Tanka? Is He not the maker of all things that have been created? Everything that we look upon, everything of the forest and the mountains already belong to Him. What have we to offer but our flesh as a sacrifice? Is this not the test of really giving of oneself? How is it that we can give Him anything less than that which would show the pain of the cost?" Spirit Walker drew deeply on his sacred pipe as it was handed back to him. He heard the agreement of the braves as they listened and considered all he had shared with them.

"All that a warrior truly owns is this body, and what we give of our flesh is the only thing we have to give. The sun dance is not only to prove one's endurance but also to vow in one's heart that his family and tribe are to come first in all things. When I participated in my first sun dance, Medicine Cloud told me these same words, and the morning before the piercing, I gave away all that I owned, even my pony. My mother was not happy, she told me that it was not necessary for me to give all to my people; I should keep some things for myself. My heart led me to do as I did, and I believe because of my sacrifice, I was given a vision of much power." Spirit Walker took a deep breath, pausing as his dark gaze rose from the pit-fire and went to the woman with the fire-curls who sat upon his sleeping couch. If he had not given all that he owned, including his flesh, to the One Above, would he have been given such a vision gift as Autumn Dawn?

"I tell you, no sacrifice is too small to give of oneself. After tomorrow, the people will look to you for protection and security. Each one among your people have the right to expect you to share with the aged and ailing, the orphans and widows. We can only survive as a people by doing as I say. The Great Spirit will look upon you with favor if you sacrifice all for Him, and His people."

"Will you not be participating in the piercing and dancing, Spirit Walker?" Panther Stalking questioned when there was a lull in the conversation. The other young men listened intently for the answer.

Spirit Walker had considered participating in this ceremony as he had four others in the past, but after praying and seeking the wisdom of Medicine Cloud's council, he had decided against it. He and Autumn Dawn had spoken only briefly about the sun dance ceremony and its importance to his people. He feared that her initial response tomorrow, upon viewing the ceremony, would be horror and fear over the supposed savagery of the ceremony. He had decided to wait until next year to participate, and then he would give his flesh over, rejoicing to the One Above for the joy he had received in being led to his vision gift. "I will be there with each one of you tomorrow. I will not participate until the next sun dance ceremony."

No one questioned his reasons, knowing that whatever they were, Spirit Walker had made them through much prayer. The piece of hide in Amber's lap went unnoticed as she listened to the men and wondered if his reasons for not participating had anything to do with her. Later in the evening, as the couple lay side by side in their bed of furs, Amber questioned Spirit Walker about the sun dance ceremony.

"I am surprised that you will not take part, Spirit Walker. Running Moon says that Strong Elk will be joining the activities, and she plans to give a flesh offering." Her hand rested against his chest, fingers absently feeling the ridges over his breasts from the sun dance piercing he had endured in the past.

"Did Running Moon explain to you what her flesh offering was for?" Spirit Walker and Amber had just lain down. His arm rested beneath her shoulder, her slender form drawn up tightly against his body. He was curious to hear her opinion of his people's beliefs.

"She only told me that her son Little Bird had been very sick last spring and she had made a vow to the Great Spirit that she would give a flesh offering if her son would live." Amber's blue eyes were wide as she turned her head to look Spirit Walker full in the face to gauge his reaction.

"This is the way of the people," he responded. "The One Above is the maker and healer of all things; it was right that she should make a vow of sacrifice."

"Do you truly believe this?" There was some surprise in Amber's tone. She and Spirit Walker had not discussed his beliefs fully; and hearing him agree with Running Moon's plans to do this thing called a flesh offering reaffirmed that her world and Spirit Walker's were very different.

"Would you not give a piece of your flesh to save a child's life?" Spirit Walker's jet eyes searched her face as she thought over his question.

"Why, of course I would," she responded with only a second's hesitation. "That is not the point, though, Spirit Walker."

"What is the point, Ptanyétu Ánpo?" He turned to his side to fully face her.

"Why should your God demand such a thing as a piece of flesh for letting a child live?"

"If that is all that the giver owns, why should He not ask it? Does the white man's God never ask something in return for His gifts?"

"Why, yes, I guess so, but I have never heard of Him asking for a piece of flesh."

"Then perhaps the white man does not listen with his heart to what his God desires. Perhaps the white man gives that which is easy for him to give."

"Many white men have given their very lives for God! Missionaries have been murdered taking the word of God to unbelievers!" Amber did not consider that she was talking to one of the true unbelievers.

Spirit Walker had seen firsthand these missionaries, known among his people as the black robes, who had come among the Indian with hatred in their hearts and condemnation in their voices. "Is it the will of their God, which leads these black robes out to bring the foolish to their God; or is it the white man's belief that their way is the only way, that only their God with the bleeding Christ has power? If the black robes die for going among those that do not wish him, is this a sacrifice to his God? Or was he foolish to believe himself wanted in a place that he does not belong?"

"I'm not sure," Amber softly confessed. "I have never considered this before." She had always believed that the missionaries were sent by God, but now she was not sure if that was the case or if they were intruding where they should not trespass. She had learned in the little time she

had been in this village that these people held a religion
in their hearts. Granted it was different from the white
man's, but they believed the Great Spirit ruled their lives,
and they adhered to certain rules because of this belief.

"Will you go and watch the ceremony tomorrow?" Spirit
Walker softly questioned, leaving behind the topic of missionaries and God.

"I am not sure." Amber was curious, but didn't know
if she could sit by and watch people purposely mutilate
their bodies. She had heard some of what would take place;
the scars on Spirit Walker's chest were evidence that the
ceremony was brutal. "I am glad that you are not going
to participate, Spirit Walker." She pressed closer to his
body. "I couldn't stand by and watch you suffer need-
lessly." Tenderly, she placed a kiss over his heart.

Spirit Walker's arms tightened around her, the kiss upon
his flesh evoking a tender response within him. He had
feared that she would feel this way about the sun dance.
He hoped that with time she would come to understand
the hardships and joys that were an everyday part of life
for the Sioux. Enough words had been shared this night.
He settled her tighter in his embrace, his mouth slanting
over hers in a breathless kiss that chased away all thoughts
of what tomorrow would bring.

Amber awoke before dawn following a restless night.
Quietly she climbed from the sleeping pallet and slipped
on her hide dress, then made her way out of the lodge.
She sat against a large oak tree not far from Spirit Walker's
lodge. The chilly morning air at the river's edge caused
her to silently rub her forearms, but it did not have the
power to chase her back inside the lodge to seek the
warmth of the pit-fire.

Last night's talk with Spirit Walker about the ceremony

that was to take place today had kept her turning restlessly upon their bed throughout the night. Every time she had tried to find sleep, Amber had envisioned the torturous pain that would be inflicted upon the Sioux people. It was a barbaric custom that these people participated in, and thoughts of it had reinforced the truth to Amber: she did not belong among Spirit Walker's people. She was a civilized woman. Talk of piercing one's flesh and making flesh offerings brought horror to her mind.

As she sat all alone, she heard the laughter of young boys farther down the river. They had probably stolen out of their parents' lodges to have an early-morning swim. It would not be much longer before the entire camp would be stirring.

She had made a mistake in ever believing that she could fit in among Spirit Walker's people. She had made friends, this was true, and over this past week she had gone daily to Sky Weaver's lodge and helped the old man with his work. On the other hand, she could not forget the attack made on her by Cut Finger, nor could she deny the fear she still held that one day he would confront her with the insane accusation that she held witch medicine. This fear, combined with the savagery of the people's belief in mutilating their bodies to please their god made Amber's decision easy: She must leave the valley as soon as possible. She would speak with Spirit Walker this very morning, and demand he take her to Harper's trading post.

She was pulled from her thoughts on how best to try and convince Spirit Walker to escort her back to civilization by excited shouts of the children. Amber pulled herself from the ground and stepped away from the tree. Something in the their voices implied that all was not right.

Before she took a step toward the shouts, a boy about ten years old came running toward her along the riverbank.

"Hurry!" he commanded her. "Help Small Bull. We cannot find him!"

"What has happened?" Amber asked in great concern.

"We were swimming, and Small Bull disappeared. The other boys are diving, trying to find him, but he is lost!"

Amber did not hesitate long with more questions, but raced in the direction of the shouts.

Amber found half a dozen boys were congregated attempting a frantic search of the river for their friend. Two stood along the bank shouting at the others who were diving in and out of the water in their hunt for Small Bull.

"Where did you last see him?" Amber called to the two boys on the bank.

"Over there." They pointed a distance out in the river. "He was racing with Black Otter and Jumping Wolf. When the other boys reached the opposite shore, Small Bull was not with them."

Amber did not tarry on the bank. A child's life was at stake, and if there was any chance to save him, she had to act fast. Unmindful of her dress and moccasins, she dove headlong into the chilled water, and with strong strokes swam toward the center of the river.

Her first dive proved discouraging. The water was too dark to see beneath; she could only search by feeling with her hands. Again and again she resurfaced, taking deep breaths of air, then kicking her way back down to the bottom of the river.

She had almost given up, in the back of her mind already believing that too much time had passed for the boy to be alive. Her lungs ached and she was quickly exhausting her energies. Amber dove one last time, her legs kicking out, taking her as far as possible. Suddenly, the tips of her fingers on one hand brushed against something that felt like grass; her mind told her to keep going, that it was nothing, that time was running out. But with a determined push, she grabbed hold of the grass, and to her utter amazement felt some weight being pulled from the bottom of the river.

Amber's heart dashed wildly against her rib cage as she pulled the small, still body to the surface by the hair. As she broke the surface, Amber quickly turned the child in her arms, one hand clutched around him as she began to swim toward shore.

"She has him! Ptanyétu Ánpo found Small Bull!" The cries of the children filled the area as those in the water began to swim back to shore and the two boys on the bank were joined by several adults.

With an inner strength borne of a desperate fear that she would not be able to save the life of the child in her arms, Amber dragged herself and the young boy to the river's edge. Making certain he was out of the water, she leaned over the small, lifeless body. "No!" Amber cried aloud. Turning Small Bull over to his side, a small amount of water spewed out of his lungs.

Hope stirred in her heart. Amber bent her head to his frail chest and listened, but no sound of a heartbeat was forthcoming. "Breathe!" she commanded, as though by sheer will she could make the child come back to life.

His chest did not move, and, looking down at him, Amber felt tears rolling down her cheeks. "Please God, make him live. I'll do anything, only make him breathe." Without second thought, she pushed against his chest. More water erupted from his body. She drew his arms up and over his head, then once again she pushed on his chest.

Nothing! No sign of life, no heartbeat, no movement. Something Bertha Poole had said to Amber years ago about having to breathe into an infant's mouth after a difficult birthing suddenly came to Amber's mind. Without hesitation, she bent over the child and covered his mouth with hers, then breathed into his throat.

Again nothing happened! Perhaps she should cover his nose, she thought, and bending down again, she pinched his nose together and blew hard into his mouth.

Again nothing! "Please God, please! I will give a flesh offering if you will just let him live!" She had no idea why she would make such a promise, but at the moment, the only thing that mattered was that this little body breathe once again!

Again and again she blew her breath into his body. Relaxing between each breath, she placed her head against his chest to listen for any sign of life.

There it was! A small, telltale movement of gurgling within his chest! She pinched his nose and breathed again. This time she heard a louder rumbling. More water expelled from his lips, then a shudder coursed over the boy's entire length.

Amber listened. Bless the Lord, for . . . a slight pulsing heartbeat! She pulled her head away from his chest and watched for movement.

One arm moved . . . then the other. The child turned somewhat, then his legs began to move.

Along the river's edge a cheer went up that Small Bull lived. Small Bull's friends, as well as several adults, had been watching in fascination as the wasicun winyan with the fire-curls breathed life back into the dead body of Small Bull.

Amber sagged against the earth as Small Bull pulled himself weakly up into a sitting position, his dark gaze puzzled, as though he held no idea what had happened.

Someone had run for Small Bull's father, and he and Spirit Walker arrived just at that moment. Lame Deer quickly gathered his son in his arms, his dark gaze flitting to the woman lying next to him on the ground.

"Ptanyétu Ánpo breathed her life into Small Bull. He had passed on, but she brought him back from the sky people!" one of the men standing along the riverbank called down to Lame Deer. The children and adults spoke in wonder of the event they had just witnessed.

Spirit Walker bent down to Amber, and helped her to regain her footing. His gaze was full of question as he wrapped an arm around her and looked back at Lame Deer and his son.

"He should rest for a while to make sure he is really all right," Amber spoke out.

Lame Deer looked from Spirit Walker to the white woman standing at his side. Silently, he nodded his head in agreement to her words. His strong arms tightened around his son, as though he still could not believe what had taken place here at the river. His son had drowned according to the young boy who had awakened him in his lodge. Now he learned that Small Bull was alive, that Ptanyétu Ánpo had not only found him at the bottom of the river, but she had done the impossible: she had brought him back from that place where death laid claim. This was the very woman who his father, Cut Finger, claimed to be possessed with witch medicine!

Twenty-two

The bone whistles held between the teeth of the dancers screeched in unison, the steady drumbeat pulsing loudly in the morning air. The dancers were led by Medicine Cloud, the chosen sun dance leader, through the village to the sun dance lodge. It was time for the ceremony to begin. Around the ankles and wrists of each dancer a wreath of sage was tied. A more elaborate wreath with two eagle feathers placed upon the crown of the head was worn by each participant. A long breech cloth which resembled a kilt, was secured around the waists of the warriors by a belt of leather.

Before the piercing of flesh, the medicine man painted a symbol of each participant's vow to Wankán Tanka on their back. The cutting of their flesh on chest and back was done quickly and cleanly, for Medicine Cloud had done this same piercing numerous times in the past.

The first dancers were pierced through their backs, the eagle claws drawn through the tendons and leather ropes secured through the skewers then tied to buffalo skulls which would be pulled along the ground until their flesh was torn and the dancers released.

Two of the dancers were placed between four poles. They were pierced through the chest twice and twice through the back underneath each shoulder blade. These ties were secured through eagle claws and to the poles. The warriors had to struggle until they earned their release.

Thunder Hawk and Running Moon's husband Strong Elk were the only warriors who were pierced through the chest and then suspended upon the sun dance pole. This sun dance ritual was the most severe of all. Until their weight tore muscular tendons and thus released them, the warriors would hang in midair.

After the piercing, the warriors sang songs of rejoicing and thanksgiving to the Great Spirit. As Medicine Cloud secured each warrior to the sun dance pole, he drew them back against their tethers causing their flesh to be pulled grotesquely out of shape.

The dancers raised their arms in prayer, the eagle-bone whistles caught between their teeth screeching loudly. All glances held upon the sun, eyes moving as they danced, their souls filling with the inner brightness of Wi. The onlookers were held spellbound in silence; no children laughed or cried, no dogs could be heard barking or fighting over a bone. No sound traveled throughout the encampment except that of the steady drumbeat, the eagle-bone whistles calling for mercy and strength from Wankán Tanka.

Spirit Walker had left his lodge earlier, after ensuring that Amber had not been harmed during her rescue of Small Bull. He had gone to offer encouragement and advice to the young men who had sought his wisdom during the earlier days of the ceremony.

After changing from her wet clothes, Amber sat alone in the lodge. She was not sure what to do. She had no desire to go to the sun dance lodge to watch these men and women torturing their bodies. But she could not forget that only a short time ago, she had promised to give a flesh offering if God would allow Small Bull to live. Spirit Walker's question the night before stalked her mind as she busied herself within the lodge. *Would you not give a piece of your flesh to save the life of a child?* Why could she not just forget his words and forget her vow?

Trying to work on the piece of hide she was painting, she heard the drumbeat resounding throughout the village and knew that the ceremony had begun. Her hands trembled as she heard the shrill whistles being blown, the hollow beat filling her head. Setting the hide and paints aside, Amber left the lodge, not sure of her intentions.

Soon she found herself standing with others outside the sun dance lodge. The piercing of the men had already finished; those with their skewers tied to the buffalo skulls were dancing around the pole. It was the time when the women presented themselves before the medicine man to give their flesh in offering to their vows.

Most of the women, like the men, had purified themselves in a sweat lodge; they wore bleached hide dresses with few embellishments. Amber saw Running Moon standing silently in the middle of the long line of women.

The women did not flinch as the skin on their arms was cut away by Medicine Cloud. They stood solemn, many holding their gazes upward to signify to the Great Spirit that their hour of payment was at hand and they were prepared.

Amber's gaze traveled around the interior of the lodge, gazing at the men who were straining against their bonds. Strong Elk as well as Thunder Hawk hung in midair upon the sun dance pole, and as Amber looked upon them, she felt her heart tremble as she viewed the torture these people forced on themselves, all in the name of religion.

From across the lodge she saw Spirit Walker wiping away sweat on a young brave's brow with a handful of sage. The brave's back had been pierced and he had been secured to four buffalo skulls. Along with his obvious pain, Amber glimpsed the pride and understanding on Spirit Walker's face.

As the long line of women slowly thinned, each turned away from the medicine man to find places to await the finish of the ceremony. Amber slowly began to approach the few women still standing in line. She had not believed she would be able to go through with her vow to God, but as she witnessed these people being so brave as they fulfilled their own vows, she wondered how she could not.

Few of the villagers appeared to take notice of her as the line left only three women, including herself, standing before Medicine Cloud. From his position across the lodge, Spirit Walker watched with amazement as Autumn Dawn stood with the women. He had been pleased she had decided to watch the ceremony; he knew she was frightened. But he had been shocked when he watched her enter the lodge to join the line of women. He did not go to her and question her, knowing that she alone had to travel the path of her closeness with the One Above. Whatever reason had drawn her, he knew in his heart that she would be forever changed from this day forth.

As the woman before Amber held out her arm and Medicine Cloud's sharp knife cut away three portions of her flesh, Amber swallowed nervously and squeezed her eyes tightly shut.

The old medicine man stood patiently as he viewed the wasicun winyan standing before him. "You would make an offering to Wakán Tanka?" His voice sounded graveled to Amber's ears.

She could not speak, her throat felt dry as parchment. All she could do was nod her head. She hesitantly held out her arm, her hand turning so her upper wrist was held upright. She watched silently as the bent fingers of his left hand revealed a long, sharp bone needle. With a swift movement, he pierced the flesh of her arm, then pulled the skin upward; it appeared as the flesh of the men upon the sun dance pole. As swiftly as he had pierced her with the needle, his glistening medicine knife flashed beneath the sunlight as he cut the piece of flesh beneath the needle. The circle of flesh he placed upon a piece of cloth at his feet as he had the skin of the other women; later the flesh and cloth would be buried during a sacred ceremony.

Amber stared at her arm and the small wound. She let her breath expel and a small smile come over her lips. It had not been as bad as she had feared. Her vow had been fulfilled and she was still alive!

Turning away from Medicine Cloud, she noticed Running Moon and Yellow Fawn smiling at her from where they sat on the ground beneath the sun dance lodge. Amber made her way to the women and silently joined them to view the rest of the ceremony. Now that she had participated it did not appear as savage as she had once believed. Now she understood more of these people's reasons for having the sun dance ceremony.

Throughout the rest of the afternoon, the warriors pulled themselves free of their bonds until shortly before dust the last participant was free and his family was helping him back to their lodge.

The last of the ceremonies were held around a large communal fire that evening shortly after dark. This was the time when those who wished to make public gifts to the poor or to reward someone for a special service presented themselves before all to announce their intentions. Spirit Walker and Amber went to the ceremony with Strong Elk's

family. Though the warrior was ailing because of his
wounds, he would never miss out on any part of the sun
dance ceremony.

Before the ceremony began, there was singing and dancing around the blazing fire, the men and women joining
in unity for this last day of the sun dance. At first, Amber
was hesitant to join in with the dancers, but Running Moon
was insistent, and as Spirit Walker and Strong Elk visited
with a group of braves, the two women joined those already
dancing in a shuffling motion around the fire.

Amber had never had a friend like Running Moon. In
fact, she had never had any friend beside Spirit Walker.
The young woman was carefree and relaxed this evening;
her husband was well after the ordeal of the sun dance
pole, and her mother was taking care of Little Bird while
Yellow Fawn sat and gossiped with the older women of the
village. Amber's laughter joined with Running Moon's as
the Indian woman attempted to teach her white friend the
steps to the dance she had learned at a very early age.

Out of breath but thoroughly enjoying themselves, the
two women stayed near the fire for the next dance, and
then the next. By the time they returned to the men, they
were laughing outright over Amber's attempts. Amber's
features were radiant as Spirit Walker reached out and
clutched her hand.

Spirit Walker's dark eyes sparkled brightly, as they had
when he had watched Autumn Dawn's every movement
while she and Running Moon danced. Looking down into
her smiling face, he marveled at his fortune. This woman
of his heart was accepting the ways of the people without
him influencing or attempting to push her.

"Come and dance, Spirit Walker. I think I have the steps
learned." Amber began to pull him away from the small
group where he was standing and lead him to the line of
dancers.

Spirit Walker was more than willing to accompany her to the dancing. To him, she was the most beautiful woman participating.

Before the two of them could take more than a few steps, Sky Weaver approached and stood directly in front of Amber. "I wish to call the elders and the wise men of the village together to witness my words this night," he called loudly. His bright gaze held upon the one who had been helping him with his work.

"What is wrong?" Amber questioned softly, looking from Sky Weaver to Spirit Walker, not understanding what was taking place. Why had the old man chosen this moment to approach her? Many of the dancers halted their steps as several of the older warriors began to make their way into the circle forming around her and Spirit Walker. An uneasiness began to settle over Amber as she glimpsed, from the corner of her eye, Cut Finger also approaching.

Spirit Walker did not respond to her question. This was the way of the people when they wished to bestow a gift or blessing upon one they believed worthy. With pride, he watched as Sky Weaver began to unbind a piece of aged hide.

With the most tender of care, the old keeper of the winter counts unlaced the leather binding that was strapped around the square of hide he held in his hand. Opening the hide, he held it where the light from the large communal fire revealed the painting.

Quiet hung over the group, as more and more of the villagers encircled them. As Cut Finger pushed his way closer to Amber, her legs began to tremble with trepidation. What she had feared over these past weeks was about to take place; Cut Finger was once again going to accuse her of having witch medicine. Gazing at Sky Weaver, she wondered if he had convinced the old man that his words were true and he had called everyone around to witness her humiliation.

"When I was a young man, Two Feathers taught me to keep the records of the people." Sky Weaver's voice carried over the people standing in expectation. "It was only two winters later that Two Feathers joined the sky people, and I was left to wonder who I would teach my craft. I prayed often about the one that must be chosen to take my place. There are many dangers that can come upon the people, and I did not know if I would join my friend Two Feathers while I was still a young man." He laughed good-naturedly. "You can all see that I did not have to worry." The villagers laughed along with him.

Amber was too nervous to enjoy the humor. She did not understand why he had confronted her and what Cut Finger had in mind.

"One day, when I had been fasting and praying for Wankán Tanka to guide me in my decision, I found that my hands were painting without my knowledge. Even now, I have this piece of hide that I painted that day so long ago. When I had finished painting this hide, I no longer questioned the One Above about who would follow my path. That one would be revealed at the proper time, I knew then."

The villagers were no longer laughing. This was an important moment for the entire tribe, and everyone waited expectantly for Sky Weaver's next words, which would reveal the one who would one day keep their winter counts.

Before saying anything else, Sky Weaver handed the aged piece of hide to one of the elders of the tribe. The old warrior looked carefully at the baded picture on the buffalo hide, his fingers feeling the material to ensure himself that the hide had been painted many years ago. After he looked his full, he passed the hide on to another standing close by.

Sky Weaver patiently waited, his gaze going back to Amber more than once, as though she played some part in what was taking place. Amber hoped that whomever he chose, that person would allow her to continue to help with the work. She derived much satisfaction from it, spending a portion of her days gathering plants and rocks, then mixing paints for Sky Weaver.

When the painting was at last handed back to the old man, he handed the piece of hide to Spirit Walker. For a few minutes, Spirit Walker looked down at it, then turned it for Amber to view the scene openly displayed.

Amber caught her breath. Her gaze swept over the delicate painting of a woman with pale skin and red hair working over hides, mixing bowls and painting materials laid out for her use. Her wide blue gaze rose up from the hide to Sky Weaver's face. "Why didn't you say something before now?"

"I was reluctant even after you came to my lodge to acknowledge that it was a woman the One Above had chosen so long ago to take over my work. There has never been a woman who has kept the winter counts."

Amber did not know what to say. The painting said it all. These people believed in visions and the hand of the Great Spirit leading them. According to Spirit Walker, it had been his vision that had told him she would one day come into his life. Now, Sky Weaver was telling his entire village that he had known long years past that she would come among his people, and that it would be her who would keep the records of the people's deeds.

"You still have much to learn, Ptanyétu Ánpo. Tomorrow we will start the record of the piercing of the sun dance ceremony."

The villagers were whispering about this turn of events.

None of the elders refuted the words of Sky Weaver. All believed that the Great Spirit had made the decision long ago, and they would never interfere with what should be.

Amber was stunned to be the recipient of such an honor. She needed more time for this to sink into her mind. It had taken place so suddenly, she could only stand and stare at Sky Weaver.

Suddenly, Cut Finger stepped closer into the group that was encircling Amber. His hand was held high to gain the attention of those who were listening to Sky Weaver's words.

Amber choked back the knot of fear that instantly filled her throat. For a few seconds, she thought that she should turn and flee, but looking around, she knew that any retreat would make her look foolish before Spirit Walker's people. They might believe his accusations if she did not stay and face his verbal abuse. With a will that was dredged up from somewhere deep in her soul, she stood her ground, forcing herself to look directly at the one who professed to be a medicine man.

To Amber's utter astonishment, Cut Finger held out a matching pair of beautiful golden eagle feathers, their tips lightly painted with vermilion.

"What is this?" She did not trust this man and held back, not reaching out to take the offering extended in her direction.

"I was wrong about you, Ptanyétu Ánpo." His words were softly spoken, and they were costing Cut Finger dearly, but he forced himself to continue. "You saved my grandson, Small Bull, this day. I am grateful that you were here in my village."

When Cut Finger had first been told that Spirit Walker's woman had saved his grandson by breathing her breath into his body, he had sat for hours in his son's lodge, watching the child for any sign that the witch woman had changed him in some way. As the morning progressed into late afternoon, and still Small Bull had acted in no way different from the day before, Cut Finger had faced the jealousy he held for the white woman. "It was a brave thing that you did, finding my grandson at the bottom of the river, then bringing him back from that life which is beyond. I give you these eagle feathers as a reward for your great deed, as is the custom of my people. I also ask that you forgive this old man and his foolish words. I know now that I was wrong about you, Ptanyétu Ánpo. You are not one that is possessed with wíhmunge." Cut Finger's voice had gradually grown louder. For one of the few times in his life, he was admitting he had been wrong, and he did not care that those standing around were listening to his apology.

Amber had been caught by surprise, and was unsure of an appropriate reaction, but as she looked at the old Indian man, pity touched her for his plight. It had taken the near death of his grandson for him to make a declaration in front of the villagers, and Amber knew she could do no less then accept his gift. Reaching out, she clasped the eagle feathers in her hand. "I will treasure your gift, Cut Finger." She smiled warmly to let him know that she was not one to hold a grudge.

Cut Finger's gray head nodded sharply one last time before he turned and strolled boldly through the crowd toward his son's lodge. He would make certain that Small Bull was resting comfortably before he retired to his own lodge for the night.

Clutching the golden eagle feathers, Amber glanced at Spirit Walker and found him smiling warmly at her. His smile told her everything; he had known that she would win over all of his people, including old Cut Finger!

Not having the chance to express his happiness for her

in words, Spirit Walker was satisfied with the thought of
being alone with Autumn Dawn, later in their lodge.

Running Moon did not hesitate to share her joy with
her friend. Hugging Amber tightly, she was thrilled to be
the first of the well-wishers. "You are honored among
women in our village, Ptanyétu Ánpo. Not only will you
keep the winter counts, but you also softened Cut Finger's
hardness. I am very proud to be your friend."

Amber hugged her in return, accepting the Indian woman's words of congratulations, then those of the other
Sioux. For the first time, Amber truly felt as though she
had been accepted. For the first time in her life, she felt
as though she belonged.

Twenty-three

The winter months in the Sioux valley passed in a busy sameness of routine for Amber. Each morning she went to the river with Running Moon. Often, Yellow Fawn remained behind in her daughter's lodge with Little Bird, the weather too cold at this early hour for the very young and the old. Returning to Spirit Walker's lodge with her water skin filled, Amber would prepare a meal, and then, make her way to Sky Weaver's lodge.

Throughout most of the remainder of the day, she would work side by side with Sky Weaver, learning much of mixing colors and drawing upon hides as he told her the stories of his people. On more than one occasion, he halted in midsentence, making certain that she was listening to his words, as well as paying attention to the work at hand. "One day it will be for you to teach the young the old ways, daughter," he would say.

She was already learning that the people of this village depended greatly upon the one that kept the winter counts. Often, she found a visitor waiting for her in Spirit

Walker's tepee in the afternoons. The man or woman requested that she recall to them some portion of the sun dance ceremony that they had not been present for, or they would question her about some other event that had taken place in the village. Eagerly, Amber would help if she was able; if not, she directed them to Sky Weaver. She had wondered if the old man had sent some of these afternoon visitors to her, especially if the topic concerned an event that had taken place during the period since her arrival in the village.

Her days were busy with helping to keep the people's records and her nights were amply busy—but more enjoyable!—as she lay in Spirit Walker's embrace. Rarely did she try to analyze her emotions where this warrior was concerned. She was happy living here among his people, and she dared not look too closely at her inner feelings. For now, she was content to share Spirit Walker's life and bed. Though she knew with assurance in her heart that with each day's passing, she and Spirit Walker were being drawn closer together by the heart, she also told herself it would be that much more wrenching when the day would come that they separated. She refused to dwell on the future. She was living for the moment, and she was enjoying every minute.

"What are you dreaming about?" Spirit Walker looked up from the arrow he was fashioning as he sat before the fire. It was a peaceful evening, as always, here in his lodge with Autumn Dawn.

Amber was working on a buffalo hide that she would make into a robe for Spirit Walker. The robe was to be a surprise. She planned to paint scenes on the robe to forever remind him of her. She would paint a few scenes of him: one as a young man hanging on the sun dance pole, another of the vision he had gained when he had walked with the sky people, and the third, the first time he had seen her. She had been lost in thought, paying little attention to the buffalo hide spread across her lap. His words had broken through her musings. "I was thinking how pleased I am that spring has finally come." She was tired of ice and snow, and the chill that was constantly in the air. This past week had been warmer, and the ice in the river had already begun to thaw.

Spirit Walker smiled warmly at her answer. "I, too, am pleased that Mother Earth will once again feel the warming rays of Wi."

Spirit Walker turned back to his quiver of arrows, studying each within to make sure that the feathers had been trimmed properly. "Now that it grows warmer, the braves are ready to go on a hunt for fresh game." Again his dark gaze went to where Amber sat on the pile of lush furs.

Since coming to the valley, Spirit Walker had not left her for more than an afternoon. His statement gave her pause to consider if he intended to go along on this hunt. "How long will these braves be away from the village?" she asked.

"As long as it takes to get the needed meat. Crow Horse and Thunder Hawk will be going; they have asked me to go along." Spirit Walker was not sure of Autumn Dawn's reaction. He hoped that she would understand the need for the warriors to go on a hunt now that the snows were beginning to melt. It had been a hard winter and many of the old people were in need of fresh meat. He would go with the hunters, because it was the way of the people. Every warrior who was capable held an obligation to do what was required to lessen the suffering of all the villagers.

"When will you go?" He still had not said he would go with the hunters, but she knew, in her heart that he would go. She knew also that she could not ask him to stay behind in the village with her.

"When Wi rises from slumber and leaves the underworld," he responded. "It is best that we go quickly so that we can return sooner." Setting the quiver of arrows off to the side against his backrest, Spirit Walker rose to his full height and made his way to Amber's side. A warm smile played across his handsome face as he added, "Perhaps the game will be plentiful, and we will be back at the village with the passing of two moons."

Two days, Amber silently thought. Looking at the bronze, godlike warrior standing in front of her, she wondered how she would be able to endure even such a short period of time without him. She was tempted to ask how long it would take if the game were not plentiful but stilled the words in her throat, not truly wanting to hear the answer.

Amber set the buffalo hide away from the pallet of soft furs and opened her arms in welcome. "If you are to leave in the morning you will need your rest," she whispered as she watched his hand drop to the tie at his waist that secured his breechcloth.

"It is not rest that I am in need of, Ptanyétu Ánpo." Stretching his length down next to her, his hungry mouth slanted over her, his heated tongue skillfully delving deeply into her sweet-honey depths.

Just when Amber thought she could take no more, his lips drifted across her cheek, along her fragile jawline to the hollow at the base of her neck, then slowly back to her mouth. His breath was warm in her mouth as his hands tore at the single garment of hide concealing her flesh.

Amber felt the heat of his skin, the abrasion of his hard body as he leaned over her. He was a powerful, imposing creature; who any woman would be powerless to resist. Reaching out to caress any part of him she could reach, she couldn't get enough of the taste and feel of him. Her own body writhed seductively beneath the onslaught of his wild hunger as he feasted upon her breasts. Her mouth met his muscular shoulder, her lips making a bold pattern of tiny kisses down toward the upper portion of his chest. Her fingers boldly glided over the strong planes of his muscled body, outlining the broadness of his sculpted back, down to his narrow hips, and over his firm buttocks. She caught and held an indrawn breath, for a breathless time as one hand brushed against the pulsing length of his maleness.

With but the slightest touch of her hand, the size of him began to enlarge as the heated blood rushed throughout his loin. A deep groan started in the depths of his chest to rumble upward.

Feeling her woman's power, Amber's slender fingers wrapped around his swollen member, and very slowly drew them up the length, then slowly, tantalizingly, traveled back down the thick, throbbing measure of him, inch by inch.

Spirit Walker could bear no more, and, reaching out, he stilled her hand with his own. "Ah, my heart . . . do not continue, or indeed we will find our rest much sooner than desired." His words were whispered against her ear, and from there, his moist tongue scorched a trail over the delicate contours of her face, down her slender throat, across the fullness of her swollen breasts, gliding over her ribs and scorching a trail over a rounded hip. As his hand boldly touched the crest of her woman's jewel, rioting sensations shot wantonly throughout her body.

With the heated contact of his lips upon her flesh, she could no longer suppress the cry that was torn free from her parted lips as she rose up and clutched Spirit Walker's thick dark hair. She was consumed by an igniting flame. She rode out this incredible journey of pure ecstasy, her mind void of all but the rippling waves of hot passion that filled her every pore, erupting into scalding pleasure. As shudder after shudder left her trembling and writhing,

fulfillment came . . . and with it, Amber's cries became
purrs of contentment.

Spirit Walker rose above Amber to spread her thighs
gently. Feeling the quivering velvet warmth welcoming
him, he groaned as blinding pleasure filled his being.

As Spirit Walker set a sensuous, luring rhythm, Amber
wound sleek arms around his neck. Her soft, berry-red
lips parted as shivers of sweet rapture set her entire body
trembling in his arms. Her body moved against him with
a silken grace.

Spirit Walker wrapped Amber's legs around his waist,
plunging deeper and deeper into the core of her.

When that moment of rapturous pleasure came, Amber
gloried in the feeling of quickening passion rushing
throughout her body. Her lips parted, and without conscious thought, words of endearment softly escaped her
throat. "I love you. I would be lost without you. Please don't
ever leave me. I love you . . . I love you . . . I love you . . ."

Looking down into her face, as her words of love softly
touched his ears, Spirit Walker knew that she was unaware
of all reason and doubted that she even knew what she
said. He swore that one day he would hear these same
words from her lips and would know that she declared
them willingly, her senses undulled by passion.

After the feeling of brilliant delight began at the center
of his being and expanded in a mighty, plunging storm
of blissful rapture, his body slowly stilled. His breathing
was still ragged, but his lips continued roaming over
Amber's face and throat. "Our hearts beat the same song
of happiness, Ptanyétu Ánpo," he murmured. His chest
was pressed against hers, and their heartbeats seemed to
join and mingle into one.

Amber wondered at the words that had slipped unbid-
den from her lips while she had been lost to her passion.
Hearing Spirit Walker's tender words, she told herself he

had not heard her declarations; if he had, he would surely want them to be shared. A soft sigh escaped her parted lips. She was not sure, even now, if she was fully ready to make such declarations of love and devotion openly. She *was* sure, though, that she would miss Spirit Walker terribly when he left the village to go on this hunting trip with the other braves. "You promise that you will return to the village as soon as possible?" Her wide blue eyes held a tender pleading.

"I will not stay away a moment longer than is needed," he reassured. "Each moment away from you, even during the days here in the village, are moments when I feel empty. My soul is only half alive when I am away from you." Spirit Walker, unlike Amber, was well able to express his inner feelings.

Relaxing back into his embrace, Amber worried about the dangers that could come up against him and the band of braves, who would leave the village early the following morning. "You will be careful, Spirit Walker? You won't take any unnecessary chances?" She remembered his fierceness the day in the meadow when the grizzly bear was attacking her, and a shudder swept over her body.

Spirit Walker's arms tightened around her as he felt the movement of her body. "We will hunt for deer and elk high in the mountains. There is no need to worry. I will return the same as I leave our lodge." He placed a tender kiss upon her lips, wishing to chase away her worries.

"I don't know what I would do if something happened to you." She snuggle against his side. His words drew comfort around her, but she would not be completely at ease until he returned from the hunting trip.

Looking down at her sleepy visage, her eyelids already beginning to lower, Spirit Walker knew contentment. Perhaps she would not allow the words of love to flow freely from her lips, but her concern and the fact she admitted she would miss him, told him more than the spoken words, told him the feelings of her heart. As his own eyes began to close, he remembered the words she had softly spoken only a short time ago, *I love you. I would be lost without you. Please don't ever leave me. I love you . . . I love you . . . I love you . . .*

"Did you tell Spirit Walker before he left the village about the baby?" Running Moon's dark eyes studied Amber thoughtfully.

Yellow Fawn was watching over Little Bird in her lodge while her daughter and her friend visited and sewed. With the other woman's words, Amber's hands stilled in their work on the buffalo robe. "What baby?" she questioned, but her voice held a slight tremor of nervousness.

Running Moon smiled warmly. For several weeks now, each morning when the women went together to gather wood and draw water for their lodge, Autumn Dawn had lingered along the pathway, her head bent over a bush as she expelled whatever was in her stomach. Running Moon had not mentioned the morning ritual until this day, having hoped that Autumn Dawn would bring the subject about first. "The baby that you carry beneath your heart," Running Moon supplied in a light tone.

Amber swallowed hard. She was surprised that Running Moon had discovered her secret. "I was going to tell Spirit Walker last night that I suspect I am carrying his child, but before I could, he told me that he would be leaving this morning with the others. I didn't want him to worry about my health. I will tell him as soon as he returns."

"He will be happy with this news." Running Moon grinned as she imagined Spirit Walker's happiness.

"Do you think he will really be pleased? We haven't talked about children yet. What we share is so new to both of us, and we have been so busy. I am always working at Sky Weaver's lodge, and people are constantly coming here to seek Spirit Walker's advice. I am not even really sure that he wishes to have children." This was not quite true. In her heart, Amber knew that Spirit Walker would be delighted with the news that she was going to have his baby. It was she who still was not sure how she felt about having his child. From the beginning, she felt that her relationship with Spirit Walker was only temporary, but it appeared that daily she was becoming more involved in his life. Having his child would be a tie that could never be broken, and Amber was not sure about her inner feelings. Did she wish the tie to be a permanent one?

"Our people are raised knowing that the survival of the people depends upon each of us. The Sioux love their children greatly, and a warrior such as Spirit Walker will know only love and pride when he looks down at his child." Running Moon knew how her own husband, Strong Elk, felt about their son. Spirit Walker would be no less proud when he heard he was to be a father.

You are right, my friend. I should have told Spirit Walker already." Amber confessed.

Running Moon did not turn back to her sewing, her gaze held steady on Amber. "How do you feel about the child in your body, Ptanyétu Ánpo?" She had never wondered how any of the women of her village felt about having a child. She had supposed they all felt as she had when she discovered herself carrying Little Bird. But this wasichu friend was different. She was never quite sure of her feeling, and even now, was not sure how she truly felt about Spirit Walker.

Amber's hand instantly went to her belly. She had had several weeks to accept the fact that she was pregnant. Now, with the other woman's question, an instant protectiveness overcame her. She was already falling in love with this tiny bit of life in her belly. In that secret portion of her heart, in that place where she had tried to harden herself in order to ensure she not be hurt, she knew that she loved Spirit Walker and could only love a child that was a part of him. Instant tears filled her eyes as she admitted her love for the handsome warrior to herself.

"Sometimes it is best that we forget the pain of our past and allow happiness to become reborn in our hearts." Running Moon's tone held great tenderness. "Many go through these steps in this life without knowing happiness. When it comes to us, we should not turn our backs but should accept it with open arms. I believe this is the way with you and Spirit Walker. I also think that this baby will be the door to this happiness for you."

"I think so, too." Amber brushed away the tears on her cheeks. "I can't wait for Spirit Walker to return to the village." She felt as though a massive burden had been lifted from her heart. She couldn't wait to see Spirit Walker to tell him about the baby, and to also tell him that she loved him.

Twenty-four

Spirit Walker had returned! Amber could feel his heated breath against the slender column of her throat, his hands caressing her shoulders as he drew her toward him. Joy sang within her breasts, her lips murmuring words of love that had been too long stilled in the darkness of her soul. Her hands attempted to push away the fur covers, welcoming the moment when his powerful body would join her upon the sleeping pallet. For a moment, her sleep-crested brow furrowed as her hands were pulled away and held tightly in a firm grip. Her eyelids fought to open, her mind sending out a fleeting warning that something was not right. A warning that was far too late for her to heed.

"Goddamn it! Now, you've woke her before we got her tied. You best cram something in her mouth before she goes a'caterwailing and wakes up the entire village!"

Amber shook the remainder of her sleep-clouded thoughts from her mind enough to recognize the voice as her stepfather's! Her eyes instantly shot open as she scrambled to the far side of the sleeping pallet and away from the hands reaching out for her.

Tate Coker leaned over her, and with a hard yank jerked her back beneath his hand. "She yaps and I'll knock her out!" His words were spoken in as low a voice as Barrow's, but their meaning was clear to Amber, who froze beneath his grip.

These two men were capable of anything. Taking a deep, steadying breath, she warned herself to use caution. "What are you doing here?" Her words were directed at Henry Barrow.

"Keep your voice low, gal, before Coker has to take his fist to you!" What the hell do you think we're here for? We've come to get you back from the heathen that stole you away from me and Coker."

Remembering the hatred her stepfather held for Indians, Amber wisely thought better than to try and explain that she had not been stolen away from rendezvous, but had gone willingly with Spirit Walker, and certainly had no desire to go anywhere with Henry Barrow and his friend. With wide, frightened eyes she looked from Barrow to Coker, unsure what she should do.

"Like I said before, gal, you don't start making noise and we'll just sneak away from this village of savages just as pretty as you please! Now, get yourself up, and get dressed. We got some hard traveling to do before daylight and I don't aim to be kept waiting!" Henry Barrow was feeling jumpy in this Indian lodge; his dull green eyes kept going back to the entrance flap, his Hawkin rifle primed and ready, rested across the crook of his arm in case of an emergency.

Amber clutched a piece of hide against her chest. Fear pulsed throughout her body. What was she going to do to prevent being taken away from Spirit Walker's village? She looked around the lodge as though expecting some help to come. She noticed that the fire in the center pit had not burned down much lower than it had been when she first went to bed. It must be fairly early. Perhaps near midnight, no later. With Tate Coker standing over her, his looming fist ready to carry out Barrow's threat, Amber silently reached down and drew her hide dress from where she had left it folded earlier in the evening. She could only hope for a little time; time in which someone might notice the two white men and rescue her before she was forced to go with them.

For a few minutes, Amber remained sitting on the bed with the piece of fur covering her naked body. Barrow looked around again, irritated by the delay, and finally questioned, "what the hell are you sitting there for? I told you to get dressed."

"And I will, if you two will go outside and wait." An idea sprang to life. Spirit Walker had sliced the back of the tent at rendezvous; she would do the same thing the minute Barrow and Coker were not watching. There was a sharp-bladed knife near the fire; she could cut a hole large enough to escape through, then run for help.

"There ain't no need for us to go outside, gal. You just dress while we turn our backs. I don't reckon as how you're going to hide yourself long from your husband anyway, but this one time we'll oblige you."

The word husband turned over in Amber's mind and settled hollowly in her stomach. She had forgotten about the ceremony that had taken place between herself and Tate Coker at rendezvous. Looking the large, bearded man full in the face, she saw the leer that came over his lips at her stepfather's words.

"Come on, Coker, let's give the gal a moment to dress." Henry Barrow nudged Tate Coker, and, showing only a moment's resistance, Coker stepped away from the sleeping pallet and followed Barrow to the fire.

Amber knew she would be allowed only a scarce few minutes to dress. Trying to think of some other way to stall the men until help could come, she slipped the hide dress over her head, and at the same time attempted to keep the piece of fur as a covering over any portion of her body that might be revealed. Watching the men's backs, she slipped her feet into the moccasins near the side of the bed. Her gaze went to the entrance flap of the tepee as she measured the distance and wondered if she would have time to make it through the doorway before they would catch her.

"Come on, gal, let's get a move on." Henry Barrow turned and caught her look of desperation as she looked toward the entrance flap. Stepping between the bed and doorway, he waited for her to follow orders.

Amber knew, that once she left the lodge with the two men, her chances of escape would be slender. Seeing her stepfather blocking her way to the door, she debated her next move. If she could reach the knife lying near the edge of the fire, perhaps she could hold the two men off until some kind of help could arrive.

Seeing her eyes travel to the fire, and glimpsing the glint of a knife, Henry Barrow's suspicion flared. "You're not thinking of trying anything stupid, are you, gal? Me and old Coker here have come some distance looking for you. Neither of us would take too kindly to your not being appreciative." His tone hardened perceptibly, the sallow skin above his scraggly beard turning bright red with growing indignation over his stepdaughter's resistance. "Now, get yourself off that Injun bed. I'd think that you would welcome rescue, like any good and decent white woman would!"

His patience had all but run its course, so Amber silently stepped away from the bed. She had seen her stepfather's impatience turn to instant rage in the past. The memory of his beatings swept through her mind, and she knew she had best do what he told her.

Tate Coker grinned with enjoyment as he viewed the fear on Amber's face. Old Barrow knew how to treat women; a firm voice and a heavy hand was what most females needed, and he would carry out that tradition once they were away from this village.

There was no way out for Amber. She was trapped before the weary regard of the two men. Slowly, she began to make her way to the entrance flap, her stepfather within a hand's easy reach of her just in case she attempted escape.

Once outside in the dark, Henry Barrow caught hold of Amber's arm, his fingers a hurtful vise which did not allow her the chance to run for freedom.

Only a short distance down the river, three horses were tied. Keeping his voice low, Barrow spoke in a gruff tone. "I aim to tie you till we clear this Injun village. Ain't no sense in taking no chances where these Sioux are concerned. They'd soon as scalp me and Coker as look at us, and we don't aim on losing our hair this night."

"I won't try anything." Amber spoke low, hoping she could convince her stepfather to leave her untied. Once she was on a horse, she would break free from the two men then ride for help; this could be her only chance!

Without comment, Barrow caught Amber around the waist and set her on the back of one of the horses. Before she could grab hold of the reins, he caught her hands and began to tie them with a piece of rawhide that had appeared out of nowhere.

"You don't need to do that!" Amber's voice was louder now. She gave no thought to obliging her stepfather in low tones. All she thought of was fleeing him and that horrible Tate Coker! She tried to kick out, to force the horse into motion.

Barrow was quicker, his hands cruel and biting as they

gripped the calf of Amber's leg while it was poised in midair ready to kick the horse. "Gag her, Coker!" Barrow called to his friend who was standing by, watching. Tying the rawhide around the saddle horn he reached up and pulled Amber low against the saddle. That allowed Coker to shove a piece of material into her mouth and tie a rag around the lower portion of her face to keep the gag in place. Amber struggled against their attempts to subdue her. Her mouth opened to scream, but the effort was strangled in her throat as the dirty cloth was pressed between her teeth. With hands tied, and now her mouth gagged, she was powerless against the two men.

"Let's get the hell out of here, Barrow!" Tate Coker pulled himself up on his horse's back, and, grabbing hold of the reins to Amber's horse, he started them into motion.

Henry Barrow was of the same mind as his partner. He wouldn't know a moment's peace till they cleared this village and put some miles between themselves and the threat of the Sioux. It had been only a stroke of luck that they had found Amber alone in the Injun's lodge. He and Coker had been watching the village for the past few days and had noticed the activity around the encampment, then had seen the band of braves leaving the valley early that morning. It had been good fortune that they had seen the large Indian who had stolen Amber away from rendezvous going with the others away from the village.

Kicking his horse's flank now, he followed up the rear, Coker leading the three along the riverbank, then into the dense forest that they had used as shelter when spying on the village.

Amber struggled against her bonds, but her stepfather had tied her wrists tightly, and she felt no give in the rawhide, nor could she force the gag out of her mouth. Along with tears of distress, fear stirred in her eyes as she turned in the saddle and made out the dark silhouette of the village of tepees set up on the valley floor. She was being stolen away from the only life where she had ever found happiness, and no one even knew what was happening. The village reposed in quiet serenity as the moon slowly traveled across the path of velvet heavens.

The hard ride through forest and over hilly terrain did not slack its pace until the sun broke through a pinkish dawn morning. It was not until then that Amber's gag was removed. While allowing the horses rest for a few short minutes, Barrow held his canteen up to Amber's lips.

"Please untie my hands," Amber gasped the moment the gag was pulled from her mouth. Her thoughts still raced with thoughts aimed at trying to get away from these two men. She could do nothing without the use of her hands.

"Drink" was Barrow's only response to her plea. Over the past hours, he had had time to think about the reception he and Coker had received when she had discovered they had come to rescue her from the savages. She had not acted like he expected a woman he had raised to act! She had seemed downright unfriendly toward him and Coker. Removing her gag would not pose a problem, but he wisely knew that untying her hands could be another matter entirely. She had already attempted to break free of them back at the Injun village. He wouldn't take a chance until they were farther away from the Sioux valley. He still felt the fine hairs on the back of his neck rise each time he heard a noise behind a tree or bush.

Late that afternoon Amber's hands were untied for a short time, while the two men stopped to fix a meal and rest their weary mounts. To her dismay, a short time later she was tied once again, and the three started on the

invisible trail that led them farther away from Spirit Walker
and his people.

As each hour passed, and Henry Barrow and Tate Coker
were not confronted by a Sioux warrior, their assurance
that no one was following behind them grew. They pressed
on, but by the next morning they were not pushing their
mounts as hard, and by that evening, they decided they
could build a small fire then get some sleep.

Weary of mind and body, Amber slumped to the ground
after her hands were freed and she was helped from her
horse. Each mile covered throughout this long day had
intensified Amber's fear that she was on her own to deal
with these two dangerous men. No help from Spirit Walker
would be forthcoming. As far as she knew, Spirit Walker
was still away from the village hunting and did not know
that she had been taken from the village. How would anyone even know what had happened to her? Spirit Walker
and his people might believe that she had wandered off
into the forest and had come to some harm. There were
bears and wolves in the woods that encircled the valley,
and it might be thought that they had devoured her. Her
heartbreak intensified when she imagined Spirit Walker's
pain upon returning to the village to find her gone.

"Get yourself up and fix a fire," Barrow ordered, his
booted foot kicking out to connect with her thigh as he
passed with an arm load of provisions. "Them savages
might have put up with your laziness, but don't be waiting
for me and Coker to be doing woman's work when you're
more than able."

With her thigh aching from the cruel kick, she quickly
obeyed her stepfather, just as she had always done in the
past. But this time, her inner mind's workings were running rampant with thoughts of escape. If she could just
get away from the two of them, she would somehow find
her way back to the Sioux valley! She would never give up

hope of returning to Spirit Walker and his people. Her hand absently went to her abdomen, and she thought of the delicate life within her body. She could not allow her child to be raised the same way she had. She had to get away from Barrow and Coker. Gathering wood around the area they had chosen for their camp, Amber's weary gaze watched for any opportunity that would provide her a means to freedom.

As the fire was started, she began to make a pot of coffee, then put on a pot of beans. Even if an opportunity presented itself, it would be a slight one, and she would be taking a chance with her own life by trying to get away.

Henry Barrow and Tate Coker watched her every movement as she bent over the flickering flames of the campfire. They spoke in low tones, discussing the fact that they would reach Harper's trading post in a couple of days. Barrow planned to go on to St. Louis to purchase his tavern. Coker would take Amber and head out for the mountains, where he would go on about his business of trapping.

"I reckon as how, right after supper, I'll be having me my wedding night." Tate Coker's tongue moistened his lips and dampened the untrimmed edges of his mustache as his glance crawled over Amber's shapely form.

Barrow nodded his fur-capped head as he also watched the girl prepare their meal. It was too damn bad he couldn't get the image of her mother out of his head. If not for this, he might have kept the girl for himself, or at least attempt to convince Coker into sharing. But though the girl was appealing enough to the eye, he felt no strong desires to bed her. "I guess you've waited long enough." Barrow patted the money belt strapped around his middle, no longer fearing that he would lose the money he had gotten from Coker at rendezvous. "Have a go at her whenever your a mind to, with my blessings." Barrow grinned widely as he leaned back against a tree and continued to daydream about the tavern he would soon own.

Amber felt the tension building throughout the evening as she finished cooking the meal, and then as the men ate. Each time her stepfather looked in her direction, his eyes glittered. Tate Coker did not bother to hide the leer that came across his features each time her blue eyes looked across the campfire. Amber felt chilled, and not from the weather. These two were up to something; she had to be on her guard!

Rising to his full, imposing height, Coker stretched his long arms upward and stated loudly, "Well, I reckon that it's time that we stretch out for a spell. We'll cut out again before dawn, so if we're to get any sleep, we had best turn in early."

Amber sat still where she was on the other side of the fire, her fear increasing, as Tate Coker stared directly at her and began to walk around the fire.

"You're right about getting back on the trail early in the morning, Coker, but I don't know any but myself who will be sleeping much this night!" Barrow stood up as he watched his partner approaching his stepdaughter.

One minute Amber was sitting next to the fire, the next, Tate Coker had grabbed her by the arms and was hauling her toward the blanket he had spread out before supper. "Let me go!" she cried. "Take your filthy hands off me!"

Her cries were ignored. Coker's large hands pawed at her body, trying to pull her clothes off, and at the same time forcing his lips over her own.

Henry Barrow made his way to his own blanket, feeling no guilt over his stepdaughter's plight. She had been a burden to him over the years, but he had done his best by her by not letting her starve. She owed him for that. She was a commodity to him, nothing more. He held no affection, or love for her; he had done his duty by her, and now she was going to do her part.

Amber's screams and cries for release circled the camp. She kicked, hit, and scratched the large man in her futile attempt for freedom. "No . . . stop . . . please don't touch me . . ." She could not bear the feel of his hard, unyielding body pressed against her own. The foul odor of his unclean teeth, beard, and mustache, overwhelmed her with revulsion as she clawed at his face in desperation.

Tate Coker enjoyed a woman with a little fire. He squeezed Amber's breast hard as he tore at the laces of her dress, his mouth trying vainly to cover hers, and with a grunt, he endured her sharp nails digging into the flesh of his face. The little hellcat would learn soon enough that he was her master! He'd soon have her whimpering softly beneath him. With that thought, he felt his prick growing in size. He was as randy as a stud horse; and the more she fought him, the more he wanted to mount her.

Amber was in total panic. She was being raped and there was no means to stop this man, no sign of help! She had no weapon, and the small amount of strength she had was slowly diminishing. But she could not give up! She would never give up! She had tasted love and tenderness in Spirit Walker's arms; her last breath would leave her body before she would lie down and submit to this brute!

Grabbing a handful of her copper hair in a tight grip, Coker brought her face closer, his mouth covering her lips, his large tongue plunging into her depths, smothering her.

Amber wanted to scream aloud her revulsion, but she was powerless to make a sound; all she could do was bring her teeth sharply down on his intrusive tongue.

With a curse, Tate Coker struck her with his fist on the side of the head. "You crazy bitch . . . I'll kill you for biting me!" Blood flowed from the wound on his tongue where Amber's teeth had inflicted a gaping hole.

His powerful fist sent Amber reeling to the ground. From the haze that encircled her mind, she heard his threats and her wide eyes reflected her terror as she saw him recoil to strike her again. Curling into a tight ball, Amber cried aloud for the life of her unborn child. "Please . . . my baby! Please don't hit me anymore! I'll do what you . . ." She could not bring herself to say the words, but at that moment, she knew that she would do what he wanted if he would let her live, let the child in her womb live.

Amber's words were like a bucket of ice-cold water being dashed over Tate Coker. Instantly, his manhood shriveled as he stood over her with fists raised. Why, the bitch was pregnant by an Injun! Looking down at her, her arms wrapped around her knees in a protective nature, his only thoughts were of revulsion; anger instantly rekindled as he turned toward Barrow. "Did ye hear what she just said, Barrow?"

"Naw, I'm trying to get some sleep. Beat her if you have to, but don't forget that we still got a lot of miles to cover, and she'll be needing to sit a horse."

"She said, she's pregnant with that savage's brat!"

Henry Barrow heard the disgust and fury in Tate Coker's voice and instantly sat up on his blanket. Slowly, he digested this news as he looked at his stepdaughter still lying on the ground. "So what if she is?" None of this concerned Henry Barrow. He had sold Amber to Tate Coker, and had done his part by going to that Injun village to get her back for him. Whatever else happened, it had nothing to do with the money in his money belt!

"My cock ain't going into nothing that's carrying one of them savage's seed! For all I know the damn thing could rot off because of that heathen! He could've had a disease or something even worse!"

"What the hell is wrong with you, Coker?" Barrow couldn't believe his friend's words.

"You heard me, Barrow. I ain't touching her as long as she's carrying a red devil in her belly!"

"Well, suit yerself, man." Henry Barrow wondered if his partner was touched in the head. Who the hell cared if the gal was taken with someone else's catch? She was still shapely enough to look upon, and her honey pot was just as good as any other woman's!

"What do you mean, suit myself?" Tate Coker turned away from Amber and his blanket as he crossed to the spot where Barrow was sitting. I paid you good money for her, I didn't bargain on taking on no Injun's seconds!"

"You bought her like we bargained, and you ain't going back on it now!" Henry Barrow eyed the larger man, his hand easing to the rifle lying next to his own blanket. "You didn't say a word about your problem before. You must have figured that one of them Injuns would be poking her good, there in that village. Fer God's sake, man, she was there all winter long!"

Even though Tate Coker was consumed with anger at being cheated out of his due, he noticed where Barrow's hand rested, and wisely told himself to use caution. Barrow was not a man to take lightly. He had already seen him kill an Injun over a drink of whiskey without flicking an eyelash. He would do the same to him if he pushed much harder. "I'm just saying that I've been cheated out of my money. It ain't right that I gave you my cash and now I've got nothing to show for it."

A flicker of pity touched Barrow's soul over his partner's plight. He had learned to like Coker over the last several months. It would be a shame if he were forced to kill him; after all, he was the first partner he had ever truly got along with for any length of time. "Well, I'll tell you what I'll do for you then. When the brat is born, I'll stove its

head in right good, and you can have the gal just like you
please.'' This was the best that Barrow would offer. He
certainly wasn't about to turn over any money.

Amber gasped aloud at her stepfather's cruel remark,
her hands automatically covering her belly in protection.

"You'd do that fer me, Barrow?'' Some of the tension
disappeared from Coker's voice. But soon enough it
returned. "How're you going to bash the kid in the head,
if you not around when it's born?''

Henry Barrow had not thought of this. After a few silent
minutes of thought, he offered, "The best I can reckon,
is that you'll have to come along with me back to St. Louis.
Sit out a few months, and after she has the kid, you can
go on back to the mountains. You might even decide to
become partners with me in my tavern.''

Barrow's offer was a hard one for Tate Coker to discard.
He had heard so much about the life Barrow planned to
lead once he left the mountains, Coker admitted that he
had been jealous. The picture that Barrow described was
one of ease and wealth; to be partners in such a venture
was an appealing thought. He was being offered a partnership in the tavern and he would also have the woman.
Then and there, he decided that he would accept Barrow's
offer. He would wait out Amber's pregnancy. Barrow would
take care of the baby, and he would take care of the gal.

Twenty-five

The hunting party returning to the Sioux valley was the cause of much excitement. Two weeks had passed since they left to seek fresh meat, and with their extra horses pulling travoises packed high with meat, there would be plenty of feasting and rejoicing throughout the camp this day and night.

As the braves rode through the encampment and were encircled by the villagers, Spirit Walker felt his own excitement mounting, attuned to the shouts and laughter of his people, his eyes sweeping over each woman as he anticipated his first glance of Autumn Dawn. He had not thought that the party would be away from the valley for so many days, but the game had been scarce at first, and each brave knew how important it was for them to bring back meat for the people. He had been one of the first to claim that they had enough provisions packed on the travoises. All had agreed finally that it was time to return to homes and families. As the minutes passed by with no sign of the woman that filled his heart, Spirit Walker felt a keen disappointment. Watching Running Moon walking next to Strong Elk's horse, her features filled with happiness because of her husband's return, he wondered if Autumn Dawn was busy working with Sky Weaver; perhaps this was the reason for her delay in greeting him.

Spirit Walker did not tarry amidst the villagers, but directed his horse to his lodge along the bank of the river. Perhaps Autumn Dawn was waiting in the lodge, wanting to share his homecoming in private. His heartbeat escalated with such thoughts. He would not fully feel alive until he looked upon her beauty, until he felt the soft touch of her hands, and heard her gentle voice.

Leaving his pony to graze on the shoots of grass growing along the edge of the river, he pushed back the entrance flap of the lodge and stepped within. An instant awareness that things were not right washed over him as he gazed around the interior of the lodge. There was no warm fire in the center fire-pit; only cold ashes greeted him. Stepping over to the sleeping pallet, his dark eyes sought out some indication of the wrong that he felt in his heart.

"Ptanyétu Ánpo," the name softly expelled his lips.

There was no response; the chilly interior of his lodge immediately justified his unease. She must be at Sky Weaver's lodge, Spirit Walker told himself, trying to push away the growing apprehension ensnaring his whole being. Or perhaps she was staying with Running Moon. That hope encouraged him to leave the lodge to search for the woman he loved more than life itself.

Even before he reached Sky Weaver's lodge, he knew in his heart that Autumn Dawn would not be there. Surely by now everyone in the village knew the hunting party had returned. Autumn Dawn would have rushed to greet him. He found the old man's lodge empty, but, unlike his own, there was a warm fire and a pot of stew cooking over the open flames. Turning around, intending to seek out

Running Moon and question her about Autumn Dawn, he was instead greeted by Medicine Cloud and Thunder Hawk.

"My friend, there is bad news." Thunder Hawk's words told of his concern, but also held promise of helping Spirit Walker through the tragedy that had befallen him.

Spirit Walker looked from his friend to the old shaman who had taught him so many things throughout his life. They had sought him out with news of Autumn Dawn; he could feel this in his heart. "Where is she?" His chest ached, his throat growing dry as his dark gaze held upon the aged medicine man.

Medicine Cloud slowly waved a fan of feathers before his face. "The woman with the fire hair disappeared the same night that the hunting party left the village."

"That long ago? She disappeared? But how? Where could she have gone?" Spirit Walker's knees weakened with the revelation Autumn Dawn had been gone so long.

Waving the fan as though to draw forth the right words to speak, Medicine Cloud continued beyond the interruption. "When it was first reported that Ptanyétu Ánpo was not to be found in the village, many warriors went in search of her. Some feared she had gone to the forest to gather plants and rocks for her paints and been attacked by a wild animal." Again the feather fan waved back and forth.

"No! I would know within if she no longer lived." Spirit Walker spoke with assurance, clutching an inner knowledge, that he would sense in his inner spirit if Autumn Dawn had breathed her last.

The medicine man nodded his head. "You would know," he agreed.

"Then what happened to her?" Spirit Walker sensed the old man knew more but was taking time to reveal all the details.

"With the passing of five moons after her disappearance,

I was awakened by the spirits and told to hold a yuwipi ceremony for the lost woman.''

"You know where she is. The spirits revealed things to you about Ptanyétu Ánpo?" Spirit Walker held great faith in Medicine Cloud and his experience as a yuwipi medicine man. A yuwipi ceremony was held to heal the sick or to find something that was lost or needed.

Medicine Cloud held out his hand; in the palm rested a shiny black stone of onyx. "This was left by the spirits." He placed the stone in a small leather pouch and handed it to Spirit Walker."The spirits say that you are to wear this around your neck. They will guide you and remain with you in your time of need. Touch the pouch with your right hand and they will speak to you secretly."

Spirit Walker took the pouch and without argument tied it around his neck. As the fingers on his right hand caressed the small bag, he felt the heat from the power within. "Where did the spirits say she is?" His ebony eyes never left the wrinkled features.

"They spoke to me as the drums beat all around me. Mother Earth vibrated with the thunder of tatanka. I saw the flashing lights of thousands of ancestral fires. The turtle rattles of the spirits shook, the sound colliding in my head with that of the drums. The spirits told me that two men took the woman with the fire hair far away. They spoke of her fighting against them, but she is alone and does not have a warrior to protect her."

Two men, two men, two men . . . The words revealed by Medicine Cloud were repeated again and again in Spirit Walker's head. His right hand absently touched the leather pouch hanging against his chest. Instantly, the features of the man Autumn Dawn had called stepfather, and the one at rendezvous who had given the man money for Autumn, came to Spirit Walker's mind.

Medicine Cloud saw understanding come into Spirit

Walker's eyes. "You must pray to the powers for protection and strength before you go after those who have taken Ptanyétu Ánpo." Medicine Cloud held no thought of trying to sway Spirit Walker from his pursuit of the woman. Autumn Dawn belonged here among the people. Her steps had led to the path of Spirit Walker's life circle by the Great Spirit. She had been chosen to keep the record of the people by the One Above. The ordeal before this warrior would be overcome and Ptanyétu Ánpo would be returned to the life she was destined to live.

"I will go with you on your journey," Thunder Hawk quickly volunteered. Spirit Walker was his best friend, and had been since earliest childhood. He would not stay in the village while his friend faced danger. He suspected that the two men who had taken Autumn Dawn were wasichus, and he knew Spirit Walker would need help to get his woman away from them.

"No, Thunder Hawk. I will go alone." Spirit Walker also knew that the trail before him would be one of great danger; but in his heart he was certain he must go after Autumn Dawn alone. "You will help to watch over the people, Cetán. Your strength is great, you are needed here."

Thunder Hawk was powerless arguing with Spirit Walker over this matter. He would not accept his friend's help.

Throughout the rest of the long afternoon, Spirit Walker built himself a sweat lodge in the sacred manner of the people. He would try to rest this night, and long before the hour when the morning star would greet the new day, he would purify himself, then beseech the powers to guide him and give him strength. His initial reaction after learning that Autumn Dawn had been taken from the village was to set out after her, but after reason calmed him he knew, he would need his strength, along with help from the spirits that ruled his life.

As the moon climbed high in the star-brilliant heavens, he lay upon the bed of furs that he had shared with the woman of his heart. He had found the buffalo robe she had been working on, and after admiring the artful description of his vision and their meeting, he wrapped himself inside the robe. The scent of clean mountain flowers that had clung to Autumn Dawn swirled around his senses as he fitfully found some rest.

Long before daylight, Spirit Walker purified himself within the sweat lodge. After the ordeal, he sat unclothed near the river's edge before a small fire of sacred sage, fanning the fragrant smoke over his body. Taking his pipe from his medicine bundle, Spirit Walker then fanned the cleansing smoke over the stem, which had been made from the leg bone of a buffalo, and the bowl of red pipe stone.

His voice was clear upon the predawn air as his hands held the pipe upward in offering. "Grandfathers, you where Wi dies each day, you of the sacred wind that is home to the great white giant, you where Wi rises and the morning star is reborn, you where all power begins, you of skan and Mother Earth, creator of the wind, the people, and the four-leggeds of the world. Behold, this warrior cries out for that which only you are the giver of. To you I offer this pipe."

Putting the mouthpiece of the pipe to his lips, he drew in deeply. Earlier, the pipe had been filled with chacun sha sha, the bark of the red willow, and had been lit. Now he offered it up to the powers of the world. The smoke of the sage and tobacco mingled and rose upon the morning breeze.

"I seek the help of my eagle spirit for this task before me. Without the powers, I will be lost and unable to find Ptanyétu Ánpo. I beg the help of the spirits, for only by their strength will I be able to spill the blood of those that stole my woman." Again, he drew on the pipe, and again, the smoke blended and rose upward.

As Spirit Walker prayed, he felt a growing inner strength. He could feel heat emanating from the stone within the leather pouch which rested against his chest. He felt the presence of the spirits encircle him, and as his gaze looked upward, his eyes followed the flight of a large golden eagle. A screeching call escaping his beak touched Spirit Walker's spirit to give him assurance.

At the finish of his prayers, Spirit Walker brushed his horse down with handfuls of sage to ensure that he would endure the ordeal ahead. Finally, he entered his lodge to gather his weapons of war.

Amber attempted to climb onto the wharf from the flatboat. A large man who had been helping another to load barrels stretched out along the dock onto the deck of a paddle-wheeled steamboat hurried to her side to offer her an arm. His dark glare briefly touched upon Henry Barrow and Tate Coker as he took the obviously pregnant woman's elbow, and cautioned, "Watch your step now, missus."

"Thank you." Amber clutched the offered hand as she placed her moccasined foot upon the wood planking of the wharf. Mavis Harper had generously given Amber a dress, the day the three had arrived at the Harper's trading post, and as Amber smoothed the skirt with an anxious hand, she knew that the man's generous assist was due to the enlarged size of her abdomen.

Amber and the two men had waited for two weeks at the trading post for a flatboat to go back down the Missouri for supplies. The days on the river had slowly turned to weeks; then one month and another passed as the occupants of the flatboat slowly made their way to St. Louis. They had spent a few weeks at a Mandan village, and several days they did not travel because of foul weather. Now that they were here, Amber's spirits were at their lowest ebb.

For several days after her abduction, she had prayed that Spirit Walker would come for her. Even while they had waited for transportation at the trading post, she had thought he would appear. Slowly her hope began to vanish. As the days wore on, and the flatboat drew closer to St. Louis, her expectation of ever seeing Spirit Walker again vanished, as did the countryside along the banks of the ever-changing Missouri River.

"She thinks she's a proper lady, now that there ain't no heathens around." Tate Coker elbowed Henry Barrow in the ribs as the two men hefted packs over their shoulders and stepped on the wharf.

"I beg your pardon?" The man who had assisted Amber outweighed even Tate Coker by a good twenty pounds. His eyes sparked flintlike as his head swung around at the two men.

Henry Barrow was in no mood to take any gruff off some do-good dock worker. Swinging his arm around with his rifle held in the crook and pointed directly at the large man's chest, he stated coldly, "You ain't got to be begging for nothing, mister. Just take your hand off the gal, and stand clear, before I blow a hole in you large enough for a fish to swim through!"

For a full minute the large man held tightly to Amber's elbow, unsure of his next move. It was obvious that the young woman traveling with these two trappers was not being treated decently, but as his gaze lowered to the rifle being pointed directly at him, he slowly began to loosen his grip.

"Come on, Jeb. Let's get these barrels loaded and then go on over to the Blessed Paradise like we been planning."

The large man's friend had watched everything from the corner of his eye, not wanting to get involved in whatever was going on between the two men and the young woman. He had seen enough bloodshed in St. Louis over women, and knew by a first glance that these two trappers were not men to be taken lightly.

"Yeah, I reckon you're right, Clem." Jeb Fugate dropped Amber's elbow as though her touch burned his flesh. Whatever the young woman's story, it did not concern him. Clem was right about minding his own business. As soon as they loaded the barrels, he and his friend would walk over to the Blessed Paradise; there he would find any number of women for the simple asking. A drink or two and he would forget he ever saw this blue-eyed beauty on the docks.

"Smart man." Tate Coker grinned as Jeb stepped away from the threesome, and once again began to load the barrels with his friend.

As the two men, with Amber following, made their way down the docks, Henry Barrow questioned his partner, "Isn't that the name of Slim Farley's whorehouse, the Blessed Paradise?"

"I heard tell that it was," Coker replied, wondering at his friend's thoughts. A slow smile tickled his lips. As if he didn't know what old Henry was thinking! The old fool hadn't gotten Miss Calico Kat out of his mind since leaving rendezvous.

"Why don't we go on over and see if old Slim has a room or two that he might want to rent to old friends," Barrow suggested.

Amber gasped, her steps slowing. Her stepfather certainly could not think that they would reside within a house of ill repute while they stayed in St. Louis!

Henry Barrow snickered loudly and turned to face Amber. "You think your too good to sleep in a whorehouse, do ya, gal, but you're willing to spread your thighs for a redskin? Why, maybe old Farley will have a job for you, too! You might be fat now, but not for long! Maybe you can get some practice from Miss Calico Kat and her girls.''

Amber's face burned with embarrassment at her step-father's words, but she stifled any response. Over the past months, he and Coker had delighted in inflicting verbal abuse upon her. She had to swallow her pride and try to ignore this hurtful attack, as she had all the others. She had to find some means to escape these two men! Now that she was in St. Louis, it should be easier to slip away from them and somehow find shelter until she had her baby. She had survived this long, and so had her child; she could endure even a whorehouse, if that was what fate demanded!

The two men grinned at her apparent discomfort. "If she learns some good tricks in pleasuring a man, I might even be tempted to sell her to old Farley; he seemed hot enough after her at rendezvous. But first, as soon as she has the brat, I aim to use her to wipe out any thoughts of that damn Injun from her mind!" Coker boasted, enjoying the crimson that flooded across the copper-haired beauty's cheeks.

Amber tried to ignore the coarse remarks. The two men would only halt their abuse when they received no pleasure in her reaction. She forced her features to calm; a stony look of indifference replaced the flushed look of hurt. They could say and do what they liked, she would never forget Spirit Walker. Nor would she ever lose the love she held for him. She would fill her mind with thoughts about the life that, even at this minute, was kicking strongly within her body. She had to be strong to protect her child. Spirit Walker's child.

Twenty-six

"Scrub a little harder right here, Jill." Tate Coker lifted his arm indicating the spot he desired the luscious woman to attend.

With a smothered giggle, the curvaceous beauty rolled her wide brown eyes at her friend Moll, who was leaning over Henry Barrow as he soaked in a steaming tub of bath water. Rubbing brisky at the sponge in one hand with the piece of soap in the other, Jill pushed the strap of her chemise back up on her shoulder. "It will be my pleasure to tend that little old spot for you." She grinned slyly as she bent over the large mountain man.

A squeal of feminine delight escaped Jill's lips as Tate Coker wrapped his brawny arms around the tempting siren and pulled her onto his lap. Water flowed over the rim of the wooden tub, splattering the floor as Jill wound her plump arms around Coker's neck and wiggled her skimpily clad buttocks against his groin.

Taking Coker's actions as a signal, Barrow grabbed the young woman attending his bath and pulled her down on his lap. His bare feet were dangling over the rim of the tub, his shaggy head resting back. With Moll perched upon him in a scandalous fashion, he quipped loudly, "Maybe I've had the wrong idea all the time, Coker. Maybe I should be thinking about opening one of these fancy houses instead of a tavern."

"Well, don't be forgetting I'm your partner, Barrow!" Coker laughed, his fingers busily unlacing the ribbon that secured the front of Jill's chemise. He liked the idea of owning a whorehouse a lot better than a tavern. He had to admit, Henry Barrow was a thinker, that was fer sure!

The pair, along with Amber, had been staying at Slim Farley's Blessed Paradise for several weeks, and both had come to the realization that they had found a spot of heaven right here on earth. Amber Dawson had been put to work, cleaning and helping with the cooking, in order to help pay her keep, while the two men had done little more than sit by and wait for her to have her baby. In the meantime, they had indulged themselves with liquor and women; the best the Blessed Paradise had to offer. After they had promised Slim Farley that the copper-haired beauty would eventually belong to him for his putting them up and allowing them unlimited credit until the child was born and disposed of, they had found their every waking moment to be pure pleasure!

Farley had agreed willingly enough, reasoning that he had plenty of girls to go around, and his watered-down whiskey would stretch a bit further than usual. He had wanted Amber to add to his stable of girls back at rendezvous, and seeing her again in St. Louis, he had been unable to resist the offer Barrow and Coker presented to him. The young woman was a beauty; her hair alone would attract men by the droves. He had seen her eyed nightly as she went about her duties of cleaning and serving. He couldn't wait for her to be slender again; she would be the making of his fortune!

In the meantime, Barrow and Coker indulged themselves with all the pleasures the Blessed Paradise had to offer. As they splashed with the two women who had willingly consented to assist their bath, Miss Calico Kat pushed the chamber door wide, and with two glasses of whiskey in her hands, she called, "I have a few extra minutes, boys. I thought one of you, or both, might want to come to my room for a little while."

Henry Barrow's hands stilled where they were fondling Moll's breasts which he knew from past experience were not nearly as generous as Miss Calico Kat's. He had been waiting for this invitation ever since he had arrived at the Blessed Paradise. Miss Calico Kat had not given him a second glance over the course of these past weeks, and he had not been able to approach her without her attention being taken by some other man.

"I do expect payment for my services, though, gentlemen." When Calico Kat, with a movement of her head, tossed back her flaming locks, both men eyed the slender curve of her creamy-white throat and the rise of her abundond bosom where her blouse lay gaping against her chest.

"Without a doubt," Henry Barrow breathed softly. A woman such as Miss Calico Kat could not be expected to give away her favors like the rest of Slim Farley's girls. She was different . . . she was special . . . she was worth every cent he would have to pay for her! Without a thought, Henry Barrow rose up from the cooled water, Moll tumbling down into the lukewarm depths with a screech of outrage. Her water-drenched face glared across the room at her rival, Miss Calico Kat.

Tate Coker gave the offer a little more thought. Why should he pay good money for a whore when he could get one free? But looking toward the doorway, his eyes filled with the lushly rounded body of the queen of the Blessed Paradise, he quickly began to reconsider. He had already had Jill on several different occasions, and, admittedly, she and some of the other girls had pleasured him beyond all expectations, but Miss Calico Kat's offer was too wickedly tempting to resist. Like his partner, he rose to his feet. His large, wet body covered with a down of pale hair, stood out stark and pale as he began to climb out of the tub. "I'm game fer a little afternoon fun." He didn't bother to retrieve his clothes, but followed Barrow toward the door to the bathing chamber.

Miss Calico Kat boldly winked at the girls sitting sullenly in the pair of tubs. "Sorry, ladies, but I'm in need of a new hat. You'll just have to make a little extra by dancing this evening." Her high-pitched laughter erupted, spilling from darkly rouged lips as she turned away from the room and led the two men down the hall to her chamber.

"Make yourselves comfortable, gentlemen." Calico gauged both men with a single glance as she opened the chamber door. "I'll just freshen up your whiskey for you."

Henry Barrow's heart hammered heavily in his chest as he entered the lavish bedchamber. Looking around, his green gaze passed over richly appointed furnishings of mahogany wood and gold-cream brocade. The carpet was plush beneath their naked feet, the orchid-peach color blending a warm contrast to the rose wallpaper with a border of dancing cherubs. This was exactly the room he would have imagined Miss Calico Kat to sleep within. The other girls at the Blessed Paradise boasted small, neat chambers; this one surpassed them all by miles. He remembered the rumor he had heard, that Slim Farley was desperately in love with Miss Calico Kat, and, looking at her accommodations, he knew the rumor was true.

"Nice place you have here," Coker said aloud Barrow's thoughts. Crossing the room, Tate Coker did exactly as

Calico had invited. He stretched full out on the oversized bed his eyes lighting as he looked upward to see the canopy of mirrors.

Calico poured whiskey from the sideboard next to the dressing table, and made her way with feline grace, to the foot of the bed. With an inviting smile, she held the two crystal glasses out to Henry Barrow. "Wouldn't you like to join your friend?" she questioned.

Barrow couldn't speak, could only nod his shaggy head. Handing Coker his glass, he sat down upon the goose-down mattress which was covered with a cool satin coverlet.

"I do feel a little overdressed." She laughed, her bright green eyes sparkling in good nature as her hand began to quickly unbutton the row of glass buttons down the front of her blouse.

Neither of the men replied as they gulped down their whiskey, their eyes held upon the slender hand traveling over the blouse, then unsnaping the skirt. Their gazes widened as the skirt, then the blouse fell to her feet. Miss Calico Kat stood naked except for black stockings, red garters with tiny roses embroidered on the side, and shiny red, high heels.

"I'll be dancing tonight. You gentlemen can pay me my fee of fifty dollars then, if you like." Her voice purred, slipping like honey over them, as the two men stared, gazes transfixed upon her ample breasts with their dark-brown dusty nipples.

Neither Barrow nor Coker flinched an eye at the extravagant price she had just demanded. Well did they know that this afternoon's experience would be one they wouldn't soon forget.

Calico grinned knowingly. The lust in their faces told her that she could easily have asked double the price. The next time she invited them into her chamber, she would do exactly that. After all, a girl had to make a living, and she wasn't getting any younger. Actually, this matter of making her living was the reason she had approached these two lazy no-goods. If not for the fact that they were the only way to get what she wanted, she would have let Farley's drabs Moll and Jill have them. But being a shrewd business-woman, she knew how to get what she wanted. Her body had gotten her this expensively furnished room at the Blessed Paradise, and her body would soon get her the whorehouse she had been dreaming about for the past year. All she had to do was play these two fools right and she would have the beautiful Amber Dawson as the number-one attraction in her own establishment. Between herself and the copper haired beauty, she would pull in most of the business in St. Louis. Slim Farley and his love-stricken poetry that he left nightly on her pillow could go hang!

Still holding the attention of both men, she cupped the underside of both her heavy breasts. With a swift motion she set them jiggling up and down, the darkened tips strutting upward. As she strode across the carpeted floor, the high heels making her legs appear very long, she swung her naked hips in a seductive fashion. The late-afternoon sun drifting through the chamber windows shone golden rays upon the flame-red bush between her legs. Running her tongue across her lips, she stood next to the bed, and with a professional glint in her hungry eyes, she feasted upon the male bodies stretched out on her bed.

Her look alone was enough to enflame any man. Barrow and Coker were mere putty in her hand as their manhoods stretched and filled with hot, rushing blood. Lowering herself between the two, her cool fingers reached out and captured them in a breathtaking hold. "You know, boys, I've been thinking a lot about Amber lately." Her emerald eyes flashed with intent as their reflection caught in the mirrors overhead.

* * *

Raucous laughter, flirtatious glances, and bold language
were the common courtesies at Slim Farley's fancy house.
From late afternoon till the early hours of morning, there
was a busy flow of men pushing through the swinging,
double, fronted doors of the Blessed Paradise.

The front room appeared much like any other saloon
in the city. There was a long bar on the immediate right
of the entryway. Behind the bar, a large, all-muscle bar-
tender and bouncer by the name of Cribs made sure that
all ran smoothly. With Cribs around, there was no rough
handling of Farley's girls, nor was there any unwarranted
gunplay. Round tables and chairs were set up around the
room for a gentlemen's pleasure. High-stakes card games
could be found, or a thick beef dinner with all the trim-
mings ordered from the kitchen.

On the opposite side of the establishment from the bar
was the dance floor. A well tuned piano played round the
hour. The one requirement upon entering the doors of
the Blessed Paradise was that each gentleman purchase
two heart-shaped dance cards at a dollar a piece; a nominal
cover charge. The Blessed Paradise was known among the
male population of St. Louis as a dollar-a-dance
whorehouse.

Each morning, the girls turned in their dance cards and
in return they earned a portion of the cover charge. The
more dance cards a young woman claimed, the more cash
in her purse. The real money came, though, when the
girls tempted their gentleman dancers into taking a stroll
up the stairs with them to their room. Cribs also kept a
watchful record of the comings and goings on the stairway;
a valuable employee, he served Farley's purse strings well.
If one of the girls tried to cheat the house, Cribs was always

ready to take the offender into the back storage room and
rough her up a little.

It was also Cribs who had been given the job of watching
over Amber whenever she was brought downstairs from
her room. The back door of the Blessed Paradise, through
the storage room, bore a large lock from within. The few
times Amber had attempted to slip through the front double doors, it was Cribs who had viciously grabbed her arm
and dragged her back into the saloon.

Life for Amber Dawson at the Blessed Paradise was just
as cruel as her earlier years living under the hand of Henry
Barrow. She worked from sunup to the late hours of the
morning, her swollen abdomen earning her no reprieve.
She scrubbed tables and floors, waited tables, serving the
men who were playing cards or needing a meal, and often
enough had to help empty and refill the large tubs in the
bathing room; where a gentleman could be helped in his
bath by one doxy or another for a shiny fifty-cent piece.

The dozen girls who worked for Slim Farley showed
Amber little kindness. Most thought of her as a threat,
even though she was heavy with child. Once the baby was
born, they knew that Farley's intent was to have her working
on the dance floor of the Blessed Paradise. Each knew that
the copper-haired beauty would greatly diminish their own
profits. With such a threat hanging over their future, their
meanness toward Amber as her time of delivery grew near
increased.

Only Miss Calico Kat showed Amber any kindness at all.
But still, this bold-talking prostitute left Amber feeling ill
at ease. She had a cold, calculating look in her green eyes,
even though she smiled sweetly, appeared to understand,
and have sympathy for Amber's sorry state. Whenever the
queen of the Blessed Paradise came upon Amber on her
hands and knees scrubbing floors, or scrubbing down the

long bar before business hours, her sympathetic concern held touches of scorn.

This early-evening hour found Amber waiting tables. Her progress around the saloon, carrying drinks or trays of food, was greatly hindered because of her cumbersome size, and also the constant threat of having to fight off the outstretched hands of the house's patrons. With an apron tied around her waist, Amber's state of pregnancy was plainly obvious, but in no way did the bulk detract from her striking beauty. If anything, her beauty appeared to grow daily, her weariness and heartache undetectable by a passing glance.

Setting the drinks they had ordered down before two men, Amber straightened suddenly, her hand going to the small of her back to rub away an aching cramp. She had not felt very well all day, but the Blessed Paradise's watchdog, Cribs, had insisted she help serve throughout the early hours of this evening before being allowed to go to her room.

"Are you all right, ma'am?" one of the gentlemen asked with some concern. He had noticed Amber's pale features as she stepped back from the table.

"Oh pooh, don't be worrying about that one!" Sara Anne, one of the house girls, spoke up. "Like her daddy says, she's strong as a horse! Why, he's only waiting for her to drop her load before he puts her back to work on her back. Next time, though, she should be more careful!" The girl's high-pitched giggle caused grins to spread over the men's faces. The man who had asked after her well-being also grinned, believing her now to be just another whore.

While the men were enjoying the attentions of Sara Anne, Amber walked away from the table. Such treatment was nothing new to her at the Blessed Paradise. Making her way to the bar, her hand lightly rubbed her belly when she could feel the babe gently kicking. Abuse like Sara Anne's she suffered on a nightly basis from the other girls. Weeks ago she had learned to harden herself to such cruelties.

"Is it all right if I go to my room now?" she asked Cribs, who stood behind the bar. She hated that she had to ask this cruel man to approve such a simple request. But standing before him and awaiting his reply, she knew that there was no other way. If she started up the stairs without permission, he would be on her within seconds. His grip upon her arm would be vicious as he dragged her back into the saloon. She had already felt the biting pressure of his powerful hands upon her arms, and would do anything to avoid enduring such abuse again; especially this evening when she was feeling so unwell.

Looking down at her, it was evident, even to Cribs, that the girl was done in. He had told Farley a few days ago that they were working her too hard. Oh, well, he wasn't the boss around here. He only followed orders. Nodding his bald head, he pulled a key out of his apron pocket and called to one of the girl's standing at the bar. "Connie, go up with Amber and tuck her in." Cribs gave out these same instructions nightly to one girl or another. Handing over the key, they knew that they were to follow Amber upstairs and lock the door behind her.

This evening, Amber didn't resent the fact that she was locked in her small chamber. She just wanted to lie down on her cot and shut her eyes. She had been working since daylight, and exhaustion was overwhelming her.

Connie opened the door to the room that Amber had been assigned when she had first been brought to the Blessed Paradise by her stepfather and Tate Coker. Without a word spoken between them, Amber stepped within and Connie pulled the door shut and turned the key in the lock.

Glancing around the dark chamber, Amber didn't bother to light the candle on the small table next to her bed. Untying the apron knotted at her back, she slipped the dark, serviceable gown over her head. Stretching full out on the cot, she rubbed the large mound of her belly. "Good night, little one," she whispered softly. "Don't worry, Mother will take care of you. I'll think of something."

Tears sprang to her eyes as her soft words were spoken aloud to an empty room. Reaching up a hand, she brushed them aside; they would not do her or her child any good. She had already shed a bucket of tears, but the effort had been wasted. She was still at the Blessed Paradise, and she knew that her stepfather and Tate Coker only waited for the baby to be delivered to make good their promised threats.

Her hands settled over her abdomen protectively. She had tried so many times to get away from the Blessed Paradise that she wondered if she could bear the effort to try again. With those disheartened thoughts, her inner consciousness tried to give her courage.

You can't give up, Amber. You must think of the child, if nothing else! You have to escape this foul place and find a life for you and your baby!

She had given up hope she would ever see Spirit Walker again. He surely believed her dead, and had months ago given up searching for her. Often, while lying on her cot here in this sparsely furnished room, she told herself that as soon as she could escape, she would find work. One day when her child grew older she would try to return to Spirit Walker and the life she had known among his people.

As the days passed, it became even more impossible for her to find a minute when she was not being watched by Cribs or one of the girls. Her hopes for the future waned. If she could get away from the Blessed Paradise before her baby was born, she would be forever grateful to the powers above. Her child was fully dependent upon her to get out of this terrible place!

Again, fresh tears came to her eyes. Too late she had realized the great love she had in her heart for Spirit Walker. Too late for her to have told him her inner feelings, too late for her to see the pleasure in his warm ebony eyes when she might whisper, "Spirit Walker, I love you with all my heart."

Twenty-seven

The night breeze stirred and seemed to call to him as Spirit Walker's hand encircled the small leather pouch hanging around his neck. The familiar warmth from the stone within pulsed down his arm to flood his body. His heartbeat intensified with a surging renewal. He could feel Autumn Dawn's nearness, almost as though she called aloud to him.

Cautiously, he tethered his horse in an alleyway. At this late hour, there were few people wandering around the streets, and those he glimpsed paid him little attention. Earlier in the day he had stolen a shirt and pair of breeches from the clothesline of a farmer's wife's. With the white man's clothes fitting snugly against his large frame and his hair tied back, the dark length tucked within the shirt collar, it would be hard for anyone to discern his true identity unless they confronted him face-to-face.

His moccasined feet silently made their way down the wood-plank sidewalk, his hand resting lightly on the hilt of his hunting knife. No one would stop him from finding

Autumn Dawn . . . No one would get between him and the woman of his heart!

Some inner sense halted his footsteps outside a large building. Light spilled onto the sidewalk as a man left the establishment through the double front doors. Spirit Walker drew back into the shadows as the man staggered past him, then down the street.

His hand went to the leather pouch, and the heat intensified. Looking up at the two-story building, he knew that Autumn Dawn was here. Silently, he walked around the building, his gaze taking in every door and window. When he came to the back door, his hand lightly tested the knob. There was no release; it was barred from within. He continued circling the building, his dark eyes studying the second-floor windows. Most were illuminated with light from the rooms within. He paused suddenly as his glance noticed a chamber window that appeared to be barred with slates of wood. His heart hammered wildly in his chest. She was in there; he could feel her closeness.

Taking deep breaths of the cool night air, his dark eyes scanned the area, seeking out some means to reach the window. The window was far too high for him to scale without a rope, he decided after a silent search.

Giving up on entering through the window, he knew that the only way to find Autumn Dawn would be to go through the front double doors. Taking his tomahawk out of its concealment place in his shirt and holding his large-bladed hunting knife in his other hand, he slowly made his way back to the front of the building.

Patiently, he waited outside, watching from the shadows as the hour drew late, and men in small groups, or alone, left the building. The music within finally halted, and, taking this as a signal to act, Spirit Walker made his way with a silent tread to the front double doors, and peered within the large front room.

His dark eyes took in everything with a single glance. A large man with no hair was walking around the room extinguishing much of the lantern light. Next to the bar stood a woman with flaming-red hair drinking from a glass. In the center of the room was a table, and around it three men sat playing cards. Spirit Walker instantly recognized the men from rendezvous. The one Autumn Dawn had called stepfather was looking hard at the cards in his hand, a frown creasing his forehead. The other man called Coker was grinning at Barrow and saying something that Spirit Walker could not hear. The slender man, dressed neatly in a suit, held his glance more on the woman at the bar than the cards in his hand.

Spirit Walker realized that any minute the large man without hair might step to the double doors and secure them from within. He knew he had little time to make a plan; he had to act. He had to find Autumn Dawn and get her out of this place as quickly as possible. For a lingering second, his glance stole up the dark stairway.

His grip upon his weapons tightened. Neither the small man sitting at the table nor the woman posed a threat for Spirit Walker. The large man would be a formidable opponent, and from all he knew about the two trappers, they would do anything to keep Autumn Dawn for them-selves. There was no doubt in his heart what he would have to do to get past the three men and up those stairs. Waiting by the doors, he drew in great gulps of air, waiting for the large man to come nearer.

One of Cribs's nightly duties at the Blessed Paradise was to close up the establishment. Usually, the evenings ended much in the same fashion. Miss Calico Kat took a nightcap at the bar, Slim sat at one of the tables watching her every movement, and, more often than not, the two men, who seemingly only Farley and a few of the girls could abide, sat playing a last hand of poker. If a gentleman lingered longer than usual upstairs with one of the girls, and the doors had already been locked, it was left up to Cribs to climb from his bed and let the man out. This evening, a grin pulled back Cribs's lips as he wondered if Miss Calico Kat would allow Slim to accompany her to her room. Earlier in the day they had been arguing, and he had overheard her telling Slim to find himself another whore to bed. Farley was smitten by the tart, that was obvious, and didn't wish to take another doxy to his bed. His eyes kept stealing over Calico with hope-filled hunger in their depths.

Reaching the doors, Cribs's hand reached out to draw them together. If he were the owner of the Blessed Paradise, he wouldn't waste his time worrying after one bawd in particular; he would have several of them entertaining him at night. His thoughts filled with the image of Amber Dawson. She would be the first in his bed if he were the boss! "What the hell are you doing?" he questioned the man who had grabbed hold of his wrist as he attempted to pull the doors closed.

Without an answer, Cribs was jerked out onto the sidewalk by a man he could not clearly see, but whose strength was far greater than his own.

For a few seconds, Spirit Walker fought with the larger man, but knowing he had little time to waste before the other men inside would be coming to check out the commotion, he hefted his tomahawk in an upward arc and brought it down on the side of the man's bald head.

Hoping to cause distraction, he flung the large man back within the saloon. Crib's body fell to the floor with a loud thud, blood from the wound seeping onto the shiny wood.

"What the bloody hell?" Coker and Barrow jumped to their feet in unison, Coker's hand instantly reaching for the knife tucked in his breeches. Coker stared at Cribs's still form, then up at the man standing over him.

"It's the goddamn Injun!" In one motion, he grabbed the edge of the table and threw it across the room, coins and cards scattering across the floor.

Slim Farley jumped to his feet, leaping away from the mess on the table, and also from the trappers. He didn't know what was going on, but he wanted no part of it. His glance darted from his fallen employee to Miss Calico Kat, who was staring pale and wide-eyed at the man who still stood near Cribs.

Coker's glance took in every feature of the intruder, starting with the dark, shiny hair that now hung down his back and over his shoulders. His shirt had been torn free of its buttons, and his wide bronze chest was heaving with power. Barrow was right! It was the Injun! The instant recognition filling his eyes gave birth to a dark rage. This was the son-of-a-bitch that had robbed him of bedding the little whore he had paid good money for! "Yeah, it's the Injun, and I aim to castrate the bastard right here and now, before I plunge my blade into his heart!" Coker slowly began to advance. Barrow nodded his head as he pulled forth his wicked-looking knife.

"What you don't finish, I surely will." Barrow began to advance in the opposite direction.

With eyes holding upon Spirit Walker, Tate Coker swung his hunting knife from hand to hand in anticipation of using it on the Indian. Drawing close enough to strike out, he threw his weight in Spirit Walker's direction as he held the knife overhead. With a harsh grunt, he brought it sharply down.

Spirit Walker would have laughed aloud at the trapper's ineptitude. He sidestepped his efforts, bringing his knife outward in a swift movement. Drawing back, he smiled coldly as he looked down at the large man's belly to see

the line of crimson blood flowing from the eight-inch
wound and dampening his breeches.

The knife cut stung only for a few seconds. Like the
Indian, Coker also looked down at his stomach, his eyes
glimpsing the stream of blood that was flowing without
letup. His lips pulled back in a snarl of fury. The goddamn
Injun had almost gutted him! "I'll kill you, right out for
that!" Coker drew his knife back and started at Spirit
Walker once again.

From the corner of his eye, Spirit Walker watched Henry
Barrow's every movement as he drew closer in the hope
of joining his friend, so the two of them could come at
him at once. Spirit Walker's arm rose high as he swung
his tomahawk wide and hard, catching the trapper sharply
between the eyes.

Coker's eyes widened in disbelief that he could go under
like this, at the hands of an Indian. That thought faded
as he paused, held upright only by the strength that held
the handle of the tomahawk.

Having no mercy in his heart for these men, Spirit
Walker jerked the weapon free from the skull of his opponent and turned upon the other man. This was the stepfather of the woman he loved. This was the man who had
treated her cruelly throughout her young life and then
had sold her, as though she were chattel. This man had
to die along with his friend!

Henry Barrow watched the Indian's tomahawk being
pulled out of Coker's head, he felt a sudden hollowness
in the center of his gut. His palms sweated as he tried to
clutch the knife tighter in his hand. His heart pounded
harshly in his chest as he watched the Indian take one step
in his direction, then another. He read the cold reality of
death there in those dark eyes, and for a second thought
to try and plead for his life. But, as the Indian stood directly

before him, Henry Barrow knew there would be no mercy to be had in his heart.

A low growl escaped his throat as he charged the Indian with all the force within his body, both men rolling to the floor. His vigor renewed with the life-or-death struggle as he slashed viciously with his knife.

Spirit Walker had been taken by surprise, but instantly all his training returned to him. With a powerful aim, he hit Barrow's right shoulder with the war axe, shattering the bone. In retaliation, Spirit Walker felt the other man's knife nick his forearm. The slight pain added flame to the already boiling cinders of hatred he held for Henry Barrow. Spirit Walker wasted no more time; with his war cry spilling from powerful lungs, he rose over the trapper and plunged the hunting knife into the center of his chest.

Henry Barrow opened his mouth as though to cry aloud at the injustice of it all. Only a few more weeks and he would have left the Blessed Paradise to find his own fancy house. It wasn't fair . . . life had been too unfair . . . the dark underworld called out to him.

Jumping to his feet, Spirit Walker's glare swept over the woman at the bar and the small man who had joined her. "Where is she?" His words were issued forth in a savage growl. If need be, he would not hesitate to take care of these two, and then take this building apart in his search for Autumn Dawn.

Slim Farley could only stare in shock at the carnage that surrounded him. He looked at the Indian and knew that he and Calico were going to be his next victims. Terror the likes of which he had never known filled his heart and intensified his trembling.

"Who is it that you want?" Calico's words came out on a strangled breath, but she knew someone had to appease this savage.

"Where is Autumn Dawn?" Spirit Walker started toward

the staircase. He had an idea of the location of the room
that he believed held his beloved. His dark gaze went from
the stairway to the two standing at the bar.

Surmising that the Indian must mean Amber, because
Barrow and Coker had both appeared to have recognized
him, Miss Calico Kat pointed to the hallway that ran to
the right of the second-floor landing.

Glaring in the couple's direction one last time before
sprinting up the stairs, Spirit Walker growled low in his
throat, "Do not move!" He hurried up the steps, knowing
that any minute he might be set upon. Running down the
hall in the direction the woman had pointed, he halted
when he stood outside a locked door. Without hesitation,
he stood back and flung his full weight at the door. It gave
way immediately, and he stormed into the room. "Ptanyétu
Ánpo!" The cry of his beloved's name burst from his lips
as he tried to see into the dark chamber.

The sound of the crashing door had instantly awakened
Amber. Hearing her name called out in the Sioux tongue,
she attempted to jump from the bed. "Spirit Walker, you
came for me!" She openly wept, trying to hurry to him,
her body's burden hindering her attempt at swiftness.

Spirit Walker's heart was close to bursting at the sweet
sight of her; yet his eyes widened at the swollen shape of
her. He said nothing as he allowed his large arms to enfold
her. With the touch of her flesh against his own, he felt
instant release from the fear that had lived with him, day
and night, since he had been told of her disappearance.
"I would die for you!" were his words in reply. "You are
unhurt?" he questioned as he led her to the doorway.

"I am well, now that you have come." Tears flowed down
her cheeks. She was rescued from her prison and her child
would not be murdered the moment of his birth! Before
going through the door with him, she turned back into the
room. "I must first fetch my dress." She hurried across

the chamber, and as she rushed back to his side, she drew
the dark gown over her head.

There was little time to waste. The man and woman
downstairs had had plenty of opportunity to go into the
streets to call for help. Taking Amber by the hand, he
started back down the hall, and began a cautious descent
down the stairs. To his surprise, they had obeyed his command, and were still standing against the bar, as though
they feared to move a single step.

Spirit Walker threw one last dark look in the couple's
direction, giving them warning to remain where they were.
Leading Amber toward the front doors, his arm protectively wrapped over her shoulders as he attempted to shield
her from the sight of her stepfather and Tate Coker's
bodies stretched out on the saloon's floor.

Amber gave only a single glance at the bodies of her
stepfather, Tate Coker, and Cribs. They had come to the
end they deserved, she would reason later. For now, she
did not allow herself to think of their fate at the hands of
the man she loved. The only thing that mattered was that
Spirit Walker was here!

Twenty-eight

Cradled in his arms, with her ear pressed to the steady beating of Spirit Walker's heart, Amber fell to sleep shortly after they had left the city of St. Louis behind. The even gait of the horse beneath her lulled her into a peaceful sleep, assured that Spirit Walker would protect her.

Spirit Walker pushed his mount as hard as he dared with Autumn Dawn sitting before him. They had made it to his horse in the alleyway without interruption, but he knew it would only be a short time before the man and woman would come to their senses and begin to scream for help. Leaving the city, he pressed the horse into the shelter of the woods that ran along the river. They would travel throughout the night, staying to the forest for protection. With luck, it would take some time for the populace to figure what had taken place at the Blessed Paradise and to gather a posse to give chase.

They would make it, Spirit Walker told himself as his arms tightened around Autumn Dawn. With the slight pressure, he felt the movement of her abdomen, and a

frown touched his dark brow. The moment he had looked
at her, he had noticed the distended shape of her belly.
The fact that she was great with child did not matter to
him. All that mattered was that he had found her, and she
was once again at his side.

As the child within her womb kicked strongly against
his arm once again, he positioned his arm at a different
angle around her. There was a sense of unease that came
over him from the life that was within her, making its
presence known.

As the moon lowered in the night sky, and the stallion
traveled through the forest at a steady pace, Spirit Walker
faced the fact that Autumn Dawn carried another man's
child in her body.

In his heart, he laid no fault for her condition upon
Autumn Dawn's head. She was blameless to the evil that
had been forced upon her. She had been stolen from his
village, abused and kept prisoner in that place she had
called by name, the Blessed Paradise. They had not spoken
about her condition, so he was unsure of her feelings
toward the baby that she carried. He knew among his own
people that when a maiden had been forced by an outsider,
or a wasichu, against her will and then found herself large
with child, often the maiden could not stand the sight of
the baby. In that case an adoptive parent was found and
the mother had nothing further to do with the infant.

A child was always loved among the Sioux, and if Autumn
Dawn held such a deep hurt over all that she had been
forced to endure and could not care for the child, than
Spirit Walker would make certain it was taken care of.
Perhaps he would take the baby to his cousin's village
farther north. He silently tried to make plans, thinking
that he would not wish to see Autumn Dawn's pain every
time she was forced to see the child growing into adulthood
there in his village.

If she could not part with the child, what then? The question filtered through his mind and left him feeling unsettled. How would he be able to look upon the child of the wasichu trapper known as Coker? Would he see the man's look upon the child's brow? Would he be forced to relive the moment he had wielded the tomahawk into his skull every time he looked upon the child? And what of the child himself? How would he accept the fact that the man who would raise him was the killer of his father? In his heart, he knew it would be the hardest thing he had ever to face if she decided to keep the child.

By morning, he had still come to no easy terms about the child nestled beneath Autumn Dawn's breasts. With her slight stirring in his arms, he smiled down into her awakening features.

"The babe?" With wakefulness, her first concern was for the child in her womb.

Spirit Walker read the worry on her face, and watched as she sat up straighter, her hand going to her stomach. As it gently stroked, she seemed to relax back against him.

"He is strong, you need not fear." He tried to sound light, but feared the words came out hollowly.

Amber did not notice Spirit Walker's preoccupation. She was too happy to be back with him to notice anything amiss. "Have we traveled throughout the night? You must be exhausted." She worried that he had not been able to sleep.

Spirit Walker smiled softly at her concern for him. After the child, she worried about his comfort; it would not be an easy thing for him to share her. "I am fine. As long as I have you in my arms, I need nothing more to sustain me."

Amber snuggled closer to his chest. "I know," she breathed lightly, inhaling his masculine scent.

Spirit Walker kissed her on the crown of the head. "We

will stop soon and let the horse rest while we eat," he offered, knowing contentment as he listened to her softly spoken agreement.

Amber was willing to do whatever he wished, she was content feeling the texture of his flesh beneath her cheek; her slender hands holding on to his forearm as though she had to be reassured he was real and that she was not caught up in some wonderful dream.

A short time later, Spirit Walker halted his mount, then helped Amber to stand on the ground. Her ungainly appearance in the light of morning, and the groan of discomfort that parted her lips, placed another worry in Spirit Walker's mind. Looking at her as she pressed both hands to the small of her back and lightly massaged the spot, he knew that they would never make it back to his village before the babe would be born.

Taking the parfleche containing food, and the water pouch from his horse, Spirit Walker took Amber by the arm and slowly led her over to a fallen log. After helping her to sit, he dug in his parfleche and pulled out a piece of pemmican.

Amber smiled brightly as she reached for the food. "You can't imagine how I have longed for this." She bit into the tasty morsel and rolled her eyes heavenward.

Spirit Walker laughed aloud, the sound seeming to break some of the tension that had built within him. "And you can't imagine how I have longed to do this." He bent toward her and pressed his lips over hers in a fiery joining that replaced separation and lost time.

"Mmm, I don't know which is better, the pemmican or you," she sighed teasingly with the release of her lips.

"Definitely you." He drew a long bronzed finger across her cheek, marveling at the softness of her flesh, lost within the depths of the blue eyes looking up at him.

"I have missed you so much, Spirit Walker." Tears filled her eyes with that soft confession.

"Never again will we be separated," he promised, and, drawing her close, they held each other close.

The traveling passed slowly after the first two days, which had been hours of flight. There was a need to travel slowly, for Amber's condition was ever-present in Spirit Walker's mind. They camped early in the evenings, and he tried not to rush her in the mornings; the days slowly passed.

This day had been even slower than the rest. Spirit Walker worried terribly over Amber's condition. His dark eyes were constantly looking to her for any sign of distress. Several times, he had caught a look of pain on her face when she had thought his gaze was not on her. They would not be able to go on much farther, and by late afternoon, he had made the decision to make a small camp and attempt to erect some type of crude shelter.

"Why are we stopping?" Amber questioned, the movement of the horse as he was pulled to a halt causing the pain in her back to worsen.

"We shall make camp here for a few days, so you can rest." Spirit Walker dismounted and reached up to help her off the stallion.

As though in desperation, she turned atop the horse and looked in the direction they had left. "But what if we are still being followed?" Her gaze was filled with worry as she looked at him.

"No one will find us now. Do not worry, I will take care of you."

This was all Amber needed to hear. She sighed aloud, and bit down hard on her lower lip as a pain, sharper than earlier, laced through her lower back. As the pain eased, she looked up to find Spirit Walker watching her, and a tender smile formed on her lips. She had seen the concern on his brow throughout the day, and she hated to think that she was the reason for his worry. She had been praying that the pain would go away and they would be able to travel a few days farther before it was time for the babe to be born. She knew her time was near, for the pains throughout the day had worsened. Now, as she looked at the man she loved, she wished she could have chased the contractions away, if only for his sake and the worry that she knew filled him.

Grabbing his blanket from the horse's back, Spirit Walker took Amber's arm and led her to a large pine tree. Spreading out the blanket, he instructed gently, "Sit here, my heart."

Amber tried to find a comfortable position on the blanket. Attempting to distract herself from the pain that was steadily consuming her, she watched as Spirit Walker started a pit-fire and then began to cut away brush and undergrowth to make a lean-to not far from where she sat.

A short time later, she was lying in the lean-to on the blanket, her pains hard and consuming; she was unable to conceal them as, her hands clutched at the blanket, lips parted. Moans like the sounds of a small animal in torment filled Spirit Walker's ears.

A terrible fear began to grow in Spirit Walker's heart as he watched her agony; he was helpless to do anything to take away the pain. Looking around, he knew that they would be needing water, and he had left the packs near the horse. With loving hands he soothed the fire-curls away from his beloved's forehead and explained that he was going to get water and would be back shortly. With quickness goading his every step, he hurried toward the river with the water pouch. With every minute that drew past, his fear increased.

How was he going to help Autumn Dawn, he wondered

as he ran to the river, that fortunately was not far away from the trail they had been traversing. He was a warrior trained in the ways of fighting and protecting his people. Even his powers as a holy man among his people did not help him with knowledge to help to deliver a child. He had never known another brave who had helped his woman deliver a child. Always there were women in the village who helped with birthings. Would he be able to help her now, in her true time of need? They had spoken little about the child since he had rescued her. He was unsure what part he would have to play in the delivery.

Filling the pouch with water, he turned back the way he had come. As he hurried, he prayed to the One Above to give him wisdom and strength for the ordeal ahead. He had already made up his mind that he would love this child because it was a part of the woman of his heart. He now swore aloud to the spirits, his vow of love and protection for the child. "Let no harm come to Ptanyétu Ánpo, Great Spirit. Protect her and the child, and I will see that the baby is loved and brought up in the way of the people. I will teach him to be a good man among his tribe, and to be strong on the hunt and at war. I will do all these things, oh Great One, if only you will help the woman that fills my heart."

Gaining the lean-to, Spirit Walker's heart quaked with fear as he bent down to the blanket. Amber lay panting, her legs drawn apart as she strained and moaned aloud with her pain and burden. Seeing her thus, a new deep-rooted fear settled over him. He had often heard stories of women who had passed on to the other life while trying to deliver themselves of a baby. Was this horrible pain normal? Was something wrong; was she going to suffer horribly before she was taken from him? A lone tear trailed down his strong, bronze cheek. As her blue eyes fixed upon him, he tried to force these evil thoughts from his mind. The Great Spirit would not take this portion of his heart away from him. Too much had already happened to them for her to be taken from him forever. He would help her. His large hands would lead this child from her body, and in doing this, the child would also become his.

Quickly, he stirred himself and began to bathe Amber's face lightly with cool water. "Ah, my heart, I am here for you. The child is anxious to view this life that awaits him here on Mother Earth."

Amber, eased somewhat by his soothing words and tender touch, tried to smile at him. She had seen the fear and the worry on his face. She felt an inner guilt over his plight as tears quickly filled her eyes. "I am sorry, Spirit Walker," she tried to apologize. Neither of them had spoken much about the child. She had hoped that he would be happy when he had found her great with his child, but she had taken his silence for displeasure. He loved her and was happy that they were reunited, but she was unsure of his feelings for the baby that would soon be delivered. Before she had been abducted from his village, she had not had the chance to tell him that she was pregnant, so she was still not sure he even *wanted* children.

Spirit Walker brushed the tears from her cheeks aside, his heart aching as he looked down at her. "You have nothing to be sorry for, Ptanyétu Ánpo." He supposed she was expressing apology for the fact that she was having another's child. "You are blameless, my heart. I will love this child because it will be a part of you. None will ever know by my action, that I am not the true father, for in my heart I will be his father."

For a second, Amber thought she had misunderstood him, but as his dark eyes held upon her, and his tender actions of soothing her brow never wavered, her heart began to leap within her breast. He believed that another was the father of the babe! She looked at him with wide eyes, trying to sort this all out. What an incredible man, she thought. He believed the child to be another's, and still he vowed to love it, because it was a part of her!

As Spirit Walker watched her features change and her eyes become brighter, he wondered at her thoughts. When a smile settled over her lips, he believed her reaction was to his promise for the babe's future.

"You are quite amazing, Spirit Walker. It is no wonder I love you so much." her eyes sparkled with joy, her words a confession of the soul.

"You do? You are sure?" Spirit Walker could hardly believe his ears. This was the first time she had willingly confessed her love for him. It seemed that he had waited forever to hear these words from her lips.

Another pain coursed through Amber's body, and for a few minutes she could not speak as she clutched his hand and endured the spasm. When they had eased, her violet eyes looked into those filled with ebony concern. A trembling smile filtered across her lips. "Our babe even now is as his father. A mighty warrior," she lightly joked.

Spirit Walker looked down at her without smiling in return. He was unsure if she was referring to himself or the trapper.

Her hand rose from the blanket and she traced her slender finger over his brow. "The babe is yours, Spirit Walker. No other has touched me but you."

Hearing her words, he still could not believe their meaning. He stared down at her, and wondered if she had taken leave of her senses because of the severe pain.

"I told Running Moon the day you left the village with the other braves. I should have told you about the baby before you left, but I was still uncertain about my feellings."

"You told Running Moon?" Spirit Walker was truly stunned. He never had considered that this child could be his own. "You speak the truth? The child is truly mine?"

His heart began to beat a wild tattoo in his chest, joy filling every portion of his heart.

"I thought you knew, but were not pleased. I wasn't sure that you wanted children," Amber softly confessed, just before another spasm of pain doubled her over on the blanket, leaving Spirit Walker to look anxiously over her.

Not pleased? Didn't wish for children? As he tenderly tried to soothe her, one hand gently massaged the small of her back. He dampened the cloth and again caressed her brow, marveling that they could hold such a deep love for one another but truly not know the other's heart. As he felt her relax, her breathing deep, he tenderly assured, "I am the happiest of men, Ptanyétu Ánpo. I desire nothing more than to see my child in your arms."

As another spasm ripped through her, much stronger than the rest, he devoted his full attention to bringing her comfort. "Remember the meadow where I viewed you in my vision, Ptanyétu Ánpo. Think to that day, and view the cool water of the pond, the flowers abounding and the cool breeze stirring your fire-curls as you danced among the tall grass. Let that coolness of the meadow touch you now, my heart. Lose yourself to that day."

Once again, Amber relaxed back on the blanket. Her eyes shut as his strong voice took her away from the agony that kept attacking her so viciously. She was again dancing with the wind in her hair, skirts flying about her as arms opened and she looked up into the warmth of the morning sun. There was peace here, there was love in the soothing voice above her, and she bound her mind with the dream-world that Spirit Walker was spreading around her. Her pain was still there, but it seemed to be some distance away. All she could hear was Spirit Walker's voice speaking of the cool, refreshing water of the pond, the earth, and the meadow. Here was shelter, in his voice and touch; here she could endure.

As her body drew up and off the pallet, everything inside her seemed to push downward. Spirit Walker knew that it was time for the babe to come. Keeping his tone light, he told her of all the beauty that he had ever seen, the beauty he viewed each time he left his village and returned to look across the Sioux valley. He spoke of cool nights with the stars of heaven dancing with wondrous brilliance over Mother Earth. His hands still touched and soothed, and he bent down between her legs, his eyes now seeing the tiny, dark head of his child making its way through its mother's body. With a fiercely beating heart, he watched as a shoulder and then another and then a small, perfect body pushed from its warm haven into his own hands.

With a shout of joy that seemed to encompass the camp area, Spirit Walker gently held up the tiny slip of life for Autumn Dawn to view. As he touched his daughter, the baby squirmed and began to cry out her wrath at the ordeal she had just been put through. With a wide grin of disbelief and purest pleasure, Spirit Walker's eyes rose from the baby in his hands to the woman of his heart. "We have a daughter, Ptanyétu Ánpo. A perfect, beautiful little girl." Their glances held, their joy overwhelming in that moment of closeness. Everything had been worth this, this precious viewing into each other's souls.

As he laid the child in Amber's arms, warm ebony eyes locked with crystal blue. "Now I have two hearts that I would die for," he whispered softly.

Epilogue

The months of winter were slowly coming to pass in the Sioux valley. Life took on a normal rhythm for Spirit Walker, Autumn Dawn, and their child. Amber had resumed her work at Sky Weaver's side drawing out the winter counts, and Spirit Walker devoted himself to his family and his people.

As Spirit Walker sat against his backrest, with his daughter sitting on his lap, he brought a piece of meat to her lips. The two-year-old child with long, inky hair laughed with happiness as her father held his attention fully upon her.

Amber looked up from her sewing at the sound of the child's laughter, her eyes filling with love for her family. As she watched Spirit Walker take up a tortiseshell comb and run it through Summer's hair, a tender memory filled her vision. She remembered the days that she and Spirit Walker had spent near the lake, away from the outside world, and how she had sat between his legs and learned of his touch and love.

As her eyes rose from her daughter, they were captured by Spirit Walker's dark gaze. There was no doubt in her heart about this mighty warrior's love for her, nor did she allow any doubt in his heart about her love for him. Daily, she told him her feelings of love. Never again would she keep her feelings locked away. She was reminded of the news that she would share with him this night after Summer was put to bed. Her hand lightly caressed her abdomen, where she knew that his seed had taken root once again.

As their gazes held, she anticipated his reaction to such news. This time he would share every moment of her pregnancy. Tonight, she would share with him her joy, and the promise of a happy tomorrow.

Sioux Glossary

Cetán	Hawk
Chacun Sha Sha	bark of the red willow
Heháka	male deer
Hetkála	squirrel
Mastínca	rabbit
Matóhota	grizzly bear
Ptanyétu Ánpo	Autumn Dawn
Skan	sky
Sunkáku Heháka	brother deer
Tatanka	male buffalo
Wáblosa	redwing blackbird
Wahpe Kalyapi	tea
Wakápapi Wasná	pemmican
Wakán Tanka	Great Spirit
Wakinyan	thunderbird
Wanági Máni	Spirit Walker
Wanági Winyan	spirit woman
Wasichu	white man
Wasicun Winyan	white woman

Wi	sun
Wicása Wakán	holy man
Wíhmunge	witch medicine
Wiwanyank Wacípi	the sun dance

SURRENDER TO THE SPLENDOR
OF THE ROMANCES
OF ROSANNE BITTNER!

UNFORGETTABLE   (4423, $5.50/$6.50)

FULL CIRCLE   (4711, $5.99/$6.99)

CARESS   (3791, $5.99/$6.99)

COMANCHE SUNSET   (3568, $4.99/$5.99)

SHAMELESS   (4056, $5.99/$6.99)

ROMANCES BY BEST-SELLING AUTHOR COLLEEN FAULKNER!

O'BRIAN'S BRIDE   (0-8217-4895-5, $4.99)

Elizabeth Lawrence left her pampered English childhood behind to journey to the far-off Colonies . . . and marry a man she'd never met. But her dreams turned to dust when an explosion killed her new husband at his powder mill, leaving her alone to run his business . . . and face a perilous life on the untamed frontier. After a desperate engagement to her husband's brother, yet another man, strong, sensual and secretive Michael Patrick O'Brian, enters her life and it will never be the same.

CAPTIVE   (0-8217-4683-1, $4.99)

Tess Morgan had journeyed across the sea to Maryland colony in search of a better life. Instead, the brave British innocent finds a battle-torn land . . . and passion in the arms of Raven, the gentle Lenape warrior who saves her from a savage fate. But Tess is bound by another. And Raven dares not trust this woman whose touch has enslaved him, yet whose blood vow to his people has set him on a path of rage and vengeance. Now, as cruel destiny forces her to become Raven's prisoner, Tess must make a choice: to fight for her freedom . . . or for the tender captor she has come to cherish with a love that will hold her forever.